Discover why everyone's talking about Charlotte Betts

Praise for *The Apothecary's Daughter*

'A colourful story with a richly-drawn backdrop of London
in the grip of the plague. A wonderful debut novel'
Carole Matthews

'Romantic, engaging and hugely satisfying.
This is one of those novels that makes you feel
like you've travelled back in time'
Katie Fforde

'A vivid tale of love in a time of plague and prejudice'
Katherine Webb

'If you are looking for a cracking good story
and to be transported to another age,
you really can't beat this'
Deborah Swift

'A thoroughly enjoyable read which will keep
you enthralled until the very last page'
Jean Fullerton

Charlotte Betts began her working life as a fashion designer in London. A career followed in interior design, property management and lettings. Always a bookworm, Charlotte discovered her passion for writing after her three children and two step-children had grown up.

Her debut novel, *The Apothecary's Daughter*, won the YouWriteOn Book of the Year Award in 2010 and the Joan Hessayon Award for New Writers, was shortlisted for the Best Historical Read at the Festival of Romance in 2011 and won the coveted Romantic Novelists' Association's Historical Romantic Novel RoNA award in 2013. Her second novel, *The Painter's Apprentice*, was also shortlisted for the Best Historical Read at the Festival of Romance in 2012 and the RoNA award in 2014. *The Spice Merchant's Wife* won the Festival of Romance's Best Historical Read award in 2013.

Charlotte lives with her husband in a cottage in the woods on the Hampshire/Berkshire border.

Visit her website at www.charlottebetts.com and follow her on Twitter @CharlotteBetts1

By Charlotte Betts:

The Apothecary's Daughter
The Painter's Apprentice
The Spice Merchant's Wife
The Chateau on the Lake
The Milliner's Daughter (e only)

The Chateau on the Lake

Charlotte Betts

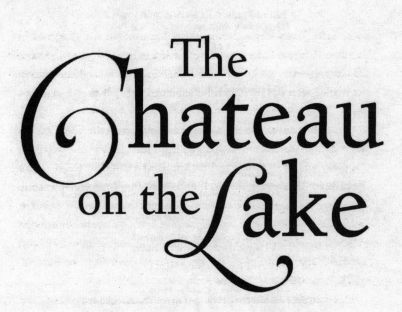

piatkus

PIATKUS

First published in Great Britain in 2014 by Piatkus
This paperback edition published in 2015 by Piatkus

1 3 5 7 9 10 8 6 4 2

Copyright © 2014 Charlotte Betts

The moral right of the author has been asserted.

*All characters and events in this publication, other than those
clearly in the public domain, are fictitious and any resemblance
to real persons, living or dead, is purely coincidental.*

A CIP catalogue record for this book
is available from the British Library.

ISBN 978-0-349-40449-3

Typeset in Caslon by M Rules
Printed and bound by CPI Group (UK) Ltd, Croydon, CR0 4YY

Papers used by Piatkus are from well-managed forests
and other responsible sources.

MIX
Paper from
responsible sources
FSC
www.fsc.org   FSC® C104740

Piatkus
An imprint of
Little, Brown Book Group
Carmelite House
50 Victoria Embankment
London EC4Y 0DY

An Hachette UK Company
www.hachette.co.uk

www.piatkus.co.uk

For our children,
Polly, Tom, James, Michael
and Katherine

Chapter 1

August 1792

It is often said that an educated woman is an abomination in the eyes of God. Since I am such a creature, my belief is that God is far too busy to worry about such things and that it is only in the hearts of men that women like myself engender such extremes of feeling. It is, however, discouraging to be constantly reminded that many of my own sex, my pupil Amelia Wainwright for example, have no wish to be other than a decorative accoutrement to hang on a husband's arm.

Barely a breath of air enters the stuffy schoolroom and my hair weighs heavy on my neck as I pace the floor, reading aloud to my pupils from Johnson's *Lives of the Most Eminent English Poets*. I can bear it no longer. I go to the window and open it wide.

Down below in Soho Square four horses drawing a landau trot by, the iron-rimmed wheels clattering and grinding over the cobbles. The scent of hot horseflesh rises up to the window along with the raucous cry of the knife grinder. Two sedan chairs are carried by in quick succession, followed by a boy driving a squealing herd of pigs.

My gaze is drawn to the garden in the centre of the square. The gravel paths and the green lawn with its central fountain appear cool and inviting. All at once I've had enough of the confines of the schoolroom.

'Come along, girls!' I say, gathering up my books.

We hurry down the staircase, chattering like a brightly coloured flock of birds, and out into the dusty street.

A moment later I'm sitting on my favourite bench in the dappled shade of a lime tree with my pupils in a circle at my feet. They make a pretty picture. Nine girls on the verge of womanhood, their cheeks delicately flushed in the warmth, their hair glossy, their brows smooth and, as yet, untouched by care.

A nursemaid runs past, calling to a small boy rolling a hoop, and a couple of scarlet-coated soldiers watch us as they loll on a bench a few yards away; otherwise we are alone in the garden. A warm breeze, delightfully scented with honeysuckle, teases my hair as I begin to read aloud again. But sixteen-year-old Amelia Wainwright is not listening. As slender and delicate as a young doe, she twists a strand of sunlit hair around her fingers. Her rosebud mouth is slightly open and her lips moist as her languishing gaze rests on the infantrymen, who laugh and josh with each other.

'Amelia!' I say, sharply.

Reluctantly, she turns her face towards me, eyes unfocused and dark with longing.

I had hoped that Johnson would be sufficiently interesting to capture the attention of even the shallowest of my pupils but it seems I am to be disappointed. I put on my most severe expression and hold out the book to her. 'You may continue, Amelia.'

Pouting, she begins to read, glancing at the soldiers all the while.

One of the infantrymen laughs and nudges his companion, who pulls a booted foot on to his knee the better to display one elegantly turned calf encased in tight white breeches. Really, he's no better than a cock robin displaying to a female of his species! The other girls begin to toss their hair and smooth their skirts and it's perfectly clear to me that they are not in the mood to improve their minds.

After a while, the two young men rise from the bench and swagger past, their swords jingling and brass buttons glinting in the sun.

Mouths turned down in disappointment, the girls watch them go and even I must confess the sight of them is enough to set any young female's heart aflutter. Silently, Amelia hands the book back to me and I resume the lesson.

An hour or so later a number of carriages roll into the square and draw up outside the three-storey townhouse that is my home and which accommodates my father's Academy for Young Ladies. The sound of a handbell, vigorously shaken, drifts out of an open window and my pupils scramble to their feet and brush grass off their skirts. I close my book with a snap. School has ended for the day.

Arm in arm, the girls hurry through the iron gates in a flurry of muslin and silken ribbons.

My mother and the school's dancing master, Signor Brunetti, are on the front steps making sure that their young charges are safely stowed into their carriages or returned to the care of their maids. When they have all left, Signor Brunetti kisses my mother's hand with a flourish and bows to me before tripping off home to his own mother.

Mama links her arm through mine and we go inside.

I find Papa standing beside the open window in his library, pouring wine into three glasses. 'Ah, Madeleine *chérie*, there you are!' he says, a smile creasing the lines around his eyes.

He hands me a glass of wine and the sun catches the gleam of the gold signet ring with its shimmering moonstone that he always wears.

'The schoolroom was so hot we went into the garden,' I say, in French. We always speak in Papa's native tongue when we are alone, but generally revert to English when Mama is with us.

'Sometimes it is necessary to enjoy the moment.' He sits down with a sigh of contentment.

Papa is dark and lean, the same height as myself, which is short for a man but tall for a woman. His high-bridged Gallic nose and penetrating brown eyes give him an uncanny resemblance to an eagle. People say that I look like him, though my eyes are an unusual shade of violet and, thankfully, my nose is less pronounced than his. Mama, fair-haired and blue eyed, was an only child and became estranged from her family before I was born, but she tells me that none of them had violet eyes. Papa, however, has always refused to discuss his family so my curiosity about my looks remains unanswered.

This infuriating obduracy of his fuelled wild fantasies in me throughout my childhood and now, at twenty-two, I consider myself perfectly mature enough to accept the truth, however unpalatable, but still they remain silent. What terrible act could have caused my parents to reject their families? Or did my mother and father do something so dreadful that their relatives cast *them* out? Papa's gravitas and natural elegance of bearing used to make me wonder if he was perhaps some by-blow of royalty, never to be acknowledged.

I am determined I will discover the truth one day.

Mama pushes open the library door and Papa rises to his feet, his eyes shining. Whatever may have happened in the past, the love my parents have for each other remains undimmed by the passage of time.

'How was your day, Philippe?' asks Mama.

'I had a visitor.'

'Mr Jephcott? I spoke to him briefly on my way to oversee the drawing class but he wouldn't tell me his business. He was most insistent that he would wait until he could speak to you.'

'He has a proposal for us and I am not sure what to make of it,' says Papa.

'What did he want?' I ask, curiosity getting the better of me.

'Mr Jephcott is a teacher of science and mathematics with an interest in philosophy, both natural and experimental.'

Mama raises her eyebrows. 'And he is seeking a position in our school? I'm not entirely sure that it's a good idea to disturb the minds of our young ladies with philosophy, natural or otherwise.'

'But why not?' I ask. 'There is no inherent reason why a girl's mind should be any less fit for such subjects than that of a callow youth, is there?'

Papa frowns. 'Not so sharp to your Mama, Madeleine.'

'I beg your pardon but you know my opinion.'

'We do,' says Papa with a wry smile, 'since you so frequently remind us of it.'

'But you do not disagree with me,' I say indignantly. 'The whole ethos of this school is to allow the girls' minds to flourish.'

Mama reaches out to touch my arm. 'But we must never forget that whilst a girl's natural intelligence must be cultivated, she will also need to find a good husband.' She smiles. 'Just as you will.'

I open my mouth to retort that once a girl has a nursery full of babies it doesn't matter how much Greek she knows, she'll never have time to continue her studies of the Classics, but Papa holds up his hand and I subside.

'Mr Jephcott,' he says, 'has nothing but praise for our Academy and wishes to invest in it. He proposes to buy the house next door and his plan is to use the drawing room as another schoolroom and to convert the attics and bedrooms into dormitories. He believes it would be beneficial for the pupils to board, affording us greater opportunities to mould their young minds.'

'But if Mr Jephcott invests his fortune in the Academy, will you still be able to call the school your own?' I ask.

Papa smiles. 'As always, my clever daughter goes straight to the heart of the matter.'

'There's a great deal to discuss,' says Mama, looking doubtful.

I glance at the clock on the mantelpiece. 'Look at the time! Sophie will be waiting for me.'

My friend Sophie kisses me, her brown curls tickling my cheek. 'I thought I might be late,' she says as we hurry towards Grosvenor Street. 'Henry didn't want me to leave.

'And is my little godson well?'

'Bouncing with energy and asking when his Aunt Madeleine will come to see him.'

Sophie Levesque is the sister I never had. Her parents belong to the silk-weaving Huguenot community and she became a pupil at my father's Academy when we were both eight years old. Small and plump, her brown hair worn in tight ringlets, she greeted me that first morning with eyes sparkling with mischief. When she smiled I stared, fascinated, at the dimples in her cheeks. She's very little changed, except that she rarely giggles any more and shadows are now ever-present under her eyes.

'Have you heard the news?' she asks.

I shake my head. 'I've been in class all day.'

'King Louis is under arrest! A great mob descended on the Tuileries and killed all the guards. They wanted to break the palace down just as they did with the Bastille.'

'I can't say I'm sorry,' I say. 'King Louis has had every opportunity to change his ways and I can attach no blame to the revolutionaries when their children are starving and Queen Marie Antoinette wears diamonds and plays at shepherdesses.'

'The royal family escaped when the mob broke in but they were brought back and imprisoned.'

I'm still pondering on this momentous news when we arrive at Lady Georgiana Woodhouse's imposing townhouse in Grosvenor Street, where she holds a fortnightly salon. Politicians, authors, artists and scientists regularly gather here to exchange ideas and opinions, and I eagerly anticipate the meetings.

The front door opens and a footman admits us into the drawing room. A buzz of conversation arises from the twenty or so people already crowded together. I recognise the Honourable Charles

James Fox, the Whig politician, holding forth to a rapt audience, Daniel Stowe, writer of abysmal poetry, and Mary Wollstonecraft, fearsomely argumentative author of *A Vindication of the Rights of Woman*.

Lady Georgiana comes to greet us, her auburn hair curled over one shoulder and her Junoesque curves barely contained in diaphanous layers of damp and gauzy muslin tied with an emerald green sash. The slim silhouette of the garment is no more substantial than a chemise, quite unlike the full skirts most of the ladies are wearing.

'The latest Paris fashion, Georgie?' asks Sophie.

'But of course!'

'I understand that society ladies in France are choosing to dress simply so as not to inspire jealousy amongst the working women. Revolutionary fashion, in fact,' I say, smiling at the pun.

'But isn't it pretty? And so delightful to be free from tight stays,' Georgiana whispers as she kisses my cheek.

Although a few years older than myself, Georgiana also attended my father's school before she went on to marry a wealthy peer. I am gratified, however, that she has not allowed the demands of the nursery to constrain her thirst for learning and enlightenment.

She slips her arms through ours and leads us towards a small group of people. 'Knowing your great interest in the Revolution in France, I want you to meet Comte Etienne d'Aubery,' she says, 'one of France's most eligible widowers. Utterly charming ... but, be warned, there's a whiff of scandal about him!'

'How interesting!' says Sophie.

'It's whispered,' says Georgiana in an undertone, 'that he murdered his wife.'

'No!' Sophie claps one hand to her mouth.

There's no time to discover more as we stop before an elegantly dressed man in a bronze brocade coat and close-fitting breeches. His hair is raven black and his olive skin darkened by the sun, unlike

7

most of the aristocratic *émigrés* who are arriving in London with increasing regularity these days.

'May I present Miss Madeleine Moreau and Mrs Levesque?' says Georgiana.

The comte is tall for a Frenchman, dark-eyed and with his curling hair cut short in the latest French style, to expose the firm angles of his jaw and long nose.

'I no longer use my title,' he says, 'since the nobility was abolished in France.' His expression is severe until he smiles, when his eyes seem illuminated from within. He speaks English with a light accent and, in spite of my dislike of the spoilt and frivolous French aristocrats, I find his looks extremely pleasing.

Georgiana turns to his companions, a middle-aged woman with bewildered eyes and a corpulent man with pudgy white hands. 'The *former* Marquis de Roussell and his wife are recent *émigrés* from the Revolution,' she says. 'Mr d'Aubery has accompanied them on their journey to London and is introducing them to society.'

I can't help studying his face covertly. There's a curiously exciting frisson in talking to a man with a disreputable past. 'So you are not an *émigré*, too, Mr d'Aubery?' I ask.

'Not at all but I often visit London.'

Sophie and I make conversation, in French, with the new arrivals since they have a poor command of English. Mr d'Aubery, I notice, watches me carefully all the while I speak. I do not take to the marquis, who is altogether too ready to talk of his plans to join the *émigré* army and 'whip the tails of the bloody revolutionaries'.

'Too late for that,' says Mr d'Aubery. 'The interference of the Duke of Brunswick's army only served to intensify opposition to the king.'

'I'm beyond caring about the king,' says de Roussell. 'He's a lost cause, anyway. But I want my estates returned to me.'

'The *émigré* army is under-funded and poorly equipped.' D'Aubery shrugs in that peculiarly Gallic fashion. 'I see little chance of success for it. And in any case, it is impossible for you to return to France now without incurring the most severe of penalties.'

De Roussell scowls. Sensing that the conversation is in danger of becoming contentious, Georgiana draws the marquis and his wife away.

'If you will excuse me,' says Sophie, 'I must find Mr Stowe. Last week he promised to write an ode to my dimples.' She flits off to the other side of the room where the poet is in earnest conversation with a red-haired man wearing a yellow waistcoat.

I turn back to Mr d'Aubery, delighted to have his sole attention.

'You speak French well,' he says, 'and your name is French, too. When did your family come to England?'

'I was born here.' I like the way he regards me so intently while I speak, as if he's really interested. 'My mother is English but my father is French.'

'And he came from . . . ?'

I hesitate. How can I tell him I have no idea, without sounding foolish? 'I have never been to France,' I say, sidestepping the question and changing the subject. 'Did you hear the news today? I understand that King Louis has been imprisoned.'

'It is a worrying time,' says the former comte. 'Whilst I support the Revolution in following the principles of freedom and equality, I fear that the working men are allowing their passions to become so inflamed that they no longer see reason.'

'It's a time of great change for France,' I say. 'But who can blame the people if they demand equality?' I'm on my favourite hobby-horse now, my views formed from endless discussions with Papa and other members of the French community in London. 'It's patently unfair if the poor are those paying all the taxes while the aristocrats, who do not, flaunt their luxurious life style in their Parisian homes, leaving the workers on their estates to starve.'

Mr d'Aubery's well-defined mouth tightens. 'It isn't always like that.'

9

'The French nobility stunt the growth of society,' I say firmly. 'And the clergy are greedy and over-privileged. I can only believe it to be of benefit to the people that Church property has been confiscated and the proceeds used to strengthen the economy.'

'Whilst there may be an element of truth in what you say, Miss Moreau, do you not think it arrogant of you to make such statements as if they are fact when you have not only never lived in France, but not even visited the country?'

Heat floods my neck and burns in my cheeks. 'Perhaps distance lends perspective.' I can hear the vinegar in my tone.

His eyes glitter, as cold and hard as jet. 'Then we must agree to differ, Miss Moreau.' The comte makes me a stiff little bow.

Mortified, I watch him walk away. How disappointing that one so well-favoured should be so haughty. Still smarting from his comment, I seek out more comfortable company.

Sophie is talking animatedly to the man in the yellow waistcoat. His copper hair is carefully tousled and he runs his fingers through his disordered curls while his gaze rakes up and down my friend's figure and comes to rest on her plump breasts.

'Madeleine, this is Mr Jack Fielding,' she says. 'May I present Miss Moreau?' Sophie lays a hand on my arm. 'Mr Fielding is an artist and has just completed his portrait of Horace Walpole's cousin.'

'How very interesting,' I say.

Jack Fielding doesn't return my smile but reaches out for one of Sophie's curls and winds it around his finger. 'There are intriguing chestnut lights amongst the brown and your olive skin tones are so much more interesting than the milky-white complexions of the native English.' He studies Sophie through half-closed eyes. 'Yes, I really think I must paint your portrait, Mrs Levesque.'

'Oh, would you?' Sophie gasps.

'I shall call on your husband tomorrow to make the arrangements.'

A quiver of unease runs down my spine as she smiles foolishly back at him and I remember that I saw just the same expression earlier that day on Amelia Wainwright's face while she was eyeing up the infantrymen.

Chapter 2

September 1792

'Again, Aunt Madeleine!' Henry's voice is high-pitched with excitement.

I glance at Sophie and she shrugs and looks away. 'Once more,' I say, 'and then you must play quietly while I talk with your mama.' Grasping the string around the spinning top, I give it a sharp pull. The top, gaily painted in red, blue and yellow, starts to spin and the colours blur together into a rainbow as it hums and twirls upon the polished floor of Sophie's drawing room.

Henry shrieks with laughter but Sophie is staring out of the window and jumps when I touch her arm. 'What is it?' I ask.

She turns to watch the spinning top until it begins to wobble increasingly violently before finally falling over.

Henry looks up at me hopefully.

'No more,' I say.

I wait until I'm sure he's absorbed in arranging his soldiers into battle formations before asking Sophie again. 'What is it that troubles you?'

'It's Charles,' she whispers, glancing at her son's dark head bent over his toys. Slowly, she pulls back the lacy frill of her sleeve and I gasp to see the ugly bruises on her forearm.

Before I can say anything, there's a quiet knock on the door and Henry's nurse enters. 'I came to see if Master Henry would like to go for his walk now?' She has a broad country face with a smattering of freckles on her nose.

Henry scrambles to his feet. 'Can we feed the ducks again, Betty?'

Sophie is smoothing down her sleeve, hiding the bruises again. 'But you must take care not to fall in the water.' She kisses Henry and he runs off hand in hand with the nursemaid, chattering excitedly.

'Betty has been with us for four months now,' Sophie says as soon as the door has closed behind them. 'Henry adores her.'

'Sophie, never mind the nursemaid! Why did Charles do this to you?'

'He's taken another mistress,' she says, her voice devoid of expression. 'My dressmaker let it slip. It seems that I share her services with my husband's new fancy piece. You can imagine the humiliation of it; the beastly girl was sticking pins into my hem and darting spiteful little glances up at me from under her eyelashes to see if I knew.'

'Oh, Sophie!' But I'm not surprised since it's well known that Charles Levesque is a philanderer. What does surprise me is that for such a thick-set man with eyebrows that meet over his nose and little small talk, he appears to have no difficulty in finding women who are happy to climb into his bed. Four years ago I begged Sophie not to marry him but her family and the Levesques had common business interests and she succumbed to familial pressure.

'Of course, I pretended that it doesn't concern me,' says Sophie unhappily. 'It's not that I care that he has other women ... well, not particularly as we've never pretended it's a love match ... but he always becomes so wretchedly fault-finding with me when he has a new mistress.'

13

Anger makes me speak sharply to her. 'And so he hurts you and soothes his conscience by persuading himself you drive him to it.'

'That's it exactly!' Sophie wipes away a tear. 'It's not as if I've ever refused him in any way ...' Her voice trails off as her cheeks blossom scarlet. 'But now that I've given him the son he wanted, I'm of no further use to him.'

'Change your dressmaker at once and keep out of Charles's way until his passion for this strumpet wanes, as it surely will.'

Sophie sighs. 'Still, Charles is so preoccupied with her that he did agree to commission Mr Fielding to paint my portrait.'

I say nothing but there's something about Jack Fielding that makes me uneasy.

Children's voices call to each other across the garden and the evening sun slants through the lime trees, highlighting my mother's hair with gold.

'An evening such as this is a gift,' she says, threading her needle with vibrant turquoise silk for the kingfisher's wing that adorns the waistcoat she's embroidering for my father.

I rest my book on my knee. 'September is always a poignant time. It's hard to imagine that it will soon be winter.'

There's a footfall on the gravel and Mama moves her sewing basket so that Papa can squeeze between us on the bench.

'I have been to Harold Jephcott's chambers,' he says, 'to further our discussions. I am inclined to consider his proposition favourably but since we would all be working closely together, I suggested that he should meet you both. He has invited us to be his guests at Vauxhall Pleasure Gardens next week. There is to be a masquerade and fireworks.'

'A masquerade!' A thrill of excitement runs through me.

'Philippe!' Alarm makes Mama grip my father's sleeve. 'You know how wickedly licentious these affairs can be.'

'I promise not to leave your side, *chérie*.' Amusement glints in his eyes.

'But what about the rakes who might make improper suggestions to Madeleine?'

Papa raises his shoulders and turns his hands palm up. 'Our daughter will stand no nonsense from any young man. Mr Jephcott will bring his wife and daughter and hire a box where we can sit safely away from the rabble. I shall, of course, defend the honour of my womenfolk with my life.'

'There's no need to descend into melodrama, Philippe,' says Mama, crossly.

I'm delighted at the prospect of such entertainment. 'I would so like to see the costumes,' I say. 'It will be as good as a play.'

Mama sighs. 'As long as we're seated in a box and stay together, I agree that it would be entertaining.'

'Then I shall send word to Mr Jephcott.'

'And I'll ask Sophie where we can hire costumes,' I say, my mind brimming with visions of Greek goddesses, water sprites and ancient queens.

'On a more sober note,' says Papa, 'on the way home from Mr Jephcott's chambers I ran into Guy Foucault and Pascal Simonet. We repaired to the Cross Keys for a glass of wine. Simonet had the news that there was a massacre at the prison de l'Abbaye in Saint-Germain a few days ago.'

'A massacre?'

Papa is grim-faced. 'An angry mob murdered twenty-four priests who were being taken to the prison. Then they forced their way inside to kill hundreds of the prisoners. The riots still continue.' Papa sighs. 'The *ancien régime* and the France of my childhood are gone for ever.'

Although brought up as a Roman Catholic Papa rarely goes to church, though he never stops Mama and myself from attending. He's always been reluctant to discuss religion, saying it's up to each man to make peace with his own god.

'Don't you ever wish to go back to France?' I ask.

'There is nothing there for me.'

'But don't you want to know how your family fare since the Revolution?'

'You know I never talk of them.' Papa glowers at me.

'But Papa ...'

'Enough!' He pushes himself to his feet. Without glancing at me again, he walks back towards the house.

'You must not worry him, Madeleine.' Mama's mouth is set in a disapproving line.

'Worry him! Isn't it my right to know about my family? What is so terrible that you make a conspiracy of silence?' My hands are curled into fists and my nails bite into my palms.

'I will not go against your father in this matter. The past is the past and we can never return to it. Besides,' Mama reaches out to touch my hand, 'we have each other. What more could we want?'

I snatch my hand away and rise to my feet. 'I need to know where I come from. Who are my grandparents? Do I have cousins, uncles, aunts? Tell me, Mama!'

'I cannot speak of it,' she murmurs, head bent again over her embroidery.

My pleasure in the beautiful evening is all gone. Angry, I stalk away from her and set off along the street, hoping that a brisk walk will dissipate my annoyance.

The following afternoon the excitement in the air of Georgiana's crowded drawing room is almost palpable.

'So that,' says Sophie, 'is the end of the French monarchy.'

All the talk is of how the Convention has declared France a Republic. The escalation in violence during the September massacres resulted in over a thousand prisoners being killed: clergy, nobles, common thieves and prostitutes all together.

'The Princesse de Lamballe was dragged out of her cell in La Force and killed most horribly,' says Georgiana. She leans forward to whisper. 'She was the Queen's close friend but that didn't stop the mob raping her, cutting off her breasts and sticking her head on a pole. They held it up outside the window of the Queen's cell, jeering and taunting her.'

'That's barbaric!' I'm sickened by the thought of it.

Sophie shudders theatrically and stands on tiptoe, scanning the assembly.

'The princess was in Bath last year, trying to raise support for the French royal family,' says Georgiana.

'She'd have done better to have stayed there,' said Sophie, peering over my shoulder. 'Even if she did end up having to scratch a living making bonnets, like some of the other *émigrés*.'

'As long as Citizen Louis Capet, as they now call the king, is alive there'll be unrest,' I say.

'Oh!' Sophie says, her cheeks flushing rose pink. 'Excuse me.'

Georgiana and I watch her as she hurries away to greet Mr Fielding.

'He's going to paint Sophie's portrait,' I say.

'Is he now?' Georgiana raises her eyebrows. 'She needs to be careful of Jack Fielding. He breaks hearts.'

'I'm sure Sophie is worldly wise enough to resist his blandishments.' But as I see the way she is laughing at some comment Fielding had made, I have misgivings.

I glance up as more guests arrive and recognise the Marquis de Roussel. He hasn't brought his wife with him this time but the Comte d'Aubery is at his side.

'Mr d'Aubery is here,' I say. I feel an odd quickening of my pulse at the sight of the darkly handsome man who had discomfited me so on our last meeting.

'He's taken a house in Conduit Street until the end of the year,' Georgiana says. 'I understand he's continuing to escort *émigrés* to our shores. Charming, isn't he?'

'I found him extremely self-important,' I say, uncomfortably picturing the disdain for me in his eyes when we last parted.

'I haven't found him so,' says Georgiana.

'Tell me, did he really murder his wife?'

She shrugs. 'There was a deal of speculation over the matter, I believe.'

But I forget Etienne d'Aubery as I watch how closely Sophie and Jack Fielding stand together as they talk.

Fielding glances over Sophie's shoulder and meets my eyes. He stares back at me, unsmiling, his fingers trailing over the bare skin of her arm as she gazes up at him.

Then I become deeply involved in discussing education and the rights of women with Mary Wollstonecraft until Mr d'Aubery joins us. I stop talking in the middle of a sentence and stand stiffly, remembering our last encounter.

'What is your opinion of recent events in France, Mr d'Aubery?' asks Miss Wollstonecraft.

'I am saddened that it has come to this. The end of the monarchy . . . ' He shakes his head sorrowfully.

'But the people of France are free from tyranny now,' I reply. I'm wearing new yellow satin shoes that have begun to pinch one of my little toes. I shift slightly from foot to foot. The shoes are very pretty but I'm still undecided if that compensates for the discomfort.

'That, of course, is true.' He regards me steadily with his dark eyes. 'But I believe that losing the monarchy will release a terrifying beast such as the French people never imagined. The different factions are each so convinced their way is the correct way that I fear for the future of my country.'

Miss Wollstonecraft glances over at Mr Fox, who is saying goodbye to Georgiana. 'Please do excuse me,' she says. 'I must catch Mr Fox before he leaves.'

I glance at Mr d'Aubery uneasily, not caring to be alone with him.

'I must apologise,' he says. 'I believe I may have spoken sharply to you the last time we met.'

I stare back at him, coolly.

The faintest tinge of pink touches his ears. 'The situation in France is complicated,' he says, 'and I doubt anyone, native to France or not, can see the way clearly through the troubles of the present time.'

I'm slightly mollified by his apology. 'I concede that I have never visited the country of my father's birth but I assure you I do keep abreast of the latest developments.'

D'Aubery bows. 'I have no wish to quarrel with you. In fact, since it has started to rain, perhaps you would allow me to convey you home in my carriage?'

I hesitate, unwilling to feel beholden to him. 'I came with my friend Mrs Levesque.'

'Then, of course, she must accompany us too.'

I glance at the window and see that rain is indeed running down the glass. It would be a shame to allow my new, if uncomfortable, satin slippers to be spoilt in the mud.

Sophie is nowhere to be found in Georgiana's drawing room. In the hall I see the door to the dining room is ajar and hear her infectious laughter, a sound I haven't heard in a long while, coming from inside.

I push open the door and discover Sophie and Jack Fielding with their arms entwined as they share a glass of wine.

She starts and pulls away from him, colour rising in her cheeks. 'Madeleine! I didn't see you there.'

'It's raining and Mr d'Aubery has offered to take us home in his carriage.'

Jack Fielding doesn't acknowledge me and my hackles rise as he drains his glass.

'Run along, Mrs Levesque,' he says.

Sophie pouts prettily. 'But I shall see you tomorrow at two o'clock for my sitting, Mr Fielding?'

He kisses his fingers to her. 'Indeed you will.'

Mr d'Aubery is taking his leave of Georgiana in the hall and a moment later we're hurrying through the rain to his carriage.

Sophie says little as we travel but stares out of the window with a half smile on her face, so that I must make polite conversation with Mr d'Aubery unaided by her.

A short while later we stop outside the Levesque house and Mr d'Aubery holds an umbrella over Sophie as she ascends the front steps.

He slams the carriage door behind him when he returns and brushes the rain off his broad shoulders. I cannot help but approve of his natural elegance.

When we arrive at Soho Square he insists on accompanying me to the front step, shielding me from the rain with his umbrella.

Papa opens the door. 'Ah, Madeleine! I was in the library and guessed it might be you.' He looks at Mr d'Aubery, his head on one side. 'And you have brought a guest? A fellow Frenchman, I believe?'

'*Exactement.*' Mr d'Aubery bows to Papa.

'Come in, come in!' Papa beams and shakes hands with him vigorously. 'I've just opened a bottle of good French wine and would welcome your opinion.'

My heart sinks. Clearly Papa is under the illusion that I have brought home a suitor to meet him.

We follow him into the library where we find Mama working on her embroidery.

'Were you caught in the rain, Madeleine?' she asks, without looking up.

'Mr d'Aubery brought me home in his carriage,' I say.

Mama glances up at my companion and hurries to put aside her needlework.

Papa and Mr d'Aubery become very animated as they swirl the wine in their glasses, holding them up to the light from the window to examine the ruby colour.

'I like the look of Mr d'Aubery,' whispers Mama. 'Is he eligible?'

'He's a widower,' I murmur, 'but I have no intention ...'

Mama smiles to herself and pats my hand.

Before very long the two men are arguing good-naturedly about recent events in Paris.

'I see now how you influence Mademoiselle Moreau's ideas on French politics,' says Mr d'Aubery to Papa with a smile.

'Never underestimate my daughter's intellect and strength of will,' he laughs. 'I assure you, her ideas are her own.' He shrugs and purses his lips. 'But perhaps, having no son, I have encouraged her to assert her intellectual opinions in a way that is more French than English for a young lady.'

'I like a woman to be interested in current affairs and to have more conversation than the choice of ribbons for her bonnet,' says Mr d'Aubery, 'even if we disagree.'

Papa claps him on the shoulder. 'A man after my own heart!'

When Mr d'Aubery laughs his whole demeanour changes and, watching him so at ease with Papa, I wonder if I should revise my opinion of his character.

'Which part of France do you come from, Mr d'Aubery?' asks Mama.

I look at my feet, wishing she wouldn't interrogate him.

'I have a town house in Paris but my estate is near Orléans,' he says. 'It was granted to my ancestor, Edouard d'Aubery, by King Louis XII in 1499.'

'And your family?' asks Mama.

'My sister lives in America. My parents unfortunately died in a carriage accident three years ago and my elder brother drowned when he was eighteen.'

'How very sad!'

'We are a family beset by tragedy.'

I notice that he doesn't mention his dead wife.

Papa uncorks another bottle of wine. 'I'd be interested,' he says, 'to hear your opinion on this vintage.'

'I wonder ... ' says Mr d'Aubery to Papa. 'I couldn't help noticing your ring. Are you by any chance connected to the Moreau family of Fontainebleau?'

I hold my breath. Am I finally to discover more about Papa's relations?

He pauses in the act of pouring another glass of wine for our visitor. 'I have no family,' he says. 'Now tell me what you think of this.'

I let out my breath in disappointment.

'Well!' says Mama a little later, after Mr d'Aubery has left. 'Not only is your friend well connected, Madeleine, but he's extremely handsome and has excellent manners.' She smiles at Papa. 'Much like you, Philippe, at that age.'

He kisses Mama's hand lingeringly and I leave them to discuss their day whilst I retire to plan tomorrow's lessons.

Chapter 3

Papa holds aloft a cane with a red ribbon tied to the tip; a pre-arranged method of ensuring that the Jephcotts will recognise us amongst the crowd of nuns, Roman gods and pirates milling around in the sunshine outside the gates of Vauxhall Gardens.

I'm effervescent with excitement as Chinese acrobats tumble amongst us, while a dwarf dressed as Pierrot collects coins from the delighted onlookers.

'How can they bear to be so energetic when it's as hot as this?' asks Mama, fanning herself.

We look very fine. Papa is a cavalier of the last century, complete with extravagantly feathered hat, lace cuffs and a sword, while Mama makes a graceful Eleanor of Aquitaine. My own costume of Queen Marie Antoinette dressed as a shepherdess is far from original, I had seen three other shepherdesses and a milkmaid even before we entered the gates, but the costume suits me. We all wear black domino masks.

A rotund Turk, brown-skinned and fearsomely moustachioed, pushes his way through the throng and claps my father on the shoulder.

'Here we are, Moreau! I thought we might never find you in such a press.' Mr Jephcott takes hold of the hands of the Queen of Sheba, a plump little woman with a ready smile under her mask, and a young woman dressed as a milkmaid. 'Mrs Jephcott and my daughter Lydia.'

Papa sweeps off his feathered hat and bows low.

As we greet each other I see that my own delight in the occasion is reflected in Lydia's shining eyes. She has her mother's petite figure and a tumble of fair curls on her shoulders.

There is some good-natured arguing between Papa and Mr Jephcott about who will pay the shilling each entrance fee and then we are admitted through the gates and into the Grove, the central area of the gardens.

'How about that for a sight, ladies?' says Mr Jephcott, opening his arms wide.

The Grove is lightly wooded and surrounded on three sides by arcades forming fifty or so open-fronted dining alcoves. The magnificent pavilion designed for the Prince of Wales, so Mr Jephcott tells us, is situated on the fourth side. An octagonal building, Chinese in style, is set before us, several storeys high, with openings all around and illuminated from within. Lively music from an orchestra situated on the top floor of the building makes a merry background to the hum of excited conversation.

Several *allées* open off the Grove, enticing us to explore.

Lydia claps her hands. 'May we walk around the gardens before supper?'

We set off, full of anticipation, along the South Walk, one of the wide avenues through the wooded gardens, lined with elms and spanned by Italianate triumphal arches.

More than a thousand other visitors are promenading in the early-evening sunshine and it's impossible not to be entranced by the costumes and the general air of gaiety. Who can tell, under their dominoes, if these elegant ladies and their masked companions are lords and ladies or light-skirts and their patrons? Even Mama is charmed by the snatches of music and singing coming from a number of Greek temples secreted in the copses that edge the walks.

'Oh, look!' says Lydia, clasping my hand.

Hurrying forward through the groups of revellers we exclaim in delight at the sight of picturesque ruins, arches and columns, with nearby a cascade tumbling over rocks into a pool edged with ferns.

'We must take our seats for supper before sunset,' says Mr Jephcott.

The shadows are lengthening as the sun lowers itself in the sky and we make our way back to the Grove, now thronged with masked guests sitting in the dining alcoves. The aroma of roasting chicken is drifting on the air and waiters are hurrying hither and thither with trays of cold meat and pies held aloft.

'The food is plain but good,' says Mr Jephcott, as we place our order. 'And we shall have a bottle of the best French wine.'

I'm amused to see that the glue adhering his enormous black moustache to his top lip has melted in the warmth and it hangs awry.

'Harold?' murmurs Mrs Jephcott, touching her top lip and giving him a meaningful nod.

'Jephcott, perhaps this is a good time for you to explain some of your new ideas for the Academy to my wife?' says Papa.

'But, of course,' says Mr Jephcott, patting his moustache back into place. 'I've long been interested in the education of women, who, I believe, are vastly underrated in what they can achieve.'

'It's so important to catch the girls while they are young and before their heads are full of foolish notions, don't you think?' says Mrs Jephcott.

Mama nods in agreement.

'I'm most impressed by the reputation of your school,' continues Mr Jephcott. 'But I believe it could be enhanced if you were to offer a boarding facility. This would allow you to foster more entirely an atmosphere conducive to learning. My dear wife would act as Matron and take responsibility for the girls' pastoral care.'

'Under Mrs Moreau's direction, of course,' says Mrs Jephcott. 'And I would also be happy to give singing lessons,' she adds.

Her husband gazes fondly at her. 'My dear Eliza has the singing voice of a nightingale.'

She blushes rosily and smiles at Mama. 'Mr Jephcott has a particular fondness for Italian opera.'

'And our Lydia studies Latin and has an uncommon interest in natural science,' he continues.

On the other side of the Grove sits a boisterous group of young men in naval uniform, singing 'The Lass Who Loved a Sailor'.

Our waiter returns with a tray piled high with wafer-thin ham, cold chicken, salads and pies. My stomach begins to growl in anticipation.

'They shave the ham so thinly here that you can read a newspaper through it,' says Mr Jephcott, holding up a scrap of meat on his fork.

The sun has almost disappeared behind the trees but it's still very warm. I pluck at my mask, which is hot and sticky against my face since there is no breeze to dispel the humidity.

'There's a surprise in store for you, Lydia and Madeleine,' says Papa, his eyes twinkling.

It's growing dark and there is a general air of expectation amongst the guests. The party of young men begins to bang their knives on the table and to chant, 'The lamps! The lamps!' Several of the other diners join in until it's impossible to speak above the din. The orchestra ceases playing Handel's *Water Music*.

'What's happening, Papa?' I shout.

Before he can answer a whistle blows and a great roar of approval reverberates around us as lights begin to glimmer almost simultaneously in the thousands upon thousands of lamps hanging from the trees and suspended around the buildings in the Grove.

I catch my breath at the magic of it. 'It's like the Arabian Nights,' I gasp. 'How do they do that?'

Mr Jephcott laughs. 'A clever trick, don't you think? A series of fuses lead from lamp to lamp and, upon a signal, men stationed all around the gardens set them alight.'

'It's as bright as day!' says Mama.

'So are you pleased you came, after all?' asks Papa.

'How could I not be? Although,' she gestures to the young men, now becoming boisterous as they call for more wine, 'I suspect it may not be a good idea to stay too late.'

'But we must remain long enough to join in the dancing after supper,' protests Mr Jephcott.

The orchestra strikes up again, this time playing a jolly rendition of 'The Lass of Richmond Hill', and many of the diners sing along, all very merry. The festive atmosphere is infectious and I breathe out a sigh of contentment. Mama and Papa are in earnest conversation with Mr and Mrs Jephcott. I'm beginning to like the couple and am not at all opposed to their breathing new life into the Academy.

'It's very close, isn't it?' Lydia pushes away her empty plate and fans her face.

'I shouldn't wonder if there's a thunderstorm later,' says her mother.

'May Madeleine and I take a little walk?'

'Not now, Lydia. I wish to continue my conversation with Mr and Mrs Moreau so I can't accompany you.'

'But we won't go far!' she wheedles.

'Perhaps if the girls stay in the Grove, in the light where we can keep an eye on them, it wouldn't do any harm,' says Mr Jephcott. 'What do you think, Moreau?'

Papa glances at Mama. 'I believe the young ladies are too sensible to stray far away.'

'Thank you, Papa.' All at once the supper box is too stifling to endure another minute and I cannot wait to walk outside in the breeze. Besides, I want to mingle with the crowd.

Lydia links her arm through mine and we stroll around the Grove, lost in the excitement of it all. There's a full moon to add to the golden glow of the lamps. Everywhere we look there are amusing sights: a nun walking with an imp of Satan, Caesar laughing with Columbine, and two sailors and a host of nymphs shrieking with laughter at the sight of a pope juggling oranges. I cannot remember when I was last so entertained.

Two highwaymen fall into step beside us, both masked and with pistols tucked into their belts.

'Evenin', ladies,' says the tallest one. 'Mind if we walk with you a while?'

'Can't stop you,' says Lydia, pertly.

Somehow the highwaymen are now one on either side of us, with arms linked through ours. Two Greek goddesses run past, screeching in delight as Harlequin and a pirate chase after them.

I glance back at the supper box but Mama and Papa are deep in conversation with Lydia's parents. I wonder whether I should give our new companions a sharp set down but really they aren't doing any harm. The conversation is light-hearted and flirtatious. I find myself enjoying it.

'If we're going to walk with you, we must know your names,' says Lydia.

'Our names?' says the taller of the men, gripping my arm. 'Well now, that's against the rules of a masquerade, isn't it? Our identities must remain a secret. Let's just say I'm Dick and this gentleman here is Tom.'

Tom bows low and Dick kisses my hand. I feel the moistness of his lips against the back of my hand and I'm not sure that I like it. 'And who might you be?' he asks.

'Antoinette,' I say, 'and my friend is Aphrodite.'

Lydia giggles.

Tom takes a bottle of wine out of his coat pocket and pulls out the cork with his teeth, never letting go of Lydia's arm. 'Here you are, Aphrodite,' he says.

After Lydia has sipped from the bottle she hands it to me. I

28

hesitate briefly then drink some too. It's vinegary, not at all like the pleasant wine we had with our supper.

There's a peculiar stillness to the overheated air and I see that Dick's forehead under his highwayman's hat is beaded with sweat.

'Let's take a turn down here, shall we?' says Tom, swinging us around to walk into one of the avenues.

We have walked a little way before I realise that it's unlit here and, except for a few couples seeking solitude in the shadows, only a few other people are nearby.

'I'm not sure ...' says Lydia.

There is a rustling and a moaning in the bushes, and a peal of drunken laughter.

'There are the ruins of a temple a little further on. We could sit there a while and talk,' says Tom, persuasively.

'It's too dark here,' I say, wondering what his face looks like behind the mask.

A giggling nun, hand in hand with a satyr, walks past us and disappears into the dense blackness of the copse beside the avenue.

A fat drop of water lands on my arm. I look up and see the moon veiled by cloud. Another raindrop falls on my upturned face and all at once I'm uneasy. We're too far away from the bright lights of the Grove. 'We must return, Lydia,' I tell her.

'Not yet,' says Dick, his breath hot on my cheek. 'You haven't paid us for your wine.'

'Paid?' Lydia looks confused.

'You need to pay us with a kiss,' says Tom, imprisoning her into his arms.

'Certainly not!' I say indignantly. 'Come on, Lydia, let's leave.'

The rain begins to fall in earnest now and in a moment Lydia's thin muslin dress is soaked and clinging to her figure, leaving little to the imagination.

Dick grips my arm. 'Not yet,' he says, pulling me towards the shadows.

I struggle against him, but every time I free one of his hands from my arm or wrist, he catches hold of me again.

Lydia is thrashing around in Tom's arms, turning her face away as he attempts to kiss her.

Dick's fingers press painfully into my upper arm.

'Let me go!' I cry.

Lydia's piercing scream is almost drowned by a monstrous clap of thunder.

I shout her name but Dick silences me by pressing his mouth over mine. He tastes of wine and raw onions. His hands are all over me, pinching my breasts and cupping my buttocks. I'm revolted and frightened now, and when the bright flash of lightning comes it only serves to illuminate his face and show me his bestial intent.

The rain begins to drum down on my head and shoulders, splashing up from the earth to soak my skirt. I hear Lydia shrieking as I scratch at Dick's face, fighting him every inch of the way as he drags me towards the deeper darkness of the shrubbery. My feet slip and slide in the thin mud forming on the sun-baked earth and I'm full of disbelief that the magical evening could suddenly have become so terrifying.

Dick pushes me against a holly bush and I scream as he lifts my skirt and then his hands are between my thighs. Twigs prick my back and spiny leaves catch at my hair as Dick grinds his hips against mine, fumbling at the buttons of his breeches as I squirm in his grasp.

Just as I think all is lost there's a great bellow of rage and Dick releases me so suddenly that I stumble and fall to the ground.

Papa, his chest heaving for breath, holds Dick's arms pinioned behind his back. Mama stands beside him, her eyes wide with apprehension and her hair sodden.

Mr Jephcott runs up to Lydia and, with a yell, kicks her assailant's knees.

Surprised, Tom lets Lydia go and she runs sobbing into her mother's arms.

Mr Jephcott snatches up a stick from the ground. 'I'll beat you within an inch of your life,' he roars.

Thunder cracks again and Tom yells each time the stick slashes down across his shoulders and head.

Dick erupts from Papa's arms and punches Mr Jephcott on the chin. 'Leave 'im alone!'

Without a word, Mr Jephcott sinks senseless to the ground.

Papa, raging in French, pulls his sword free and runs at Dick.

There's a flash of silver and Dick yells, 'Damn your eyes, you've run me through, you bastard!'

Papa jerks the sword out of Dick's thigh and readies himself to strike again. 'You have dared to attempt to dishonour our daughters and you will pay the price.'

Dick's knees buckle and he falls down, arms over his head, begging for mercy, while the blood spurts from his thigh into a dark pool on the earth.

Tom rears up from the ground with rain and blood running down his cheeks in rivulets, his highwayman's pistol levelled at Mama. 'Get away from him, you damned Frenchie,' he shouts, 'or I'll shoot her!'

Ice cold with terror, I see how his hand shakes. 'Don't!' I shout, but my voice fails me and comes out as a whisper.

Stopped in his tracks, Papa looks at Mama and lets his sword arm fall to his side. 'You are the scum of the earth, preying on women weaker than yourselves . . .'

'Philippe, I implore you . . . ' Mama gasps as Papa kicks viciously at Dick's supine form.

Dick screams and Tom lifts his wavering pistol arm, pointing it at Mama.

It all happens so fast. Papa, sword raised, leaps at Tom.

Mama runs forward and clings to his back to restrain him.

There's a sharp crack and a blinding flash.

'Philippe!' screams Mama.

Then there is silence, save for the rain falling from the black sky and hissing on to the ground.

Chapter 4

I draw the curtains to close out the shaft of sunlight that falls across Mama's face where it rests on the pillow. 'Is that better?' I whisper.

She nods and I stroke her hair off her brow. Fever blazes in her cheeks.

'Madeleine?' she murmurs.

'Can I fetch you something?' If there is anything she wants I will go to the ends of the earth to find it, but nothing I can do will ever assuage my guilt. If I had not so foolishly allowed myself to be beguiled by the enchantment of that evening, I'd never have gone walking with strange men.

'Madeleine, bury me next to my dearest Philippe.' She loses control for a moment. 'Oh, my Philippe!'

'You're *not* going to die!' I grip her hand fiercely and pull it to my lips.

'It's too late for me, sweetheart.'

In my inmost heart I know she speaks the truth but I cannot accept it. 'You *will* get well, Mama!'

'Papa's ring ... after I'm gone, you must wear it.'

She twists his signet ring around her finger and I close my eyes to shut out the painful memory of removing it from his finger even before his body grew cold. The bullet had penetrated his heart and killed him instantly. Mama had been pressed so closely against his back as she tried to restrain him from attacking Tom that when the bullet had exited Papa's body it had lodged in her chest. The surgeon had removed it but within a few days infection had set in.

'Mama, should I write to Papa's family?'

Wearily, she shakes her head. 'There is no one he would wish to contact.'

'But surely . . .'

'He always said that the past is past and we must look only to the future.' A tear rolls down her cheek. 'I know nothing of Papa's family except that they came from near Fontainebleau,' she says. 'He always refused to talk about them to me.'

Mama's hand reaches out for me and as I curl my fingers around her wrist I feel the pulse there beating as fast as the wings of a trapped bird. Suddenly her face crumples in distress. 'I always meant to make peace with my own parents before they died but I left it too late. My father was a good man but too proud to seek me out to forgive me.'

'What happened between you?' I hardly dare to ask but I must know.

She sighs. 'On the day I was to have married the man he chose for me, I eloped with your father, leaving my intended at the altar.'

I gasp. The very idea of my gentle mother behaving so outrageously is inconceivable to me.

'After Philippe arrived in England he came to work at Maitland Hall, my parents' home, as my French tutor. We fell in love but Father refused to consider the match.' Mama's mouth twists into a small smile. 'A penniless French tutor had no place in his plans. Don't cry, sweetheart,' she says. 'I never regretted marrying your father.' Weakly, she reaches up to touch my hair. 'It is imperative now that I write to my lawyer.'

To humour her, I bring her paper and ink and prop her up against the pillows. When she's finished, I fold the letter and set it on the dressing table, amongst the medicine bottles, bandages and basins.

There is a knock on the door and our maid Sarah beckons to me from the doorway. 'Mrs Jephcott and Miss Jephcott have come to call upon you.'

Mama's eyes are closed.

'I'll be back in a few minutes,' I say.

She nods her head and I stand up carefully, so as not to disturb her.

'Madeleine?' Her voice is no louder than the rustle of dry leaves stirring in a breeze. 'It breaks my heart to think of you alone, but I love you, sweetheart. Never forget that.'

I kiss her hot forehead and wipe away my own tears.

Hurrying downstairs, my footsteps echo as I cross the hall. The Academy has been closed since that dreadful night when Papa was murdered and the house is eerily quiet.

Mrs Jephcott and Lydia are waiting in the drawing room.

'We came hoping for better news of dear Mrs Moreau,' says Mrs Jephcott.

'The doctor called again this morning to dress the wound,' I say, 'but ...' My face crumples as the tears flow. 'He says that the infection has spread and that she cannot overcome it,' I sob.

Mrs Jephcott murmurs condolences while Lydia hovers nearby.

'We'll come again tomorrow but send for us at once if ...'

'Thank you.'

Mrs Jephcott hesitates a moment and then says, 'Mr Jephcott went to witness your father's murderers hang this morning. Both of them snivelled and wailed like the cowards they were but now they'll never have the opportunity to prey on innocent young women again.'

'I can't find it in my heart to forgive them yet,' I say.

I return to the sickroom to find Mama moaning softly in her sleep.

Her breath comes in shallow gasps and I whisper endearments to her until she quietens.

She dozes through the night, waking only to mutter confused questions about Papa's whereabouts. Her cheeks and chest are flushed with fever and the whites of her eyes are yellow.

At last exhaustion overwhelms me and I rest my forehead upon our clasped hands and sleep.

The sound of a cart rattling over the cobbles below awakens me. Dawn light filters through the curtains as they wave softly in the breeze from the open window and dances upon the bedchamber wall. My neck aches from my awkward position hunched over the bed and I let go of Mama's hand and stretch out my back.

Her face is pale and I reach out to touch her forehead and find that the fever has gone and her skin is cool.

The room is very quiet and Mama continues to sleep peacefully. All at once my heart begins to thud.

'Mama?' I stand up and lean over her, my hand to her nose. Not a breath stirs. 'Mama!' Her eyes don't open when I shake her. Sobbing, I gather her into my arms but I know that my worst fear has come true. Both my mother and my father are dead and I am entirely alone in the world.

A gust of wind sweeps clouds across the stormy sky above the grave-yard but then the sun emerges, making me squint in the unexpected brightness. My eyes are gritty from weeping and the unyielding black wool of my new mourning clothes chafes my neck. All the Academy staff, many pupils, their parents, our neighbours and a great number of the French community in London have come to pay their respects as Mama is laid to rest beside Papa.

Silent tears blind me as I sprinkle a handful of earth upon her coffin. I shall never see either of my beloved parents again and a piercing stab of anguish makes me falter. Sophie grasps my elbow as my knees threaten to give way.

After Mama is buried I lead the mourners in a silent procession back to the house where I stand, dazed, in the hall greeting the guests. A sea of faces passes in front of me but my eyes are blurred by tears as I accept their kisses and kind words. I wish that they would all leave me in peace. There is a hovering blackness on the edge of my vision and my eyes close as I begin to sway.

A warm hand grips mine and a voice speaks to me in French. I blink as I realise that it is Mr d'Aubery's dark eyes I see looking into my own.

'Enough,' he says, taking my arm in a firm grip and leading me to a chair. He raises a finger to the maid who is carrying a tray of wine glasses amongst the guests. Lifting a glass of red wine from the tray, he holds it to my lips. 'Drink,' he commands.

Obediently, I sip.

'When did you last eat?' he asks.

'Eat?' I shrug. 'Yesterday, perhaps.'

He walks away and Signor Brunetti comes to offer his condolences. 'What is to become of us?' he asks, twisting a lace-trimmed handkerchief in his hands. 'Will you close the Academy? I must think of my Mammina.'

'I don't know.' I've been too shocked even to think about that.

Signor Brunetti pats my hand, tears welling in his eyes. 'I'm so sorry, *carina*. We will talk of it another time.' He draws a shuddering breath and tiptoes away.

'Miss Moreau?'

Amelia Wainwright's parents stand before me.

'We were sorry to hear the sad news of your parents' passing,' says Mrs Wainwright.

'But we must ask you what arrangements have been made for the school?' adds her husband. His coat is stretched tightly across his paunch and his purple cheeks bear testament to his enjoyment of fine wines. 'Now that your father is no longer Director ...'

'I don't know.' I press a hand to my chest. The room suddenly feels airless. 'I haven't thought.'

'I don't wish to press you unduly but Amelia's best interests must be protected.' Mr Wainwright's cold blue eyes bore into me.

Mr d'Aubery arrives at my side with a slice of veal pie on a plate. 'Excuse me,' he says, shouldering his way between Mr Wainwright and myself. 'Miss Moreau is faint with grief. I must insist you allow her to rest.'

Mr Wainwright's mouth tightens in irritation. 'But it's important ...'

'Most certainly,' says Mr d'Aubery curtly.

Wainwright starts to speak, sees Mr d'Aubery's forbidding stare, and stops. 'We shall discuss this further very soon, Miss Moreau.' Mr Wainwright takes his wife's arm and they walk away.

'Eat this,' says Mr d'Aubery, handing me the plate of pie.

It's easier to nibble at the pastry than to resist him. Surprisingly, a few moments after I have forced myself to swallow, I realise I'm hungry.

'Very good!' says Mr d'Aubery approvingly as he takes the empty plate from me a few moments later.

'Mr Wainwright is quite right, however,' I say. 'I must decide what is going to happen to the school.' The future, frightening and lonely, opens up like a chasm before me.

'There is time for that tomorrow,' says Mr d'Aubery. He looks around the crowded room. 'Do you have no family here?'

I shake my head. 'I have never known any family other than my parents.'

Sophie hurries up to us with a glass of negus. 'There you are.'

My friend has been very kind to me. She came to take me to stay at her home, arranged the funeral and held me all night when I couldn't stop shaking.

'I shall leave now,' says Mr d'Aubery, 'and perhaps some of the other guests will follow.' He takes my hand and lifts it to his lips. 'I am so very sorry that such a tragic event has occurred and feel privileged to have had the opportunity to meet both your parents. The world will be a sadder place without them.'

Tears that are never far away start to my eyes again at his unexpectedly kind words.

Sophie hooks her elbow through mine and stays by my side for the rest of the afternoon until, one by one, the guests leave.

Mr Jephcott approaches me with his wife and Lydia, to say goodbye. 'My dear Miss Moreau, I cannot adequately express the distress I feel at what has happened. I wish more than you can know that I had never suggested visiting Vauxhall Gardens.'

'I keep imagining what it would be like if it was Lydia who had lost both her parents,' says Mrs Jephcott, dabbing her eyes.

Lydia's gaze remains downcast, as if she cannot bear to look at me.

'I have no wish to add to your burdens,' says Mr Jephcott, 'but we should discuss plans for the Academy.'

I nod my head. I don't want to think about that now. 'Tomorrow at two o'clock? I need to ...'

'Of course.'

Later, Sophie and I close the door behind the last of the guests.

'You're as frail as a leaf,' she says with a worried frown. 'Won't you come home with me again tonight?'

'Thank you but I must become used to being on my own.'

Sophie sighs. 'I must go home to Henry now but if you change your mind, no matter what time of the night, send for me and I'll come at once.'

I hug her, grateful for her kindness but too close to tears to speak.

My feet are heavy as I go upstairs. Hesitating a moment, I open the door to my parents' room and go inside.

It's quiet and the dressing table is still crowded with the paraphernalia of the sick room. Papa's slippers are tucked under a

39

bedside table and Mama's nightgown is thrown across the end of the bed, as if they have just left.

There's a knot of pain in my chest so tight that it's hard for me to breathe. I hold Mama's nightgown to my face. It still smells of her skin and the perfume she used to wear. In my head I hear the last words that she uttered to me.

'*I love you, sweetheart. Never forget that.*'

Sobbing, I bury my face in the softness of her nightgown.

At last I am drained of tears and so tired that all I can do is curl up in Mama and Papa's bed. The last thing I see before I fall asleep is Mama's note to Mr Thimbleby propped up on the dressing table.

Mr and Mrs Jephcott arrive promptly at two o'clock the next day.

Mr Jephcott comes straight to the point. 'If your father's Academy is to retain its good reputation, it must re-open very soon. Would you allow me to assume the position of Director?'

I'm relieved that he's made the suggestion that appears to offer the most satisfactory answer. Papa liked Mr Jephcott and stated that he'd be happy for him to be closely involved in the running of the school. The staff will be relieved not to be turned off, but where does this leave me?

'You would, of course, have a home and a position here for as long as you need it,' says Mrs Jephcott, just as if she's read my mind.

It's a terrible decision to make, to give up the place that my parents worked so hard to build together, but is it possible for me to carry on here alone? More to the point, do I want to?

Silence stretches out until at last I speak. 'The Academy will lose more pupils if it remains closed any longer. Perhaps we could work side by side for a few weeks? To give us the opportunity to see if the arrangement suits us all.'

Mr Jephcott claps his hands. 'An admirable idea!'

Chapter 5

I gaze listlessly out of the classroom window while my pupils whisper and giggle amongst themselves. I have resumed my teaching duties again over the past weeks but a terrible malaise has settled over me. It's hard for me to comprehend that my life has changed so dramatically in such a short time.

I'd made the effort to attend Georgiana's salon but the political discussions failed to engage me. I'd looked for Mr d'Aubery to thank him for his kindness to me at Mama's funeral but there was no sign of him. Sophie, her eyes sparkling and her complexion positively glowing, was so entirely taken up by flirting with Mr Fielding that I became quite out of temper and left early, alone.

One of my pupils drops her book with a thud and I'm startled out of my reverie. I pull my thoughts back to matters in hand and ask Clarissa Gardiner to recite the poem she has supposedly been learning.

At last the bell rings and I'm thankful that lessons are over for the day.

I'm crossing the hall after the girls have all gone when Mr Jephcott calls me into Papa's library. Mrs Jephcott smiles briefly at me from her seat beside the window.

'Ah, Madeleine,' he says. 'As a courtesy I thought it time to appraise you of the changes I'm about to instigate in the Academy.' He peers at me over the top of his glasses.

It's strange to see this portly little person seated behind the desk, instead of Papa's lithe figure. 'Changes?' I ask.

'Of course there must be changes,' he says, a trifle impatiently. 'I've discussed the sad situation of your parents' passing with the landlord and he is happy for me to take over the rent payments from the next quarter day. Additionally, my purchase of the adjacent property is now complete.'

'That's good news,' I say, even though I find it hard to be excited by it.

'So at last we can move forward with the improvements,' says Mrs Jephcott.

'As you'll be aware,' says Mr Jephcott, unrolling a large drawing, 'I've been in consultation with an architect who has produced plans of the new arrangements.' He beckons me closer and Mrs Jephcott comes to join us.

'There will be new openings here between the two buildings on all four floors,' he says. 'The greater space will allow not only for additional classrooms on the ground and first floors but also for dormitories. The kitchens in the basement will be enlarged to serve the girls' dining room, which will be here.'

'In our drawing room?'

'There's no need for a drawing room in this side of the house any more since Mrs Jephcott, Lydia and I will have our own spacious private quarters in the new house.'

'I see.' And where am I to sit in the evenings? I wonder. 'And the new dormitories?' I ask.

Mrs Jephcott points to the second-floor plan. 'All these large bedrooms on the second floor will comfortably house six girls each.'

'But this one is my own room,' I say. A flicker of fear or anger, I know not which, kindles in my breast.

42

Mr Jephcott smiles. 'We can charge parents extra for those whose daughters would like a view overlooking Soho Square.'

'So where do you intend me to sleep?'

'The attics will provide a dormitory for twelve of the younger girls and further dormitories for staff and servants. We might squeeze in a partition to allow you some privacy, in respect of your former privileged position with the school.'

'I imagine you would prefer a room of your own, however small?' says Mrs Jephcott.

'So I'm to be relegated to a poky cupboard in the attics?' Outrage makes my hands and voice tremble.

'Madeleine, dear,' says Mrs Jephcott, a steely glint in her eye, 'you must see that Mr Jephcott will be put to a great deal of expense to make these improvements? It's essential that we use the space economically and make provision for as many girls as possible to bring in the necessary income. Your own salary depends upon it.'

I clench my fists and fix Mr Jephcott with a baleful glare. 'And do I have no say in how matters will be arranged?'

'Your teaching skills are known and acknowledged,' he says, 'and we would, of course, be very sorry to lose you.'

I hear the implied threat in his words and a wave of fear overwhelms my righteous anger, forcing me to drop my gaze. There is nowhere else for me to go.

Mrs Jephcott sighs. 'I do hope you aren't going to be awkward, Madeleine. Changes are often difficult to accept at first but it's necessary to do what is required for the greater good.'

I'm too furious and unhappy to answer. I leave the room before I say something I may regret.

The proposed building works commence and before long there is enough banging and hammering all day to wake the devil. Sometimes I have to shout over the noise to make myself heard in the classrooms.

As I walk downstairs one day, I find two workmen carrying Mama's favourite chaise-longue out of the drawing room.

'Where are you going with that?' I demand. I glance through the doorway and see that the carpet is being rolled up too.

'Mrs Jephcott's orders,' says one of the men. 'We're to strip this room and take the furniture to their new apartments. Excuse me, miss, but we've got a job of work to do.'

I retreat to my bedroom and weep, wondering how long it will be before I lose that too. I'm powerless to fight against the implacable Jephcotts.

I call upon Sophie several times in the ensuing weeks but rarely find her at home. My loneliness and despair mount and, if I had hoped to find solace in friendship with Lydia, I have been disappointed. One Saturday in November I make another overture towards her.

'It's a perfect day for a ride in Rotten Row,' I say. 'Will you come with me, Lydia?'

She bites her lip and looks away. I know already that she'll refuse.

'Why do you always rebuff me?' I ask.

Shrugging, she looks at her feet.

'Please tell me!' My feelings are hurt.

'I can't,' she mumbles.

'Have I offended you?'

Lydia sighs. 'I can't look at you without remembering that terrible night when your father died. I want to put it all behind me. I'm sorry, Madeleine, but it's too uncomfortable for me to be your friend.'

Feeling miserable, I retire to my lonely bedroom. I must face up to the fact that there is no comfortable position for me in the school any more. I twist my father's ring around my finger, losing myself in the changing colours of the luminous depths of the moonstone. It used to be said that anyone who looked deep into a moonstone could see into the future but I'm not sure I want to know what is going to happen to me. I do know there must be change ahead.

The change, when it arrives in early-December, comes in an entirely unexpected way, in the form of a letter. I remove the wax seal and unfold it. It's a response to Mama's letter that I posted to her lawyer, Mr Thimbleby.

Dear Miss Moreau,

May I offer my sincere condolences for your recent tragic losses? During her last illness your mother, the late Mrs Caroline Moreau, asked me to write to you and explain certain circumstances.

Upon the death of her parents, Mrs Moreau received an inheritance, which your father did not wish her to accept. The funds were therefore invested for you, to be made available for such time as you might have need of them. My client's instructions were for ourselves to release some of the trust funds to you immediately. You may find it reassuring to know that there is a sum available to you that is sufficient, if you live frugally, to allow you a modicum of comfort for the next few years.

Furthermore, when you attain the age of five and twenty you will inherit your grandfather's home, Maitland Hall. In the meantime, the property is tenanted and the income invested with the remainder of your grandfather's estate. These funds will in due course allow you to maintain Maitland Hall and enjoy a life of ease.

Arrangements have been set in train for you to collect an allowance from the Mercantile Bank in Threadneedle Street.

Please do not hesitate to write to me should you require further advice.

I remain your obedient servant,

Josiah Thimbleby

Carefully, I fold the letter and put it away in my pocket, only to take it out and read it again a few minutes later. Nothing can bring back my beloved parents but at least this legacy will bring me a measure of independence. All at once a tiny bubble of hope begins to swell inside me and I long to share it with the only person I know who will be happy for me.

Ten minutes later I'm buttoning my coat against the chill winter air and hurrying towards Sophie's house, hoping that for once she will be at home.

It seems that my wish is to be granted. However, when I'm admitted to the drawing room, I'm shocked to see that one of her eyelids is purple and swollen and there's a cut on her cheek.

I turn her face to look at her bruises in the light. 'Sophie, what happened? Was it Charles?'

'I'd prefer not to talk about it,' she says.

'But . . .'

'It's only been once this week. It's just that he caught my face this time.'

'Can't you tell your father?'

'I have,' she says brusquely. 'He tells me I should practise being a better wife.'

I'm appalled that Charles Levesque beats his wife and there is nothing in law that she can do.

'Never mind that. I have something to show you.' Sophie takes me by the hand upstairs to her bedroom and points to the large painting hanging over the bed. 'What do you think?'

I draw in my breath. I have to admit that Jack Fielding has talent. His portrait of Sophie shows her languorously reclining on a chaise-longue, her form draped in almost transparent gauze. He's captured her mischievous expression and enigmatic smile but also imbued her with a brooding sensuality.

'It's wonderful! You look . . .'

Sophie smiles faintly. 'Charles says it makes me look wanton and wouldn't let me hang it downstairs.'

Privately I agree with him.

We return to the drawing room and after Sophie has called for tea I tell her my own news. 'So now that I have an income,' I say, barely able to take my gaze off her bruised face, 'I thought we might go on a trip together. We'll take Henry with us and go to Bath, to drink the waters and visit the Assembly Rooms.'

The smile fades from Sophie's face. 'Ordinarily I'd be delighted but my diary is too full for me to leave town at present. I'm so sorry, Maddy.'

'I can't go unaccompanied.'

'And I've neglected you shamefully of late, haven't I? Perhaps Lydia would go with you?'

I shake my head. 'Sophie, I'm so miserable, I can't stay at Soho Square much longer!'

She bites her lip but still doesn't offer to accompany me to Bath. I try not to let my disappointment show but my pleasure at the exciting news has faded.

It is a few days before Christmas and the Academy is closed. The rain has pelted down all day and I have no inclination to walk through the downpour to visit Georgiana's salon. Instead, I remain by the fire in my bedroom since I cannot intrude upon the Jephcotts in their new apartment. I stare into the flames, wondering if I should leave the school and rent a room somewhere, but such a course of action would do my reputation no good. In three years I shall have more independence but how am I to endure living with the Jephcotts until I inherit Maitland Hall? Sighing, I pick up my book.

I'm dozing over Burke's *Reflections on the Revolution in France* when I hear the grandfather clock strike eleven and then a carriage draws up outside in the street. Within a few moments I hear a staccato knock on the front door.

Curious, I go downstairs and see that Sarah has opened the door to a visitor.

'Mr d'Aubery!' I say. 'Whatever brings you here?'

'I apologise for arriving at such a late hour but it's Mrs Levesque.' Rainwater drips off his hat and on to the floor.

'What has happened?' I ask, alarmed.

Mr d'Aubery hurries outside again and returns a moment later carrying Sophie in his arms. Silently, he places her on the hall chair and wipes raindrops from his eyes.

'Sophie, what is it?' I'm distressed to see that her face is contorted by sobs and she's quite unable to respond to my question.

'Perhaps it would be advisable to put Mrs Levesque to bed?' says Mr d'Aubery.

I can only agree. 'Sarah, bring a hot brick and a clean nightdress to my bedroom.' I attempt to pull Sophie to her feet but she's half-fainting from exhaustion.

'Permit me,' says Mr d'Aubery. He swings her into his arms as if she were no heavier than a child and makes for the stairs.

Once he has deposited Sophie upon the bed in my room he retreats and I peel off her damp clothing. Aghast, I study the livid bruising on her arms and stomach.

Her eyes are shocked and her mouth trembles so much that I don't ask her if her husband has done this.

Sarah brings towels, one of my nightgowns and hot bricks wrapped in flannel. I rub Sophie dry and slip the nightgown over her head. Once she's in bed and the blankets are tucked under her chin, she closes her eyes and a moment later she's asleep.

Downstairs, Mr d'Aubery is in the library with Mr and Mrs Jephcott.

'Mr d'Aubery, please tell me what has happened,' I say.

'Mr d'Aubery found your friend in a distressed state,' Mrs Jephcott intervenes, lips tight with disapproval.

'She's overwrought so I've put her to bed.'

'This is a disgraceful state of affairs,' says Mr Jephcott, 'and I sincerely hope none of the pupils' parents come to hear of it. You will remove Mrs Levesque from my school first thing in the morning and she will not be admitted here again.'

My school, he'd said! Hatred washes over me in a scarlet tide.

'It's late,' says Mr d'Aubery, standing up and saving me from making an unseemly and unprofitable outburst.

'I shall see Mr d'Aubery out,' I tell the Jephcotts through gritted teeth.

'What really happened?' I ask as soon as the library door closes behind us.

Mr d'Aubery shrugs. 'I was at Lady Woodhouse's salon this evening when I saw Mrs Levesque talking to Mr Fielding. The tone of the conversation was ... heated. I thought nothing of it at the time but later, when I left the house, I found your friend collapsed against the railings along the street. I went to assist her but she talked so wildly of drowning herself in the river that I dared not leave her.'

'Oh, poor Sophie! And thank you. I don't know what might have happened if you hadn't rescued her.'

'I shall call upon the Levesque household tonight to convey the news that she is safely in your care. A twisted ankle might suffice as a suitable excuse, I believe? Besides,' says Mr d'Aubery, his mouth curving in an ironic smile, 'I wish to avoid Levesque challenging me to a duel if he discovers I have run away with his wife.'

Chapter 6

The following morning when Sophie awakes she stares at me uncomprehendingly for a moment and then sits up.

'Oh, Madeleine!' she says, eyes tragic. She covers her face with her hands. 'I've been so foolish!'

'Tell me.'

'It would never have happened if Charles weren't so cruel ...'

'I saw your bruises.'

'Madeleine, it's unendurable! A few months ago I told him I knew about his mistress. Do you know what he said? "What business is it of yours?" And then yawned in my face. So I slapped him.' The corners of Sophie's mouth lift in a wan smile. 'For one moment I felt so powerful. But then he began to hit me. Since then he beats me all the time for the slightest thing and I'm so frightened he'll kill me.'

A hot rush of anger races through my veins. Sophie's position is even more intolerable than my own.

'So when Jack Fielding began to flatter me I lapped it up,' she continues. 'He told me I was beautiful, and the way he looked at me made me *feel* beautiful. All those afternoons when he was painting my portrait his eyes ran over my skin like a warm caress.' Her own eyes are defiant. 'I fell in love with him, Maddy, and he said he loved me, too.'

It's worse than I had realised. 'What does he think of the way Charles beats you?' I say carefully.

She shrugs. 'I think in some strange way it excites him.'

'Does Charles know about Jack?' Anxiety makes me bite my lip. If Charles Levesque knows, Sophie will certainly risk losing her son.

But she shakes her head. 'It would be certain death for me if he did.'

'What happened last night?'

'Yesterday I discovered from that odious gossip Mrs Hill that Charles has set up his mistress in a town house in King Street.' Her mouth twists into a bitter smile. 'Still, I didn't care because I knew that Jack would be waiting for me at Georgiana's salon last night. You see, we'd talked about running away to Italy and setting up home together.'

'You hadn't!'

'I thought that if I took Henry, then I'd be free from Charles for ever.'

'But you argued with Jack last night,' I say, remembering what Mr d'Aubery told me.

'I saw him flirting with Laetitia Bowes, persuading her to have her portrait painted. Hard words were exchanged between us. And then he told me he'd never loved me after all.' Tears well up in Sophie's brown eyes. 'He laughed and said he'd never had any intention of running away with me. He said ...' She breaks off and gulps for breath. 'He said he makes love to all the ladies he paints because then their skin glows and their eyes shine.'

I rock her in my arms as she sobs, and reflect on the cruelty of men and the foolishness of women.

'I'll put your box here, miss.' The workman hefts the box containing all my worldly possessions off his shoulder, crashes it to the bare floorboards. 'Shall I close the door?'

'No! No, thank you,' I say.

He nods and departs.

I look around me in dismay at the claustrophobic compartment. A narrow bed is pushed against the flimsy partition wall and there is, perhaps, two feet of space all around it. A row of hooks on one wall and a triangular washstand jammed into the corner complete the furnishings for my new bedroom. Panic begins to flutter in my chest. A small window looks out over the rooftops and I hurry to open it, but it's stuck fast.

Confined spaces have made me anxious ever since a mischievous school friend shut me in the coal cellar. Sophie had come looking for me, heard me sobbing and released me. I've never forgotten the fear I felt then and even now an icy shudder runs down my back at the memory. How can I possibly bear to live in what is little more than a cell for the foreseeable future?

Full of hatred for the vile Jephcotts, I hang up my clothes on the hooks and then go downstairs to sit in one of the classrooms while I prepare tomorrow's lessons.

When I have completed my task and tidied the books away I set off for Georgiana's salon. Sophie, following her return to her husband, has begged me to discover if there has been any gossip following the end of her affair with Jack Fielding. Since I'll do whatever I can to delay my return to the horrid cell, I'm pleased to have an excuse to go out. Besides, I have another reason for attending.

Georgiana comes to greet me with a kiss. 'Is Sophie not with you tonight?' she asks.

'I believe Henry had toothache,' I lie.

'Poor little boy!'

Since Georgiana is an inveterate gossip and she isn't questioning me about Sophie's affair with Jack Fielding, I am encouraged to hope that she has no inkling of my friend's collapse.

'Is Mr d'Aubery or the Marquis de Roussell here?' I ask.

'The marquis is here.' Georgiana leans towards me and lowers her voice. 'Though for my part I find him very dull company and rather hope he'll take himself off before too long.'

She drifts off to greet a new arrival and I make my way through the throng.

The marquis is talking in his execrable English at Daniel Stowe and when the poet sees me coming he grasps the opportunity to escape.

'I wonder if you would assist me in a small matter?' I say to the marquis, in French.

'If I can, Mademoiselle Moreau,' he says. 'And it is always a pleasure to converse in my own language rather than this barbarous English.'

I hold out my hand. 'I wonder if you would look at my ring?' I've been thinking about something Mama said as she lay dying and then I remembered that Mr d'Aubery had questioned Papa about his signet ring.

The marquis takes out his quizzing glass and peers at Papa's moonstone ring.

'It belonged to my father,' I say. 'He died recently and, since he never cared to talk about his family, I wondered if you might know anything about them? He said that this ring had been passed down from father to son for generations in his family.'

De Roussell studies the crest of the leaping deer engraved on the stone and then glances up at me. 'It's a very fine moonstone and I believe I recognise the crest. Which part of France did your father come from?'

'My mother said he originated from Fontainebleau. His name was Philippe Moreau.'

'Ah! Then I'm right. Philippe Moreau is the name of the eldest son of Louis-François Moreau, Duc de Limours. The family seat, Château de Lys, is near Fontainebleau, I believe.'

Stunned, I shake my head. My father, the son of a duke! During my childhood I had woven stories in which I was a long-lost princess, but this was no less fantastical.

'Is the Duc de Limours still alive?' I ask.

De Roussell shrugs. 'As to that I cannot say. But there is another son, I believe.'

I hardly remember taking my leave of the marquis or saying my goodbyes to Georgiana in my hurry to tell Sophie of the news.

When I arrive, quite out of breath, at Sophie's house, she's in the drawing room and looks up at me with an anxious expression. 'Did you hear any gossip about me?' she asks.

'None at all.' I run and clasp her hands. 'But you can't imagine my news,' I say. 'I showed Papa's ring to the Marquis de Roussell and he tells me that Papa was the son of a duke and that I may have an uncle, too!'

'No!' Sophie shrieks in delight. 'You *must* seek them out.'

It's an exciting but breathtakingly impossible idea, travelling to revolutionary France to find them. 'I couldn't. It's so far away, and they probably don't even know I exist.'

'Maddy, you've wondered about them all your life. And now that your parents aren't here to stop you ...'

I close my eyes as a shaft of pain pierces my heart again.

She hugs me, sympathetic tears welling in her own eyes. 'Whatever difficulties life presents us with, Maddy, at least we will always have each other.'

We talk about my discovery until it's too late for me to stay out any longer.

I return to Soho Square and eventually fall asleep in my nasty cell, my mind full of images of unfamiliar places and shadowy, faceless relatives.

Christmas Day comes and, although the Jephcotts dutifully include me in their festivities, I'm desolate. Echoes of earlier Christmases haunt me. I cannot help but remember the affection between the three of us when Mama and I sat by the fire roasting chestnuts, while Papa serenaded us with carols. Soho Square holds too many loving memories for me not to feel miserable now that Mama and Papa have gone. The school they established together is no longer my beloved home.

The day after Christmas I walk to the Levesque house to take my gift of a set of pewter soldiers to Henry, who throws his arms around me in delight.

Sophie has tears in her eyes as she greets me.

'Henry,' I say, 'perhaps you would take your soldiers up to the nursery?'

'What's the matter, Sophie?' I ask as soon as the door has closed behind him.

'Maddy, I don't know what to do,' she whispers.

'Is it Charles again?'

She shakes her head. 'I'm going to have another baby.'

'But that's wonderful news!'

'No, it isn't. It's not Charles's child.'

'Not . . . ' Shock silences me.

'Charles hasn't been near my bed for months.' She looks at me now, her eyes full of fear. 'It's Jack's baby. If Charles finds out he'll kill me.'

I don't doubt it. At the very best he'll turn her into the streets and never let her see Henry again. 'Sophie, what will you do?'

'What can I do, apart from take Henry and run away?'

'Charles wouldn't rest until he found you.'

'Maddy, come with me?' Her eyes plead with me. 'You want to find your papa's relatives. We could go to France together.'

I'm aghast. 'Sophie, talking about it is one thing, actually travelling on our own to France is quite another.'

'Mary Wollstonecraft did. And several other ladies of our acquaintance.' She grips my wrist, a fevered light in her brown eyes. '*Please*, Maddy! I'm so frightened.'

A tingle of excitement begins to runs through my veins. I cannot bear to remain in Soho Square for much longer and, more than ever, I want to find my French family. Could we really find a way to travel to France in its present state of upheaval? 'I suppose we could ask Miss Wollstonecraft's advice on how to go about it,' I say.

'We must call on her today,' urges Sophie.

'But, Sophie, if Charles hears what we're intending, he'll put a stop to it. You must ask his permission to travel. If you can persuade him to allow you to go, he'll have no need to come racing after you. If we leave here before your condition becomes apparent we can live quietly in France until the baby is born. And then ...'

'And then what?' asks Sophie.

'You must have the baby adopted.' She makes a mew of distress and I grip her hand. 'If you want to keep Henry at your side, you have no other choice.' I watch her face crumple. It hurts me to be so brutal but she must face facts.

'So the price of my adultery is that I must choose between my children?'

I don't answer. Nothing I can say will change that cruel truth. 'Let's ask Charles now,' I say.

'Will you do it?' Sophie's face is full of fear.

Five minutes later I knock on the door of Charles Levesque's study. Sophie grips my hand as I ask his permission for her to undertake the journey.

Charles shakes his head so that all his chins wobble and glares at Sophie. 'Go if you want to, Madam, but you're not taking my son.'

'Oh, but ...'

'Henry stays in his nursery. I'm not having him dragged about all over the place and at risk of contracting some foreign disease. The continent is full of vermin and dangerous fevers.' He glances at the clock. 'You've delayed me. I doubt I'll return for dinner tonight.'

After he has gone, Sophie weeps on my shoulder. 'I've no choice but to leave Henry behind, have I?'

'Not if you want to see him again,' I say.

A week later, Sophie and I are in my cell at Soho Square, poring over the packing list suggested by our travelling friends. We're arguing over the necessity for a rhubarb grater and two pairs of leather sheets when the maid comes to tell us that a gentleman has called to see us. Hurrying down to the drawing room, I'm surprised and secretly rather pleased to find Mr d'Aubery.

'Forgive me for calling on you unexpectedly,' he says, 'but I've heard a disturbing rumour.'

'Whatever can that be?' I ask. Mr d'Aubery is looking very handsome today in a chocolate brown velvet coat, a colour that matches his eyes.

'Lady Georgiana tells me that you plan to visit France.'

'I intend to seek out my father's family,' I say.

'And I shall accompany Madeleine,' says Sophie.

'I cannot permit this extremely foolhardy course of action.'

The smile fades from my face. 'I *beg* your pardon? By what authority do you forbid us?'

'Miss Moreau, France is in turmoil.' He speaks slowly as if we are dimwits. 'There are riots in the streets. Strangers are regarded with suspicion. And for two young Englishwomen ...'

'We both speak the language fluently,' says Sophie. 'We have French names and there is no reason for anyone to suspect we are not citizens of the Republic.'

'I beg to differ, Madame Levesque,' says Mr d'Aubery. 'Your spoken French has a Huguenot accent. And yours, Miss Moreau, although you are fluent ... there are times when you use an outmoded vocabulary. It may be enough to draw attention to you.'

Stung by his accusation, I say, 'I converse regularly with the

French community here in London and no one has ever mentioned that before.'

Mr d'Aubery shrugs. 'Do you have the necessary travel papers, proving that you are French citizens?'

I glance at Sophie. We hadn't thought of that. I tell him, 'It has become impossible for me to remain at the Academy any longer now that my parents are dead, and I have no remaining family in this country. I understand from the Marquis de Roussell that my father was the son of the Duc de Limours and that I have an uncle. Surely you can understand now why I must go to France?'

'De Roussell told you that?'

'He recognised my father's ring. As I believe did you.'

Mr d'Aubery looks at me impassively.

'Didn't you?' I insist.

'Your father had no wish to discuss the matter.'

'Nevertheless, I intend to visit Fontainebleau and meet the only family I have left.'

'This is not the time for such a visit. I implore you to reconsider.'

I lift my chin and fold my arms.

'Who travels with you?'

'We have no need of a great retinue of servants,' I say, forestalling him before he can argue the point. 'We shall not seek out any trouble,' I say. 'My intention is only to carry out my lifelong desire to meet my relatives and to for us to broaden our education by travel.'

'I beg you to desist.'

'Our minds are quite made up,' I said firmly.

He rubs his hands wearily over his face. 'If you are so determined,' he says after a long pause, 'and since I expect to return to France in the next fortnight, then I had better accompany you as far as Paris. I would never forgive myself if I discovered that your obstinacy had led you into difficulties.'

A great sense of relief washes over me. Despite my brave words it had occurred to me that this was not the best time to be travelling to France, but Sophie has no choice. Now we shall not have to make the journey into the unknown by ourselves.

Sophie lets out a cry of delight. 'Mr d'Aubery, that is the very thing! Think how merry we shall be all together.'

Mr d'Aubery sighs. 'I suggest I arrange false identity papers for you both and we shall all travel from Dover on the same packet.'

Chapter 7

Mr d'Aubery comes for me at first light one raw January morning.

I have slept poorly, worrying about the wisdom of venturing into a strange land in the company of a man who is reputed to have murdered his wife. Eventually, however, I decided that nothing in his demeanour leads me to believe he is likely to murder us. Besides, Sophie's plight permits no delay.

'I'll ask you once more,' says Mr d'Aubery, 'are you quite sure you wish to make this journey?'

The severity of his expression causes me another pang of doubt but I'll not back down now. 'I am.'

'At least you have followed my instructions regarding your luggage,' he says, lifting my single travelling bag into his carriage.

He'd warned us to bring nothing more than we can carry ourselves and to wear sombre clothes in the new French peasant fashion so as not to draw unwelcome attention. Sophie had argued but Mr d'Aubery had been so fierce in reminding her that the revolutionaries might otherwise believe us to be aristocrats and set upon us, that she had quietened her complaints.

'You must take off your father's ring, Miss Moreau,' says Mr d'Aubery. 'The crest may be recognised.'

Obediently, I slip the ring from my finger. I shall thread it on to a ribbon and wear it around my neck under my fichu.

A moment later we are rolling out of Soho Square.

I peer out of the rear window of the carriage at the house that has been my home for most of my life until it is lost from my view. Blinking back tears, I wonder if I have made a terrible mistake. But then I remember the look of relief in Mrs Jephcott's eyes as she'd glanced at her husband when I'd said my goodbyes the previous night and know that I cannot go back.

Before long we draw to a halt outside the Levesque house, where Sophie is waiting for us. There is no sign of Charles but Henry and his nursemaid come to see us off. After five minutes I have to remind Sophie that we'll miss our boat if she doesn't disentangle herself from her son's little arms.

Tearfully, she waves her handkerchief as we drive away and our last glimpse of him is when Betty lifts him up and takes him inside.

'Oh, Maddy, what have I done?' weeps Sophie, sinking back against the velvet cushions.

We travel all day, stopping only to change horses and eat a hasty supper at an inn. Sophie is pale and silent and at one point we stop the carriage as nausea threatens to overwhelm her. At last, we arrive at Dover.

I cannot help but be relieved that Mr d'Aubery is familiar with the harbour. It's dark already and we descend from the carriage and wait, shivering, on the bustling quayside while he takes the carriage to the stables.

Once on board the packet, our cramped, windowless cabin smells of salt and tar but we are so tired we can do no more than undress and fall into the bunks. We expect to set sail on the dawn tide.

Late the following morning Sophie and I stumble up on deck. The sea is still high but the packet edges closer to the shore as a flotilla of rowing boats comes to greet us.

'The tide is too low to risk sailing into the harbour,' explains Mr d'Aubery.

I look over the rail at the churning sea so far below, to where a boat awaits us. I've always been frightened of heights and the boat looks very small. 'But how will we ...'

'There is a ladder.'

'I can't!' Sophie says, horrified.

'You must,' he says.

'No!'

I grip Sophie's arm and give her a shake. 'Will you return to England then?' Her face crumples and she shakes her head. 'Mr d'Aubery will go down first,' I say, 'then I'll help you.'

Trembling from head to toe, she allows us to set her feet upon the flimsy rope ladder.

'Close your eyes and keep moving,' I say, smiling encouragingly at her, although my own heart is knocking fit to burst.

Sophie screws her eyes shut and lowers herself, step by step, down the ladder.

A sailor helps me over the side and I have to resist the urge to cling, whimpering, to the deck but I follow my own advice, close my eyes and set off.

Once our baggage has been lowered, the boatman starts to pull on the oars. Even if our clothes weren't already miserably damp, we would soon have been soaked by the persistent drizzle and the salt spray.

Eventually, to my great relief, the boat battles into harbour and jolts against the quayside. Chilled to the bone, I set foot for the first time in my father's homeland.

The stench of Paris assails our nostrils as soon as we reach the outskirts in the public coach, a thick mixture of coal smoke, excrement and rotting vegetation. The air carries something indefinably different from the smell of London ... garlic and tobacco and strong cheese, perhaps. All this had once been a part of Papa's life.

Three days of travelling in a draughty diligence and two nights in damp sheets infested with bedbugs have left both Sophie and myself scratching and sneezing. Our noses are streaming, my hair is a bird's nest, and I would give half the gold coins sewn into the hem of my petticoat to be able to lie in a clean bed in a darkened room.

The news that greeted us on our arrival in France, that King Louis has been charged with treason and sentenced to death in a few days' time, has alarmed us all but we dare not discuss it in front of our fellow passengers, several of whom wear the red, white and blue cockade of the revolutionaries.

In a whispered aside as we waited to board the coach, Mr d'Aubery said that any hint of concern for the king might cause our new travelling companions to condemn us as well.

'You must call me Monsieur d'Aubery, and if you must speak at all make sure it is only in French. And do not let your guard down,' he instructed, 'even for a moment.'

I've had plenty of time whilst travelling to mull over my misgivings about this journey and my thoughts on the Revolution. Whilst I still believe that France has no room for a simpering, extravagant queen and a spoilt king utterly out of step with his people, it has shocked me to the core that they are to be executed and not merely exiled. It appears that Monsieur d'Aubery is right and I lack the necessary knowledge, at present, to make proper judgements.

Monsieur d'Aubery, looking annoyingly healthy and well groomed this morning, pulls down the window of the coach and peers outside.

Tall houses line the mean streets and a gang of ragged street children race past, banging their fists on the sides of the diligence, shouting demands for sous. The coachman swears and cracks his whip, scattering the screaming urchins.

Sophie, her eyes fever-bright, presses her fingers to her mouth, her face so pale it's almost green. 'Please, the smell . . . '

Monsieur d'Aubery closes the window and the elderly woman sitting opposite hastily draws back her skirts as Sophie is wracked by another coughing fit that makes her retch into her handkerchief.

I sneeze violently into mine.

'Mademoiselle Moreau, I cannot in all conscience leave you both in your current state of health to seek accommodation once we arrive in Paris,' says Monsieur d'Aubery.

'I'm sure we'll manage.' But I dread the thought of tramping the streets to find lodgings.

'You shall come and stay with me until you are both well,' he says.

His tone might be dictatorial but I'm more than happy to accept his invitation, at least until we have recovered from our chills.

A stout gentleman eating raw onions and pungent goat's cheese is pressed against me and I peer around him to look out of the window. We travel slowly, our coach's progress impeded by hawkers of all kinds shouting their wares, selling everything from lottery tickets and kindling wood to rabbit skins. An oyster seller with a large basket on her back wrenches open the diligence door and offers us a dripping oyster shell. One of the young men casually kicks her off the step and slams the door again.

Suddenly we grind to a halt as a noisy group of men in loose trousers swagger down the narrow street, their hoarse cries reaching us even through the closed windows.

'Give us bread! Give us candles! Give us soap! Give us sugar!' they chant, over and over again.

The diligence rocks as they surge past us and two of the male passengers wearing the cockade rise to their feet and hang out of the windows, waving their fists in the air and shouting their support.

The elderly woman sniffs. 'The grocers who hoard supplies to inflate prices should be hung up by their ears above their own doorways.'

Once the protesters have passed, the two young men plump down in their seats again, eyes bright with excitement.

The diligence moves off and after a while the crowded, refuse-strewn thoroughfares give way to wide streets of shops and fine houses. Before long we draw to a halt.

We alight, stiff from hours of travelling, and the coachman throws our baggage down from the roof.

'It's not far,' says Monsieur d'Aubery, picking up Sophie's bag out of the mud. He sets off and I take her arm, shivering in the cold, damp air.

Rue de Richelieu is lined with substantial stone houses several storeys high and soon we arrive before an elegant mansion. A footman admits us and we are shown into the salon while Monsieur d'Aubery goes to find his housekeeper.

Sophie and I sink into red velvet chairs and regard the delicately carved and gilded *boiserie*s on the walls, the high ceiling and ornate chandeliers. Our feet nestle into claret and gold carpets set upon intricately patterned parquet flooring.

'I hadn't realised that Monsieur d'Aubery lived in such grandeur,' I whispered.

'At least we can expect clean sheets here,' says Sophie.

All I want is to lie down quietly somewhere, anywhere, until my thunderous headache has gone.

Monsieur d'Aubery rejoins us, bringing his housekeeper. 'Madame Guillet will take you to your rooms. Please ask for anything that will make you more comfortable.'

He dismisses our thanks with a wave of his hand and leaves us to follow the housekeeper upstairs.

Sophie's room adjoins my own and Madame Guillet casts a sharp-eyed glance around to check that all is in order. Ewers of hot water are steaming on the dressing table and snowy white towels warm by the fire.

'Please use the bell if there is anything you require.' The housekeeper closes the door behind her and I strip off my travel-stained clothes, wash and fall into bed.

The sheets, of exquisitely fine linen, are indeed not only clean but lavender-scented. I fall into a deep and dreamless sleep.

Chapter 8

I awake during the night to hear Sophie coughing. The fire has died down to glowing coals. Padding barefoot across the soft rug, I open the door to the next room.

'Sophie?' I whisper.

She mutters something I can't understand and her forehead is very hot. I curl up beside her on the bed in case she needs me but when dawn comes I creep back into my own room.

I awake when a maid brings in fresh hot water. A fire already crackles in the marble chimneypiece.

'Good morning, Mademoiselle. Shall I open the shutters and bring you some chocolate?'

Later, in spite of a continuing headache, I'm miraculously fortified by a cup of chocolate and a freshly laundered dress. I knock on Sophie's door and hear her feeble response. When I go in I see that perspiration beads her forehead as she's caught up in a paroxysm of coughing.

I prop her against the pillows and help her to sip water. 'Sophie, you need a doctor.'

'I don't want to be any trouble . . .'

'You'll cause even more trouble if you don't get better soon.'

I go out into the corridor and look over the balustrade into the cavernous hall below. I creep down the curving staircase and tiptoe across the black and white marble. Hesitating, I turn the handle of the salon door and start when I hear a voice behind me.

'Good morning, Mademoiselle Moreau. I trust you slept well?' Monsieur d'Aubery is freshly shaven and lightly scented with lemon verbena.

'I'm worried about Sophie,' I say, coming straight to the point. 'The chill has settled on her chest and she should see a doctor.'

'Then I shall send for Dubois,' he says. 'He is the family doctor and we can trust him.'

I return to sit beside Sophie, whose breathing is laboured. Nothing I do eases her discomfort so I greet the arrival of Dr Dubois with relief. A jovial man with shrewd grey eyes, he questions Sophie patiently while he takes her pulse and listens to her chest.

'We'll soon have you right again, Madame Levesque,' he says. 'I'll send round the apothecary's boy with some bronchial mixture.' He snaps his bag closed, bows to Sophie and nods to me before leaving the room.

Soon after, I slip away from her bedside and follow him. The door to the library is open and I stop in the action of raising a hand to knock on the door when I hear the deep tones of Dr Dubois.

'The king has his appointment with Madame Guillotine at ten o'clock tomorrow morning in the Place de la Révolution,' he says. 'They'll bring him from the Temple prison and parade him through the streets.'

'So soon, Armand? Is there no prospect of a reprieve?' asks Monsieur d'Aubery.

'Unlikely. And afterwards there is no going back.'

'There will be bloodshed while the different revolutionary factions fight for control. I fear for everyone, from the highest aristocrat in his château to the paupers scrabbling for crumbs in the gutter.'

'History will be made tomorrow,' says Dr Dubois.

Suddenly the door opens. I step back, my hand still raised to knock. 'I beg your pardon,' I stammer. 'I came to ask if I could fetch Sophie's medicine from the apothecary, to save time?'

'Certainly not!' says Monsieur d'Aubery. 'The streets of Paris are no place for a lady at present.'

'You would be wise to take heed of your host's warning,' says Dr Dubois. 'But never fear, Mademoiselle Moreau, I shall attend the apothecary immediately.'

The doctor is as good as his word and within the hour Sophie's medicine has arrived. The day drifts by in the routine of sick-room care. I read to Sophie from my book of poetry and watch the clock to be sure she has her medicine on time. In the evening when she's asleep, I join Monsieur d'Aubery in the dining room for supper.

I feel a certain awkwardness in dining with him *à deux*. It's perfectly proper as there are two footmen in attendance but, apart from a short journey in his carriage, we have never been alone together until now. We sit formally at either end of a long table with glittering candelabra set between us. The table is set with starched linen and gleaming silverware just as if we are at a banquet, even though the food is simple: soup, bread and cold chicken.

Monsieur d'Aubery smiles wryly. 'My mother would have been mortified to see such plain fare,' he says, 'especially when a guest is present. But life is different now.'

'And we dine in comparative luxury while so many in Paris are hungry,' I say, remembering the ragged children who chased after the diligence.

'Bread is criminally expensive and soap and other necessities are scarce.' His eyes gleam in the flickering candlelight. 'I always think that, without soap, man is quickly reduced to the level of the beasts.'

As I finish my dinner I wonder how much soap his housekeeper has squirrelled away and what would happen if the protesting *sans-culottes* came to look for it. I cannot imagine my urbane host, murderer or not, behaving like a beast.

'I must thank you again, Monsieur d'Aubery,' I say, 'for your assistance in accompanying us on this journey and for your kind hospitality. Truthfully, I don't know how Sophie and I would have managed if you had simply left us to fend for ourselves.'

'Perhaps I am not so unmannerly as you first thought me?' There is a hint of amusement in his eyes.

I'm covered in confusion. Perhaps he sees more than I have imagined. 'Please rest assured,' I say, 'that we have no wish to trouble you for longer than necessary. I'm anxious to meet my father's relatives as soon as Sophie is well.' I blot my mouth with a napkin and smother a yawn.

'Tired?' His voice is kind.

'I do beg your pardon,' I say. 'Although my chill is better it has left me fatigued.'

'Then I suggest you retire.'

We say goodnight and I experience a brief moment of regret that I'm not joining him in lingering over a glass of brandy.

Upstairs, Sophie is still asleep and I go to my own room. The bed has been warmed and I sigh with pleasure as the sheets enfold me. I lie in the dark, illuminated only by the fire, and ponder on the conversation I overheard between Monsieur d'Aubery and Dr Dubois. *History will be made tomorrow.* The knowledge reverberates around my head. *History will be made tomorrow.* At last I fall asleep, my thoughts full of vivid pictures of King Louis mounting the scaffold.

The following morning as soon as I'm dressed I visit the sick room.

'The king is going to the guillotine today,' I say as I pour out a spoonful of Sophie's medicine. 'It's hard to believe that such a terrible thing can happen.'

'I only want to sleep,' she says, swallowing her medicine.

I plump up her pillows and wash her face and she's asleep again as soon as I've straightened the sheets.

Outside the church clocks strike the hour. Nine o'clock. In one hour, on the twenty-first day of January 1793, history will be made.

In the Rue de Richelieu below a number of people are hurrying by and I wonder what King Louis is thinking in the Temple prison. Are the soldiers coming for him even now, to tear him from the arms of his sobbing wife and children and bundle him into a coach for his final journey? Has his priest listened to his last confession? It's impossible to grasp that these momentous events are taking place less than a mile from here. When I am old my grandchildren will ask me what I recall of this long-ago day. And what will I tell them: that I sat by a sick friend's bedside watching her sleep, while less than a mile away history was being made?

Almost without thinking, I find myself hastily buttoning on my coat and tucking my hair inside the deeply frilled cap that has become the revolutionary wear *de rigueur*. Closing Sophie's door behind me, I skitter downstairs and across the vast hall. The front door is locked. Nonplussed, I set off down the corridor towards the back of the house. I hear vegetables being chopped and the clatter of dishes through the open door to the kitchen and slink past before anyone notices me. The back door is unlocked and outside, at the end of the walled yard, is a bolted gate. The bolt draws back smoothly and a moment later I'm in an alley. I lose my bearings for a moment but then weave my way through a maze of lanes until I'm in the Rue de Richelieu again.

Men and women are running past and the frosty air vibrates with their excited chatter. In the distance I hear the tramp of feet and the banging of drums, and a wave of exhilaration washes over me. I'm swept up with the hurrying throng past the Palais Royal and into Rue St Honoré, carried along by the high spirits of the crowd. The wide road is lined with *sans-culottes* and soldiers of the National

71

Guard, while the teeming mass of people behind jostles at their backs.

I stand on tiptoe and catch a glimpse of thirty or so militiamen marching towards us, banging their drums as if on the way to a battlefield. The clamour is deafening and I put my fingers in my ears but the sound still resonates in my head. The crowd is shouting but the beat of the drums, the stamp of marching feet and the clatter of the cavalry who ride past with swords held aloft, drown the cries.

A woman standing next to me wearing a drab brown coat clutches at my arm and says something I can't hear. I shake my head and she shouts in my ear.

'The king's carriage is coming!'

I jump up to peer over the heads, my heart thudding in time with the drums. Amongst the cavalry escort I see a green coach making its way slowly along the road and the roar of the crowd swells.

I'm knocked flying by a great bull of a man carrying a fearsome pike. He curses at me. 'Get out of my way, Citoyenne!'

Suddenly frightened, I drag myself to my feet from the muddy cobbles before I'm trodden underfoot by others racing past. Catching my breath, I lean against the window of an umbrella shop and glance at the patriotic display of red, white and blue silk parasols. Then I'm caught up again by the noise and the excitement and the sense of urgency, and shoulder my way through the horde rushing towards the king's destiny. Today history is being made and I'm never, never going to forget the heart-stopping excitement of this moment.

Battered and bruised, at last I reach a great open square surrounded by classical buildings. The Place de la Révolution. Some way off is a raised scaffold surrounded by blue-coated soldiers with revolutionary cockades in their hats, all armed with rifles and fixed bayonets.

The square is heaving with a teeming multitude carrying pikes and guns and the noise is overwhelming. I elbow my way determinedly through the crowd and after twenty minutes or so I have a place near the front and can see the scaffold clearly now. It's higher than the height of a man and the guillotine looms fifteen feet above it. I supress a shiver as I see four executioners waiting impassively below, with their arms folded. They wear coats in the revolutionary style and tri-coloured cockades in their three-cornered hats.

The insistent drumming is growing faster, and louder, and in only a moment the soldiers step back to make way. The king's carriage rolls slowly into view and halts at the foot of the scaffold. A guard wrenches open the door and King Louis descends while the crowd roars in delight.

I see only a glimpse of his pale face before the executioners step forward to take off his coat. The king shrugs them off and calmly removes his own necktie and arranges his shirt to expose his neck. He's slightly plump and looks disappointingly ordinary. The executioner ties his hands with a handkerchief and then the king slowly climbs the ladder to the scaffold while the drums throb and the crowd jeers and shrieks in a hideous cacophony.

Once upon the platform King Louis crosses from one side to the other with a firm step and stares at the twenty or so drummers. They falter and one by one fall silent. The crowd, too, settles into an expectant hush. I hold my breath.

The king throws wide his arms. 'I die innocent of all the crimes laid to my charge,' he declares in a clear, strong voice. 'I pardon those who have occasioned my death and I pray to God that the blood you are about to shed may never be visited upon France.'

Sudden tears spring to my eyes at his last-minute bravery but then there is a great bellow from a cavalry officer.

'Beat the drums, damn you!'

The drummers begin to pound furiously again and hoarse shouts come from the crowd.

'Get on with it!'

'Death to Citoyen Capet!'

My mouth is dry as I watch the executioners grapple with the king and drag him under the blade of the guillotine. Suddenly I feel sick and my heart rattles rapidly behind my ribcage.

Then I hear a swish and a thud as the blade falls.

The king's head is severed from his body and drops into the basket below.

An artillery salute booms out over the square.

The crowd roars in an orgy of excitement. 'Long live the Republic!'

It isn't until this moment, this terrible moment when one of the executioners holds up the king's head by his hair, that the true horror of what I have seen hits me with the force of a lump hammer. The youngest executioner dances around the scaffold, shrieking in glee and swinging the severed head so that drops of royal blood sprinkle the spectators, while with his other hand he makes obscene gestures.

A woman standing next to me is jumping up and down, shrieking in delight. Turning aside, I vomit on to the ground.

Chapter 9

All around me people are whistling, cheering and kissing each other. Trembling with shock, I wipe my mouth. Am I the only person in the crowd who is sickened by what has happened?

A woman in a tricolour sash is standing next to me, watching. 'Aren't you pleased the king is dead, Citoyenne?' Her eyes narrow as she questions me.

'The sight of blood makes me ill,' I say, but I can tell from her expression that she doubts me.

'Now there will be freedom for everyone.' She throws back her head and yells, 'Death to the queen!'

A handful of people take up her cry.

She prods me with a grimy forefinger. 'You ... say it with me!'

I open my mouth but can't bring myself to shout the words.

The woman grips my wrist, her nails digging into the skin. 'Don't you want the royal bitch to die?' She frowns. 'Who are you? You don't speak like a citizen.'

I spin on my heel, snatching my wrist from her grasp, and began to shove my way through the crowd.

'Don't let her escape!' shouts the woman. 'She's a traitor to the Revolution!'

Others take up the cry. 'Traitor!'

I scream as hands clutch at my clothing and snag my hair. Sheer terror gives me the strength to propel myself onwards. A man grabs my arm, but then the cannon fires again close by and he looks up to watch a cannonball fly in an arc across the grey sky above. I twist out of his grip and force my way through the multitude until I reach the edge of the square. Glancing back, I see the woman in the sash screaming and shaking her fist at me. Heart hammering, I duck down and weave away through the crowd, panic lending me strength. At last I leave the square behind and run as blindly as if the devil is chasing me.

Breath rasps in my throat as my feet pound over the cobbles. At any moment someone might catch hold of me and drag me back. At last I collapse against a wall, chest heaving, while I press my fists against the stitch in my side. Sobbing, I glance over my shoulder but don't see anyone I recognise. A horde of people rushes past, buffeting me with their elbows and treading on my toes, but I'm so relieved to have lost my pursuers that I don't care.

The stitch in my side has eased but as I look around I see nothing that is familiar to me. The masses stream past, punching the air and singing bawdy songs. I'm lost in a strange city and no one knows, or cares, where I am. I flinch as a sudden crack of gunfire ricochets from building to building and a woman screams. A flutter of panic makes my stomach clench. I daren't ask anyone for directions. Skirting the walls, I sprint to the end of the street and turn into the next road.

My attention is caught by a display of red, white and blue in a shop window and a wave of relief washes over me as I recognise the parasols I saw earlier. I glimpse my reflection in the window and realise that I have lost my frilled cap and my hair is tumbled around my shoulders. Forcing my way through the chattering masses surging along Rue St Honoré, I set off, against the flow, towards the safety of Rue de Richelieu, desperate to be back in the safety of Monsieur d'Aubery's house.

A gang of twenty or so youths, singing at the top of their voices, is marching towards me. I shrink back against the wall to let them pass, but one of them snatches hold of me and plants a kiss on my mouth. I recoil while the youths cheer, clap their friend on the back and continue on their way. Shuddering, I wipe my mouth on the back of my hand.

All at once someone seizes my upper arm in a grip of steel and spins me around. I gasp, terrified again as a voice hisses in my ear.

'What the hell do you think you are doing?' Monsieur d'Aubery's handsome face is taut with anger and his eyes blaze.

'Monsieur d'Aubery! The king, I saw the king ...'

He shakes my arm violently. 'Didn't I tell you that the streets of Paris are too dangerous for a lady?'

Relief gives way to distress. 'I only wanted to ...' Tears start to my eyes and I can feel my face turn scarlet as I try not to cry.

'Don't speak to me! I'm too angry to listen.' Still clutching my arm, he sets off at such a pace that I nearly trip over as I trot along trying to keep up, all the while shaking with shock.

Before long we arrive back at the house and the front door opens seconds after Monsieur d'Aubery hammers a tattoo with the knocker.

The maid flinches when she sees the thunderous expression on his face and steps away as, still gripping my arm, he drags me up the staircase.

Sophie is propped up in bed, her cheeks flushed and sweat glistening on her brow. She cries out when she sees me and Dr Dubois rises from the chair at her bedside.

'Are you hurt, Mademoiselle Moreau?' he asks.

I notice that the buttons have been ripped off my coat but I shake my head, trying to forget my terror.

'We have all been extremely concerned for your welfare,' says Dr Dubois. The reproach in his voice is enough to make me drop my gaze and my knees are trembling so much I fear they will give way.

'I expected to return before you awoke, Sophie.' Surreptitiously I wipe away tears with my finger.

'Dr Dubois called by to see how I was and that's when we found you were missing.' Sophie's voice is faint and she closes her eyes as if the effort of speaking has exhausted her.

Monsieur d'Aubery strides from the room. We hear his booted footsteps clip down the stairs and then a door slams.

I glance at Dr Dubois, who shrugs. 'He was concerned for you.'

Sophie begins to cough so violently that I can hear the breath whistling in her lungs and I'm overtaken by new anxiety. She presses a handkerchief to her lips and falls back against the pillows when the fit is over.

Dr Dubois indicates that he wishes to speak to me and I follow him from the sickroom.

'Madame Levesque has not shaken off the fever as quickly as I'd expected,' he says.

His face is grave and fear stirs in my breast. 'But she will get well?'

Dr Dubois is silent for a moment and then picks up my hand and pats it. 'I will do all in my power. Watch her carefully, especially as I believe it is not only her own life that is at stake. Is that not so?' He studies my face carefully.

I stare back at him and then lower my gaze. 'Yes,' I murmur.

He nods in acknowledgement. 'Feed her chicken broth, keep her cool and send for me if there is any change.' He smiles. 'And remember to look after yourself too. I prescribe a glass of red wine with your dinner and you should sleep whenever your patient does.'

'I've made Monsieur d'Aubery very angry.' I'm close to tears again.

'He has suffered many tragedies in his life, and feared the worst might have befallen you.' Dr Dubois pats my hand again. 'Go and see him this evening. He'll be himself again by then.'

I sit beside Sophie all afternoon with my aching head full of dreadful images of the king's beheading. In my mind's eye I picture the glint of the guillotine's blade and hear it hiss and then see the head fall into the basket, over and over again.

When it grows dark I close the curtains and bathe Sophie's over-heated face.

Later, the maid comes to tell me that supper is ready and I put on a clean dress and fichu before going downstairs.

Monsieur d'Aubery is already seated at the vast dining table. He stands as I enter the room and waits while the footman draws out my chair.

We sit in uncomfortable silence while the footman ladles soup into our bowls and then Monsieur d'Aubery dismisses him.

Dismayed, I watch him leave and wish I could run after him but know I must face up to what is sure to come.

'I believe I owe you an apology,' Monsieur d'Aubery says. His posture is stiff and his face unsmiling.

I'm completely taken aback. 'On the contrary,' I say in a low voice, feeling thoroughly chastened, 'I understand why you were angry and I'm sorry I put you at risk, too. I know now that it was extremely foolish of me to leave the house today.'

'You escaped very lightly,' he says, slightly mollified.

I shiver at the memory of the murderous crowd clutching at my clothes and hair. 'I would do it again, though,' I say.

'Again?' He stares at me.

'Don't you see?' I appeal to him. 'History was made today and I was there to witness it.' I close my eyes for a second as I remember the executioner dancing around the scaffold with the king's head in his hand. 'Although I shall be for ever haunted by the terrible memory of King Louis's beheading...'

'My God!' Monsieur d'Aubery pushes back his chair and surges to his feet. 'You *saw* him go to the guillotine?'

I push away my soup as queasiness overwhelms me. 'It was a dreadful event but not so dreadful as the bloodlust of those watching.'

'A lady like you should never have experienced . . .'

'Monsieur d'Aubery, you told me a while ago that I had not the knowledge to have an opinion upon the Revolution in France. I realise now that you were correct. But however shocking it was today, I am at least a step closer to gaining that knowledge.'

'I made a very great mistake in allowing you and Madame Levesque to come to France.' Monsieur d'Aubery sits down again, his brow furrowed.

'We would still have come, whatever you had said.'

Monsieur d'Aubery sighs. 'You are extremely stubborn, Mademoiselle Moreau.' He returns to his soup and we barely exchange another word until I excuse myself to attend to Sophie.

My friend remains very ill and I'm exhausted from tending her through the nights, but after several days her fever breaks. Although I'm relieved by this, she has become thin and frail with bruised shadows under her lack-lustre eyes. We make our own little world in our adjoining rooms, toasting our toes by the fire and reading books from Monsieur d'Aubery's library, but her spirits remain very low. My own thoughts are occupied with imagining myself meeting Papa's family for the very first time and wondering what I shall say to them. Will I sense echoes of him in the château in which he grew up? Sometimes he spoke fondly of his nurse. Perhaps she will still be at Château de Lys.

One day, while Sophie is dozing, I am standing by the window looking down at the street below when a battalion of ragged soldiers march by. A motley collection of civilians runs along beside them, most of them wearing red caps. I open the window and listen to the tramping of soldiers' feet and the raucous shouts and jeering cries of the followers. Three or four street dogs chase after them, barking excitedly.

There is a soft knock at the door and I open it to see Monsieur d'Aubery.

'I must speak to you straight away,' he says.

Alarmed by his grim expression, I glance at Sophie and see that she still sleeps

Silently, I follow him downstairs into the library. He gestures me to a leather chair beside the hearth.

'What has happened?' I ask.

'France has declared war on England and Holland.'

I draw in my breath sharply. 'First Austria and Prussia and now this! I've just seen soldiers in the street.'

'New conscripts, I daresay.' He rubs his temples as if he has a headache. 'The question is, what am I to do with you and Madame Levesque? If anyone suspects you're English, you'll be accused of being a spy. They'd imprison me too, or worse, for harbouring you.'

'But no one need suspect that we're not French.'

Monsieur d'Aubery rubs his thumb over his chin. 'It's one thing to pass as a native Frenchwoman travelling through Paris, quite another to live here. The city is extremely volatile at present and, as a member of the former aristocracy, my house may become a target for the revolutionaries. I have decided to retreat to the country.'

I swallow, suddenly conscious that Sophie and I will then be left to find somewhere else to stay.

'I shall take you with me,' he says.

'Oh, but ...'

He holds up his hand. 'Please do me the courtesy of not arguing, Mademoiselle Moreau. You are not yet fully aware of the danger you and I could find ourselves in if I leave you at large in Paris or travelling alone to Fontainebleau before Madame Levesque is fully recovered.'

I consider what he's said. I'm impatient to find Papa's relatives but it's quite possible that we'll receive an uncertain reception and, as Sophie is still unwell, I don't wish to exhaust her by subjecting her to the vagaries of public transport. Perhaps it is more sensible to remain under Monsieur d'Aubery's protection for the present. 'Thank you, then. We will be happy to accept your kind offer.'

He nods. 'We shall leave in the morning before first light.'

Chapter 10

It's bitterly cold and Sophie and I huddle together under a blanket as Monsieur d'Aubery's carriage jolts along the road. It was snowing when we left the inn this morning but now only an occasional flurry patters against the windows. The leaden sky has given way to bright sunshine and the countryside is blanketed in white, rendering it beautiful but hard to read.

'Not far now,' says Monsieur d'Aubery, blowing on his fingers. 'I hope Madame Viard received my note and has lit the fires to welcome us.'

I glance at his face and see that the tense set of his features has softened. We've barely spoken during the journey, his forbidding expression making me too nervous to disturb him.

A moment later the carriage grinds to a halt before two stone pillars flanking ornate ironwork gates. A boy runs from the lodge and heaves open the tall iron gates, pushing back the snow. The coachman flicks his whip and the horses set off again at a brisk pace into a dense pine forest.

After several minutes we emerge from the darkness into the dazzling light reflected from snow-covered parkland.

Monsieur d'Aubery pulls down a window. 'Château Mirabelle,' he says, the freezing air transforming his breath into a cloud.

Shivering, I lean out of the window to look. The carriageway continues straight ahead between an avenue of oak trees and, in the distance, silhouetted against the pristine expanse of sunlit snow, is a substantial building of honey-coloured stone. The grey slate roof glistens with frost. A turret topped by a conical tower rises from each corner of it.

'Oh!' I breathe. 'It's like a castle in a fairy tale.'

Even Sophie, who has barely spoken all day, sits up and looks out of the other window with a semblance of interest.

I observe with interest that Monsieur d'Aubery's smile is as fond as a lover's as he gazes at his country home.

My own delight mounts as we draw closer. Formal gardens are laid out to the front, with low hedges forming an intricate knot garden no less attractive for being covered in snow. The carriage drive leads to a large turning circle with a stone pool as its centre-piece, in which a prancing horse, a collection of mythical sea creatures and several cherubs adorn a fountain. Icicles hanging from the sculpture glitter like daggers of diamonds.

'How beautiful!' I say, and am rewarded by Monsieur d'Aubery's smile. I'd forgotten how attractive he is when his eyes light up with pleasure.

The carriage stops and the coachman unfolds the steps. As I descend my eye is caught by the figure of a man hurrying down the steps from the front entrance to the château.

Monsieur d'Aubery waves and calls out, 'Jean-Luc!'

The man's feet crunch in the snow as he bounds towards us and claps Monsieur d'Aubery on the shoulder. He's tall and powerfully built with thick brown hair, and wears an elaborately embroidered silk waistcoat, I see.

'We thought you were never coming back to Château Mira-belle!' the man says. 'How the devil are you, Etienne?' His teeth are very white when he smiles and he exudes good health and humour.

'I'm well, although glad to be out of Paris.' Monsieur d'Aubery is darker and more slight of figure than his friend, but the two of them are fine-looking men.

'Difficult times?' asks Jean-Luc.

'Indeed.'

'And you have brought us two lovely guests?'

'Madame Levesque and Mademoiselle Moreau, may I present Monsieur Jean-Luc Viard, my estate manager?'

I conceal my surprise that Monsieur d'Aubery appears to be on such familiar terms with his employee. I had assumed Monsieur Viard to be a former member of the nobility also.

'Enchanted to make your acquaintance,' he says, bowing. His hazel eyes shine and it's impossible not to respond to his infectious smile. 'You must be cold after your journey. Please come inside and warm yourselves.' He offers me his arm. 'Take care not to slip on the snow.'

I glance at Monsieur d'Aubery to see if he appears to be discomfited by his position as host being usurped but he merely offers to escort Sophie up the steps.

The portico leads into a grand hall and our footsteps echo as we cross the white marble floor to warm our hands before the flames leaping in the great stone fireplace. There are marble busts of Roman emperors standing on plinths in each corner of the hall.

'Has all been well here while I've been away, Jean-Luc?'

Monsieur Viard smiles. 'Have I not always looked after the château as if it were my own? Of course all is well. Except for poor Antoine Gerard, who passed away of a seizure.'

Monsieur d'Aubery frowns. 'I'm sorry to hear that. I shall visit his widow tomorrow.'

The two men continue to discuss estate business and I take the opportunity to study my surroundings discreetly. An elegant double

85

staircase curves up to the first floor, past walls lined with ancestral portraits. Gilded console tables and mirrors enhance the impression of opulence. As the heat begins to thaw my fingers, I glance at Sophie to see if she is as overwhelmed as I am by the grandeur all around but she stares into the flames, looking half-dead with exhaustion.

Footsteps tap across the marble floor and a handsome woman dressed in black approaches.

Monsieur d'Aubery acknowledges her with a nod. 'Madame Viard.'

'Welcome home, sir.' She glances at Sophie and me. 'All is ready for your guests.' She has an hourglass figure and the frilled lace cap she wears doesn't entirely conceal thick black hair with a single white streak at the front.

'I apologise, Mademoiselle Moreau, but I have estate matters to attend to,' says Monsieur d'Aubery.

'Please do not trouble yourself on our account,' I say.

'Madame Viard will show you to your rooms now and I shall see you at breakfast.' Monsieur d'Aubery bows. 'Please make use of the salon and the library, if you wish.'

We follow the housekeeper up the wide staircase while I wonder about her name. She is of mature years yet doesn't appear to be old enough to be Jean-Luc's mother, but surely she's too old to be his wife? Puzzled, I study her curvaceous figure as she walks in front of us. His elder sister, perhaps?

Upstairs, she opens the doors to our rooms. 'I believe you will find everything you require,' she says.

After she has left, I sit on Sophie's bed and bounce up and down to test the mattress. The richly embroidered bedcover is faded but the carpet is thick and the silk wall hangings delicately painted.

Sophie sinks down on to a velvet chair and peels off her gloves. 'I'm going to lie down.'

'Let me draw the curtains then.' I move to the window and pause as I look outside. 'Sophie, come and see this!'

Our rooms are at the back, facing out over the gardens and parkland. Rooks circle in the air, calling mournfully to each other. To one side is a wooded copse but what immediately draws my attention is a large lake. Ice-covered, it sparkles in the sunshine and I see that there is an island in the centre, on which are the ruins of what appears to be a Greek temple.

'Very pretty,' says Sophie listlessly.

On the far side of the lake is an elegant stone building with shuttered windows, which looks like a perfectly proportioned doll's house.

I close the drapes, help Sophie to remove her outer clothing and settle her into bed. She curls up on her side without another word.

'I'll come and see you later,' I say.

She murmurs something I cannot hear and I leave her.

In my own room I sit on the window seat, reading and occasionally looking out over the silvery lake and the backdrop of distant snowy hills. A few months ago I could never have imagined that I would be a guest of a man I hardly know in a château in France, soon to meet relatives I hadn't realised existed. I have always wanted to find Papa's family but I would trade the opportunity in an instant to be at home again in Soho Square with Mama and Papa beside me.

The following morning I persuade Sophie to come downstairs for breakfast and we find Monsieur d'Aubery waiting for us in the dining room. Sunshine streams through the window and I can smell the aroma of coffee and fresh bread.

'Good morning,' he says. 'Did you sleep well?'

'Indeed I did,' I say. 'At least, until the cock crowed at first light.' I note that he's dressed in tight-fitting riding breeches that show off his lithe form to perfection.

He smiles. 'I love the peace and fresh air here after I have been in Paris or London.'

I pour coffee from a heavy silver pot and pass a cup to Sophie. She wrinkles her nose and shakes her head. 'Are you going out riding, Monsieur d'Aubery?' I ask.

'I must visit my tenants and ride around the boundaries of the estate.'

'It's a beautiful day.' I glance wistfully out of the window at the snowy gardens.

'Then why don't you both come with me?'

'Oh, no, I couldn't,' says Sophie, crumbling a morsel of bread.

'I should love to,' I say, 'but unfortunately I have no riding habit or boots.'

'My sister left behind a wardrobe of clothes when she went to live in America,' says Monsieur d'Aubery. 'Madame Viard will find a suitable outfit for you.'

Fifteen minutes later she has laid out a green velvet riding habit on my bed and I hasten to try it on. The jacket is close-fitting and there's a matching skirt with black braid to the hem. Since I'm taller than most women the skirt is a little short on me.

'The colour suits you,' says Sophie, as I button the jacket. 'But won't you be cold?'

'The sun is shining and I have gloves and my wool scarf,' I say, pulling on the black riding boots. 'These are too small but I shan't be walking far in them. Come down to the stables and see me off, will you, Sophie?'

She sighs. 'I suppose so.'

I suppress a sigh of irritation and wish she would make more effort.

Monsieur d'Aubery is pacing up and down in the hall, clearly impatient to start the business of the day.

The air outside is crisp and cold. The stables are set to one side of the château, next to a walled vegetable garden and pig stys. White chickens strut through the stable yard where several horses look out from their boxes. A tabby cat is washing itself on the yard wall and looks up enquiringly as we approach.

Monsieur d'Aubery strokes the muzzle of a big black horse, murmuring endearments as he opens the stable door.

'Isn't he beautiful!' I say as the powerful creature steps delicately into the snowy yard, his black coat gleaming in the sun.

'This is Diable,' says Monsieur d'Aubery. 'And I must warn you to keep your distance. He has an unpredictable temper.'

'He looks gentle enough,' says Sophie.

'He's well-mannered with me,' says Monsieur d'Aubery, 'but it took some time to teach him his manners.' Gently, he fondles Diable's ears and then takes a carrot from his pocket and holds it out to him on the flat of his palm. 'He once had a habit of bolting and throwing his rider, but he knows who is his master now.'

The groom, Colbert, opens another of the boxes and leads out a pretty chestnut mare.

'This is Minette,' says Monsieur d'Aubery. 'You need not worry about her temper as she is the most biddable creature imaginable.'

Certainly from the limpid look that Minette gives me I have nothing to fear.

The stable boy helps me to mount and Sophie, shoulders drooping, returns inside. I sigh. Her unhappiness taints my enjoyment of the day.

Leaving the stables behind us, we progress along the bridleway running around the perimeter of the park. There is a bitter wind but the sun is on my face, the air is pure and clean, and I'm filled with a sudden sense of well-being. I'll try and talk Sophie out of her low spirits later, I decide.

'When we're out here,' I say, 'where it's so peaceful, it seems unimaginable that this is a country at war, doesn't it?'

Monsieur d'Aubery's expression is sad. 'My childhood was so free and safe but I wonder now if life will ever be the same again. Even here, where everything looks the same as it always did, there are unhappy undercurrents.'

We trot through a gateway and on to a lane between fields that gradually rise to form a backdrop of low hills.

Monsieur d'Aubery points to one of the slopes and the low stone building at its base. 'There's my vineyard,' he says, 'and that's the *chai*, where we store the wine. We've extended the vineyard in the last couple of years. You shall try some of the Chateau Mirabelle 1789 tonight.'

'The year the Revolution began. A year to remember,' I say.

A flock of sheep cluster together in one corner of another field and Monsieur d'Aubery leans down from his saddle to unhook the rope that secures the gate.

'Fox prints,' he says, nodding his head at tracks in the snow. 'I must warn the shepherd or the new lambs will be lost before they've barely seen the light of day.'

A wide river flows along the side of the field, its reedy banks crusted with ice and snow. We close the gate behind us and walk the horses along a lane bounded by an avenue of elms. Despite the bright sunshine, my fingers are numb with cold and I'm sure the tip of my nose is glowing. Minette is warm beneath me and the smell of horseflesh and well-worn leather is peculiarly comforting. At the end of the lane we enter a copse and continue in single file. I duck several times to avoid the leafless branches knocking my hat awry. In the distance is the sound of children's voices.

As we emerge from the copse the scent of wood smoke drifts towards us and soon we see a village nestling into a little valley. It is a collection of neat houses with thatched roofs clustered around a frozen duck pond. Children are screaming in delight as they slip and slide across the surface, pushing and pulling at each other.

'I remember having fun on the ice with Jean-Luc and my brother Laurent when I was a boy,' says Monsieur d'Aubery, smiling at the memory.

It's pleasing to see him so at ease. 'So you have known Monsieur Viard for a long time?'

'All my life. He's a few months older than I and he shared our tutor. We grew up together so he is almost like a brother to me.'

So that explains Jean-Luc's familiarity towards Monsieur d'Aubery. 'And Madame Viard?' I ask.

'Jean-Luc's mother.'

I cannot conceal my surprise. 'She doesn't look old enough.'

'I believe she was only sixteen when he was born. Her husband Marcel works in the vineyard.'

A slight curl of Monsieur d'Aubery's lip as he speaks leads me to wonder if he doesn't care much for his friend's father.

'Most of the estate workers live here,' he continues. 'I must visit the Gerard family. Poor Antoine, a carpenter, has died of a seizure and leaves a widow and children.'

'May I come with you?'

He looks at me in surprise. 'If you won't find it distressing?'

'I know what it's like to lose loved ones.' My heart constricts momentarily with a pang of grief. Perhaps I'll be able to ease the meeting for the grieving widow. Her tenuous position must be making her extremely apprehensive and I imagine Monsieur d'Aubery's severe manner will only increase her anxiety.

He loops the horse's reins over a gatepost and knocks on the door of one of the cottages. A small boy opens it. Wide-eyed, he steps back to allow us to enter.

The plain little room has a freshly swept floor and cooking dishes and bowls neatly arranged on shelves. Washing, mostly children's clothes as far as I can see, is drying on a clothes horse before a meagre fire. Small children are squabbling amicably over a pile of bricks on the floor, while two older girls peel potatoes at the table.

Their mother is nursing her baby. She blushes and the child is pulled from her breast and propped up against her shoulder as she hastily adjusts her clothing and bobs a curtsey.

'Please, we have no wish to disturb you,' I say.

'My dear Madame Gerard,' says Monsieur d'Aubery. 'I returned from Paris to hear the sad news of your husband's passing and came to offer my condolences.'

'Thank you, sir,' she says with quiet dignity. Her bottom lip quivers. Her eyes look frightened.

'I wanted to reassure you straight away that you are welcome to remain in your cottage.'

'Oh, sir!' She bursts into noisy sobs and the baby on her shoulder begins to wail too. 'I've been so worried.'

Hastily, I proffer my handkerchief and she dabs at her eyes. I'm surprised and relieved that Monsieur d'Aubery is so sensitive in his dealings with the poor widow. He has a more gentle side to his nature than I had supposed.

The door bursts open and a gangly youth of about fifteen drags in a sledge piled with firewood.

'Mama, look . . .' He stops short as he notices the visitors.

'Good morning, young man! Victor, isn't it?' says Mr d'Aubery.

The boy says nothing, pulling his too-short sleeves down over his thin wrists until his sister pinches his arm. 'Yes, sir.'

'I'm pleased to see that you are a help to your mother.' Mr d'Aubery puts his hand in his pocket and pulls out a small bag, which he places on the table. 'This should see you through the rest of the winter, Madame Gerard. There will be no rent to pay at present, but once your baby is weaned call on Madame Viard. She will find work for you.'

We leave the cottage with the clamour of thanks in our ears and Monsieur d'Aubery hands a coin to the boy minding our horses.

'That was very well done,' I say as we ride away. I've warmed to Monsieur d'Aubery; it seems that despite his severe manner, he has a kind heart.

Two hours later we have made a circuit of the whole estate and trot back towards the stables. My hands and feet are frozen and I'm looking forward to warming myself by the fire.

'I'm impressed by how well cared for everything is,' I say as we dismount.

'I'm determined to look after the estate and my tenants as well as my father did,' says Monsieur d'Aubery.

'You were young to inherit.'

'It wasn't until Laurent died that I realised that one day it would be my responsibility. Even then, I expected my father to grow old first,' he says, his expression sober. 'But, for me, tradition is everything and I hope with all my heart that one day I shall be able to hand on the estate to my son,'

We ride back in silence. When I glance at the bleak set of his face, I dare not disturb him with idle chatter. I reflect that there is a great deal more to Monsieur d'Aubery than I had imagined.

Chapter 11

I'm worried about Sophie who has remained in bed for several days, growing increasingly morose and rejecting all my attempts to improve her spirits.

She glances up at me from the pillows, her eyes puffy again from weeping. 'You're not a mother and cannot possibly imagine how much I miss Henry,' she says, plucking at the embroidered rosebuds on her nightgown.

I curb my irritation. We have talked of nothing else all morning. 'I do see how miserable it's made you to have left him behind,' I say in calm tones. 'But in the long term your decision to come to France is in his best interests.'

'I know what you think,' continues Sophie, 'that I've made my bed and now I must lie in it.'

That, of course, is exactly what I do think but it wouldn't be helpful to say it.

'Will Henry even remember me when I return? Meanwhile, Charles is free to set up his mistress in a fine house and to beat me when he's out of humour. Because I made one mistake, I stand to lose everything and society condones it! *It isn't fair!*' my friend exclaims.

'I agree,' I say, 'but for women it was ever thus.'

Sophie glares at me. 'Have you any other platitudes to offer, Madeleine?'

'You know you are as dear to me as a sister. I hate to see you so unhappy but you have no other choice now, if only for Henry's sake.'

'I thought you were my friend?' Her lips thin to a line and she looks at me as if she hates me.

My annoyance boils over. 'I'm trying to help you, Sophie, but your ever-lasting self-pity makes it impossible.' My voice rises in anger.

'Then why don't you just go away and leave me alone?'

My patience snaps. 'Stew in your own juice then!'

In my own room I pace up and down, quite unable to settle. I haven't argued with Sophie for years, not since we'd had a childish squabble over whose turn it was to play with a rag doll. All at once I'm overwhelmed with loneliness, a horrid, empty feeling that aches under my breastbone. My parents are dead and I've quarrelled with my best friend. I'm staying in the house of a man I hardly know, who is reluctantly providing us with shelter from dangerous revolutionaries, and I can't go home, wherever that is now.

I curl up on the window seat and stare outside. There's no sun today, only a heavy mist that hangs over everything like a damp sheet. Rooks circle above the trees, their harsh cries audible even though the window is closed. The snow is beginning to thaw, leaving the gardens in an untidy patchwork of green and white. Irritated and unhappy, I decide to take a brisk walk to burn off my agitation.

Buttoning up my coat, I let myself out of the front door. The icicles suspended from the fountain are melting and dripping on to the frozen pool below. The stone horse's teeth are bared in a rictus of terror as it rears up from the mythical sea creatures insinuating themselves around its legs. Shivering in the damp air, I set off along the path to the knot garden.

Mist clings to everything, forming diamond droplets of moisture. There's a bench at the furthest reach of the knot garden and I dry the seat with my handkerchief and sit down to look back at the château, wreathed in ghostly fog. The damp is making my hair curl and my shoes are soaked but at least the fresh air has shaken me out of my bad temper.

A movement at the edge of my vision makes me turn and I watch as a great black horse bolts from the back of the château. Diable. Mr d'Aubery's black riding cape billows out behind him in the swirling mist as the horse races hell for leather towards the copse of trees on my left. A moment later they're gone. I wonder where he's off to in such a hurry, or is he, perhaps, simply enjoying the exhilaration of the moment? He intrigues me and I'm curious to discover more about him.

'Mademoiselle Moreau!'

Jean-Luc Viard strides towards me through the vaporous air and waves when I smile at him.

'Good morning,' I say.

The bench judders as he sits down beside me and stretches one arm along the backrest. His cheeks are glowing from the cold and he exudes a sense of male strength. It's impossible not to give him a wide smile.

'Enjoying the view?' There's a distinct twinkle in his eye.

The warmth rises in my cheeks. He's very engaging and also easy to read, quite unlike Monsieur d'Aubery who gives away little of his feelings. 'This place looks so mysterious in the mist, doesn't it?' I say.

'But very beautiful.'

I see the same fond expression in his eyes as I saw in Monsieur d'Aubery's when we arrived. 'Have you always lived on the estate?'

He nods. 'It's my home and I intend never to leave it. But tell me about yourself. Where do you and Madame Levesque come from? You don't sound as if it's from around here.' He smiles. 'Everyone in the château wants to know who the mystery guests are. And why it is that Madame Levesque travels without the protection of her husband?'

I hesitate, unsure what story Monsieur d'Aubery might have fabricated to explain our presence.

'She's but recently widowed,' I improvise, with some sense of satisfaction at having done away with Charles Levesque and explained Sophie's unhappy demeanour at one stroke.

Then we hear a shout and a small figure runs towards us. It takes me a moment to recognise the boy from the stable.

He comes shuddering to a halt before us, heaving for breath. 'Monsieur Viard, sir ... ' he pants.

'What is it, Jacques?'

'It's Diable. He's gone! I was polishing the saddles when I heard a horse trotting out of the yard, but by the time I ran outside I saw Diable's box was open and he'd gone.'

'I saw Monsieur d'Aubery ride him away a few moments ago,' I say. 'He went into the woods over there.'

'But he can't have,' says the boy.

'I know it was Diable. It was misty but I would swear it was Monsieur d'Aubery riding him at breakneck speed.'

'But Monsieur Alphonse arrived only half an hour ago to visit the master and his horse is still in the stable.'

'Are you sure?' asks Monsieur Viard.

Jacques nods vigorously.

The boy scurries off back towards the stables and Monsieur Viard and I return inside.

We cross the hall and Monsieur Viard knocks on the door to the estate office before opening it.

Monsieur d'Aubery is sitting at his desk beside another gentleman, bent over some architectural drawings. He looks up at us with raised eyebrows.

'I apologise for the interruption, Etienne,' says Monsieur Viard, 'but someone has ridden Diable out of the stables.'

Monsieur d'Aubery rises to his feet, scraping back his chair in alarm.

'I thought it was you I saw galloping off a few moments ago,' I say, perplexed. 'The rider was wearing a black riding cape like yours.'

'I've been closeted here with Monsieur Alphonse studying the plans for the new cottages.' Monsieur d'Aubery's jaw clenches. 'Whoever stole Diable may rue the day.'

'I apologise,' he says to his visitor, 'but we will have to reconvene.' He strides from the office, closely followed by Monsieur Viard.

Monsieur Alphonse sighs and begins to fold up his plans.

At the stables Jacques comes to greet us, his eyes wide and frightened.

'Where is Colbert?' demands Monsieur d'Aubery.

'My father went to see the blacksmith,' stutters Jacques. 'I was polishing the saddles when I heard a horse in the yard. I knew they were all in their stalls so I went to see what was happening and there was Diable galloping off. I'm sorry, master . . .'

'It wasn't your fault,' says Monsieur d'Aubery. 'But you didn't see who was riding him?'

Jacques shakes his head. 'I knew it wasn't you, though.'

'How was that?' asks Monsieur Viard.

'Too small.' Jacques sucks his teeth. 'And not a good rider.'

'One of the village children, do you think?'

'None of them would dare,' says Monsieur Viard.

I stroke Minette's velvety muzzle. Suddenly she blows through her nose and lifts her head, shaking her mane. I glance behind me and see Diable emerging from the woods. 'Look!' I say.

'Thank God,' says Monsieur d'Aubery. 'You all stay here and I'll catch him.'

He approaches slowly, calling out to the horse and slowing as Diable snorts and tosses his head. At last Monsieur d'Aubery manages to sidle closer, catch hold of the trailing reins and lead the horse back to us.

'Whoever tried to steal him will be sorry for it,' says Monsieur d'Aubery, running a hand down Diable's fetlocks, 'if he isn't already dead.' He stops and pulls free a shred of material tangled up in one of the stirrups. 'Oh!'

'What is it?' asks Monsieur Viard.

'It seems our thief was wearing clothing embroidered with pink rosebuds.' He smoothes out the scrap of fabric on the palm of his hand.

Monsieur Viard snorts with laughter, his expression incredulous.

I gasp. 'But that's from Sophie's nightgown.'

Monsieur d'Aubery gives me a sharp glance. 'Where is she?

'I left her in bed this morning. We argued ...'

'Go and see if she's still there. Hurry now! And, Colbert, go with Monsieur Viard and start searching the woods.'

I run as fast as I can, race up the stairs two at a time and burst into Sophie's room. The bedclothes are flung back and the room is deserted.

Guilt floods over me for arguing with her when she was distressed. If anything terrible has happened ...

My stomach is knotted with anxiety as I run downstairs and rap on the housekeeper's door. Without waiting for an answer I turn the handle.

Madame Viard is sitting at a table and looks up at me, mouth pursed in annoyance. 'Is there something you require, Mademoiselle Moreau?'

'Have you seen Madame Levesque?'

'But no. Not since she sent the maid away with her luncheon uneaten. Again.'

'She's missing. And I'm very afraid she may have met with an accident. Please will you ask the rest of the servants if they've seen her in the last hour or so?'

'As you wish, Mademoiselle.'

The stables are deserted when I return. The mist is thickening as

99

twilight approaches. There's no time to waste. I run towards the woods.

The ground is uneven beneath the trees and I stumble several times as I call Sophie's name. There's no sign of the others although I hear the echoes of their cries in the distance. It grows darker as I venture deeper into the woods and panic flutters in my chest. What if we don't find her? Or what if Diable has thrown her and trampled her underfoot? Brambles tear at my clothing as I fight my way through the undergrowth and a sob bubbles up in my chest.

A piercing whistle makes me stop in my tracks.

'Here! She's here!' shouts a voice.

A volley of calls respond and I run towards them, ducking under tree branches and scrambling over snow-covered logs. I don't see the tangle of ivy until I trip and fall headlong. The ground comes up to meet me, slamming into my chest with the force of a sledge hammer. It feels as if a giant hand is squeezing my lungs and I remain face down on the snow, heaving for breath.

Strong hands pull me into a sitting position. 'Breathe slowly,' says Monsieur d'Aubery in the same tone of voice that he used to calm Diable. His dark eye look into mine, willing me to obey.

I focus on his irises, umber with flecks of gold, until I begin to breathe evenly again.

'Can you stand?'

I scramble to my feet. My chest aches and my coat is crusted with ice and pieces of twig but there isn't time to brush myself down.

He keeps a firm grip on my elbow and I'm thankful for it since I have begun to shake, whether from the shock of my fall or from fear of what we might find, I don't know.

Monsieur Viard is kneeling on the ground, while Colbert, Jacques and three other men are gathered in a circle around him. I run to them, my heart in my mouth.

Sophie lies unmoving on her back, eyes closed, looking innocent and childlike in her rose-embroidered nightgown with the black wings of the riding cape spread out beside her. Blood seeps from her head, staining the icy ground with scarlet.

I fall to my knees beside Monsieur Viard. 'Is she . . .'

'Unconscious,' he says.

I pick up one of her hands and chafe it in mine. 'She's frozen!' I wrap the black cloak over her torn nightgown.

'We must take her back without delay,' says Monsieur d'Aubery. He unbuttons his coat and lays it over Sophie.

Monsieur Viard pushes him aside then, gathers Sophie into his arms as if she weighs no more than a feather, and sets off.

I stifle a sob as I see blood dripping from her dark hair, leaving a trail of crimson drops in the snow.

Later, the door to my friend's room opens and the doctor emerges.

'How is she?' I ask.

'Awake,' he replies, rocking his portly figure slightly on his heels.

'Will she be all right?'

'Once the wound to her temple has healed there should be no lasting physical damage.'

Sophie lies propped up in bed, her head bandaged, and the sight of her makes me forget my annoyance. 'Why did you do it? You must have known that Diable might have killed you?'

She heaves a deep, sobbing sigh. 'I hoped a fall would make me miscarry.'

'Oh, Sophie!' I hug her tight, full of miserable guilt. 'But the fall hasn't damaged the baby?'

She shakes her head. 'The doctor says not.' She yawns. 'Oh, Maddy, I'm so very tired!'

I sit beside her until her eyelids droop and at last she sleeps. Quietly, I leave the room.

Monsieur d'Aubery is in the estate office, resting an elbow on the mantelpiece while he pushes the logs further into the hearth with the toe of one shoe. I watch him unobserved for a moment from the doorway. Something about the elegance of his wiry figure reminds me of Papa and I try to ignore the swift shaft of pain in my heart.

'Monsieur d'Aubery?'

He glances at me, his brow furrowed with anxiety. 'How is Madame Levesque?'

'Better.'

'I'm relieved to hear it. The thought of another tragedy at Château Mirabelle was almost too much to contemplate. Did she say why she did it?'

'In her misery I'm not sure she even knew what she was doing today. You know how wretched she was after her ...' I hesitate '... after her friendship with Mr Fielding came to an end. She wanted to escape from London but now that she has, she misses her son terribly.'

'And, of course, since England and France are at war, she cannot return home.' He pulls out a chair for me beside the desk.

'Monsieur d'Aubery, as soon as Sophie has recovered from her fall, we'll thank you for your hospitality and move on. My purpose in coming to France is to seek out my father's family. If it's not convenient for us to stay with them we shall rent a country cottage where we can live quietly until the war is over.'

He's silent for a moment, gaze fixed on the flickering flames in the hearth. 'It may be too unsafe for you and Madame Levesque to travel alone. Should it be suspected that you have come from England your situation would be perilous indeed.'

'And you're concerned you'd be accused of being a traitor to France because you brought us into the country?'

Monsieur d'Aubery sighs and picks up a pen. 'I don't think you understand how vulnerable we all are. I should like to escort you to visit your father's family in Fontainebleau. If they invite you to stay then I shall be happy for you, but if there is any ... awkwardness, then I can bring you back here.'

'Awkwardness?'

Monsieur d'Aubery lays down his quill pen and moves the bottle of ink a fraction, lining up both items precisely with the blotter. 'You should ask yourself why your father left his family all those years ago and never returned.'

'But that's just it,' I say. 'All my life I have yearned to know. And now it's even more important that I meet Papa's relatives. I miss my parents more than I can say. Nothing can take away that pain, but to know that I have a link, a blood connection, to someone else is essential for me. Family is everything. Surely you can understand that?'

'Yes, I do.' He sighs. 'I know a little about the Moreau family. Louis-François, your grandfather, died some years ago. His wife survives him, I believe, and there is another son, Auguste.'

'Uncle Auguste,' I say. 'And I have a grandmother too.' I smile as I try to picture her. Will we bear any resemblance to one another? Perhaps she'll tell me stories of Papa's childhood?

'And nothing will change your mind about going to visit them?'

'Nothing.'

Mr d'Aubery turns up his palms and shrugs. 'Then so be it.'

Chapter 12

Two days later, at first light, Sophie, Monsieur d'Aubery and I make an early start for Fontainebleau. I'm so full of excited anticipation that it's hard for me to sit still. I try to concentrate on watching the sky bloom pink and gold as the sun rises, while I plan what I'm going to say to my father's family.

'Nervous?' asks Sophie, placing her hand over mine.

I realise I've been twisting the fabric of my skirt into creases. 'I've waited all my life for this day,' I say.

'What if they don't believe who you are?'

'They must.' I reach into the neckline of my dress and pull out a ribbon with the Moreau ring threaded on to it.

I watch the countryside rattle past while I consider different ways to introduce myself to my grandmother and Uncle Auguste. I wonder if he will look like Papa. Will they tell me what caused the family rift? Surely at least my grandmother will welcome me?

It's late-afternoon when we arrive at Villeneuve-St-Meurice, the village near Fontainebleau where Château de Lys is situated. Driving slowly along the rutted road it's hard not to be dismayed by the rotting thatched roofs and general air of neglect. Pigs root in front of a tumbledown cottage and the acrid stench of dung makes my eyes water.

A young woman holding a ragged child by the hand stands beside the road and Colbert stops the carriage to ask for directions to the château.

She looks up with dull eyes and points along the road. 'You can't miss it,' she says. 'It has great stone gateposts with eagles on top.'

Monsieur d'Aubery leans out of the window and drops a coin into her outstretched hand. As the carriage rolls away, I see her spit on the ground.

Monsieur d'Aubery is watching me, a tense expression on his face. When I return his gaze, he opens his mouth as if about to speak then turns away to look out of the window. Too anxious to question him, I continue to imagine what my relatives will look like and how they will receive me.

Five minutes later, we find the stone eagles. They stand sentinel, wings spread, on either side of a pair of impressive wrought-iron gates, staring fiercely at approaching visitors from hooded eyes.

We wait for the lodge keeper to unlock the gates and then we turn in at a long carriage drive through rolling parkland studded with mature oaks. My heart begins to thud in anticipation. What will I say to my uncle and grandmother? Will there be a sense of connection between us?

I jump as Sophie rests her hand on mine, and realise I've been drumming my fingers on the seat.

'So much time has passed since the quarrel that I'm sure it will be forgotten now,' she whispers.

I look out of the carriage window again and there, in the distance, is a vast edifice on top of a hill, its numerous towers silhouetted against the sky.

'Surely that's not Château de Lys?' asks Sophie, eyebrows raised.

Monsieur d'Aubery nods.

I'm speechless with shock. My father's family must be immensely rich.

As we draw closer the château appears to grow in size. Massive grey-stone walls loom above us, all reflected in the wide moat. It's impossible to count the number of windows but they're on five floors, from a slit in the tallest turret to a small barred opening a few feet above the mossy waterline of the moat. The forbidding appearance of this place makes me shiver. It looks like a prison or a fortress and I cannot imagine a stronger contrast to the welcoming aspect of Château Mirabelle.

Our carriage rattles over the wooden drawbridge and crunches to a halt on the gravel. Twin stone staircases curve up to a wide balustraded terrace.

Sophie and I glance at each other. All at once I wish I hadn't come. I'm totally unprepared for such grandeur.

Colbert opens the carriage door.

'Will you wait here while I announce you?' says Monsieur d'Aubery as he alights.

A footman in a powdered wig and a splendid blue and gold coat is hurrying down the steps and Monsieur d'Aubery goes to meet him. We watch as the footman hurries back up the steps and then Monsieur d'Aubery returns and says we will be summoned.

We wait in the coach for a considerable time and my apprehension increases. I reach out for Sophie's hand and cling to it.

Monsieur d'Aubery remains silent but I notice that his fists are clenched in his lap.

'What if they refuse to receive us?' asks Sophie, voicing my own thoughts.

'It probably takes a while to find anyone in such an enormous place,' I say.

'At least your uncle can't say they haven't room for us,' giggles Sophie.

Happy to see her in recovered spirits, I laugh, the tension broken.

At last the footman reappears and asks us to follow him.

I glance at Sophie and we descend from the carriage.

Monsieur d'Aubery looks at me, his expression unreadable. 'If you wish, it's not too late to leave, Mademoiselle Moreau?'

I bite my lip, sorely tempted, then shake my head. 'I haven't come all this way to lose my courage at the last moment.'

The footman leads the way up the stone steps to the terrace with its far-reaching views. Solid oak doors, twice as high as a man, lead into an echoing cavern of a hall. I gain a fleeting impression of inlaid-marble floors, ormolu-framed mirrors and lavishly gilded furniture. Silently, we mount the ornate staircase that curves up to the floor above, while my pulse begins to race. In only a moment I shall meet Papa's family.

The footman opens double doors into a vast drawing room and announces us.

A middle-aged man and an elderly woman sitting on a sofa by the fire at the other end of the room are dwarfed by their surroundings. My mouth is dry with anxiety as I see these members of my family for the very first time.

Monsieur d'Aubery escorts Sophie and me, offering us each the support of his arm, and we make sedate progress across the sea of sumptuously thick carpet, finally coming to rest six feet in front of the sofa. Monsieur d'Aubery bows and Sophie and I drop curtseys. I feel as if I am being presented to royalty and wonder if my rapid heartbeat is audible. I force a wavering smile, trying to catch my grandmother's eye.

Slowly, the man I assume to be my Uncle Auguste rises to his feet. He is younger than I expected, perhaps eight or ten years younger than Papa. His richly embroidered waistcoat is stretched across an ample stomach and he wears a heavily powdered wig. There is something about his aquiline nose that reminds me of Papa.

He ignores Sophie and myself and speaks directly to Monsieur d'Aubery. 'I remember you,' he says. 'What is the purpose of your visit, d'Aubery?' I'm dismayed to find that his voice is as cold and distant as the meagre fire burning in the hearth. 'I've heard of your exploits in escorting lily-livered nobles out of France. I do hope you haven't come to persuade *me* to leave the country?' He presses one plump white hand to his breast and smirks.

'You may be certain that I have not,' says Monsieur d'Aubery.

I take an instant dislike to Uncle Auguste and a chasm of bitter disappointment opens up inside my heart.

'It's nonsense to run away,' says Uncle Auguste. 'The peasants simply need a firm hand to confine them to the gutter. Keep their wages low and they will work hard.' His lip curls. 'Equality, indeed!'

'In the current climate I can only warn you that there are very real dangers for you in inflaming the passions of the bourgeoisie and the peasants,' says Monsieur d'Aubery. 'But that is not why I am here today. As your manservant will have explained, I have accompanied your niece, Mademoiselle Moreau . . . '

'I have no niece.'

'You may not have been aware of her existence before now but, I assure you, she exists. Allow me to present her to you.'

'You have been taken in by an imposter, d'Aubery.'

I step forward, my cheeks burning with sudden fury at the insult. 'I assure you, I am no imposter. I am Madeleine Moreau, daughter of Philippe Moreau. And I believe you to be my father's brother, Auguste.'

He looks down the length of his nose at me as if I am something unpleasant deposited at his feet. 'Indeed?'

'Yes,' I say firmly. 'Delighted to make your acquaintance.' Next I face the elderly lady dressed in black. 'And am I correct in believing you to be my father's mother? My grandmother?' I smile hopefully.

She glances at my uncle. 'I have only one son and he stands beside me.'

I gasp as if she has slapped me. 'Surely you do not deny the existence of your son Philippe?'

'Philippe has been dead to me for many years.' Her voice is as cold and as sharp as crystals of ice.

'How can a mother . . .'

Auguste Moreau surges towards me then. 'Imposter!'

I take a step back, crushed to find that this meeting I have anticipated nearly all my life is going so badly.

Monsieur d'Aubery steps between us.

'You will leave immediately!' My uncle's voice echoes shrilly through the glacial chamber. 'How *dare* you come here, claiming to belong to this family?'

'I do belong to this family,' I say, reaching desperately into the neckline of my dress and pulling out Papa's ring, threaded on a silk ribbon. 'Here's my proof. The Moreau ring.' I must make him believe me.

Moreau's eyes bulge and he pushes Monsieur d'Aubery out of the way and snatches the ring.

I gasp in shock as my head jerks forward and the ribbon chafes my neck. I feel his breath on my cheek and quake before the animosity in his eyes. Whatever I expected, it wasn't violence.

'Who did you steal this from?' he whispers, staring at the engraved crest.

'Apologise at once to the lady,' thunders Monsieur d'Aubery.

'This ring is mine,' I say, pulling it free from Uncle Auguste's grasping fingers.

His face is scarlet with rage and, despite the chill in the room, sweat beads his forehead. 'You're lying! You've come here with the intention of making a claim on my estate.'

'I did not! I didn't even know of your existence until a few weeks ago. Since both my parents are recently dead . . .'

Grandmother Moreau gasps and presses one hand to her mouth.

Uncle Auguste becomes very still, his gaze penetrating. 'Philippe is dead? Are you sure?'

'Of course I'm sure.'

'Have you any brothers?'

I shake my head. The smile on my uncle's face makes me feel sick.

'Thank God,' he says, wiping one palm over his sweating face. 'So you have no rights.'

Grandmother Moreau stirs in her seat and looks at me directly for the first time. 'Why have you come here to stir up old sorrows?'

I catch my breath. My grandmother's eyes are violet, the same colour as the eyes that look back at me from the mirror every day.

'Well?' barks Uncle Auguste.

'I had hoped you might welcome me as a member of your family,' I reply. The mere idea of this now seems ridiculous. All I want is to leave Château de Lys and never again see these two unpleasant specimens of humanity. And I want to leave before I break down and cry.

'There is nothing for you here,' says my father's mother. Her voice is full of pain.

'I can see that,' I say, voice icy. 'We'll not take up any more of your time.'

'Not so fast,' says Uncle Auguste. 'I want the Moreau ring. It's mine by right.'

I tuck it safely away again. 'On the contrary. It's mine and you shall never have it.'

The fury and hatred on Uncle Auguste's face are truly terrifying. I flinch as he launches himself at me, tearing at my fichu and scrabbling for the ring between my breasts. I panic, fighting off his hands, suddenly reliving Dick's assault in Vauxhall Gardens.

Sophie screams and Monsieur d'Aubery roars with anger as he drags my uncle away.

The doors open and the footman bursts in.

Monsieur d'Aubery has Uncle Auguste by the throat. 'Stop there,' he shouts to the footman, 'if you don't want to see the your master throttled!'

The footman skids to a halt.

Monsieur d'Aubery thrusts his face close to his prisoner's. 'Apologise to Mademoiselle Moreau!'

I'm astonished to see that Monsieur d'Aubery's aloof manner has entirely deserted him as he comes passionately to my defence.

Uncle Auguste whimpers.

'Careful! You're squeezing his throat too hard!' warns Sophie.

Monsieur d'Aubery makes a visible effort and loosens his grip. 'Apologise! Now!'

Uncle Auguste's face is pale green and he glances at me briefly before muttering, 'I apologise,' towards his feet.

I notice the footman's hastily suppressed grin.

Monsieur d'Aubery pushes Uncle Auguste away and wipes his hands disdainfully on his breeches. 'Shall we go?' he says to Sophie and me.

'Get them out of here!' shouts Uncle Auguste to the footman.

I'm trembling with distress and outrage as I glance at Grandmother Moreau, hoping to appeal to her better nature.

She's staring at her folded hands in her lap but, as if she feels the intensity of my gaze, she glances up. I see a flicker of something in her violet eyes, regret or fear perhaps; I'm not sure.

'I said, get them out!' bellows Uncle Auguste.

Monsieur d'Aubery briefly touches his finger to my cheek. 'Are you all right?' he whispers.

I nod and cling tightly to his arm as he leads us away.

Sophie catches her breath on a whimper as half a dozen male servants hurry into the room and closely surround us.

'What makes you think I'll allow you to leave, Etienne?' calls Uncle Auguste from the other end of the room. He laughs. 'Perhaps I should lock you in the dungeon again?'

All at once I'm very afraid.

Monsieur d'Aubery stops walking. He elbows aside one of the manservants and turns to face Uncle Auguste. 'You were an unpleasant youth and maturity hasn't improved you.' His voice is full of disgust. 'You still hide behind the power your wealth bestows on you and prey on those weaker than yourself.'

'So you remember the dungeon, then?' Uncle Auguste smirks. 'I remember how you snivelled. And how I laughed!'

'A great deal of water has passed under the bridge since then, Moreau,' says Monsieur d'Aubery. 'A word of warning, though. Be careful. Be very careful. If you continue in this vein, you will regret it.'

Uncle Auguste takes an involuntary step backwards at the implied threat.

Monsieur d'Aubery takes my arm again. We continue the long, slow walk out of the drawing room. My knees tremble and the back of my neck prickles as if Uncle Auguste's hot gaze is burning into me. If Monsieur d'Aubery weren't gripping my arm so tightly, I would lose my nerve and run.

At last the door closes behind us and I breathe more easily out of my uncle's presence. We walk through the château, surrounded by servants, and all the while my back is rigid. I wonder if my uncle is irate enough to have us apprehended. At last we reach the front door and our guard accompanies us in threatening silence down the steps to the carriage.

It isn't until we have departed through the eagle gateposts that the tension in my muscles begins to ease. Tears roll down my cheeks. All my dreams of meeting my family are shattered and I feel ashamed to share the same blood as Uncle Auguste. A yawning emptiness opens up in my soul. Sophie's hand creeps into mine and I clutch at it gratefully.

When I have composed myself, I study Monsieur d'Aubery's profile as he stares out of the window. In the miserable time since my parents' deaths, no one has really cared what happened to me but today Monsieur d'Aubery leapt to my defence, with no thought at all for his own safety, purely to protect me. Ever since we left London he has gone to great lengths to shelter Sophie and me from the consequences of our reckless actions. Perhaps he feels my scrutiny because he turns to look at me.

'I apologise for subjecting you to such a disagreeable scene,' I say, 'and I am more grateful to you than you know for defending me. If you hadn't fought off that madman, I dread to imagine what might have happened.'

'I feared such a reception,' he replies, and I'm surprised to see compassion in his eyes. 'But it would have been wrong of me to forbid you to meet your uncle and grandmother, however unwise I believed it to be.'

'What did that unpleasant creature mean by asking you if you remembered the dungeon?' I ask.

Slowly, he drags his gaze away from the window. 'I was six years old when I first met Auguste Moreau,' he says. 'My father and I were very close and I often used to accompany him on visits to tenants and neighbours. When he visited Château de Lys on business one day, I went with him. I was left to amuse myself in the gardens, and it was there that I met Auguste. He was about thirteen years old.' A rueful smile passes over Monsieur d'Aubery's lips. 'I remember being fascinated by his face, which was covered in pimples.'

'What happened?' I ask.

'He offered to take me on a tour of his home. We walked for miles along the corridors, looking into the maids' bedrooms which seemed to be of special interest to him. In the kitchens he stole cake from the pantry and then he took me through the storerooms, down to the cellars. He showed me the dungeon, a miserably dark and damp cell with only a barred window slit.'

I shudder. 'I saw one like that from the outside,' I say.

Monsieur d'Aubery nods. 'Auguste showed me that the moat was only a few inches below the window and told me how his ancestors used to imprison their enemies there. "When they opened the sluice gates the moat rose and filled the dungeon with water," he said.

"The prisoners drowned." Then he rushed past me and slammed the gate shut behind him.'

I gasp in horror.

Monsieur d'Aubery swallows. 'He laughed at me. "I'm going to open the sluices," he said, and left me alone. I was terrified. I fancied I could hear the screams of drowning prisoners. I beat on the walls and shouted for Papa but he didn't come.'

There's an unexpected vulnerability in his voice. Tears start to my eyes and my heart aches for the small boy he had been. My own experience of being confined in the coal cellar pales into insignificance against his suffering.

'You were barely older than my Henry,' says Sophie, with a shudder.

'They didn't find me until dark. I couldn't speak for a week afterwards.'

'Didn't you tell your father what Auguste had done?'

'Not until years later. My father mentioned that the Duc de Limours, Louis-François, had died. It seemed that he was to be succeeded by Auguste. It was then that my father mentioned there had been an elder son, Philippe, who'd left the family many years before.'

'Did he say why?' I'm desperate to find out all I can about Papa.

'Apparently Philippe had intervened when his father violently beat one of the estate workers, nearly killing him. Since the duc was unrepentant and refused to offer restitution to the man or his family, Philippe renounced his position as heir and threatened to leave for ever.'

'Which, of course, he did.'

'Your grandfather,' says Monsieur d'Aubery, 'wished to avoid a scandal so he had Philippe locked in the dungeon until he came to his senses. A week later he discovered his son had escaped. Philippe was never heard of in France again.'

'Your papa made the right decision, Madeleine,' says Sophie. 'Imagine living with a family like that!'

'We won't have the opportunity, even if we wanted to,' I say. Suddenly I'm overcome with melancholy and despair. Coming to France, to find the last part of the jigsaw puzzle about my family, has brought me nothing but misery and now uncertainty as to the future.

'But you can be very proud of your father, Mademoiselle Moreau,' says Monsieur d'Aubery. His voice is gentle and his expression so full of concern for me that my eyes well up again. 'He was a man of great principle and forfeited a life of ease to do what he believed to be right.'

'I am proud of him,' I say. I look out of the carriage window, fighting back the tears, as we pass through the unkempt village of Villeneuve-St-Meurice, so very different from the village near Château Mirabelle.

We travel in silence, each of us absorbed in our thoughts. If Monsieur d'Aubery had not been with us, Sophie and I would now be in considerable difficulties. I owe him an enormous debt of gratitude. A shiver passes down my back as I imagine the absolute terror of being shut up in the dungeon of Château de Lys.

Chapter 13

In the days following our return I'm full of restless malaise. One morning I take a walk before breakfast. The wind is bitingly cold but the skeleton trees are touched silver with frost and the beauty of the scene goes some way towards soothing my unhappiness.

I walk along the lakeside path until I come to the little boathouse. On the jetty I rest my forearms on the handrail while I study the view and reflect that it would be pleasant to take the boat over to the temple in the summer but, sadly, Sophie and I must be long gone before then.

As I pass the stables on my return Monsieur d'Aubery is riding Diable into the yard.

'We are both early birds today,' he says. 'If you don't mind me in my riding clothes perhaps we could breakfast together?'

My spirits lift immediately and I return inside to remove my coat. The cold has pinched colour into my cheeks I notice as I tidy my hair before the mirror.

I've already poured the coffee when Monsieur d'Aubery arrives in the dining room. We exchange pleasantries about our morning excursions and I thank him again for escorting us to Château de Lys.

'I couldn't sleep last night for mulling over our meeting with the Moreaux,' I say. The bitter disappointment of it still hurts.

'Best to put that loathsome uncle of yours out of your thoughts,' he says.

'I should not have liked to be there without your protection,' I admit, remembering how fearless he had been, 'and I understand now why you were insistent on accompanying us. I'd very much hoped for a warmer welcome.'

'I'm sorry that your search has brought you nothing but unhappiness.' His tone is sincere.

'So it's time to move on,' I say, with a heavy heart. 'I wonder if you would advise me how Sophie and I might find a cottage to rent?'

'But is it wise for you to live alone?'

'What do you mean?'

The tips of Monsieur d'Aubery's ears grow pink. 'If I'm not mistaken Madame Levesque is expecting a happy event?'

I remain silent for a moment. 'How very perspicacious of you, Monsieur d'Aubery.' It's too late now to pretend that Sophie isn't expecting, but since she's married at least there's no need to explain that the baby is Jack Fielding's.

'I have a proposition for you,' says Monsieur d'Aubery. 'It is, perhaps, not fitting that you and Madame Levesque should remain at Château Mirabelle but no one would look askance if you rented my grandmother's old house.'

My spirits soar. There is no doubt that to be independent, but to remain within a stone's throw of the only friend we have in France, would give me a great deal of comfort. 'But we wouldn't wish to be an embarrassment to you,' I say. 'As strangers, while the country is so unstable ...'

'We shall invent a connection between our families,' Monsieur d'Aubery assures me.

'Monsieur Viard has already asked where we come from.'

Monsieur d'Aubery puts down his coffee cup. 'What did you tell him?'

I shrug. 'Only that we were travelling on our way to visit my relatives. I didn't know what you might have told him.'

Monsieur d'Aubery nods in approval. 'I would trust Jean-Luc to the ends of the earth but he must never know you have come from London. One careless word could put us all at risk.' He rubs his fingers over his chin while he thinks. 'The difficulty is that he knows my family so it won't be possible to pass you off as relatives.'

'He asked why Sophie's husband isn't travelling with us. I'm afraid I told him that Charles Levesque is dead.'

'How inventive of you,' says Monsieur d'Aubery, eyes dancing with sudden amusement. 'But perhaps we'd better agree on our story?'

When Monsieur d'Aubery smiles his whole face lights up in the most attractive way and his demeanour is not severe at all. I find myself watching, and liking, the way his well-shaped mouth curves as he speaks.

We discuss various ideas and finally decide that, if asked, we'll say that Sophie is the daughter of a childhood friend of Monsieur d'Aubery's mother, who lives in a village near Lyon.

'And since she is such a recent widow, she needs a complete change of scene because Lyon holds such sad memories for her. That should serve the purpose, don't you think?'

Monsieur d'Aubery nods in agreement. 'It's as well to say as little as possible. Now, when we have finished our breakfast, shall I take you to see the house?'

Half an hour later we approach the little house along its gravel drive.

'I have asked Madame Viard to arrange for the shutters to be opened,' says Monsieur d'Aubery.

The house has windows to either side of the front door and pale green shutters that are folded back against the creamy stone of the walls. The roof is of slate, like the château's, and, although not large, the house has elegant proportions. Clipped box trees are placed either side of the porch.

'It's beautiful,' I say.

'I used to love visiting my grandmother here when I was a boy. Then it always smelled of lavender polish and *gâteau à la vanille*.' He smiles at the memory.

The front door is ajar and we enter a square, stone-floored hall. The doors are open and I step into the drawing room. A pair of tall windows afford a view of the lake and reflected light floods the room, even though there is no sunshine today.

Monsieur d'Aubery whisks two of the dustsheets away to reveal a lady's satinwood writing desk and a daybed upholstered in rose silk. 'If the furniture is not to your liking, I'm sure we could find other items for you.'

I stroke the inlaid veneer of the pretty little desk and pull open one of the drawers by its tiny ivory knob. 'I wouldn't want to change a thing.'

Monsieur d'Aubery smiles again. 'Let me show you the rest.'

As we walk through the house, despite the chill in the rooms, excitement bubbles in my breast. There is a dining room, also with a lake view, a study and morning room, and the usual kitchen offices at the back. A staircase leads to four bedrooms with attics above. The garden is bounded by stone walls and there's a small orchard at the end.

Standing by the window looking at the silvery expanse of the lake, I know that I want to live in this perfect little house so much that it hurts.

'I would be pleased if you and Madame Levesque would rent it,' says Monsieur d'Aubery. 'It distresses me to see it empty. I remember it as such a happy place.'

'It is impossible not to love it,' I say.

He clears his throat and mentions a rent that seems to be absurdly low. 'I prefer it to be lived in and kept aired, especially during the winter months. Naturally, for that sum, I would include sufficient wood for the fires and my carriage is at your disposal.'

'You are too kind,' I say, really meaning it.

'May we shake hands on our agreement?'

Monsieur d'Aubery's hand is warm as I clasp it and all at once the miserable disappointment of my meeting with Auguste Moreau seems less sharp. 'Thank you,' I say, elated that Sophie and I will live in this charming house.

As we walk back I reflect that my opinion of Mr d'Aubery has quite changed from the first time I met him. I'm grateful to him for his kindness to Sophie when he found her collapsed in the street and for his fierce defence of me at Château de Lys. I've seen how kindly he helped grieving Madame Gerard and her family. Even his anger towards me, born out of fear for my safety after the king's execution, seems more understandable when I consider the suffering he has endured after the untoward deaths in his own family. He is not always the arrogant man I had believed him to be and his stern expression and sometimes overbearing manner hide a generous heart.

A few days later we move our scant possessions into the little house and Sophie professes herself as pleased with our new home as I am.

Madame Viard stands in the hall directing operations as two maids make up the beds with clean linen and give a final polish to the windows. A basket of provisions has been sent from the kitchens and these are now arranged in the larder. Fires burn brightly in every hearth and the slightly musty odour of a house closed up for too long has been replaced by the scent of lavender and beeswax.

'I hope you will find everything to your satisfaction,' says Madame Viard after she has shooed the maids outside.

'I'm sure we shall,' I say.

She looks around the hall, her eyes missing nothing. 'A pretty house,' she says. 'I would be happy to live here myself. Is there anything else you require, Mademoiselle Moreau?'

'There is one thing,' I say. 'When is market day?'

'Morville on a Thursday. If you're wanting a lift Jacques will take you in the cart together with the cook, Madame Thibault.'

After she has gone, Sophie and I rearrange the chairs in the drawing room so that we have a view of the lake and she sets out her pencils and sketchbook on a table while I examine the books on the shelves beside the writing desk in the study.

I hear footsteps on the gravel outside and am delighted to see Monsieur d'Aubery approaching the front door. Hastily I glance in the hall mirror and pat my curls into place before opening the door.

'Welcome!' I say.

'I called to see if you are settled or if there is anything you require?' He lifts his head and sniffs. 'Lavender! Grandmother always kept that scent in this house.'

'The furniture is newly polished. Please, come into the drawing room.'

'Good afternoon, Madame Levesque! You're ready to start a masterpiece, I see,' he comments as he enters the room.

Sophie looks up from her sketchpad and gives him a brilliant smile. 'Hardly a masterpiece but this view of the lake with its little temple is so peaceful that I shall enjoy the labour, whatever the result.'

'Will you stay for tea?' I ask. 'We have no maid so I'll see to it myself.'

'Then I shall come with you to carry the tray.'

Laughingly, I protest but secretly I'm pleased when he insists.

The coals are glowing in the kitchen range and before very long the kettle is singing and the cups are set out on a tray. It amuses me to see a former comte filling up the sugar bowl and pouring boiling water on to the tea leaves. We return to the drawing room and make toast by the fire.

'Perhaps next time you come to call I shall be able to offer you *gâteau à la vanille*,' I say.

'I can see I will have to pass by at four o'clock every day,' says Monsieur d'Aubery with a smile. 'I was also going to tell you that ...'

There is a loud rat-a-tat on the door and I hurry to open it.

Monsieur Viard stands on the step. 'Maman told me you were both safely ensconced in your new home. I was passing and couldn't help glancing in at the window and seeing you all so snug around the fireside.'

I hold the door wide open in welcome.

Monsieur Viard beams and follows me into the drawing room, where he looks far too large to fit its neat proportions. 'Madame Levesque ... Etienne.' He bows. 'I hope you will forgive the intrusion?'

'You're very welcome,' says Sophie. 'I'll fetch another cup and we shall make you hot buttered toast.'

Monsieur Viard holds his hands out to the fire. 'Well, this is very agreeable!'

It pleases me to have the company of two such personable men. Both of them are fine-looking; Monsieur d'Aubery leaner, darker and more intense than Monsieur Viard, who always has a ready smile to bestow. Sunshine and shadow, I think to myself, both pleasing in their different ways.

'Jean-Luc, when you arrived I was about to mention that I have employed a new carpenter to replace Antoine Gerard,' says Monsieur d'Aubery. 'And he's happy for Victor to be his apprentice.'

'But that's wonderful!' I say. I'm delighted that he hasn't forgotten the Gerard family. 'I had an idea about them, too,' I say. 'I was wondering whether to call on Madame Gerard to see if she could spare me her eldest daughter to be our maid?'

Monsieur d'Aubery's expression is doubtful. 'Babette is very young and untrained.'

'I'm used to girls of that age and shall train her myself. Then, when we've moved on, she'll be useful at Château Mirabelle.'

'An excellent idea,' says Monsieur d'Aubery, 'and, Heaven knows, another wage coming into the Gerard household will help a great deal.' He smiles so warmly at me that I blush.

Our guests drink several cups of tea before leaving, promising to return in a day or two. As Sophie and I stand on the doorstep to say goodbye, Monsieur d'Aubery invites me to go riding with him later in the week.

'I should like that very much,' I say.

'Once the weather is warmer I'll row you across the lake to the island,' says Monsieur Viard, apparently not to be outdone. 'And we'll take a jaunt into Morville one day soon, if you'd like?'

'You must all come to dine, too,' says Monsieur d'Aubery, 'and a hand of cards afterwards.'

'They're most attentive,' says Sophie, looking at me from under her eyelashes after the men have left. 'I do believe they're vying for your attention, Maddy.'

'They're very kind,' I say, blushing.

'And uncommonly attractive,' says Sophie. 'Ah, well! Time will tell.'

It's growing dark and I light the candles and close the shutters, wondering how it would be to have either Monsieur d'Aubery or Monsieur Viard as a suitor. I like them both. Monsieur Viard is light-hearted and makes me laugh but there is something about Monsieur d'Aubery's serious manner that makes me want to discover more about him. Perhaps a person needs to earn his trust, but then I suspect he would be a faithful friend for ever.

Sophie and I sit companionably by the fire chatting about our new friends until the coals glow orange and the ashes fall into the hearth.

Chapter 14

March 1793

We settle into our new life and now that Sophie has been forced to face the inevitable, I see how hard she's trying to make the best of it. Her baby has quickened and frequently I see her resting her hand on her abdomen, a faraway expression on her face. She occupies herself with her drawing, while I have decided to write a treatise on education for girls. I'm sure Papa would have approved.

Young Victor Gerard walks his sister to our house each morning on his way to work. Often I invite him to join Babette for breakfast, hoping that this will lessen the financial burden for poor Madame Gerard. It brings a lump to my throat when the boy talks so earnestly of his intention to work hard at his apprenticeship and assume responsibility for his family. Babette, too, is eager to please and I'm finding her quick to learn her duties.

Monsieur d'Aubery regularly calls on us in the afternoons, sometimes bringing Monsieur Viard with him. I look forward a great deal to these tea parties as a cheerful interlude in our quiet life and am flattered by the banter between the two men as they compete for my attention.

On most mornings I join Monsieur d'Aubery for his morning ride. Sophie says the fresh air and male company puts colour in my cheeks.

I cannot deny it. My waking thoughts have begun to be filled by Monsieur d'Aubery, or Etienne as I call him to myself. As we come to know each other better, his formality towards me diminishes. I like the way he listens to me so intently and his occasional flashes of humour. I anticipate our times together with great pleasure.

On a fresh spring morning, Babette and I set off from the house with our shopping baskets in hand to visit the market. Sophie stays behind, fearful that the potholed country lanes will make the trip too uncomfortable for her now that her waistline is expanding.

We present ourselves in the stable yard, where Jacques is ready with the *charrette*, hitched up to the piebald cob. The tabby cat winds itself around my legs, purring loudly, as we wait for Madame Thibault. I notice that the cat's belly is swollen. Her kittens must be due.

'Did I remember to add butter to the shopping list, Babette?' I ask, as I bend down to rub the cat's ears.

She holds out the list to me.

The cat's purring grows louder. 'You look,' I say, 'since Madame here is demanding my attention.'

A moment later I glance up and see that our maid's eyes are welling with tears. 'What is it, Babette? Have I upset you?'

'I can't,' she says.

'Can't what?'

'I can't read.'

I curse myself for my insensitivity. Living in a country village, there is no reason at all why the daughter of a carpenter should be able to read. 'Don't worry, Babette. Shall I take the list? And we might as well sit in the cart to wait.'

A moment later I sit up straight with a smile on my face as Etienne trots into the stable yard on Diable.

'Off to market?' he asks. He sits well on the great black horse, his posture relaxed and confident.

'We look forward to our little shopping expeditions to Morville,' I say.

Etienne smiles. 'Enjoy yourselves.' He wheels Diable away and then the small black-clad figure of Madame Thibault hurries into the yard. Out of breath, she climbs up to sit on the bench seat beside me. 'Oh, dear,' she says, 'I do hope I haven't made us too late. We don't want to find that all the best goods have been sold.'

Jogging along the road to Morville with the breeze in my face and the early-spring sunshine warm on my knees, I'm filled with a sense of well-being. The trees are just beginning to unfurl their new leaves and there are primroses in the hedgerows. I haven't felt as settled as this since my parents died.

Madame Thibault breaks into my reverie. 'Have you heard about the happenings in the Vendée? I had a letter from my cousin.' The cook clasps her plump little hands over her bosom. 'She says her son was called to join the army. He's only just seventeen and now they want to send him off to war.' She clicks her tongue in disgust.

'Surely boys that young aren't needed?'

'Three hundred thousand men are to be raised from all parts of the country to fight with the English, Austrians, Spanish and Prussians. The men have to find their own provisions as they march, plundering and stealing, so in some areas there isn't any food left for families to buy.'

'I knew it was bad in Paris but didn't realise the difficulties had reached the country, too.'

Madame Thibault shakes her head. 'The people won't stand for it and they're going to take up arms against the government.'

'Civil war?' I ask, shocked.

Madame Thibault nods, her eyes full of tears. 'I shouldn't have said anything but I'm worried for my cousin's family. Please forget I mentioned it. Of course I'm loyal to the Republic and wouldn't want anyone to think otherwise.'

'There have been so many changes since the storming of the Bastille that it's hard to keep abreast of them all,' I say. 'Revolution will always upset the order of things but, at the end of it, we should expect many lives to be improved.' I hope I'm right. Certainly events in France are not following the course I expected in my earlier, more idealistic life.

'Except those who die in the course of the changes,' says Madame Thibault, sniffing. 'Still, please forget what I said. I'm upset for my cousin, that's all.'

When we arrive at the market square in Morville, Madame Thibault trots off with her basket leaving Babette and myself to wander amongst the stalls. Although the square is crowded, very little merchandise is available.

On previous visits the stalls had been piled high with firm green cabbages, baskets of eggs and walnuts, pyramids of apples polished to a russet shine, preserved confit of duck glistening in bowls of goose fat, and pats of creamy goat's cheese wrapped in vine leaves. Today, instead of dozens of plump chickens for sale there are only a couple of scrawny hens in moult, who regard us listlessly through the wooden bars of their cage.

We manage to find a cabbage, carrots, onions and some flour, but the butter has all been sold and there is little choice at the butcher's stall.

'Shall I run to the baker's and see what he has left while you buy the oil?' asks Babette.

'That's a good idea.' I hand her a few coins.

Once I've bought olive oil and salt, I visit a stall selling household goods and buy a small and rather grey-looking piece of soap at exorbitant cost. I have no idea if soap will be available again in the near future but I remember Etienne saying that without soap man is quickly reduced to the level of the beasts.

Babette returns to my side with a baguette tucked under her arm.

'I need to look at the haberdasher's, Babette, and then we've finished.'

Sophie has already let out her skirts as far as they will go and I've promised to buy some material for a new dress. I find some sprigged muslin in a flattering shade of blue and reflect how much less expensive it is to make a dress in the new fashion since we no longer wear extravagantly large skirts.

'Isn't it pretty?' says Babette, fingering the soft material.

'A little cool for this time of year but Madame Levesque can wear her quilted petticoat underneath it for now and it will be summer before we know it.'

While the stallholder is measuring and cutting the muslin I see some rose pink Indian cotton and hold it up to myself. 'What do you think, Babette?'

'It's beautiful,' she says. 'And it makes your cheeks look pink.'

All at once I feel reckless. Who knows if it will be available again next time we come to the market? 'I'll take a dress length,' I say. 'And, Babette, would you like me to make you a dress, too?'

Her hazel eyes widen. 'For me? I've only ever had Maman's clothes cut down before.'

'Then you shall definitely have a new dress all of your own.'

As we leave the stall an elderly man, shabbily dressed in rusty black and leaning heavily upon a cane, approaches us. 'Good morning, Babette.'

'Père Chenot.' Babette drops a curtsey.

'And your poor mother and all the little ones, are they well?'

'Yes, thank you, Père. And this is my new mistress, Mademoiselle Moreau.'

The old man bows. 'Enchanted to make your acquaintance, Mademoiselle Moreau. So Babette is now your maid?'

'And proving to be most diligent.'

Père Chenot smiles and a latticework of wrinkles spreads across his tired face. 'I would have expected nothing else of her.' He lays a hand on Babette's head for a second and murmurs under his breath. 'Go in peace, my child.' He bows again to me and then limps away.

'Let's sit down for a moment while we take stock,' I say.

There is a *lavoir* at the corner of the square, adjacent to the river that runs through the centre of the town, where the women gather to gossip and do the washing. Today, since it is market day, the wash house is deserted.

Babette and I perch on one of the low granite walls that surround the building, which is open to the elements at the sides, under a tiled roof supported with heavy oak beams. We examine our purchases and, suddenly anxious that it may not be readily available again, I send Babette back to buy another piece of soap.

I sit quietly listening to the rushing sound of the river, diverted to make a constant flow of water through the vast stone wash trough, and reflect that a year ago I could never have imagined I would soon be living in the land of Papa's birth.

We return to the cart to find Jacques fast asleep with his cap over his face. The piebald horse has finished his nosebag and is dozing, too, with one hoof tipped up.

'Will you stay here, Babette, while I go and find Madame Thibault?'

She is at the dry goods stall paying for her last item, a sack of flour, when I find her.

'Let me help,' I say, taking one of her laden baskets.

She nods in thanks. 'Supplies are short,' she whispers, 'but I've some useful contacts and have made a good deal here.'

The grocer's boy heaves the flour on to his back and follows us to the cart, where Babette is hugging her parcel of primrose cotton to her chest.

Once the flour sack and the baskets are safely stowed between our feet, Jacques clicks his tongue at the horse and the cart rolls away.

'I wonder if you can advise me, Madame Thibault?' I say. 'In July Madame Levesque will require the services of a midwife.'

'Then you must speak to Widow Berger in the village.' Madame Thibault nods. 'She delivers all the babies hereabouts and only ever loses the sickly ones.'

'Thank you. I'll visit her.'

'You do that,' says Madame Thibault, 'but I must tell you the latest news. I met the housekeeper from Château Boulay in the market just now. She says the marquis and his family have run away to London.' She shakes her head. 'The state confiscated the château and a lawyer has bought it for a song but he won't keep such a large household as the marquis. Half the staff are out of work.'

'What will they do?'

'Starve, probably. The young men will join the army, of course, but there isn't enough work for everyone. So many of the former nobility have gone to Paris or London and their châteaux sold to the gentry.'

'At least Mr d'Aubery still remains at Château Mirabelle.'

'He's generally liked in these parts, despite the talk about his wife.' She clicks her tongue. 'And that was a sad thing and no mistake, when the old comte and his wife died.'

'What happened?'

'It was a carriage accident. Something frightened the horses and they bolted. The carriage tipped over when they reached the ford. The horses were mad with fear and the master was killed outright when they trampled him but the poor mistress was trapped under the carriage wheels. No one was there to hear her cries and eventually she couldn't hold her face above the river any longer.' Madame Tibault crosses herself. 'She drowned, God rest her sweet soul.'

There's a lump in my throat as the cart jogs along through the countryside and I imagine Etienne's distress at the shocking manner of his parents' deaths.

The drawing room at Château Mirabelle has high ceilings and carved *boiseries* covering the walls, all painted in the softest shade of green. I perch on the edge of a silk-upholstered sofa and pass the time while I wait for Etienne by studying the delicate satinwood furniture and the swirling pattern and soft colours of the Savonnerie carpet.

Footsteps approach briskly across the stone floor of the hall and I just have time to pinch some colour into my cheeks before Etienne enters the room.

'How delightful to see you, Mademoiselle Moreau!'

'I hope I do not disturb you?'

'Not at all.' He sits down on an adjacent chair and smiles expectantly at me.

'I'm hoping you'll approve of a scheme I have in mind,' I say. 'I discovered the other day that my maid Babette cannot read.'

'It's not uncommon for villagers to be illiterate.'

'But this is the Age of Enlightenment!'

'I suppose they don't miss what they have never had.'

'Are you afraid of the villagers becoming too educated and having ideas above their rank?'

Etienne smiles wryly. 'I'm not sure, since the Revolution, that the villagers need to be able to write to gain ideas of aggrandisement.'

'In my opinion every person should be literate, no matter what level of society they come from.'

'And you do have a great many opinions, Mademoiselle Moreau,' says Etienne.

I'm just about to retort when he continues.

'But I agree with you on this matter. Everyone should be literate. Even the girls.'

'Oh,' I say, exhaling. I'd been readying myself for a confrontation.

'So you would have no objection if I were to teach the village children to read and write?'

'None whatsoever. In fact, I would encourage it.'

'I could fit four or five children around our dining table.'

'I have another idea. Will you follow me?'

He leads me out of the drawing room, up the stairs and along the landing to a part of the building I have not seen before. We walk down a green-painted corridor lined with paintings and then he opens a door to a large room, plainly furnished with wooden tables and scrubbed floorboards. There are two windows and he unlocks the shutters to admit the light. The walls are covered in maps, and collections of small animal skulls are arranged in a glass-fronted cupboard and butterflies pinned to a board in a display case.

'My old schoolroom,' says Etienne. 'You may use it for your lessons, if you wish.'

I look around me, filled with delight, while I imagine a young and rather earnest Etienne studying in this very room.

'Laurent and I, together with Jean-Luc, learned our lessons here,' he says, 'but there is plenty of room for fifteen or so children. What memories this room brings back!' He takes a book from a shelf and opens it. 'Ah, yes! Mathematics. I always dreaded the subject. Jean-Luc used to torment me because he found it so easy.'

'All children have their strengths and weaknesses and I daresay there were subjects in which you excelled and Monsieur Viard was less able?'

Etienne smiles. 'I loved to read and could often be found on the window seat in my father's library. Jean-Luc was never interested in literature.'

'But how would you feel about a gaggle of children coming into your home every day?'

'The place is large enough.' His face grows sad. 'I'd hoped to have a son of my own to use this room. God knows, it feels like a mausoleum here sometimes. It's a house that should be full of life.' He takes a step closer to me and reaches for my hand. 'And I believe you, Mademoiselle Moreau, may be just the woman to achieve that.'

His gaze is penetrating and I'm quite unable to look away. The rest of the room fades into a blur and all I see is the deep brown of his eyes. Slowly, he lifts my fingers and then brushes his mouth against the back of my hand, sending a shiver down my spine. I moisten my lips. I want him to kiss me properly.

But then he drops his gaze and releases my fingers.

Disappointment and embarrassment make me turn away. I spin the globe on its axis with trembling fingers, feigning a deep interest in the African continent and wondering if he'd seen the longing in my eyes.

'When do you intend to begin the lessons?' he asks, as if nothing had happened between us.

The heat in my cheeks dies away sufficiently to allow me to face him.

'There's no time like the present,' I say. 'I shall walk to the village tomorrow and seek permission from the children's parents.'

'I wish you every success in your endeavour, Mademoiselle Moreau.'

I follow him down the stairs and bid him goodbye.

Chapter 15

A couple of days later, after supper, Sophie sits beside me, reading, while I prepare my lesson plans for the following week when my first pupils will join me in the schoolroom. Initially I will have twelve children, aged between six and eleven, every Tuesday and Thursday. Not all the parents were in favour of the idea but, if the lessons go well, perhaps other children will follow.

There are some useful things in the schoolroom that I'll be able to use, slates, books and a globe. That globe. I remember spinning it to hide my awkwardness after the breathless moment when I'd been sure Etienne was about to kiss me. I can't stop wondering what caused him to draw back at the last moment.

'You'll never finish your work if you keep daydreaming,' says Sophie. 'Is it of Monsieur d'Aubery?' She laughs. 'Your face is a picture, Maddy. Of course it's of Monsieur d'Aubery.'

'Is it so obvious?'

'I've known you too long for you to be able to pull the wool over my eyes, but anyone looking at the two of you together can see that you only have eyes for each other. And I gain the impression that Monsieur Viard doesn't care for that at all.'

'I haven't noticed.'

'That's because you're far too taken up with Monsieur d'Aubery to notice anyone else.'

I can't stop myself asking the next question. 'Do you really think Monsieur d'Aubery likes me?'

'Of course he does! But we'll just have to wait and see what happens, won't we?'

Sophie retires early to bed and a little while later I'm finishing my notes when I hear the doorknocker. I wonder if Babette has forgotten something but when I open the door my heart leaps when I find Etienne standing on the step.

'Forgive me for calling so late,' he says, 'but I saw a light still burning.'

'Please, come in!' Hastily, I smoothe down my hair as he follows me into the drawing room. I hope he hasn't noticed the ink stains on my fingers.

'I'm preparing my lessons,' I say, fumbling to tidy up the open books and scattered papers.

'That is part of the reason for my visit.'

My heart sinks. 'Is it no longer convenient?'

'I have been called away unexpectedly but I came to assure you that there is no reason not to hold your lessons, as planned.'

'Called away?' The smile fades from my lips.

He thrusts one hand into his pocket and holds out a key. 'This opens the door to the servants' quarters and rear staircase. I have told Madame Viard that you have free access if you wish to go to the schoolroom at any time.'

'That's very thoughtful of you,' I say, hoping he doesn't hear the despondency in my voice. 'Will you be away for long?'

'A week or two, perhaps.'

'I see.' The time stretches before me like a desert.

'An old friend has arrived.' Etienne idly picks up a small volume of poetry that had been my papa's and strokes the worn leather cover with his thumb. He seems in no hurry to leave. 'My friend is a chevalier of noble blood and travels with his wife and young son. Life here has become intolerable for them and they have been forced to flee their estate in fear of their lives. I have promised to escort them to London.'

My stomach clenches in sudden fear for his safety. 'But isn't that very dangerous, in the current circumstances?'

'Of course.'

I daren't ask him if it's essential for him to go. 'You will be careful?'

'I always am.' Etienne grins boyishly and I can see that part of him is excited by the prospect of the adventure. 'I couldn't leave without saying goodbye to you.'

Slowly, I lead him back to the hall and open the front door. It's very dark outside and the candle on the hall table gutters in the draught.

'I have told no one else where I am going, not even Jean-Luc,' he says softly, 'in case I'm accused of collaborating with the British. I could be guillotined for less.'

I shiver in the cold night air and pull my shawl more tightly around my shoulders. 'No one will hear from me what you're planning.'

'I know that.'

I'm flattered that he trusts me. I will miss him very much.

We stand close together in the open doorway in our own small cocoon of light and his cheekbones are burnished by its glow. 'I can't bear to think of you taking any risks,' I say, my voice husky.

'Don't look so worried.' He reaches out to caress my cheek with the back of his fingers.

My breath catches as his butterfly touch sparks a tremor that runs all the way through me, leaving my knees trembling. I press my face against his hand. 'I wish you didn't have to go,' I whisper.

'I'll come and find you the moment I return.' And then he draws me into his arms.

He holds me for a long moment, our cheeks just touching. The comforting warmth of him is against my breast and I wonder if he can feel the thudding of my heart.

Sighing, he drops a kiss on my forehead and releases me. 'Until we meet again,' he says.

'Good night.' I don't want him to go.

He sets off along the path. I glimpse the pale blur of his face as he turns to lift a hand in farewell.

'Godspeed,' I murmur, as he melts into the darkness.

After he has gone, I stroke my cheek with trembling fingers where his touch still lingers.

The key Etienne gave to me turns easily in the lock and I enter a vestibule giving access to the kitchen passage and a bare wooden staircase to the upper floors. A rich meaty smell of stew and cabbage pervades the air and the sound of clattering pans and female voices comes from the kitchen.

Upstairs, the schoolroom smells faintly of ancient dust and mildewed books. My footsteps clip across the bare boards as I walk to the window. Down below the carriage drive stretches away into the distance through the parkland and finally disappears into the woods. Watching from my bedroom window early this morning, I saw a carriage driving away with Etienne riding ahead on Diable. Now, pressing my forehead against the cool glass of the schoolroom window, I wonder how long it will be before he'll come riding back to us and if he will come straight away to see me. There had been an implied promise in our parting that makes my heart beat faster to remember it.

Sighing, I turn away and start to arrange the tables and chairs ready for my pupils. There are slates in the large oak cupboard and

I chalk a child's name on each one, before setting them out on the tables.

'The schoolmistress in her lair!' says a teasing voice behind me.

I whirl around, thinking that it is Etienne's voice and he has returned early. 'Oh, Monsieur Viard!'

'Did I startle you?' Jean-Luc Viard is leaning against the doorpost with his arms folded as he watches me.

'Just a little.' I try not to let my disappointment show.

'I came home for lunch and Maman mentioned that she saw you coming up here.' He studies his fingernails and says, 'Etienne visited you very late last night.'

'He only stayed a moment or two,' I say, suddenly wary.

A smile flickers across Monsieur Viard's face. 'I happened to be passing.'

My face flares scarlet as I realise that he might have seen me in Etienne's arms. 'He came to give me the key to let myself into the schoolroom.'

'I just wondered,' says Monsieur Viard, 'if he said where he was going? He left so early I didn't have a chance to speak to him.'

'I believe a friend and his family came to visit, passing through on their way to Paris. Monsieur d'Aubery mentioned he also had business there and decided to travel with them.'

'What kind of business?'

I open my eyes wide and attempt to look guileless. 'He didn't speak to me about that.'

'I'm surprised.' Monsieur Viard's gaze is piercing. 'I thought you and Etienne had a particular fondness for each other?'

'He ... he's been very kind to Madame Levesque and myself,' I stutter.

'Well, I shan't tease you about it any longer, then. Would you like me to show you the schoolroom's secret? Unless Etienne has already told you about it?'

I shake my head.

139

Monsieur Viard grins, all at once more like his usual self. 'Come with me.'

There is a door in the corner of the room, which I had taken for another cupboard, and he reaches up and feels along the top of the architrave until he fetches down a key. 'Still here!' he says, triumphantly. He unlocks the door and opens it, revealing a steep and winding stone staircase only as wide as our shoulders. 'Shall I go first? There might be spiders' webs.'

'I'm not afraid of a few spiders,' I lie. I manage not to flinch as I follow Monsieur Viard up the stairs and catch drifts of sticky webs across my cheek but I'm far more anxious about being in such a confined space. I'm out of breath by the time we emerge into a small, circular chamber pierced by four windows. The wooden floor is thick with dust and the air smells musty.

'It's years since I've been up here,' says Monsieur Viard. 'Laurent, Etienne and I used this turret as our secret hideaway. I wonder . . .' He steps closer to the wall and a floorboard suddenly lifts in the centre of the room. Bending down, he puts his hand in the space underneath and withdraws a small cloth bag together with a bow and a quiver full of arrows.

'What have you there?' I ask.

'Childhood treasures.' He loosens the drawstring on the little bag and tips out a handful of marbles, which roll across the floor in all directions.

I pick up an extra-large marble as it comes to rest by my foot. It's a beautiful thing made of polished agate.

Monsieur Viard takes it from me. 'The floor slopes away here so the marbles always ended up in a pile against the wall.' He struggles with the rusted catch on one of the windows until the casement opens with a squeak. 'Come and see.' A cold breeze blows through, banishing the stale air.

We are at the highest point of the building, matched only by the other three turrets, and we can see for miles beyond the parkland.

Rubbing the dust off a second window, I see the steeply pitched roof of the château like a dark sea of slate stretching away towards the other turrets.

Monsieur Viard opens a second window and there is the lake, shining in the light and as glassy smooth as my father's moonstone ring. The little house nestles beside it and beyond that are the neat rows of vines on the gentle slope of the vineyard.

'It's wonderful,' I say.

'I love it up here.' Monsieur Viard leans out over the windowsill and breathes in deeply.

'Careful!' I say.

'Look down there.'

I rest my hands on the sill beside Monsieur Viard's and peer out of the window. It's a very long way down to the ground and it makes me dizzy. I never did like heights.

'Look!' Monsieur Viard holds my arm tightly and points to the carved stone dragons with entwined tails that embellish the turret. Beneath them is a stone ledge a foot wide running around the tower about six feet below. 'We used to climb down and sit on that ledge to shoot arrows at the rooks. It runs all the way around the building.'

I shiver. 'You could have killed yourselves!'

Monsieur Viard throws back his head and laughs. 'That's what Maman used to say but we never came to any harm.'

'Nonetheless,' I say as I close the window firmly, 'I shall make sure the door to the staircase remains locked while the children are in the schoolroom.'

Monsieur Viard closes the other window, places the childhood treasures back under the floorboard and we begin the descent. I'm relieved when we're out of the close confinement of the spiral staircase and back in the schoolroom.

'All ready for your class tomorrow?'

I glance around at the neatly arranged tables and nod in satisfaction.

Monsieur Viard watches me with his mouth pursed. 'Have you taught children before?'

'For some years now, although only girls.'

'You don't look like a schoolteacher. Where did you work?'

I bite my lip, trying to remember the story Monsieur d'Aubery and I had concocted. 'My father and mother had a school near Lyon,' I say, 'and I helped them with the younger girls for many years before I conducted classes on my own.'

'And what made you leave Lyon?' He sits down on a corner of the table and folds his arms over his broad chest.

He's watching me closely and I do my best not to look anxious. 'The counter-revolutionaries make it an uncomfortable place to live. And then there is Sophie, my oldest and closest friend,' I say. 'When her husband died from a sudden illness she sank into a despair so deep and terrible that I feared for her life.'

'And it seems that you were right to fear for her since she nearly killed herself riding off on Diable.'

'She said that everywhere she looked in Lyon she was reminded of her dear, dead Charles.' I paste a mournful expression on my face and draw in a deep sighing breath. 'In the end I decided that the only thing to do was to take her away from all the sad memories until she recovered. So we went to Paris to visit friends.'

'But what exactly made you come to Château Mirabelle?'

It makes me anxious, being questioned like this. 'Sophie's mother knew Monsieur d'Aubery's mother very well when they were children and she bade us call on him at his town house. Paris was in turmoil following the execution of the king . . . '

'Citoyen Louis Capet.' Monsieur Viard corrected me with a half smile.

'Of course. And when we mentioned that we wished to retreat to a cottage somewhere in the country, Monsieur d'Aubery kindly offered to rent us a house.'

'And I believe Madame Levesque is expecting a happy event?'

'Her husband's last gift to her,' I say. 'Thankfully, her spirits are much improved now.' I straighten my lesson notes neatly on the teacher's desk. 'Everything is ready here.'

'And I'm late for luncheon.'

We leave the schoolroom and I close the door behind me.

'Maman doesn't like me to be late,' says Monsieur Viard with a wry smile as we hurry along the corridor. 'I have my own suite of rooms next to hers but we always take our meals together in the housekeeper's parlour.'

'I hope the children won't make too much noise as they come and go,' I say as we start down the stairs.

Angry voices drift up from below and as we reach the bottom step I wonder if it's an altercation between the servants.

Monsieur Viard stands still and I see that an angry flush colours his cheeks.

Then the door to the housekeeper's parlour is flung back against the wall and a small man in a greasy-looking jacket and wooden *sabots* staggers out.

Madame Viard appears in the doorway with her hands on her hips. Her high-crowned cap is crooked and its silk ribbons loosened. 'Don't you ever try that again, you lecherous bastard! You're drunk, Marcel, and I won't have you in this room until you've sobered up.'

Marcel glares at us with bloodshot eyes. 'What are you looking at?' he demands.

Monsieur Viard's jaw is set as he steps forward, his fists clenching as he towers over the smaller man. 'Get back to work!' he says.

The man stares back at him belligerently and there is an uneasy moment while I wonder if they will come to blows, but eventually Marcel drops his gaze and shambles off down the stairs.

'Are you all right, Maman?' Monsieur Viard takes his mother in his arms.

She clings to him for a moment, crimson spots of anger on her cheeks. 'He's a good-for-nothing peasant!'

'I'll come back in a moment,' he says, kissing her forehead.

She nods and wipes away a tear before retreating into her quarters.

Silently, Monsieur Viard and I walk down the stairs side by side.

'Thank you for showing me the tower,' I say, as we reach the servants' lobby.

'I'm sorry you had to witness that unpleasant scene,' he says. A muscle still flickers in his jaw.

'As long as your mother is unharmed ...'

'I would never let anyone hurt Maman.' The intensity of feeling in his voice leaves me in no doubt that he means what he says.

'Goodbye, then.'

Unsmiling, Monsieur Viard inclines his head in the smallest of bows. I've barely stepped over the threshold when the door closes behind me.

Sophie and Babette are sewing in companionable silence at the table in the dining room.

'I've eaten,' says Sophie. 'I was too hungry to wait for you but yours is on a covered tray in the kitchen.'

'I'll fetch it and sit beside you,' I say.

A few moments later I'm eating my cold meat and bread. 'Babette? Who is Marcel?'

Our young maid looks up from her stitching. 'Marcel Viard? Madame Viard's husband?'

Carefully, I put down my fork. 'I suppose he must be.' Thoughtfully, I chew on a piece of bread. It's hard to imagine that weasel-faced Marcel can be the housekeeper's husband, or indeed

Jean-Luc's father. Perhaps, before he developed his fondness for the bottle, he'd been a more prepossessing young man? Whatever the case may be, Jean-Luc appears to feel little affection for his father. And who can blame him?

Chapter 16

The following afternoon I wait outside the servants' entrance until the children begin to arrive from the village. The smallest hold their older sisters' or brothers' hands and the others chatter together in groups.

At last all twelve children are here and I clap my hands to gain their attention. 'Good afternoon, children. I am Mademoiselle Moreau and you may call me Mademoiselle. First of all, are there any of you who would like to visit the privy before we start our lessons?'

Twelve pairs of solemn eyes study me.

One little girl comes forward and stands before me, twisting her skirt in embarrassment.

'Good girl.' I smile at her. 'It's just around the corner behind the hedge. Run along now and we'll wait for you.'

Half the other children step forward then and I shoo them off. They run, laughing and squealing, to the necessary house. I call one boy back after I see him push another child.

'And what is your name?' I ask the miscreant.

'Emile Porcher.'

'You will not push the other children again, Emile, unless you wish to spend the next two hours standing in the corner. Do you understand me?'

'Yes.' He pouts and refuses to meet my gaze.

'Yes, *Mademoiselle*.' I tip up his chin until he is forced to look at me.

'Yes, Mademoiselle.'

'Good. Remember that I will be watching you. Off you go!'

Emile swaggers away and I sigh. We haven't even started our lesson and already I've found the class troublemaker.

Once the children are all assembled again I make them stand in an orderly line and bid them to be silent until we reach the school-room. As we tramp up the stairs I notice that the door to the housekeeper's parlour is firmly closed.

Inside the schoolroom I call the children forward, one by one, to sit before the slate that bears their name. I set them to work making a fair copy. Soon a dozen little heads are bent over their slates and I experience again the thrill of believing that perhaps I can make a real difference to young minds.

Nearly two hours later I finish reading the children a story and then draw the lessons to a close. I'm preparing to escort them downstairs again when the door opens.

'Children, please rise as we have a visitor,' I say.

Dutifully, they scramble to their feet.

'Good afternoon, children,' says Jean-Luc Viard. He stands with his powerful legs apart and his arms held behind his back and fixes them one by one with a stern eye. 'Have you all been good?'

There is an answering chorus of, 'Yes, sir,' and 'Very good, sir.'

'Is this the truth, Mademoiselle Moreau? Or do I need to bring my birch switch to teach them another lesson?' He regards me with a quizzical eye and it's all I can do not to smile.

'The children have been most attentive,' I say, glancing at young Emile, who squirms on the bench and attempts to look nonchalant.

'I am very pleased to hear it.' Monsieur Viard's face splits into a wide grin. 'In that case ... ' From behind his back he brings a plate mounded with slices of bread, liberally spread with jam.

A moment or two later the children's smiling faces are also smeared with jam.

I clap my hands and chivvy my charges into a crocodile. 'Now remember, not a word until we're outside!'

They clatter downstairs and Monsieur Viard and I follow.

The children line up to shake my hand before dismissal. 'Now all go straight home and no dawdling on the way! I'll see you here again on Tuesday afternoon.'

'And I shall call by to see that you are behaving yourselves,' says Monsieur Viard as the children scamper off.

'That was thoughtful of you, to bring the bread and jam,' I say. 'Some of the poor little mites look as if they don't have enough to eat.'

'They probably don't, with the price of bread what it is these days. Still, I'm not sure I needed to come and threaten them, after all. You appeared to have everything perfectly under control.'

I smile. 'I've been teaching for long enough to know how to manage a classroom of children.'

Monsieur Viard looks serious again. 'There's something I wish to discuss with you. May I walk you home?'

He takes the basket of books from my arms and we set off along the path towards the house.

'What is it you wanted to say?'

Monsieur Viard rubs his nose and sighs. 'First I apologise for the unpleasant confrontation with my father yesterday. I suppose all families must have their crosses to bear. For Maman and myself, it is my father.'

'Think nothing of it,' I say lightly.

Monsieur Viard glances at me sideways. 'There's something else,' he says, 'of a delicate nature. I hesitate to raise the subject but

148

I feel it is my duty to do so.' He appears to be agitated and begins to walk much faster until I am obliged to trot along beside him to keep up.

I experience a flicker of fear. Could he have somehow discovered the secret of where Sophie and I have come from?

'As I said, it is of a delicate nature and I have no wish to cause you embarrassment. Quite the opposite, in fact.' Jean-Luc's usually laughing eyes are serious.

Nonplussed, I say nothing.

'Etienne and I have known each other all our lives and I believe no one understands him better than I. It is clear to me, even though he denies it, that he has become uncommonly fond of you. And why would he not? You are very beautiful . . .'

'Monsieur Viard!' I protest.

He holds up a hand. 'I state that not as flattery but as fact. Besides, I saw you in the doorway together the other night.'

Embarrassed and annoyed that he had witnessed that special moment, I look away.

'In truth,' says Monsieur Viard, 'I believe you have stolen Etienne's heart, but the sincere feelings of friendship I hold for you will not allow me to stand by and watch him make you false promises.'

I'm alarmed. 'But he has made me no promises.'

'I have seen how he looks at you and I believe you return his sentiments. It's unfair of him to show you affection that might lead you to hope that he *will* make you promises.'

Irritation is mixed with my unease. 'I don't understand.'

'Then I must be cruel to be kind.'

'Please tell me what it is,' I say frostily.

'You should be aware that Etienne is not, and may never be, in a position to offer you marriage.'

My cheeks flare. 'Such a subject has never been discussed between us.'

'Maybe not,' says Monsieur Viard unhappily, 'but I am making it my business to tell you so that it never *will* be discussed. You see, I have to tell you that Etienne already has a wife.'

'A *wife?*' I stare at him and the silence stretches out. 'But he's a widower,' I say at last.

Monsieur Viard spreads his hands, palms up, and shrugs. 'Nobody knows that for sure except perhaps Etienne himself. His wife disappeared one day and was never seen again. There is no indication that she has died and so he is not free to offer you marriage.'

All at once I find it hard to breathe, as if there's a great weight pressing down on my chest. I recall the time Georgiana told me that it was rumoured that Etienne had murdered his wife. I'd dismissed that as idle gossip but she'd never said that there was any question of his wife being missing.

'I'm sorry,' he says. 'The news has shocked you. Please believe me, I have told you this out of friendship, to avoid your being hurt, but I fear I may already be too late.'

I draw in a deep breath. 'Nonsense!' I say. 'I owe a debt of gratitude to Monsieur d'Aubery for all his kindness to Sophie and myself but there's no question of my having lost my heart to him.'

'Really?' Monsieur Viard looks at me doubtfully.

'Absolutely.' I smile brightly and hope the crushing unhappiness that is making my stomach churn doesn't show in my face.

'Nevertheless I can see that the news has come as a great surprise to you and I confess I'm disappointed that Etienne didn't tell you himself. I do believe that a true friend would never have concealed such knowledge from you.'

'There was no need for him to tell me,' I say, 'since there is no understanding between us.'

'Then I can only say that I am very relieved.'

I begin to walk faster, suddenly desperate to be alone with my misery, somewhere Jean-Luc will not be watching me and waiting for me to break down.

We reach the house and Monsieur Viard hands me my basket as I open the door.

I do not invite him inside. 'Thank you for escorting me.'

'Perhaps . . .'

'Yes?' I step into the doorway.

'Perhaps, tomorrow, when I visit Morville, you would care to accompany me? There's an inn where they serve a very good chicken pie.'

I just want him to go. 'Sophie needs me tomorrow.'

'Please don't let me stop you!' says her voice from behind me.

Monsieur Viard bows. 'How delightful to see you, Madame Levesque!'

'Won't you come in?' asks Sophie.

My heart sinks but Monsieur Viard glances at me and says, 'Thank you but I'm sure Mademoiselle Moreau will wish to tell you all about her new pupils.' Lifting a hand in farewell, he sets off back along the path.

Sophie closes the front door. 'Did the lessons go well? Come into the drawing room and tell me all about it.'

'Oh, Sophie,' I say, unable to hold back the tears any longer. 'It's Etienne.' I fall into her arms.

'Whatever is it?' she asks, patting my back as I sob on her shoulder. 'Is he ill?'

'No. He's married!'

Sophie draws in her breath and holds me at arm's length to look at my face. 'But I thought his wife was dead? Where is she? Not here at Château Mirabelle, surely?'

'Monsieur Viard said nobody knows.'

Sophie stares at me in amazement. 'But that's ridiculous. Surely Monsieur d'Aubery would have told you if he still had a wife? I shall ask Monsieur Viard about it myself.'

I catch at her sleeve in alarm. 'No! I don't want him to know my affections are engaged.'

'I'm sorry to say that it appears Monsieur d'Aubery has not been open with you.' She kisses my cheek. 'Now, shall we have our tea and play piquet to take your mind off this supposed wife?'

We pass an uneventful evening but I am so distracted that I lose all but one game to Sophie. Afterwards, we retire to bed and I lie with my arms folded behind my head, staring into the darkness. I can no longer deny to myself that I'm halfway to falling in love with Etienne and the knowledge that he may still be married has cut me to the bone.

'Did you sleep badly?' asks Sophie as I toy with a piece of bread at breakfast the next morning.

'Hardly at all.' I sigh. 'But I've come to a decision. I can't ask Monsieur Viard to tell me more about Etienne's wife but perhaps his mother will tell me the truth of the situation.' I'm hoping that my awkwardness at asking such a question will be outweighed by her embarrassment since I witnessed the confrontation with her drunken husband.

After the breakfast dishes are put away and Babette has arrived, I put on my coat and walk to the château. I let myself in by the servants' entrance and peer round the kitchen door.

'Is Madame Viard here?' I ask Madame Thibault.

She shakes her head. 'She's in the housekeeper's room.'

I walk up the back staircase and tap on the door. Madame Viard's voice calls for me to enter and I see quickly suppressed surprise on her face when she sees who is calling on her.

'I wonder if you would spare me a minute?' I say.

'Of course, Mademoiselle Moreau.' Her tone is bland and polite. 'Would you care to take coffee with me?' The silk of her skirt swishes as she pulls out a chair from under the table and takes another cup from the sideboard.

'I was talking to Monsieur Viard ... your son, that is, not your husband ... and he said something that surprised me.' I run my finger around the rim of the coffee cup, noting that the porcelain is unexpectedly fine for a housekeeper.

'Jean-Luc mentioned that he told you about Monsieur d'Aubery's wife,' says Madame Viard. She looks at me appraisingly. 'It's no secret here but he believed you didn't know. And, in the circumstances, he felt it his duty to bring it to your attention.'

So it is true then. A crimson tide of distress floods my face. 'Monsieur Viard appeared to be under the misapprehension that I might have had some kind of special understanding with Monsieur d'Aubery,' I say. 'It isn't the case but, nevertheless, I confess to curiosity and hope that you might enlighten me further. Your son said that no one knows the whereabouts of Madame d'Aubery?'

Madame Viard regards me with shrewd dark eyes. 'It caused a great deal of scandal at the time and we never have found out exactly what happened. Finish your coffee and I'll show you something that may interest you.'

I drain my cup of scalding coffee and follow her from the room. We go through the servants' door into the château. A long corridor stretches away in front of us and our footsteps fall softly upon thick carpet. Finally we reach the end and Madame Viard opens the last door.

The room is shadowy dark and the air still. There is the faint scent of dried roses, sweet but slightly musty. Madame Viard opens the casements and unlocks the shutters.

I blink as light floods in, revealing blush pink wallpaper and a carpet woven in soft shades of green, pink and gold. The gilded furniture is delicate and the bed covered with gold damask. A lady's bedchamber.

'Look here,' says Madame Viard.

The light coming through the window falls upon a gold-framed portrait on the wall. A beautiful young woman, her fair hair elaborately curled, sits at a painted writing desk with a half smile on her face. A sapphire pendant nestles between her full breasts and her white shoulders are set off by artfully draped silk gauze. She holds a rosebud between her fingers. A bud as perfect as her own features.

'Isabelle d'Aubery,' says Madame Viard.

Isabelle's cool blue eyes look deep into mine, as if she is peering into my very soul.

'Where is she now?' I ask, my voice barely above a whisper.

'No one knows.'

'But surely she didn't simply vanish?'

'It was summer and she said she was going to take her paints to the temple on the island. She didn't come back and, later, the rowing boat was found upside down on the lake.'

'So she drowned?'

Madame Viard shrugs. 'There was no body. Monsieur d'Aubery had the lake dragged but no trace of her was discovered. Everyone turned out to search the estate.'

'What do you think happened?'

'Some people thought that she ran away with a lover. And perhaps she did, but others believe ... '

'What?'

Madame Viard picks up a rose petal from the bowl of pot pourri on the dressing table and it crumbles to scented dust between her fingers and drifts on to the silk carpet. 'Who is to say if Monsieur d'Aubery might not have discovered Isabelle in the arms of her lover? Rumour has it that he murdered his wife in a fit of jealous passion.'

'The very idea of such a thing is impossible!' But is it? How well do I truly know Etienne d'Aubery?

Madame Viard raised her eyebrows. 'I have known Monsieur d'Aubery since he was a child and he has an extremely volatile temper. If he discovered his wife was unfaithful to him, who knows what he might have done?'

'I cannot believe that of him,' I say, my voice quivering.

'Isabelle's portrait used to hang in the hall,' says Madame Viard, as if she hasn't heard my outburst. 'But he moved it up here. Do you see how her eyes follow you wherever you go?'

I look up at the painting again. Isabelle's painted eyes look into my own with an intensity that makes me uncomfortable. I step aside but she's still looking at me.

'You see?' says Madame Viard.

'It's a trick of the light,' I say, uncertainly.

Madame Viard gives me a pitying smile. 'Sometimes I ask myself if Monsieur d'Aubery moved the portrait to avoid her gaze because he's guilty, or if it was because he loved her so much that it pained him to be constantly reminded of her.'

I drag my gaze away.

'Perhaps you should ask Monsieur d'Aubery yourself what happened to Isabelle?' says Madame Viard.

'I have no wish to distress him by reviving painful memories.'

'A place such as this is full of secrets but it's usually best to know the truth,' says Madame Viard.

A sharp stone of loss lodges itself under my breastbone. Whatever the truth is, whether Etienne is a murderer or is still married to a woman who has disappeared, he's lost to me for ever.

I meet Isabelle's challenging stare again while Madame Viard secures the shutters and then I follow her from the room.

Chapter 17

The sun is shining and I sit by the open window listening to the birds while I attempt to write another chapter of my treatise on education for girls. The lovely day is quite at odds with my melancholy mood and I'm screwing up yet another blotted page when there's a rattle of gravel on the windowpane.

Jumping up, I see Monsieur Viard grinning at me from the garden. I open the casement.

'You look far too serious for such a beautiful morning,' he says. 'I've come to persuade you to change your mind about accompanying me to Morville today.' He smiles at me winningly. 'I have one small errand to make but you could pass the time very pleasantly sitting in the square or visiting the shopkeepers until I've finished.'

Undecided, I chew my bottom lip. I'm too overset to achieve anything in my present state of mind.

'Do, please, give me the pleasure of your company.'

Damn Etienne! It's pointless wallowing in misery over a man I can't have. 'I do need some more chalk for the children's slates,' I say.

'Then that's settled! Shall we meet in the stable yard in half an hour?'

A short while later I'm dressed in my new pink dress with a cream fichu around my shoulders and my hair tucked up inside my favourite frilled cap. I say goodbye to Sophie and hurry towards the stables.

Monsieur Viard, elegant in a claret cutaway coat with a damask waistcoat, is waiting for me in the stable yard.

'How delightful you look, Mademoiselle Moreau!' Monsieur Viard hands me up the steps of the carriage, smiling. 'And not an inky finger to be seen.'

'You're dressed extremely fine today. I do hope the *sans-culottes* don't mistake you for an aristocrat and pelt you with mud.'

Laughing, he climbs up and sits beside me, his large frame rocking the carriage.

Colbert jumps up on to the coachman's seat and flicks the reins.

Monsieur Viard keeps me entertained with an easy flow of conversation as the countryside rolls past the window and before long we arrive at Morville. The carriage drives into the courtyard of the Lion d'Or and we alight.

Monsieur Viard takes my arm and we walk towards the square. There is no market today but the shops are open.

'I have an appointment with the mayor at the Hôtel de Ville,' says Monsieur Viard, 'but I expect to be finished within the hour. Shall we meet then back at the Lion d'Or?'

'That will give me plenty of time to carry out my errands,' I say.

Monsieur Viard lifts my hand to his lips. 'Until later then, Mademoiselle Moreau.'

I watch him for a moment as he strides across the square towards the Hôtel de Ville, the imposing building that is the centre of government for the town and reflect that the day is proving to be more agreeable than I'd anticipated.

The greengrocer's shop is tucked in between a bakery and a butcher. Beside it, a long queue of people snakes out of the bakery and halfway around the square.

Inside the greengrocer's the display of stock is disappointing. A small pyramid of wrinkled apples holds pride of place but apart from a basket of turnips and a few carrots the counter is bare. I fear Sophie's craving for fresh greens will have to go unanswered.

The shopkeeper, as old and withered as his apples, comes forward to greet me. I notice that he wears the red, white and blue cockade of the Revolution.

'Do you have any spring cabbage?' I ask.

He shakes his head. 'The army strips the fields wherever they go and there's little left.' Bending down, he heaves a basket up on to the counter. 'There are potatoes,' he says. He holds up his hand before I can speak. 'I know what you're going to say: potatoes are only fit for feeding to the hogs.'

Delving into the basket, he lifts out a large potato coated in mud. 'But try it, you might be surprised.'

I remember that in France no one eats potatoes and bite my lip to prevent myself from telling him that in England my mother had an excellent recipe for potato pudding. 'I'll take half a dozen,' I say.

Tucking my purchase into my basket, I say good morning and seek out the hardware shop. I buy sticks of chalk for my pupils and go to look at the queue for the bakery again but it has barely moved. We still have flour left so I'll make bread myself rather than wait all afternoon.

I sit on a bench under one of the lime trees that edge the square and watch the world go by. The church, which is situated on one side of the square, is boarded up, like so many others in France. In spite of that, the clock is still working and I have half an hour to wait for Monsieur Viard.

It's very pleasant to sit peacefully in the sun. I watch some thin and ragged children crouched in the dust playing jacks with a handful of stones.

'Mademoiselle Moreau?'

I look up to see Père Chenot, his weathered old face wreathed in smiles.

'May I sit beside you for a moment?' Carefully, he lowers himself down on to the bench and rests his stick against his knee. 'I've been waiting in the bread queue since eight o'clock this morning,' he says. 'I'm too old to stand any longer so I shall have to eat my soup without bread.'

I uncover my basket and take out the largest potato. 'Would you like this? If you cut off the skin, grate it and make it into a little cake, you can fry it in goose grease or pig fat. I promise you it will be delicious eaten with your soup.'

Dubiously, Père Chenot takes it from me. 'I'll try it.' He smiles. 'If it's good enough for a pig, one of God's creatures, it must be good enough for me.'

'I came to find some spring cabbage,' I say, 'but there are none to be had. My friend is expecting and she had a sudden craving for it.'

'Cabbage, you say? Well, I may be able to help you there. Will you come with me? It's only a step or two away.'

Slowly I walk beside the old man as he hobbles across the square to a small stone house. He turns the iron ring in the door and we enter a shadowy hallway.

'Berthe?' he calls and an elderly woman dressed in black comes through the doorway. She eyes me suspiciously.

'Mademoiselle Moreau, may I present my sister, Widow Mathieu?'

She frowns at her brother. 'Citoyenne Mathieu, remember, François!'

'Yes, of course, my dear.'

I curtsey to Citoyenne Mathieu, who makes the merest inclination of her head back to me.

'Where is the bread, François?'

'There is no bread today. I wish to show Mademoiselle Moreau our garden.'

'*My* garden.'

'Just so, my dear.'

I follow him through the passage and out of the back door into a small walled garden. There are fruit trees at each corner, apple, plum and cherry. The ground between is divided into squares by gravel paths with a circular herb garden at the centre.

'How delightful!' I say.

'When the authorities turned me out of the priest's house and forbade me to preach, my sister took me in.' Amusement twinkles in his eyes. 'She had no mind to see me sitting on her doorstep with a begging bowl in my hand.'

'I'm sure she didn't!'

'She was recently widowed and so I took on the garden.' He leans towards me to whisper, 'Between you and me, I'm happy to keep out of her way as much as possible and the garden is the perfect excuse since then she cannot accuse me of laziness.' He chuckles.

It is true; the garden is perfectly tidy and all the shrubs are neatly trimmed. The earth is freshly turned in all the squares except one, which is planted with rows of spring cabbage.

'You see?' Père Chenot nods at the cabbages. 'I can let you have a few leaves.' He takes a penknife from his pocket and deftly cuts several leaves from the largest plant while a robin, head cocked, watches us with beady eyes from the apple tree.

'Tuck them in the bottom of your basket, my dear.' He taps his nose. 'There's no reason why my sister need know you have them.'

'Are you sure . . . '

'I paid for the seeds and planted and weeded them myself so I say you shall have them.'

The sound of the church clock drifts over the wall.

'I forgot the time!' I say. 'I'm meeting Monsieur Viard at the Lion d'Or.'

'Then I shall let you out through the gate.'

I'm halfway across the square when I see Monsieur Viard coming down the steps of the Hôtel de Ville two at a time. I wave to catch his attention.

'Dear Mademoiselle Moreau, I do hope I haven't kept you waiting too long?'

'Not at all. I finished my errands and then met Père Chenot. He took me to . . .'

Monsieur Viard frowns. 'He's no longer a priest. You must know you can no longer call him Père Chenot? He is simply Citoyen Chenot.'

'Old habits die hard,' I say evasively. How unthinking of me to let down my guard, even for a moment! It saddens me that such a gentle old man as Père Chenot could be considered a threat to the revolutionary powers but I forbear to make any comment. 'Did your business go well?'

Monsieur Viard nods. 'Since Etienne is away, the mayor called on me as the representative of the estate to discuss the numbers of men that can be spared to join the army. Each department is obliged to raise their quota of eligible volunteers.' He rubs his hands together. 'Shall we see what is for dinner?'

The dining room of the Lion d'Or is empty and we sit at the table by the window. A fire smokes in the hearth and a shaggy dog lies asleep before it. I'm slightly ill-at-ease that we appear to be dining alone and wonder what I'll find to say to Monsieur Viard when my thoughts are so full of Etienne.

'I've confit of goose or roast chicken today,' says the innkeeper, 'but, alas, no bread, which you'll know if you look at the queue outside the bakery.'

'Then we shall count ourselves fortunate that we can still feast on goose,' says Monsieur Viard.

'I can't help feeling sorry for the peasants,' I say, after the innkeeper has returned to the bar. 'I saw some children in the square and they looked so thin.'

'The peasants have always been thin,' says Monsieur Viard, 'but in time the Revolution will change that. Now that we are free from the tyranny of the king and his court, there will be a period of adjustment, of course, but the bourgeoisie will bring order and contentment back to France.'

'I do hope so.'

He smiles at me. 'But we haven't come here today to worry about that. I hoped that our little outing would take your mind off your disappointment.'

'I'm not ...'

He holds a finger to my mouth. 'We'll speak no more of it.'

A pretty serving maid brings Monsieur Viard his goose. 'And how are you today, monsieur?' she asks. 'Haven't seen you in a while.' She bends over to put the plate in front of him, displaying a generous amount of her plump breasts. 'See anything else you'd like?'

'Saucy minx!' says Monsieur Viard, good-naturedly.

The girl pouts at him.

'Be off with you and bring my lovely guest her dinner, too. And a bottle of red wine, if you please.'

The serving maid flounces off and I reflect that it's not hard to understand why her head has been turned by a man as robust and well-favoured as Jean-Luc Viard. She returns a moment or two later with the wine and bangs a plate of roast chicken down in front of me.

Monsieur Viard's lips are pressed together as he tries not to laugh. After she has gone again he says, 'I made the mistake of passing the time of day with her the last time I took my dinner here. I was on my own and she made pleasant company for a while.'

The girl, polishing glasses behind the bar, glowers at me while we eat.

A party of half a dozen men arrives and soon the dining room is filled with cheerful chatter and bustle.

Monsieur Viard entertains me with anecdotes and droll comments on the other diners. 'Do you see the man over there in the brown coat, the one draining his wine as if it's the answer to all of life's problems?'

I glance at the other table and identify the man.

'Well, I heard from his tailor that ... '

I hardly listen to all of Monsieur Viard's flow of light-hearted conversation but I'm grateful to be able to put my unhappiness aside and let him flatter and entertain me. Gradually, my sombre mood lifts.

After we have concluded our meal with apple tart and some cheese, Monsieur Viard leans back with a sigh of satisfaction. 'If Etienne is experiencing half the pleasure with his friends that I have enjoyed in your company today, he is a lucky man.'

My cheeks are glowing from wine and laughing at Monsieur Viard's jokes but I feel the smile fade from my face then.

'That was thoughtless of me,' he says, placing his hand over mine on the table.

'I assure you ... '

'Despite your protestations, I believe you've developed a fondness for him.'

'As I said before, as a friend, he's been very kind.'

'It's hard for you,' he says, sympathetically, 'so far away from your home and friends.'

Fleetingly, I picture my mother's face and am assailed by a wave of sorrow and homesickness. I have no home in England any more and I have lost my long-cherished hope of being welcomed by Papa's family. The future is uncertain.

'I should like you to know that you can call on me at any time,' Monsieur Viard says. 'It is good to have a *trustworthy* friend, is it not?'

'Indeed it is,' I say. He seems concerned for me and I experience a sudden rush of affection for him. I'm very much in need of friendship at present.

He smiles. 'Then, as we are to be friends, will you call me Jean-Luc?'

It's hard to refuse his appeal when he smiles at me so warmly. 'Please call me Madeleine, Jean-Luc.'

He squeezes my hand. 'Then that's settled! And now perhaps we had better return. Since Etienne is away I'm doubly busy with the estate.'

Half an hour later we arrive again in the stable yard at Château Mirabelle. Young Jacques runs to hold the horses while we alight. 'Mademoiselle,' he says, 'there is something I'd like to show you.'

'And what can that be?' asks Jean-Luc, ruffling the boy's hair.

We follow Jacques to the corner of the stable yard and find the tabby cat curled up on a pile of clean straw with five kittens, two ginger and three tabby, mewing beside her.

'This is the first time she's brought them out of the stable,' says Jacques.

'Aren't they delightful?' I sit on the straw beside the cat and stroke her cheek.

Jean-Luc comes to sit beside me and picks up one of the little balls of ginger fluff. The kitten opens its mouth and mews loudly.

I gather the remaining kittens on to my lap, stroking their thistledown fur. A bold little tabby climbs up my front and another clambers up my arm to perch on my shoulder. It tumbles off and clings, mewing pitifully, to a lock of my hair.

Laughing, Jean-Luc moves closer and tries to disentangle it.

'Ouch! Jean-Luc, quick, she's got claws like needles.'

'Keep still, Madeleine! I can't do it if you keep squirming around.' He restrains me with his arm and attempts to tug my hair free from the kitten's claws.

'It's hard to believe such sharp claws can belong to something so soft, isn't it?' I'm suddenly aware of how close he is to me and the strength of his arm around my shoulder.

'Very soft,' says Jean-Luc, as he pulls my hair free. He returns the kitten to its mother and then slowly caresses the tress of hair on my shoulder, allowing his hand to rest there. 'Your hair feels like silk,' he says, his voice suddenly husky.

His face is very close to my own and I find myself curiously unable to move away.

Then a shadow passes over us, breaking the spell. I glance up and my heart lifts for a second when I see Etienne silhouetted against the sun, looking down at us. But then I'm filled with dismay that he should have found me in Jean-Luc's arms, however innocent it may be.

'Etienne!' says Jean-Luc, making no attempt to release me. 'I didn't hear you arrive.'

'I couldn't bear to be away another day.' Etienne's eyes are dark and unfathomable. His boots are mud-spattered and his breeches powdered with dust. 'But then Diable cast a shoe some three miles away. I left him at the farrier's and walked from the village.' His voice is taut and his face grey with exhaustion.

'Madeleine and I have just returned from dining at the Lion d'Or,' says Jean-Luc.

Discomfited, I move so that Jean-Luc's hand falls from my shoulder, conscious of how it must look to Etienne. 'Have you seen these delightful additions to the stable yard?' I say. I'm unable to meet his eyes and bend my head over a kitten to conceal the blush racing up my cheeks.

'Let's hope they earn their keep by keeping the vermin away,' says Etienne brusquely. 'I've had a long ride and I'm tired and dirty. If you'll excuse me, I'll go and change.'

'Please, don't let us detain you,' says Jean-Luc, a half-smile playing about his lips.

Etienne walks away but speaks to Jean-Luc over his shoulder. 'If you can tear yourself away, I'll see you in the estate office in half an hour, if you please, Jean-Luc. I want you to explain the monthly accounts. Damn things don't make any sense.'

'But of course, Etienne. And I'll look forward to hearing what business you had that was so important you had to leave for Paris in a hurry.'

Etienne stalks away, his back ramrod straight.

'Well,' drawls Jean-Luc, 'the master seems to have been drinking vinegar, don't you think?'

I don't like his tone and feel uncomfortable that I might have been the cause of rivalry between old friends. Placing the kittens back at their mother's side, I stand up and brush down my skirt. Etienne may not have been open with me about his wife but I don't like to see him so tired and angry. And it seems to me that Jean-Luc deliberately tried to taunt him by displaying the new closeness between us.

Chapter 18

I'm sitting at the writing table staring out of the window. I'd planned to work on my treatise but my thoughts keep returning uncomfortably to Etienne's expression when he returned unexpectedly and found me in Jean-Luc's arms.

The last time I'd seen Etienne, he'd held me so tenderly and I'd believed that it promised more. Now, knowing about Isabelle, my cheeks burn at the thought that I could have been so misled. It's painful but the sensible course of action is to put aside my romantic feelings for Etienne, which can only result in unhappiness for me.

Sophie comes into view on the path to the house. I hear her open the front door and go to greet her in the hall.

'I've been drinking coffee with Madame Viard and she's given me this to make nightgowns for the baby,' she says.

I take the bundle from her, a folded sheet, and finger the material, feeling the softness of linen washed a hundred times.

'It's old but there's plenty of good in it,' says Sophie. 'If I have to give my baby away, at least I shall send him off with clothes sewn with love in every stitch.' Her bottom lip quivers.

I hug her tightly. 'You must think of little Henry. Once the baby is born and as soon as the war is over, we'll be able to return to London. Only think of how happy Henry will be to have his mama returned to him.'

'If he even remembers who I am by then.'

'Of course he will!'

'Despite the war, I must find a way to return home as soon as possible,' she says, close to tears. 'Only Henry can save me from the utmost misery.'

'Let's think about one thing at a time. I'll help you to cut out some of the nightgowns and you can start sewing the layette.'

Keeping up a flow of bright chatter, I manage to divert Sophie's unhappy thoughts and keep her busy with the sewing. Meanwhile, I'm wondering how to save her from further distress by taking it upon myself to discover a suitable home for her baby, ready for when the time comes.

At the end of our afternoon class, the children clatter downstairs and outside through the servants' lobby.

'Now all go straight home, mind!'

'Yes, Mademoiselle.'

Emile, of course, races off with never a word.

Babette is waiting to collect her younger sister and she hurries forward to take her by the hand. 'Sylvie, say thank you to Mademoiselle Moreau.'

Sylvie lisps her thanks and I wave goodbye as the two girls skip off home.

'How are the lessons progressing?' says a voice beside me.

My heart skips a beat. I knew I couldn't avoid Etienne for ever. 'The children are responding well,' I say, in as even a tone as I can manage, unwilling to let him know how his presence flusters me.

'Good. I'm pleased to hear that they appreciate the opportunity.' His expression is grim and unsmiling.

'I've not seen you alone since you returned,' I say. 'Did you manage to arrange a passage to England for your friends?'

Etienne rubs his fingers in a circle against his temple and I wonder if he has a headache. 'I saw them on to the boat but, just as it made ready to sail, Bernard persuaded me that they didn't need me to accompany them. I confess, I wished to return here as soon as possible.'

I lower my gaze as he looks at me. Had he been eager to return to see me or was it purely estate matters that concerned him?

'It was too late in the day by then for me to start the return journey to Paris so I rested at an inn,' he continues. 'When I went to breakfast the following morning, the innkeeper was imparting the news to other guests that there had been a skirmish at sea with a British warship the previous night.'

'Oh, no!'

'The boat that carried my friends was blown up with all crew and passengers.'

I stare at him, seeing the shadows under his eyes, and my stomach knots when I think of how close to death he came himself. 'I'm so very sorry to hear that.'

Etienne looks away. 'I had a lucky escape but I feel terrible guilt that I wasn't there when my friends needed me.'

'You couldn't have changed what happened.'

'I shan't risk travelling to England again. Too many people depend on me here.' He sighs. 'Allow me to carry your books back to the house.'

He takes my basket from me and we walk side by side along the path without speaking.

Etienne never actually declared any special feelings for me, I reflect as we walk, no matter what I may have hoped for. Can I then really accuse him of treating me badly? Certainly this is not the time to upbraid him for his lack of openness about his wife.

'What other news from Paris?' I ask to break the awkward silence that thickens the air between us.

'The Jacobins are gaining strength,' says Etienne, wearily. 'The journalist Marat continues to write inflammatory articles in his newspaper *L'Ami du Peuple* and to stir the emotions of the *sans-culottes* with his pamphlets. Paris is in a state of turmoil and everyone is suspicious of everyone else's motives.'

'The Revolution has become a runaway wagon and no one appears to have control over it any more,' I say. It's easier to discuss politics than to raise the subject of his marriage. 'When it all began I applauded those who took strength into their own hands to stop the excesses of the royal family and the nobility, but look where that has led.'

We come to the lake and stop for a moment to watch a dragonfly dart over the surface of the water and settle on a bulrush swaying in the breeze.

'The king is dead and the peasants are no better off.' Etienne's voice is bleak. 'France is bankrupted by her wars.'

'Even if you have money, it's not always possible to buy what you want,' I say. 'Bread is in short supply and there were no eggs to be had again in the market last week.'

The dragonfly flits away in a flash of metallic blue and Etienne turns away from the lake. 'All this scrabbling for power by the different factions exhausts me. I simply want to manage my estate well and look after the families who work here.'

He sounds so despondent that I long to hold him in my arms, but that is impossible, I know now.

When we arrive at the house he hands me my basket. 'Is Madame Levesque keeping well?' he asks.

I nod. 'The midwife has visited her and all is progressing normally. She's making clothes for the baby.'

'I trust that her coming child is a comfort to her in her grief. Now, if you will excuse me, I have work to do.'

I stand in the porch and watch him walk away. His shoulders are bowed as if he has the weight of the world on them and I cannot help but feel compassion for him.

Two days later Victor and Babette arrive for their breakfast as usual. There are only some crusts of bread to spare but they eat them hungrily and then Victor nudges Babette.

'Go on, you tell her,' he whispers.

Babette, a wide smile on her face, looks at me. 'Will you come outside with us, Mademoiselle Moreau?'

Curious, I follow them into the garden to find a chicken coop on the grass. Victor carefully opens a wooden flap and I peer in to see two white chickens with pale pink combs on their heads. 'These are for you. The master asked me to make the coop and he chose the chickens himself.'

'They're called Agnes and Alouette,' says Babette, hopping up and down with excitement. 'The master said I could choose their names.'

'They're lovely!' I'm touched that, despite his melancholy mood, Etienne had taken note of my complaint about the lack of eggs in the market.

'You need to keep them shut up for a day or two,' says Victor, 'so that they know where their home is. Then you can let them out to roam in the garden.'

Delighted, I say, 'I've never kept chickens before as I've always lived in ...' I stop myself just in time from saying London, 'a town'.

'I made the coop to my own design,' says Victor proudly. 'Do you see, you can lift off the roof to clean out the inside and there's a little ladder for the chickens to climb up. There are handles here so you can lift it on to a new patch of grass every day.'

I run my hand over the little roof and find it has been sanded smooth before being painted the same pretty pale green as the shutters on the house. 'You've made it beautifully, Victor.'

He blushes. 'I'm pleased you like it.'

'But you'd better hurry now,' says Babette, 'or you'll be late for work.'

'And we need to start the washing,' I say, 'or it will never have time to dry today.'

It's still dark a few days later when Madame Thibault, Madame Viard and I climb into the *charrette* in the stable yard.

'I need some dressmaker's pins and some muslin to make a new cap and fichu,' says Madame Viard. 'And I promised Jean-Luc to deliver a note to the mayor.'

'And I'm determined to be first in the queue at the baker's,' says Madame Thibault as we jog along.

Madame Viard turns to me. 'And how is life in the house by the lake, Mademoiselle Moreau?'

'It feels like home already,' I say.

'And do you think you'll stay long?' Her dark eyes are watchful.

'We have no reason to leave, at present.'

'And Madame Levesque is in an interesting condition so will be happy to settle for a while, I daresay.'

We lapse into silence until we arrive at the market square in Morville.

'I can hardly believe it.' I say. 'Look at that!'

It's barely light but it's dispiriting to see that twenty or so women are already lined up outside the bakery. The door is firmly closed and the window shuttered.

'I shall carry out my errands and meet up with you later,' says Madame Viard. I watch her walk away and it strikes me again how attractive she still is. She must have been lovely in the flower of her youth.

'There's nothing for it but to join the bread queue,' says Madame Thibault.

I smile at the young matron who is in the queue before us. 'Have you been waiting long?' I ask.

'Twenty minutes or so.' She sniffs. 'I thought I'd arrive before anyone else today as I was kept waiting four hours yesterday, and still went away empty-handed, but it seems I wasn't the only one with the same idea. At least the baker must have flour today because I can smell the bread baking.'

I lift my head and sniff the air. The delicious scent of hot bread makes my stomach growl.

An hour later the baker unlocks the doors. The crowd surges forward, jostling for position with their elbows and shopping baskets. At last the young woman in front of us reaches the counter.

'Eleven sous?' she says, outraged. 'Eleven sous! That's more than half of what my husband earns in a day. How can I feed my family when bread is eleven sous a loaf?'

The baker sighs and folds his hands over his floury apron. 'Do you want it or not?' he asks. 'There's plenty that do if you don't.'

'I'll take one loaf,' says the woman, begrudgingly counting out the coins.

'Next!' says the baker.

'I'll take three loaves,' says Madame Thibault.

The baker shakes his head. 'One each, that's the limit.'

'But I've got a household to feed! Don't you recognise me? I'm Madame Thibault, the cook at Château Mirabelle.'

'Madame, it wouldn't make any difference if you was Queen Marie Antoinette herself, it's still only one loaf.' He chuckles. 'In fact, if you was Marie Antoinette, I'd tell you to go and eat cake.'

Grumbling under her breath, Madame Thibault tucks the loaf into her basket.

'Have you any flour for sale?' I ask the baker.

Somewhere in the distance I can hear a drum begin to beat.

The baker shakes his head. 'You might try the dry goods store but I know Monsieur Albert was running low.' He looks over my shoulder. 'Next!'

Madame Thibault and I push through the throng and step outside into the square again.

'We'd better see if there's any flour,' she says, her expression grim. 'This loaf won't go very far.'

'What's happening at the church?' I ask.

A large group of men are gathered in front of the building, which is bedecked with red, white and blue flags. Soldiers, a dozen or so, all wearing blue coats, white breeches and with revolutionary cockades in their hats, are mingling with the public. Another soldier beats a drum with an insistent rhythm.

'Look, there's the mayor,' says Madame Thibault, pointing to a man standing at the top of the church steps, framed in the doorway.

The man steps forward, holds up his hand for attention and begins to speak.

We step closer to listen.

'Citizens, until the enemies of France have been chased off the territory of the Republic, every French person must stand ready to serve and support our armed forces. Young men will go to fight ...'

'Huzzah!' shouts a man in the crowd.

The mayor smiles and bows to him. 'Young men will go to fight, husbands will forge weapons and manage the transport services, wives and daughters will make tents and uniforms and serve in the hospitals, old men will inflame the bravery of our soldiers and preach the hatefulness of kings, the unity of the Republic ...' His words are drowned by the roar of patriotic approval from the crowd.

One of the soldiers fires his musket into the air and the noise subsides. 'Now let's see what you are made of!' he shouts. 'Come forward and volunteer and together we'll see off our enemies with their tails between their legs.'

174

A man steps forward, waving his fists in the air, and his friends whistle and clap him on the shoulder.

A cry of 'Long live the Republic!' is heard over the shouts. One by one, the men come up to volunteer and each is greeted by rousing cheers and the furious banging of the drum.

I swallow a surge of bile and close my eyes as, just for a moment, the noise of the drum and the clamour of the crowd remind me of standing in the square and witnessing the execution of King Louis.

Madame Thibault catches hold of my arm and pulls me away. 'Perhaps we'll find the queue for flour is shorter while this is going on.'

Glancing over my shoulder at the crowd, I catch sight of Madame Viard watching the men join up. I follow Madame Thibault as she walks briskly across the square to the dry goods store. The owner is standing in the doorway watching the volunteers but steps aside to allow us to enter.

'Do you have flour?' asks Madame Thibault.

'I have the new *égalité* flour,' says the merchant. 'It's not possible to buy white flour. All flour is mixed brown and white so everyone eats the same quality.'

'We'll take a sack each,' I say.

Monsieur Albert purses his lips. 'It's rationed.' He bends down to lift two small bags of flour on to the counter. 'One each.'

Madame Thibault looks at me, aghast. 'We're all going to starve.'

'Thousands are already doing so.' Monsieur Albert turns his hands palm up. 'If I don't ration the little flour I can get hold of, there'll be riots.'

'When will you have more?' I ask.

'Try next week.'

'We can't wait that long!' Madame Thibault is pale with shock.

Monsieur Albert raises his eyes to the heavens. 'We none of us have any choice in the matter.'

'Have you any sugar or dried beans?' I scan the almost empty shelves behind him. 'Or oil?'

The corners of Monsieur Albert's mouth are turned down.

'What do you have?' I ask, in desperation.

'There are still some chestnuts and, yes, a few haricot beans.'

A short while later Madame Thibault and I leave the shop with a few pitifully small packages in our baskets.

Madame Viard is waiting for us outside. 'Is that all you've bought?'

'I can't go on like this,' says Madame Thibault, shaking her head. 'Rationing indeed! I shall have to make enquiries about other sources of supply. Madame Viard, will you go into the shop, too, and buy whatever the grocer will let you have or there won't be enough to feed everyone?'

'There's one other call I want to make,' I say. 'I'll meet you back at the *charrette*.'

I hurry away across the square, my footsteps beating in time to the soldier's drum until I reach the gate in the wall. Rapping my knuckles on it, I wait. I'm just about to knock again when I hear slow footsteps on the gravel. The bolt scrapes back and the gate opens a fraction.

'Yes?' says a quavering voice.

'It is I, Mademoiselle Moreau.'

The gate swings open and the former priest is peering out at me. 'What is it?'

'Please, don't be alarmed, Père Chenot.' The poor man is pale and shaking.

He glances both ways into the square and then steps back to allow me to enter. 'Forgive me for my lack of welcome. The mayor and his men called on me yesterday.' He bolts the gate behind me with trembling fingers. 'I'm under house arrest. If I am seen outside these walls . . .'

'What?'

Père Chenot runs his finger across his neck in a slicing motion. 'Apparently I'm a dangerous counter-revolutionary.' A flicker of a smile races across his face.

'But that's terrible!'

'Far worse happened to Our Lord. Meanwhile, is there something I can do for you?'

'I wondered if you had any spare vegetable seed for sale?'

Père Chenot smiles. 'The season is advancing so you'll have to act quickly.' He hobbles away towards the tiny wooden shed in the corner of the garden.

Ten minutes later I shake the old priest's hand and slip out of the garden gate with another handful of cabbage leaves, and carrot, lettuce, turnip, bean and marrow seeds in my pocket.

The children are restless. I've been a teacher for long enough to know when trouble is brewing. Out of the corner of my eye I see Emile elbow little Lisette Marchand in the ribs and she bursts into noisy tears.

'What is the matter, Lisette, apart from Emile being very naughty?'

'It's Papa!' Lisette begins to howl in earnest.

Hurrying to her side, I take a handkerchief from my pocket to wipe away her tears.

'He's gone to be a soldier and Emile says he's going to die and never come back!' She buries her face in her arms.

Shocked, I pull Emile to his feet by his collar. 'That's a very unkind thing to say to Lisette.'

He shrugs off my hand. 'My papa's gone to beat the bastard British, too. And he said he might not come back.'

I bite my lip while I consider the best way to deal with the situation. 'A war is an unhappy and worrying time for whoever is involved in it,' I say. 'But the British are people like us, you know.

Their children are just as frightened as you when their papas have to fight for what they believe in.'

Emile stands in front of me, hands on hips and his face mutinous. 'I'm not frightened but my papa says the British are stupid. *And* they eat babies.'

Lisette and two other girls scream.

'That's utter nonsense, Emile!'

'My papa doesn't lie.' There's a dangerous glint in his eye.

'I'm not suggesting he does but . . .'

Emile kicks the table leg and runs from the schoolroom, only to come to a sudden stop in the doorway.

'Are you causing trouble again, Emile?' says Jean-Luc.

'No, it's her!' Emile points at me, rage turning his face crimson.

'I tell you what,' says Jean-Luc, gripping the boy's shoulder, 'why don't we go and have a talk, man to man?'

Emile's eyes are brimming with tears but he nods.

'Any of you other boys want to come with us?' Jean-Luc asks the rest of the class. 'Women think about war in a different way from us men.'

One at a time, the other boys stand up and gather around Jean-Luc.

'We'll be a little while, Mademoiselle Moreau, if that is agreeable to you?' Jean-Luc raises one eyebrow and looks at me with a wry smile.

Grateful that he appears to have handled a difficult situation in such a sensitive way, I nod.

'After we've had our discussion, I'll accompany the boys back to the village.'

'Thank you, Monsieur Viard.' It's comforting to know that I can rely on him in times of difficulty.

The boys' footsteps clatter away and I go to soothe the weeping girls.

Chapter 19

On my way home after school I visit the kitchen garden. The wooden door in the wall is ajar and, as I've never ventured inside before, I'm curious. Shivering a little, I look around me. There couldn't be a greater contrast to Père Chenot's *potager*. The garden is large and must have been very fine, once. Now it's neglected and the espaliered fruit trees have become overgrown. Loose branches wave unrestrained in the wind. The earth is crowded with weeds and only one small area of ground has been dug. A glasshouse leans drunkenly against the south-facing wall and a wooden barrow rests on its side, the wheel missing.

A drift of smoke is rising from the glasshouse and I hurry towards it, anxious that it might be on fire. Much of the glass in the windows is broken and the door hangs off its hinges, grating across the ground as I push it open. Smoke clouds the inside of the glasshouse and I wave my hands in front of my face to dispel it. Dead vines hang in thick curtains from tangled wire supports and I have to push them aside as I walk.

The source of the fire is a brazier sulkily belching out smoke. Since there is little glass in the roof above, it doesn't seem to be any danger to the structure. Wryly, I smile to myself, thinking that the glasshouse is so dilapidated that burning it might be the best answer.

It's as I make to leave that I see Marcel Viard lying on a bale of straw nearby. He sits up and scratches his head, a bottle of wine clutched to his chest.

'What are you doing here?' he asks, bleary-eyed.

'I saw the fire.'

'It's cold today.'

I nod in agreement. 'I wonder if there's a spare garden fork I might borrow?'

'You?' Viard's expression is incredulous.

'I have some seeds to plant.'

He scratches his head again. 'You can help yourself.' He nods at the far corner of the garden. 'There's a shed.' He takes a swig of wine from the bottle and wipes his mouth on the back of his hand. 'It's dark in the shed. D'you want me to come and help you?' His face twists into a leer.

'I can manage,' I say, and escape as fast as I can.

Later that afternoon Sophie is sitting warmly wrapped in a shawl on the garden bench under the apple tree while I start to clear the weeds from the little vegetable patch at the end of the orchard. The delicate perfume of apple blossom surrounds us as Alouette and Agnes strut around my feet, contentedly pecking at the freshly turned earth and squabbling now and again over a juicy worm. They have grown plump and sleek and their combs have turned scarlet.

The day is cool but digging has made me very warm and I stop to lean on the spade for a moment while I push a strand of hair off my forehead. Then I notice Etienne standing under the apple tree, watching me, and my heart begins to race.

'I knocked on the front door,' he says, 'but Babette told me to let myself in through the side gate.'

'How lovely to see you,' says Sophie. 'I'm languishing for want of company.'

'Are you keeping well, Madame Levesque?'

'The country air suits me.'

Etienne carries a lidded basket and holds it out to me. 'I have brought you these, if you would like them?'

Curious, I lift the lid and cannot help smiling. Inside, curled up fast asleep, are a ginger and a tabby kitten.

'Aren't they adorable!' says Sophie.

'Delightful,' I agree, stroking the soft fur.

The ginger kitten yawns widely, showing the pink inside of its little mouth, all lined with teeth as sharp as needles.

'I hope they'll keep you company,' says Etienne to Sophie.

'Oh, they will!' She lifts the ginger kitten to her breast, her eyes shining.

'Thank you, Monsieur d'Aubery,' I say.

He reaches out and swiftly runs his thumb along my cheekbone. 'A smudge of earth,' he says.

His touch makes me quiver and I force myself to look away.

'So you're planting a garden?'

'It's a waste of good land not to grow vegetables.'

'I agree.' He sighs. 'Our kitchen garden is in a deplorably neglected state. When I was a child it was so orderly that a weed dared not show its face. But then we had an army of gardeners. Two years ago we reduced the number by half. Now, since so many of the estate workers have joined the army, we can only spare Marcel Viard.'

'I saw him today when I went to borrow the garden tools.'

Etienne's mouth lifts in an ironic smile. 'And no doubt he was working hard to plant the seeds that will save us from starvation this summer?'

'No doubt.'

Suddenly Sophie squeals. 'Quick! He's running away!'

The ginger kitten is clinging to the trunk of the apple tree. Before we can stop him, he's run up into the branches.

'He'll come down when he's hungry,' says Etienne.

'But we can't leave him there!' cries Sophie.

The kitten peers down at us, framed by leaves, and then begins to mew.

'Please, Monsieur d'Aubery, will you fetch him?' Sophie looks up at him imploringly.

Etienne sighs, unbuttons his coat and hands it to me. Then he steps up on to the bench and heaves himself into the canopy of the tree.

Etienne's coat retains his warmth as I hug it to my chest. It smells faintly of the stable, overlaid with a hint of the vetiver pomade he sometimes wears.

Apple blossom showers down on us like fragrant snow as he climbs higher and higher while the kitten continues to mew pathetically.

Sophie slams the basket lid shut as the tabby kitten reaches out an inquisitive paw.

There's a muffled curse from above. 'Come here, you little hellcat!' mutters Etienne, and then there's a triumphant cry. 'Got you!'

A moment later he jumps down from the tree and lands, crouching, on the ground with a thump. There is a leaf in his tousled hair and blood beads up from a long scratch on his wrist. He looks impossibly handsome.

'Where is he?' asks Sophie.

Etienne reaches into his shirt and retrieves the squirming kitten. I take the cat from him, while he sucks blood from his hand.

'Come into the house and I'll wash it,' I say.

He shakes his head. 'It's only a scratch. Besides, I'm on my way to the vineyard. The first leaves are beginning to unfurl. Would you like to accompany me?'

I'm sorely tempted but I have determined not to break my heart by becoming involved with a man who may be married. 'I've too much to do here,' I say.

The smile fades from Etienne's face. 'As you wish.' He bows to us both and walks away without looking back.

I pick up my spade again and begin to hack viciously at the stony ground.

As spring moves towards early summer I continue to work in the vegetable garden, weeding and watering and waging a bitter battle with the slugs that dine upon my delicate seedlings. Sophie accuses me of cruelty as I collect the slugs every evening and drop them into a bucket of salted water. But, eventually, as food in the shops becomes even more scarce, she joins me in my hunt for the enemy.

I'm hoeing the beans one sunny morning and worrying about how Sophie and I are going to find a home for her baby when I hear a footstep on the path and Jean-Luc comes through the garden gate. He's carrying a basket over his arm.

I tuck a stray curl behind my ear and smile a welcome.

'You're working as hard as a peasant,' he says. 'But today I'm going to row you over the lake to the island where we'll have a picnic.' He holds up his hand. 'And don't argue with me as I won't take no for an answer.'

'I have no intention of arguing with you,' I say. The prospect of Jean-Luc's amusing company is very welcome. 'I have a blister on my palm and I've been trying to think of an excuse to cease my labours. I must wash first, though, and see if Sophie wants to join us.'

Jean-Luc's smile fades a little and I realise that she hadn't been included in his invitation.

Sophie, however, is resting with the kittens curled up beside her on the bed and merely bids me to enjoy myself.

I scrub the earth from under my fingernails, change into a clean dress and tie a ribbon in my hair.

'You look delightful,' says Jean-Luc as I come downstairs.

His compliment pleases me. I'm looking forward to an hour or two when I can cast aside my cares in favour of simple, uncomplicated pleasures.

He picks up the picnic basket again and offers me his arm.

We come to the jetty and go inside the boathouse, where Jean-Luc climbs the rickety ladder up to a makeshift platform between the roof trusses. He throws down a couple of cushions and I brush off the dust and spiders' webs.

A rowing boat is tied up at the jetty beside the little boathouse and the lake is as smooth as green glass. Jean-Luc places the cushions on the seats and steadies me as I step into the boat. Taking off his coat, he rolls up his shirtsleeves before beginning to row us towards the little island.

I relax in the sunshine, trailing my fingers in the limpid water and watching the muscles rippling in Jean-Luc's strong arms as I listen to the rhythmic squeak of the oars. Drops of water sparkle prettily in the light as they drip from the oars and a moorhen runs across the surface of the lake in its haste to remove itself from our course.

Soon the boat scrapes on to the shingle beach. Jean-Luc pulls off his shoes, jumps into the shallow water and drags the boat out of the water. 'We'll have our picnic in the temple, shall we?' he says. He carries his shoes in one hand and the picnic basket in the other, and we amble along the path that winds amongst the scrubby undergrowth.

Crowning the highest point of the island and set in a grove of silver birches, the temple is open to the elements at the front. Four columns support a pediment and as we grow closer I notice classical carvings on the frieze beneath it. We climb half a dozen wide steps and go inside. The flagstone floor is unswept and a few dead leaves rustle as they drift in the breeze.

'No one has been here since last summer,' says Jean-Luc. 'It's been too cold for picnics until now.' He puts the picnic basket down on one of the stone benches built against the back wall and unfolds a metal table.

I open the basket, shake out the embroidered tablecloth and align the starched creases neatly across the table. Soon a feast of cheese, olives, rolls, apples and slices of raisin cake is laid out before us. Jean-Luc opens a bottle of Château Mirabelle and pours the golden wine into two glasses.

'What a delightful place,' I say, wondering how on earth Madame Thibault had been able to provide us with such a spread given the current shortages.

'Etienne's grandfather travelled in Italy and Greece to study architecture as a young man. You may have noticed the marble busts in the hall?'

'The ones that look like Roman emperors?'

'The old comte brought them back with him. He found some of them around ancient ruins and local peasants sold him others. He was very taken with the classical style and determined to build a folly as soon as he came into the title. The lake and the island were made first and then he planted the grove of silver birches as a setting for the temple.'

'What a big project!'

'He had plenty of serfs to do the work for him, while he drifted about in his curled wig and velvet coat giving orders.'

'You sound as if you didn't like him very much.'

Jean-Luke shrugs. 'He was typical of the *ancien régime*. Once the temple was built he used to bring his mistresses here. Sometimes he exercised his *droit du seigneur* and brought the prettiest serving maids where no one could hear their screams.'

'His poor wife!' I put down my piece of bread, suddenly no longer hungry.

'Once she'd produced the requisite heir, I daresay she had lovers of her own.'

It's uncomfortable to imagine Etienne's grandmother behaving in such a way, though perhaps things were different then.

'More wine?' Jean-Luc holds the bottle over my glass.

I shake my head.

He crosses his legs, resting one ankle on his knee as he eats a piece of cake.

I can't help looking at his bare foot. There is sand on the sole and his toenails are rimmed with grey mud from the lake. Fine black hairs grow on his toes. I glance away, curious but at the same time made slightly uncomfortable by such intimate knowledge of him.

Sipping my wine, I watch the birches dancing in the breeze and wonder if these same trees witnessed the seduction and rape of frightened young girls. I shudder as I'm suddenly reminded of the sylvan grove at Vauxhall Gardens where Papa was murdered protecting my honour.

Jean-Luc refills his glass and leans back, regarding me through half-closed eyes. 'You're looking very pensive, Madeleine.'

'I was thinking of my father,' I say, before I can stop myself.

'The school teacher from Lyon.'

I nod, my eyes welling up as I picture again the terrible scene that deprived me of both my parents.

'Tell me about him.'

'He was a man of honour.' Surreptitiously I wipe a tear away with my finger. 'He always stood up for what he believed in.'

'So he supported the Revolution, then?'

I banish the memory of blood spurting from Papa's heart and blossoming on his shirt as he lay on the ground. 'He never had any time for the greedy rich and always believed hard work should be rewarded.'

'I should like to have met him.' Jean-Luc smiles. 'I could have taken him to the Jacobin Club with me.'

The sense of aching loss that I always carry in my breast intensifies then and my throat closes as I try not to weep. I turn my face away as tears overflow, rolling down my face and dripping off my chin.

'I didn't mean to make you cry,' says Jean-Luc.

'I still miss him so!'

And then Jean-Luc catches me in his arms and holds my head against his broad shoulder. 'You have a good cry,' he says, rubbing my back.

Eventually the storm of weeping is over and I'm embarrassed that my tears have soaked his shirtfront. I pull away, unable to look at him.

'Let me see.' Jean-Luc holds me at arm's length and tips up my chin. He dabs at my cheeks with his handkerchief. 'That's better.' He continues to hold my chin, studying my face. 'You're very lovely,' he says.

'My eyes must be all red . . .'

Before I can draw breath, he leans forward and kisses me.

Frozen with surprise, I feel the prickle of his stubble on my chin as his full mouth presses against mine. It isn't unpleasant, not at all, but I'm completely taken aback. Then he buries his hands in my hair and I can't move away, at least, not without shoving him in the chest and I'm not quite sure that I want to do that.

Gently, he releases me. 'I'm sorry,' he says. 'I caught you unawares, didn't I?'

I nod, my fingers pressed to my lips.

'Are you angry?'

'No.'

'Good. Then I suggest we finish our picnic.'

He refills my wine glass and this time I drink.

Jean-Luc, apparently entirely at ease, makes light conversation while I relive his kiss, all the while attempting to understand how I feel about it.

'Madeleine?'

I jump and see that Jean-Luc is regarding me with amusement.

'I said, the wind is getting up. It looks as if it might rain.'

Glancing up at the sky I see that grey clouds are rolling across the sun. I begin to pack the remains of the picnic into the basket but as I fold up the tablecloth I notice that there are splashes of paint on the table underneath and pause, staring at it.

'What is it?' asks Jean-Luc.

'Paint,' I say. 'Your mother mentioned that Monsieur d'Aubery's wife came here to paint on the day she disappeared.'

'She often used to come here. Or so she said.'

'What do you mean by that?'

'Perhaps it was a pretext to enable her to meet her lover without causing suspicion?'

'Do you think she had a lover?'

Jean-Luc packs the empty wine bottle into the basket. 'I was never quite sure why Etienne married her. Of course, she came with a good dowry but it wasn't necessary for him to marry for money. The marriage was an unfortunate mismatch.' He stares out over the lake, a slight frown between his eyebrows.

'Your mother showed me her portrait. She was very beautiful.'

'But also shallow and frivolous.' He turns to look at me. 'On the afternoon she disappeared I was in the woods. A horseman galloped past and out of the château's gates with a cloaked figure sitting behind him.'

'Isabelle?'

'I prefer to believe she ran away with her lover rather than that Etienne found them together and . . .' He leaves the sentence unfinished.

'And what?'

'Etienne is always so certain that he's right in everything he does and, as an only child, Isabelle had been very indulged. She wanted to live in Paris while Etienne wanted to be here. They often had bitter quarrels.' Jean-Luc looks directly at me. 'It's a sight to behold when Etienne's temper is unleashed.'

At once I remember the ferocity of his rage when he grabbed Auguste Moreau by the throat. Might he have lost his temper with Isabelle and perhaps killed her by mistake? It's an unbearable thought, as unbearable as the thought that he still has a wife. 'And no one has ever seen Isabelle again?'

Jean-Luc shakes his head. 'No, but if she ran away with a lover, she'd hardly return here to pay a social call, would she?' He sighs. 'Still, enough of all that. This picnic was to have been a light-hearted occasion.'

I glance up at the sky again. 'We'd better hurry.'

We walk briskly down the stony path to the beach and Jean-Luc pushes the boat into the water before climbing aboard. The surface of the lake is choppy now as the gusty wind whips up white horses on the unfathomable water.

Chapter 20

May 1793

The kittens, Minou and Mouche, gambol around the garden, play-fighting and chasing butterflies on the mignonette. Sophie makes a pretty picture as she sits, with head bent over her sewing, on the garden bench in the dappled sunshine.

I'm hot from watering my vegetable garden. 'The lettuces are coming on well now,' I say, sitting down beside her. I lift up one of the tiny garments she's placed in a neat pile and examine the dainty stitches.

'I hope your hands are clean!' she says in a mock-severe tone.

'You've made far too many nightgowns for one baby to wear.'

'They aren't all for my baby,' she says. 'I had plenty of linen left over and I thought I'd make some for the orphans and the poor. Heaven knows, I've nothing else to do with my time other than grow fatter.' She stretches and rubs at her back.

'Uncomfortable?'

'A little.' She rests her hand on her abdomen. 'He's growing so fast now.'

Taking my hand she presses it to the mound of her stomach and

I feel a hard little lump. Suddenly it moves and she laughs. 'There, did you feel that?'

'I did. He's going to be strong if he kicks like that.' It's a curious thought that a new life is forming so close to us but out of sight.

'He had hiccups early this morning, making it impossible for me to sleep.' She smiles indulgently.

I say nothing, anxious that already she appears to have formed a bond with this child and fearful for her distress when she is parted from it.

The garden gate clicks and I see a man dressed in loose blue work clothes with a battered straw hat pulled down over his eyes. My heart does a somersault when I realise that it's Etienne.

'Please excuse my attire,' he says. 'I've been working in the vineyard.'

'You look like a *sans-culotte*!' I say. 'But then, I suppose I look like a peasant in my old gardening dress.' I'm quite unable to find anything interesting to say, only drinking in the sight of him, looking at the way stubble shadows his chin and thinking how handsome he is, despite his shabby clothes.

'But why are *you* working in the vineyard?' asks Sophie.

'So many of the men have gone to fight that I'm needed there.' Etienne sighs. 'Everything is growing so fast now that there's too much work for the few men and boys that remain.'

I'm curious. 'What are you doing to the vines?'

'They need to be tied in and trained to grow neatly along the wires.'

I notice that there is a pruning knife in his belt and his hands are engrained with dirt, just like a peasant's. 'Couldn't the village women do that?' I ask.

He stares at me in amazement. 'Women help with the harvest, but this is man's work.'

'Is it any more difficult than gardening? Surely,' I say, 'the women could be trained to do that? Many of them would welcome the extra income while their husbands are away.'

191

Etienne steps over to my vegetable plot and studies the neat rows of lettuces. 'You seem to be managing very well.' He looks up at me and smiles.

I glance away, fearful he'll see the yearning in my eyes.

'The reason for my visit is to ask if you would both care to come and take your dinner with me tomorrow?'

'That would be delightful,' says Sophie.

I can't help the smile that spreads across my face.

'And now I must go home and wash off the day's grime,' he tells us.

'I'll come to the front gate with you.'

Etienne bids Sophie good evening and we walk around the side of the house and up the lavender walk to the front gate.

'Until tomorrow then,' he says. He makes no move to open the gate, as if he wishes to delay our parting as much as I do.

I snap off a head of lavender, bruise it between my fingers and sniff the aromatic oil. I hesitate then decide to go ahead. 'There's something else I wanted to ask.'

'Yes?'

'Is there an orphanage near here?'

Etienne gives me a searching look. 'An orphanage?'

I nod and attempt to look nonchalant. 'Sophie has made a number of baby nightgowns. She thought they might be of use to the orphans.'

'Oh, I see. Well, there is one half an hour away on the road to Orléans.'

'Thank you.'

'Good evening, then.'

'Goodnight, Etienne.'

He walks away and I close the gate behind him.

The following morning Sophie and I visit the stables where Colbert has the *charrette* waiting for us. The piebald cob has his nose in a bucket of water but, as soon as we are settled, Colbert flicks the reins and we start off.

'I haven't left the house in months,' says Sophie.

'You're sure it won't be too much for you?' I ask.

'Babette tells me the road to Orléans is much better than the rough country lanes to Morville. Besides, I should like to give the nightgowns to the orphanage myself.'

She becomes quiet, concentrating on the road ahead, and I can't help wondering if she's aware of my ulterior motive for this journey. We can't put it off any longer; it's time to find a prospective home for her baby.

The orphanage is a dark stone building set back from the road behind iron gates. Colbert drives into the weedy forecourt and pulls up in front of the house.

'There are bars at the windows,' whispers Sophie as I help her to descend.

'The children must be kept safe,' I say but, privately, I can't help thinking that it's a sinister-looking place.

A young serving girl opens the door and bids us wait on the wooden bench in the hall. The sound of children singing drifts down the stairs and Sophie smiles faintly.

Footsteps tap briskly along the corridor and an imposing woman approaches, dressed in black with her grey hair tucked severely into her white cap.

'Good morning, Mesdames. I am Madame Boudin, *directrice* of this institution. How may I help you?' I see the woman's sharp eyes glance at Sophie's swollen abdomen.

Sophie stands up. 'I have made some nightgowns for the orphans,' she says and holds out her parcel.

'How kind! We are always in need of more clothing for the children.' The *directrice* takes the proffered parcel but Sophie doesn't let it go. 'Is there something else?' Madame Boudin enquires.

'Yes. I should like to see the children.'

There is a momentary silence. Then: 'Of course, Madame. We are always happy for our benefactors to see the work we do here. Please, come with me.'

She crosses the tiled floor and opens a door. Girls in identical grey dresses, sitting at long trestle tables, glance up at us as we enter. An older girl stands on a raised platform with a birch rod in her hand, supervising her charges.

Sophie puts her hand over her nose at the unpleasantly greasy smell arising from the mounds of hair in various colours heaped on the tables before the girls.

'There is still a demand for human hair to be made into wigs,' says Madame Boudin, 'but fashions are changing rapidly and before long we may need to find other work for the girls.'

We watch the orphan girls for a moment as they collect and comb the hair, tying it into neat switches of uniform length and colour. The girls work quickly, without speaking, some of them frowning in concentration.

Madame Boudin nods to the supervisor, who bobs her a curtsey.

We follow the *directrice* from the room and she leads us upstairs.

'The boys work in here,' she says, opening a door. There are more trestle tables but this time they are laid out with heaps of straw, which the boys are stuffing into large canvas bags. Some of the inmates are sewing together the open ends of the bags to make mattresses. The air is full of dust and I sneeze three times in succession. Several of the children have reddened eyes and runny noses, I observe.

The next part of the tour takes us to a room crammed with children too young to work. A few toys are scattered on the floor: a doll with one arm missing, a pile of bricks and a spinning top. A gaunt woman with a hare-lip supervises them, along with a couple of nursery maids.

We proceed in silence to the attics where there are thirty or so cots filled with infants up to two years old. A number of older, grey-uniformed orphanage girls are feeding and changing the wailing infants under the watchful eye of a matron.

'All the girls are trained to earn their living in the outside world doing domestic work,' said Madame Boudin, raising her voice over the noise. 'We do all our own cleaning and cooking and laundry. The girls gain plenty of experience as nursery maids and then the boys, as soon as they are old enough, are apprenticed to cloth weavers, blacksmiths and carpenters.'

'Admirable,' I say, faintly.

Sophie leans over a cot and picks up a baby of perhaps five or six months old. He regards her gravely and she tickles his ribs but he doesn't smile. 'Do the children ever find new families?'

Madame Boudin sighs. 'Regrettably, very few of them. There is too much poverty for people to take another child into the family. But not all these children are orphans or foundlings. Some are here because their parents cannot afford to feed them. Others are crippled or not in full possession of their faculties. It's a constant difficulty for us to raise enough funds to support our inmates.' She looks speculatively at Sophie. 'That's a good-natured child. He rarely cries. I don't suppose you'd like to take him home with you?'

'I cannot,' says Sophie, placing the baby back in his cot.

'Can you make a donation? Or perhaps you have friends who may help us?' Madame Boudin pleads.

'I'm far from home and have no friends nearby.'

Reaching into my pocket, I pull out a handful of coins. Madame Boudin puts them in her pocket. Silently we walk downstairs to the hall. The young maid materialises and opens the door.

'Thank you for bringing the nightgowns,' says Madame Boudin. Her gaze drops to Sophie's stomach again. 'Perhaps we'll see you again before long.'

As we drive out through the gates Sophie's hand creeps into mine. She looks at me with tear-drenched eyes. 'Oh, Maddy! How could I have even imagined I would abandon my baby in an orphanage?'

Chapter 21

June 1793

Still in a reflective mood following our visit to the orphanage, Sophie and I walk out as dusk is falling. Château Mirabelle soars in front of us, floating on a sea of mist curling up from the parkland. The moon is a narrow crescent of silver suspended in the deepening blue of the sky.

'It's lovely, isn't it?' says Sophie. 'Such a shame that there isn't a family to live in it.'

'There might have been be if Isabelle were still here.'

'Poor Etienne,' says Sophie. 'He's been left in a terrible quandary, not knowing if his wife is dead or alive. Unless he *did* murder her, of course.'

'He didn't!' I snap. But should I put my belief in him?

'It wouldn't have been very clever of him to leave her body somewhere it could be found. Either way, he cannot marry again,' Sophie pronounces.

'I'd prefer not to discuss this.'

She catches hold of my arm and makes me look at her. 'I don't want you to suffer the same pain as I did by loving the wrong man, that's all, Maddy.'

I nod at her in the gathering darkness but do not say I fear that it's already too late.

The maid leads us into the drawing room, which is blazing with candles, and our host hurries forward to greet us. Etienne wears his pale blue silk coat and the silver buckles on his shoes gleam.

'I'm so glad you came,' he says, kissing our fingers. 'May I introduce Monsieur and Madame Rochefort?'

I hadn't expected any other guests. I see that my pink muslin dress is a much plainer affair than the full-skirted and flounced evening dress worn by Madame Rochefort. Her powdered hair is dressed in elaborate curls and decorated with feathers and seed pearls. Clearly Madame has no intention of following the simpler revolutionary fashions.

Madame Rochefort inclines her head to Sophie and then stares at her with eyebrows raised. Sophie's dress, even though loose and unwaisted, cannot begin to conceal the curves of eight months of pregnancy.

Older by some years than his wife, Monsieur Rochefort is also formally dressed and wears a powdered wig and extravagantly embroidered waistcoat.

Once Sophie and I are seated side by side on gilded chairs, she catches my eye. 'I'd never have come, in my condition, if I'd known Monsieur d'Aubery had guests,' she whispers.

'Perhaps he doesn't realise that women who are increasing aren't invited to formal dinner parties,' I whisper back.

We make polite conversation, side-stepping questions from Madame Rochefort about our families and where we have come from.

Then the drawing-room door opens again and Jean-Luc enters. His white silk stockings are pristine, as usual, and his brown hair is arranged in carefully disordered curls. He gives me a mischievous smile and then turns to Etienne. 'Apologies for my late arrival,' he says, 'but I'm able to accept your invitation after all.'

'Did the Jacobin Club cancel their dinner then?' asks Etienne.

Monsieur Rochefort's eyebrows rise so high that they almost disappear under his wig but he refrains from commenting.

'There'll be plenty of other occasions for a Jacobin dinner in the future. It's been some time since I've been invited to dine in such charming company,' says Jean-Luc. He looks directly at me. 'Ladies, what a vision of loveliness you are!'

Madame Rochefort simpers and pats her powdered curls into place while Monsieur Rochefort makes a face as if he has a bad smell under his nose.

Jean-Luc catches my eye and it's hard for me not to laugh as he copies Monsieur Rochefort's expression.

The maid brings a tray of glasses and we sip sparkling wine while Etienne leads us to talk of less controversial subjects than the Jacobin Club. After a while a footman announces dinner and we remove to the dining room.

There is a delicious aroma of roast chicken and I'm suddenly hungry. We've rarely eaten meat in the past weeks, unless Victor brings us a rabbit. Fortunately, Etienne turns a blind eye to poaching, especially while his workers are short of food.

The dinner is not extravagant but Madame Thibault has made the best of simple ingredients. By the time we finish our cauliflower soup, however, it's plain to me that Monsieur Rochefort must once have been an aristocrat. No wonder he has no love for the Jacobins.

'Château Beaubourg is rapidly falling into disrepair since the younger men joined the army,' he complains. 'And now that the Convention has imposed such fierce taxes on the estates I've little money left to employ even the ageing men who remain.'

'The old order is changing,' says Jean-Luc, leaning back in his chair, 'and for the better, I believe.'

Underneath the table I feel his foot touch mine and when I glance at him he sends me a secret little smile. It's impossible to resist smiling back but I draw my foot away and tuck it under my chair when I see that Etienne is watching us.

'I've been out in the vineyard every day,' he says. 'If every able-bodied man who remains in the area doesn't work on it now, the harvest will be negligible. And I need the income from this year's vintage to carry out essential roof repairs and to pay the new taxes.'

'Are you censuring me for not joining you in the vineyard, Etienne?' asks Jean-Luc.

Etienne doesn't reply directly.

'I cannot imagine you setting aside your embroidered waistcoats and silken stockings to don ragged work clothes.'

Jean-Luc regards his friend with a lazy smile. 'Don't forget *some-one* has to keep the accounts up to date if the estate isn't to go to rack and ruin.'

'*You've* been working in the vineyard, Comte?' asks Madame Rochefort. 'With your own hands?'

Etienne laughs ruefully and holds them out for inspection. 'As you can see.'

'Good God, D'Aubery,' says Monsieur Rochefort, 'you'll have the women working there next!'

'Mademoiselle Moreau has already suggested that.' Etienne lifts his glass to me. 'I've thought it through and it's an excellent idea.'

A glow of pleasure makes me smile back at him.

'Well!' says Madame Rochefort. 'You certainly won't find *me* work-ing like a slave in the fields, Edouard.'

'No, I don't suppose I shall, my dear.' Monsieur Rochefort looks amused.

'Mademoiselle Moreau,' says Etienne, 'I wonder if you would act as my ambassador and sound out the village women to see if they would be interested in your idea?'

'I'd be happy to,' I say, pleased that he has entrusted the task to me.

We discuss the work the women might do until Jean-Luc inter-rupts us.

'I hoped you might open a bottle of the Château Mirabelle '89 tonight, Etienne,' he says. 'A portentous year, wasn't it? The year the Revolution began.'

Monsieur Rochefort opens his mouth as if he is about to make a disapproving comment but then thinks better of it.

Covertly, I watch Etienne and Jean-Luc as they talk, discerning a subtle undertone of discord between them. It's not the first time I've noticed this since Etienne returned from his trip to the coast and found me in Jean-Luc's arms. On the surface, their differences appear to arise because Jean-Luc is more involved with the politics driving the Revolution forward, while Etienne is only interested in maintaining the estate. Nevertheless, I can't help wondering if there is another cause for the tension between two old friends.

Several bottles of wine later, the candles have burned out in the chandelier, dripping wax on to the table below. Sophie, barely keeping her eyes open, has withdrawn from the conversation. Monsieur and Madame Rochefort, however, appear to be firmly entrenched for a long evening.

I'm sleepy and a little light-headed too from drinking more wine than I'm used to. 'We keep country hours and it's time Sophie was in bed,' I say, 'so we must thank you for your hospitality and take our leave.'

'Of course,' says Etienne. 'We would not wish to overtire Madame Levesque.'

'I shall escort you both back to the house,' says Jean-Luc.

We say our goodbyes. As Etienne bends over my hand to kiss it, I have to restrain myself from reaching out to touch his dark curls. It's a constant ache in my heart that there can be no future together for us.

'It's been delightful,' he says, still in possession of my hand and his gaze holding mine.

Jean-Luc is watching. Regretfully, I release my fingers.

A few moments later we are outside in the cool night air.

Jean-Luc holds up a flickering lantern to guide our way. 'Old Rochefort is a pompous fool. He represents everything the revolutionaries despise. I don't know why Etienne invited him tonight. We never liked him even when he was a boy.'

'Perhaps,' I say, 'Etienne clings to his old acquaintances to discover how other former nobles are managing? It's a delicate path to tread since the Revolution.'

'He should be careful if he doesn't want to lose Château Mirabelle,' says Jean-Luc. There is a sharp edge to his voice. 'I've warned him but he doesn't listen.'

My head is swimming from the wine and I stub my toe in the darkness, causing me to stumble.

'Steady!' Jean-Luc grips my arm, drawing me close to his side. His thigh brushes against mine as we walk. Muzzy-headed, I welcome the strength of his arm and lean on him for support.

We walk the rest of the way in silence.

'Thank you for lighting our way,' says Sophie.

'The pleasure is mine.' Jean-Luc squeezes me against his side again and whispers in my ear, 'Goodnight, *mignonne*.'

'Goodnight, Jean-Luc,' I say.

He lifts my hand and presses it lingeringly to his lips. 'Until tomorrow.'

His footsteps crunch away over the gravel and we watch until the light from his lantern fades into the distance.

I yawn, suddenly very sleepy.

'Do look!' says Sophie.

The sharp brightness of the scimitar moon is reflected in silver on the still black water of the lake and we stand motionless to wonder at the beauty of it.

'I watch the waxing and the waning of the moon every night from my bedroom window,' says Sophie, her voice quavering a little. 'Two more full moons and my baby will be here. And then what will I do?'

The question shimmers in the air between us, the silence stretching to breaking point until an owl hoots in the trees above.

I tuck Sophie's arm firmly through mine to still her trembling. 'It's growing cold,' I say. 'Let's go in.'

The next morning I fetch a handful of corn to sprinkle on the ground for Agnes and Alouette. My head throbs from the previous night's wine and I blush as I remember how Jean-Luc had to support me home and the warmth of his breath on my cheek as he whispered in my ear. He's handsome and attentive. If only I could stop thinking of Etienne, perhaps I'd give him more whole-hearted encouragement.

Agnes doesn't come running as usual when I scatter the corn and I call out to Victor, who is building a picket fence so that the chickens cannot ravage our precious vegetables. 'Have you seen Agnes?'

He puts down his saw and we look in all her favourite places. I peer into the chicken coop while Victor lifts the lid on the nesting box.

'She's here!' he says. Agnes puffs up her feathers and aims a peck at his fingers. Very gently, he reaches under her and extracts a prize. We look at each other in delight.

'I must show this to Sophie,' I say, cradling the warm egg in my hands.

Babette has finished her duties so we sit at the kitchen table for our daily reading lesson. She's making good progress and her confidence is growing.

'It won't be long before I can read to my little brothers and sisters,' she says, face glowing with pleasure. 'Perhaps I can teach them to write, too.'

'That's my hope for the future,' I say. 'If every child who learns to read and write teaches another three or four, that would be a big step towards the whole population becoming literate, and education and betterment being available to all.' I reflect that Babette's achievement gives me a far greater sense of satisfaction than anything I previously felt at the progress of my pampered pupils at Papa's Academy for Young Ladies.

After the lesson is finished, I accompany Babette back to the village. The sun is still hot and we walk side-by-side, keeping to the shade of the trees.

When we arrive at the cottage, her younger siblings are playing with their hoop outside and crowd around her, clamouring for their supper.

'But can you not see we have Mademoiselle visiting us?' she says. 'Now play quietly and I'll call you when supper is ready.'

Babette's mother smiles a welcome and pours us a cup of water to slake our thirst.

The baby whimpers on his mother's shoulder and Babette gathers him into her arms and props him on her hip as she starts to prepare a chickpea stew.

'Madame Gerard,' I say, 'I've come to ask your help. Monsieur d'Aubery is working in the vineyard so he couldn't come himself.'

'I've heard that,' she says, shaking her head in wonder. 'Who'd have thought that the master would end up working in his own fields?'

'That's the point. He doesn't ask anyone to do anything he wouldn't do himself. There aren't enough men to work in the vineyard and the *vendange* will be very small if there aren't more people to help. I said I thought the women from the village might be prepared to turn out.'

'That's man's work.'

'But it's work women can do too. The vines are blossoming now. Some of the leaves need to be removed to allow the sun to ripen the grapes.'

She looks at me with a small frown. 'That can't be too hard.'

'And as it's so warm, the vines must be watered. Mr d'Aubery will

204

pay two-thirds of a man's wage to any woman who comes to help and there will also be a share of the profit once the wine is sold.'

Madame Gerard nods slowly while she considers the matter. 'That's very generous. But what about the children?'

'We can set up some sheep hurdles to stop the little ones from wandering off. One of the grandmothers can mind them with the help of some of the older girls, and we can set up a temporary kitchen in the *chai*. Madame Thibault will provide soup for everyone in the middle of the day.'

'You've thought of everything.'

'I hope so. Would you speak to the other women and let me know?'

She chews her lip. 'Some might not like the idea but I'll see what I can do. Heaven knows, we all need more income.' She nods decisively. 'Give me a week or so and you'll have your answer.'

Chapter 22

It's a hot and sultry day and the children are shiny-faced in the stifling schoolroom as they bend over their slates. There's a pervasive odour of unwashed clothing. Is this what poverty smells like? I wonder. I adjust the window shutters to keep out the harsh light of the sun and stare longingly outside at the fresh green of the grass and the splashing fountain in the courtyard.

I remember a day the previous August, before everything in my life changed. Then, my pupils were the daughters of the wealthy, their silky tresses braided with pretty ribbons and their chatter as noisy as a flock of tropical birds as we escaped the schoolroom in a flurry of muslin and silk. Today my charges are more like dusty little sparrows in their dun-coloured clothes and ragged haircuts. But there's no reason why we shouldn't escape, too.

I clap my hands. 'We're going outside and I'll read you a story there. Leave your slates on the table and I'll look at them later.'

The children look up at me, faces bright with expectation.

'Hold hands and file out of the schoolroom two by two in an orderly manner, please! Emile, you will stay close to me where I can see you.'

Jostling and giggling, the children hurry out down the stairs and into the open air. They follow me in a more-or-less neat crocodile and once outside I allow them to sit on the edge of the fountain pool and splash their hot little hands and faces with the cool water. It's refreshing to listen to the water spouting from the fountain and the children stare at the prancing horse and the naked cherubs around its feet and nudge each other and giggle.

Emile, of course, has to be the one who jumps into the pool with a joyous whoop and splashes the rest of the children so violently that they scream in shocked delight. My protests go entirely unheard and I'm beginning to think I'll have to wade into the water myself to pull him out when the air is rent by a shrill whistle.

The laughter and squealing fade away and an uncomfortable silence prevails. Someone whispers, 'It's the master!'

Etienne, stern-faced, comes forward with his hands on his hips. He looks every inch the master, in spite of his shabby work clothes. 'And what is happening here?'

One of the little girls, her wet hair in rat's tails, begins to tremble.

'It's so hot . . .' I begin, anxious to protect my charges.

'Indeed it is extremely hot,' says Etienne. He kicks off his shoes. 'And I can see a lot of grubby little urchins all in need of a good wash. Shoes off, all of you!'

I don't think it's the right time to say that half the children don't have any shoes.

Etienne jumps into the fountain, making a great splash, and water slaps against the sides of the pool. 'Come on! Hurry up now!'

I laugh to see him gasp as the cold water soaks him to the skin.

One of the braver boys dips his toes in the water, recoiling at the cold, and then one by one the others follow. Only a moment later all the children are paddling and splashing and running under the fountain. The bolder ones have their hair plastered across their faces as they come up for air after diving below the surface of the pool.

'Aren't you coming in?' Etienne, his wet shirt clinging to his muscular chest, wades towards me where I stand beside the pool.

'If I do,' I say, 'I don't believe I'll ever have any authority over the children again.' I can't take my eyes off him and the sun feels hotter than ever on my overheated cheeks. 'It's different for you, you're the master.'

'You could paddle a bit. In a lady-like way, of course.' His brown eyes are alight with mischief and I glimpse the small boy he once was.

Hesitantly, I take off my shoes then sit on the side of the pool and lower my feet into the water. Closing my eyes in ecstasy for a fraction of a second, I wriggle my toes in the delicious coolness.

Etienne holds out his hand to me and I stand up.

'There, that wasn't so difficult, was it?'

'Oh, dear,' I say, glancing over his shoulder and seeing Emile climbing high up on to the statue of the prancing horse.

Etienne sighs, releases my hand and goes to haul the trouble-maker back to safety.

Lisette Marchand pulls me over to one of the stone cherubs at the base of the fountain. 'Look!' she says. She presses her hand over the cherub's mouth to stop the water, giggling with glee.

Suddenly water spurts out in a great stream and hits me full in the face. I gasp and then laugh as I see Lisette's frightened expression. 'It's all right, *chérie*, I'm not cross, only surprised.'

I'm wringing water out of my hair when Etienne returns to my side.

'Well, well,' he drawls. 'A veritable water sprite! You look just like a lady of fashion about to enter a Parisian salon with your muslin dress all damped down.'

I glance down and see that the fine cotton of my dress has been rendered almost transparent and is clinging to my figure. Hot with embarrassment, I pull the wet muslin away from my body. Turning aside, I call out to the children.

'That's enough now! Time to come out of the water.'

Grumbling, they cease their frolics and begin to climb out of the pool. They stand shivering while water drips from their clothing into puddles around their feet.

'We must get you dry again before your mothers see you,' says Etienne. He points to the other side of the park. 'Do you see that oak tree?'

The children nod, their eyes fixed on his face.

'When I give the signal, I want you to run to it and sit in the sun. Off you go!' He puts two fingers to his mouth and emits an ear-splitting whistle.

The children race off into the distance, their skinny little legs going up and down as fast as the shuttle on a Spinning Jenny.

'Wherever did you learn to whistle like that?' I ask, as we amble after them.

He smiles. 'It's the result of a misspent youth.'

'I must thank you for allowing the children to sully your fountain. It was good to see them so happy.'

'I used to love paddling there on a hot day when I was a boy.' Etienne chuckles. 'This was an excuse for me to recapture the fun we used to have, my brother Laurent and I.' His smile fades. 'I still miss him but perhaps he would not have been able to adapt to our changing circumstances in the new order of things. He had a clear sense of his position in life, like our father.'

I glance at his face, which is serious now. 'It must be hard for you to see that world slipping away.'

'What other choice is there? I must bow to the revolutionary forces and do whatever is necessary or Château Mirabelle will be confiscated by the state and sold to someone who has no appreciation of its history or any idea how to manage it.'

'And there's no turning back from the Revolution now, is there?'

He shakes his head, flicking droplets of water over my face.

When we reach the oak tree, the children are lying in the sun, basking like little lizards.

I lean against the tree trunk while I read aloud from Jean de La

Fontaine's book of *Fables*. The lilting cadences of the story combined with the warmth of the sun lull several of the children to sleep. Even Etienne, who lies on the grass nearby with his hands behind his head, is dozing. The air is very still. After a while I stop reading and close my eyes too.

Some time later the sound of a waggon rattling along the carriage drive wakes me.

'I wonder why a waggon is using the main drive instead of the kitchen entrance,' says Etienne, rubbing sleep from his eyes. 'I'll go and see what it's about.'

He yawns widely. His hair has dried in spiky tufts, I see, with a pang of affection for him.

'Are your clothes nearly dry, children?' I ask.

There's a chorus of assent.

'Then it's time for you to run along home.'

The children line up to shake my hand and then skip away towards the village.

Etienne remains deep in conversation with the driver of the waggon and I go over to discover what is happening. There are two other men in the vehicle, which is piled high with rusty metal and old railings. As I draw closer, the driver walks his horse around to face the opposite direction then jumps back up on his seat. The waggon rolls towards the main entrance again.

'What was that about?' I ask.

A muscle tightens in Etienne's jaw. 'He's come to collect the gates.'

'What do you mean?'

'Mayor Prudhomme has decreed that all citizens must give what metal they can to be melted down and made into arms and ammunitions. They will return tomorrow to denude the kitchen of Madame Thibault's saucepans.'

'But they can't!'

Etienne's face is white. 'Yes, they can. They'll come to your

210

house, too, I expect. I'm going to walk up to the gates now and see that those ruffians don't damage the posts while they're about their business.'

'I'm coming, too.'

He turns away without a word and marches off along the drive and I trot beside him. We hurry along, passing through the coolness of the pine woods until the gatehouse comes into sight.

The three men are shouting instructions to each other as they struggle to lift one of the great wrought-iron gates off its hinges.

'My grandfather designed these gates,' says Etienne. 'Do you see the family crest in the central cartouche and our initials in the filigreework?'

'They're very beautiful,' I say, saddened to see them being manhandled.

'They were made in the forge in the village.' There are tears in Etienne's eyes. 'Every time I return from a journey my heart lifts when I see these gates because they signify that I'm nearly home.'

Grunting and arguing as they work, the men manage to free the top hinge.

'Can't you stop them?' I ask, seething with indignation.

Etienne simply looks at me until I realise the stupidity of my question. Any former noble who doesn't conform will be accused of anti-revolutionary behaviour. The mayor and his committee would confiscate Château Mirabelle before Etienne could draw breath.

There is a hoarse warning shout as the heavy gate twists from the workmen's hands. There's a screeching sound as it falls sideways, still secured at the bottom.

'Look out!' calls Etienne, as the gatepost shudders and then topples.

Blocks of stone tumble to the ground with a thundering crash.

One of the workmen tips his hat on to the back of his head and scratches his ear. 'Ah, well,' he says philosophically, 'you won't be needing a gatepost if you've got no gates to hang on it, will you?'

The others roar with laughter.

'I can't stay and watch this act of desecration,' mutters Etienne. He stalks back up the drive.

I long to hurry after him but I know nothing I can say will soothe him. Instead I return to the house and hide all of our saucepans, except one, in the chicken house.

The sun beats down on my head and the air is still and silent, as if every living thing is dozing. The long grass sighs gently as I meander across the meadow. Even the river is flowing sluggishly, as if half asleep.

I carry a covered basket containing cake and a handful of the cherries from the orchard that Jean-Luc brought me earlier this morning. He'd found me in the garden and made me put down my hoe and sit beside him on the bench.

'As sweet and red as your lips,' he'd said, as he fed me cherries, one by one.

Perspiration beads my upper lip as I walk slowly up the stony slope of the vineyard. After Etienne's distress at the destruction of the gates I'm pleased to be able to bring him some good news.

I find him crouched over examining the soil at the base of one of the vines. He starts as he looks up at me, squinting into the sun. Standing up, he brushes the dusty earth off his hands. 'It's very dry.' He lifts a vine shoot and supports it in his palm. 'Look here,' he says.

I peer closely at the vine and see that the raceme is covered in tiny greenish-white flowers.

'The vines are blossoming,' he says. 'Before long we'll see minute green grapes and in about a hundred days the harvest will be ready.'

'I brought you a slice of cake,' I say, 'and Babette sends you a message from her mother. Several of the women have agreed to help with the vines.'

Etienne's face breaks into a wide smile. 'That is most welcome news. Shall we go and sit in the shade?'

At the bottom of the hill he draws up the bucket from the well beside the *chai*. Removing his hat, he bends over and tips water over his head and hands. Shaking it from his eyes, he lowers the bucket again and then uses the cup tied to the side of the well to gulp a long draught of water.

'Thirsty work?'

He nods, smiling, and offers the cup to me.

The water is sweet and cool and I drink it down greedily.

We go inside the *chai*, stopping in the doorway for a moment while our eyes adjust to the shadows. Sunlight paints a bright lozenge on the beaten earth floor. Stepping out of the sun, the temperature is suddenly several degrees cooler.

Our footsteps echo around the high-ceilinged chamber as Etienne leads me over to a long wooden table. We perch on a bench at one end. I unwrap the fragrant *gateau à la vanille* and offer it to him.

'What a picture!' he says, studying the golden cake and the glossy crimson cherries resting on the starched white linen. He falls on the cake and devours it in seconds, eyes closed in appreciation.

'Here, have mine,' I say.

He needs no further urging but eats the second slice more slowly, savouring every morsel, sighing when it's all gone. We sit together quietly, eating the cherries and enjoying the peace.

Somewhere in the distance I hear a murmur of sound and then a snatch of song.

'What's that?' I ask.

Etienne cocks his head to listen, frowning in concentration. 'Singing. Is it soldiers?' He stands up rapidly and runs to the open door.

I follow him and we see a column of women processing along the lane towards us, followed by a gambolling tribe of ragged children, all singing the *Marseillaise* at the top of their voices.

'I thought it might be soldiers,' said Etienne, relief plain to see in his face, 'coming to take whatever provisions they could find from the village and the château.'

The women, a dozen of them, come to a stop before us.

Madame Gerard steps forward. 'We've come to work,' she says.

Etienne goes to shake her hand. 'You are all most welcome.'

A short while later the women are moving slowly across the vineyard removing some of the leaves from the canopy of vines to allow the sun to reach the budding fruits.

I watch them for a while, pleased to have played my part in finding a way to help both Etienne and the village women.

A few days later I return to the vineyard. A baby wails as I walk past the *chai* and there are several small children playing in the doorway with Widow Berger minding them. She waves at me as I pass. The younger village women are already at work and I seek out Madame Gerard.

'How is it?' I ask.

She pushes away a lock of damp hair that has escaped from her sunbonnet. 'No one is complaining.' I see that there are freckles sprinkled across her cheeks. 'Not too much anyway. It's hot, and bending makes your back ache.'

'I've come to help,' I say.

'You, Mademoiselle?'

'It would be terrible to allow the harvest to fail if we can prevent it.'

We work alongside each other for the next couple of hours and Madame Gerard is right; it is backbreaking work. It's also a fine balance between leaving enough of the canopy to prevent heat stress on the vine and allowing the fruit to ripen and sweeten without risking mildew.

In the middle of the day, when the sun is at its highest, we hear a bell ringing and go down to the *chai* where Madame Thibault and a kitchen maid are ladling out bowlfuls of soup. Madame Gerard and another woman retreat behind a makeshift curtain to nurse their babies.

The men huddle together at the far end of the table. Uncertain of my reception amongst the women, I take my soup and place myself next to some of the older children. Lisette Marchand shyly asks if she may sit beside me.

The young woman opposite me at the table nudges her neighbour and whispers something under her breath as she looks over my shoulder.

The chatter and laughter fade away and I see that Etienne is standing in the doorway. He walks down the room, exchanging a few words with everyone.

'I didn't expect to find you here,' he says when he reaches me. The sun has touched his high cheekbones and his loose blue trousers are powdered with dust.

'I want to help.'

'Thank you. We need every pair of hands available.' He smiles as he watches some boys running around whooping as they play tag. 'Even Emile has a part to play.'

He moves on and it is only when he has spoken to all the workers that he collects his own bowl of soup and sits down with the men.

I finish my soup, disappointed that he doesn't talk to me again.

Madame Thibault brings out platters of cherries and the girls hook them over their ears like earrings, while the boys challenge each other to see how far they can spit the stones.

All too soon we finish our meal and are wending our way back up the slope to continue work.

At the end of the day, on my way home, I pass the walled vegetable garden and see that the door is slightly ajar. Inside the ground is overgrown but I notice that Marcel has planted some seeds, albeit in haphazard rows, before he was called to work in the vineyard again. I bend over and pull up a handful of groundsel and dande-lions. The weeds are thick and lush while the seedling lettuces and bean plants are frail, but the saving grace is that the weeds have at least sheltered them from the sun.

An hour or so passes. Finally, when I stand with my hands on my hips to ease my aching back, I realise that I've cleared several rows. The sun is beginning to set as I dip a watering can into the cistern of water beside the greenhouse and then start to walk slowly up and down the rows, watering the thirsty plants.

At last it's too dark to see and I slip out of the walled garden and close the door behind me.

Chapter 23

July 1793

I close the schoolroom for the summer to allow the children to help in the vineyard. The days turn into weeks, all blending together in a blur of heat and backache, thirst and blisters, as we continue to tie in the vine shoots and trim back the wilder excesses of the tendrils, to allow the strength of the plant to go to the grapes. Once the grapes begin to swell we remove some of the smaller fruits to allow the others space to grow. Etienne tells me this is called the 'green harvest'.

And then there's the watering. We must prevent the vines dying from drought, but too much water might result in grapes without sufficient sweetness and flavour. Our palms blister and then grow calluses as we draw up the buckets countless times from the well and put them on a cart drawn by the piebald cob. We take it in turns to lead him up the hill, which the children think is a fine game as they hitch a ride, and then we deposit the contents of the buckets, one by one, along the rows of vines, leaving dark stains on the dusty soil.

At the end of each day Jean-Luc has fallen into the habit of coming to meet me to accompany me back to the house and I've begun look forward to his lively company. Today is Saturday and Jean-Luc sits at a table in the *chai* with his account book and a strongbox as the women queue up to collect their earnings. At first I demurred when Etienne asked me to join the women in the queue, but he insisted and I cannot deny that the extra money is useful since my supply of gold coins is dwindling.

The men, as usual, are paid first. The children, pleased to see their mothers again, gambol noisily around our feet while we wait our turn.

'What a relief to be out of the sun,' I say to Madame Gerard and Emile's mother, Madame Porcher.

'I don't remember a summer as hot as this for many a year,' says Madame Porcher, her face shiny with sweat.

Madame Gerard takes baby Albert from Widow Berger with a tired smile and settles him on her hip. 'Still, the master has promised us a share of the profits when the wine is sold.'

'But that's at least a year away,' says Madame Porcher. 'Emile!' She turns to shout at her son, who is climbing on a stack of oak barrels. 'Get down from there at once or I'll give you a clout round the ear!'

'At least Victor and Babette are bringing home a wage now,' says Madame Gerard. 'And Albert,' she kisses the baby's cheek, 'will be weaned in a few months. I must speak to Madame Viard about finding some work in the kitchens for me.'

'It's all right for the master though, isn't it?' says Madame Porcher, her mouth twisted by resentment. 'He's got a cellar stacked to the roof with earlier vintages he can sell, not to mention a palace full of gilded furniture and priceless paintings, any one of which would feed the whole village for a year.'

'But he's a good master, isn't he?' I say, quick to rush to Etienne's defence.

Madame Porcher shrugs. 'Well enough, I suppose, if we can be sure he's not a murderer.' Her eyes gleam with spite. 'No one ever did find out what happened to that wife of his, did they?' She looks at me speculatively. 'But I suppose he's told you all about that, you being so friendly with him and all?'

'I know his wife is missing,' I say, stiffly.

'And unfortunately for you, the position of the next chatelaine isn't available until Isabelle d'Aubery is found, either dead or alive. But perhaps you'll settle for Jean-Luc Viard as second best, eh?'

Heat races into my cheeks and Madame Gerard puts a hand on Madame Porcher's arm. 'Claudette!' she murmurs.

Then the queue shuffles forwards and Claudette Porcher turns away to talk to another of the women.

Scarlet-faced, I stare at my feet while I reflect that Madame Porcher speaks only the truth.

'I'm sorry, Mademoiselle,' whispers Madame Gerard. 'Claudette has always looked for something to complain about, even as a girl. You're new here and people are suspicious of strangers, especially in these times of war and want.'

Albert begins to wriggle in his mother's arms and then to cry and there is no more conversation.

At last it's my turn to receive my wages and Jean-Luc checks his ledger for the number of hours I've worked and then places a pile of coins on the desk for me. 'I've nearly finished here,' he says. 'I'll walk you home.'

I tuck the coins in my pocket and step aside while the last two women are paid.

I watch Jean-Luc as he closes his ledger and locks the cashbox. He has a commanding presence and looks every inch the gentleman in his well-tailored coat.

He must sense me looking at him because he glances up and smiles. Tucking the cashbox under his arm, he strides towards me.

'Shall we go?' He rests his hand on the back of my waist to guide me and I notice Claudette Porcher watching us with a cynical expression. She raises her eyebrows and nudges her companion with one elbow.

A fiery blush stains my cheeks again, just as Etienne steps out of the shadows by the door of the *chai*. He looks weary and sports a smudge of dust on his jaw. His shirtsleeves are rolled up and he wipes the perspiration from his forehead with a sun-browned hand. 'Good evening, Mademoiselle Moreau. And Jean-Luc.'

'And to you, Etienne,' says Jean-Luc, taking my arm in a proprietorial way.

I glance back over my shoulder as we walk away and see that Etienne is still watching us, his face closed. An ache in my breast makes me yearn to go to him but that way lies only misery.

As we walk through the fields Jean-Luc stops to pick me a bunch of hedgerow flowers, presenting them with a flourish. 'Beautiful flowers for a beautiful lady.'

I take them from him and sniff their sweet scent. I must not allow myself to think of Etienne but concentrate instead on Jean-Luc, an eligible man whose attentions make me feel cared for.

At the house we stop by the gate and he kisses me gently. I don't resist. If Etienne's weary face weren't constantly in my mind's eye, perhaps I'd even respond with fervour. Maybe I will next time. As Sophie keeps reminding me, I must look to the future.

'Until tomorrow, Madeleine,' says Jean-Luc. In the sunshine, his hazel eyes are flecked with green, I notice.

Impulsively, I reach up and press a swift kiss to his lips, grateful for his attentiveness. He laughs and tries to catch me in his arms but I slip away from him and shut the gate between us. 'Until tomorrow,' I echo, and go inside.

Sophie has prepared dinner and we eat in the garden, now burgeoning with summer flowers, and talk over the small events of the day. Afterwards I water and weed my vegetable plot and then wander over to the château and the walled vegetable garden.

I water the beans, walking slowly up and down the rows, swinging the watering can rhythmically. I notice the pretty scarlet flowers unfolding and smile in satisfaction at the sight of the frilly little lettuces growing visibly every day.

I love this secret time: the stillness in the air, the damp scent of the earth rising from the ground and the residual heat of the day emanating from the brick wall that surrounds the garden. I allow my thoughts to drift, remembering the musky scent of Jean-Luc's hair pomade when I kissed him. Could my friendship with him grow into something more? To lose the aching void inside me and be really happy again, I must find a husband and make a family of my own. Perhaps Jean-Luc could be the one I seek?

The metallic click of the latch on the garden door makes me look up, startled. Framed in the doorway is a black figure silhouetted against the orange globe of the setting sun. I recognise his profile straight away and my heart leaps with pleasure.

'So it's you who is keeping the garden!' says Etienne. 'I thought it must be Marcel.'

'I don't believe he's been here since you asked him to return to work in the vineyard.' A warm glow of pleasure at Etienne's unexpected presence spreads through me and all my resolutions to put him out of my thoughts evaporate like mist in sunshine.

Etienne looks at the weed-free beds and the sturdy little plants. 'You've wrought miracles,' he says.

Glowing with pride, I walk him up and down the rows. 'They aren't straight,' I say. 'Marcel must have been drinking when he sowed the seeds. I found a whole stack of empty wine bottles behind the greenhouse. And half a dozen full ones.'

'He's a disgrace,' says Etienne, scowling. 'I only keep him on because it would be shaming for Jean-Luc and his mother if I turned him out.' He sighs. 'My father would never hear a word against him, though. He said Marcel used to be a good worker, if a little dour, and hinted at some sadness that made him turn to drink.'

Etienne pulls up a large dandelion and stuffs it absentmindedly into his pocket. 'I think we deserve a drink at the end of another day of hard work, don't you?'

We walk through the lengthening shadows and I show him Marcel's hidden cache. Inside the greenhouse we find a chipped wine glass and a corkscrew. While Etienne opens the bottle, I rinse the glass in the cistern and dry it on my skirt. We carry our prizes over to the iron bench, the metal still warm from the sun.

'Marcel must have stolen this,' says Etienne, examining the label on the wine bottle. 'It's the Château Mirabelle 1789.' He smiles wryly. 'At least we know it's decent quality.'

I hold the glass up to the sun and see how the pale liquid becomes infused with gold. I sip the wine, allowing it to roll around my tongue, and savour the crisp, refreshing fruitiness of it before handing the glass to Etienne. I feel at peace.

We sit in companionable silence, our faces gilded by the light of . the setting sun as we take it in turns to sip from the glass. The sky is a deep orange now, streaked with gold and peach. All around us the cicadas are beginning their evensong, rasping away in the vegetation.

Etienne turns slowly to face me, frowning slightly. 'You are particular friends with Jean-Luc, I think? I know that he calls you by your given name.'

I'm unsure how to answer. 'He's always very friendly.'

'Yes, I've noticed.'

The green paint is flaking off the decorative ironwork scroll that forms the arm of the bench and I run my hand over it, feeling the edges sharp against my fingers. And I close my eyes in sorrow as I remember again how Etienne held me before he went away and how, when he returned, he found me in Jean-Luc's arms.

'Aren't we friends, too?' asks Etienne.

'Of course.' I wish with all my heart that we could be more than mere friends.

'Then, would it be presumptuous of me to ask you to call me Etienne?'

The air is heavy with the honeyed scent of the jasmine that scrambles up the wall behind us. I'm drowsy and loose with wine and that sweet sensation when your muscles are relaxing after physical exercise. 'Not at all,' I say. 'If you will call me Madeleine.'

He smiles at me with such warmth that it's hard not to reach out and touch his hand beside mine on the bench. Instead, I focus on the sun as it slides down behind the wall. Then the golden light rapidly fades and the sky, a milky haze at the horizon, deepens to sapphire blue above. And then it's dark.

'I suppose we should go in,' murmurs Etienne after a while.

I don't want to go indoors. I want to stay here in the warm darkness with him. I want him to explain why he didn't tell me himself that he had, or has, a wife. And I want him to kiss me.

'We should go in,' says Etienne again.

'In a moment,' I say, but the spell is broken and I cannot bring myself to ask him why he has never told me about Isabelle. I take a last sip of the wine and hand the remainder to him.

He drains the glass and stands up. 'Come on,' he says, his voice soft in the dark, 'I'll walk you home or Sophie will be anxious.'

Reluctantly, I stand up.

The moon is a pale disc above us and two or three bright stars glimmer in the heavens. Silently, we step through the door in the wall, leaving behind our secret world, and walk side by side in the silvery moonlight while my heart aches with longing for him.

A lamp is burning in the porch of the house to light me home.

'Goodnight, Madeleine,' says Etienne, and before I can answer, he has gone.

I remain in the porch, listening to the sounds of the night and watching the moths singeing their wings in the flame, just as I risk burning myself if I approach the flame of my love for Etienne.

Sighing, I turn the door handle to go inside. It's then that I sense someone watching me from the trees nearby. I peer into the darkness and see the outline of a man leaning against an oak tree.

'Etienne?' I whisper. Forgetting all thoughts of caution and decorum, I run towards him.

In the blink of an eye the shape melts into the shadows.

My fingers reach out to touch the rough bark of the oak but there is no one there.

An owl hoots mockingly from the branches above.

Sophie and I sit in the sun, shelling peas. Agnes and Alouette are crooning gently nearby as they take a dust bath under the hedge.

'It's so peaceful here, isn't it?' says Sophie. 'I was thinking about London and the noise and the smell of summer drains.'

'I don't miss the city at all,' I say. 'Except, perhaps, for the lively conversations we used to have in Georgiana's salon.'

'Living here is an island in time,' says Sophie. She stares at the empty peapod in her hand, lost in thought. After a moment she says, 'I've had such a wonderful idea. At the orphanage Madame Boudin offered us a child to adopt.'

I know immediately what is in her mind. 'You can't Sophie!' I say, aghast. 'Charles will know.'

'But why should he?' She leans forward, her eyes sparkling. 'We can tell him my baby is an orphan of the Revolution.'

'What if the child looks just like you? Charles will guess then that you had a lover. There must have been rumours at the time . . .'

The corners of Sophie's mouth turn down. 'He paid me so little mind, I doubt he noticed.'

'People will talk. Even if he doesn't realise the baby is yours, what if he confines it to the servants' quarters or makes you send it to the workhouse? Knowing Charles, he won't want to bring up a child of unknown provenance as his own.'

'I've thought of that,' she says triumphantly. 'I'll tell him the baby is of noble blood.'

Shaking my head, I say, 'Supposing he makes enquiries?'

'It'll be far too difficult for him to do that while we're at war with France. Don't try and persuade me to give up my child, Maddy, because I won't!'

Looking at the mutinous set of her mouth, I know I'm wasting my breath. Then I hear a voice calling my name and see Jean-Luc striding towards us.

'Babette told me you were in the garden. I brought you these,' he says, holding up a couple of rabbits hanging upside-down from a string knotted around their feet. 'I went out shooting early this morning.'

'They'll make a perfect dish with these peas,' I say.

'Why don't you come back later and share it with us?' says Sophie.

Jean-Luc flashes her a wide smile. 'I'll bring a bottle of wine,' he says. 'And my mother sends a message. Tomorrow she's intending to make a new revolutionary flag to present to the mayor in Morville for the Bastille Day celebrations. Maman is hoping you will both join her in her endeavours.'

'I'll be working in the vineyard again tomorrow, Jean-Luc,' I say.

A flicker of annoyance passes over his face. 'It's an honour to be asked and not to be turned down lightly.'

There's a slight edge to his voice that puts me on my guard. 'Perhaps I won't be missed for one day,' I say.

'And I shall be happy to join Madame Viard,' says Sophie. 'I'll enjoy the company.'

'That's good, then,' says Jean-Luc, his usual good humour restored. 'I'll give the rabbits to Babette.'

After he's gone, Sophie and I return to the kitchen. The rabbits lie on the table and a trickle of blood runs over the edge and makes a sticky puddle on the floor. We watch Babette deftly peel off the skin, then paunch and joint the rabbits ready for a stew.

'It's lucky we hid the big stock pot in the hen house before the mayor's men arrived,' whispers Sophie. 'We'd never be able to fit all the joints into the one small pan they left for us.'

'It's sad to imagine the gates being melted down with saucepans, isn't it?' I say.

'And wicked for something so beautiful to be made into weapons.'

Later, after Babette has left for the day, Sophie bustles about in the kitchen with a clean apron stretched over her stomach. It's not long to her time now and I worry that she should rest more but she says she prefers to be busy.

We lay the table for dinner in the garden and she insists we bring out a starched tablecloth and the best china with the d'Aubery crest. There are fine crystal goblets, too, that we have never used, and I pick flowers from the garden.

'You could do worse than Jean-Luc, you know,' says Sophie. 'He is increasingly attentive to you. He has an important position here and would be able to provide for you very well.' Her cheeks dimple as she smiles roguishly at me. 'And he really is *very* good-looking, in case you hadn't noticed.'

'Oh, yes, I've noticed,' I say. It's impossible not to notice a man like Jean-Luc.

Later, the rich aroma of rabbit stew fills the house as I change into a clean dress and confine my curls in a blue silk ribbon Jean-Luc gave me. Studying my reflection in the looking glass, I sigh ruefully as I notice that my skin is lightly bronzed by the sun. I wouldn't do at all in Georgiana's salon but, secretly, I like the way that the colour in my face deepens the violet of my eyes and whitens my teeth. I look like a healthy peasant.

If I gave Jean-Luc some encouragement, could I have a future with him? I wonder. If I were to remain here after Sophie returns to her family, I'd be able to stay near to Etienne. But could I bear to be so close to him, knowing that he is for ever out of my reach?

The doorknocker sounds and I hurry downstairs to find not Jean-Luc as expected on the doorstep but Etienne, a rolled-up newspaper tucked under his arm. His shirt is rumpled and his shoes dusty.

'You are looking very fine,' he says. 'Are you about to pay a social call?'

I laugh. 'Where would I go to do that?' I open the door wider to allow him to enter.

'Something smells good.'

'Jean-Luc brought us some rabbits. He's coming for dinner.'

The smile fades from Etienne's face.

'Perhaps you would care to join us?'

The kitchen door opens and Sophie comes into the hall, drying her hands on a cloth.

'I've invited Etienne to dinner,' I say.

'Oh, I see. How lovely.' Sophie smiles brightly at him. 'Perhaps you'd go through into the garden while Madeleine and I are busy in the kitchen?'

After he has gone outside, Sophie grips me by the wrist and gives me a shake. 'Why did you invite him?' she hisses. 'It's all set up for you to have a quiet little dinner with Jean-Luc. I was going to plead a headache and leave you alone together.'

'Please don't act as matchmaker on my behalf, Sophie.'

She sighs heavily. 'No matter,' she says. 'Perhaps it's not such a bad thing after all. It will focus Jean-Luc's mind if Etienne is making sheep's eyes at you.'

'He doesn't make sheep's eyes at me!'

'You let me be the judge of that! Now come and help me in the kitchen.'

A short while later the doorknocker bangs again.

'Good evening, Jean-Luc,' I say. He's freshly shaved and wears pristine white linen at his neck. His hair is perfumed with pomade. 'Come through to the garden. Etienne is waiting for us.'

Jean-Luc frowns. 'I didn't know he was going to be here.'

'Neither did we.'

Etienne is sitting on the garden bench with his eyes closed and his face turned up to the evening sun. Minou is asleep on his knee.

Jean-Luc claps him on the shoulder, making him start. 'Did I wake you, Etienne?'

'I confess you did,' he says, lifting the kitten gently to the ground and rising to his feet. 'I began early in the vineyard today, before the sun grew too hot.' He yawns. 'As soon as I sit down these days, I fall asleep. It must be much harder for the women, especially those who have children to care for.'

Sophie calls to me through the window and I hurry back to the kitchen to carry out the tray of covered tureens to the table set up beneath the apple tree. I lay an extra place setting and despatch Etienne to bring another chair from the dining room.

'Will you open the wine, Jean-Luc?' asks Sophie.

He obliges, sniffing the cork and swirling the wine around in the crystal goblet before tasting it and pronouncing it to be excellent.

The rabbit stew is thick with onions and scented with sage, and the peas are small and tender. We still have half a loaf left to mop up the gravy with.

'A feast!' says Etienne later, wiping his mouth on his napkin.

'It's a shame you didn't change out of your peasant garb before inviting yourself to dinner,' jests Jean-Luc. 'Madeleine, however, looks ready to step into a Parisian drawing room, despite her labours today in the vineyard and vegetable garden.' He leans back and stretches one arm behind me to rest on the back of my chair.

Etienne's eyes flicker towards Jean-Luc's hand behind my neck. 'I hadn't intended to intrude,' he says. 'I merely came by to see if Madeleine and Sophie would like to have this copy of the *Moniteur*.' He offers me the rolled-up newspaper.

'I prefer *L'Ami du Peuple* myself,' says Jean-Luc. His hand is resting lightly on the nape of my neck now and I shiver slightly as he toys with one of my curls.

'I was reading about the Committee of Public Safety,' says Etienne, his gaze following the movements of Jean-Luc's hand.

'What exactly does the Committee do,' asks Sophie, 'apart from maintaining public order? I haven't read a newspaper in weeks and, tucked away here in the country, it's hard to know what is happening.'

'The Committee is essential to keeping order in wartime,' says Jean-Luc. 'It plays a crucial role in organising the provisioning of the army ... and of the people, come to that. It appoints the generals, and also the judges and juries for the Revolutionary Tribunal.'

Etienne runs his finger contemplatively around the rim of his glass. 'The Tribunal is handing out increasingly harsh treatment to those who are believed not to support revolutionary ideals.'

'It *must* do so,' says Jean-Luc, leaning forward. 'France is in great peril and we must be aware at all times of traitors and spies lurking in our midst and plotting our destruction from within. We are threatened not only by invading foreign armies but by the anti-revolutionary revolts in the west and south.'

Sophie glances at me. 'But despite the Revolution the people are still struggling to find enough to eat.'

'Don't you see?' says Jean-Luc, looking intently at each of us in turn. 'That is the very reason why much stricter controls must be instigated. The anti-revolutionaries marching to Paris from all over France mean that soldiers are deployed in supressing internal strife instead of fighting off the marauding British and Dutch.'

'But why does there have to be fighting?' asks Sophie, pressing a hand to her temple. 'It's frightening, never knowing if the army or the anti-revolutionaries are going to pass by or if someone we know will turn out to be a spy.'

'Perhaps we've spoken enough of this for now,' I say, glancing at her shaking hands.

Etienne gives me a barely perceptible nod and refills our glasses. 'There are to be fireworks in Morville next week,' he says, 'to celebrate the anniversary of the storming of the Bastille. Perhaps we should make up a party and go and watch?'

Sophie clasps her hands against her breast. 'How lovely that would be!'

'But, Sophie,' I say, 'won't the journey be too uncomfortable for you?'

She looks at me with her eyes shining. 'I'm prepared to put up with that for the chance to have some fun. I'm so very tired of being imprisoned here.' She smiles dazzlingly at Etienne. 'Forgive me! This house is a most elegant gilded cage but I long for a change of scene.'

Etienne inclines his head to her. 'Then we shall take the carriage and convey you as gently as possible to Morville, where you shall enjoy the sights of the town celebrating.'

Sophie and I present ourselves at the housekeeper's parlour the following morning.

'How delightful that you are to join me in my endeavours,' says Madame Viard. 'My son told me that Mayor Prudhomme requires a flag and we can be proud to demonstrate our loyalty by making this important emblem of the Republic.'

We exchange pleasantries while she spreads out the red, white and blue linen on her dining table and then we start to cut and sew the pieces of the flag together.

'Madame Levesque has taken coffee with me on several occasions,' says Madame Viard, passing me the scissors, 'but it's time for you and I to come to know one another better, Mademoiselle Moreau.'

I return her smile and bend my head over a piece of hemming.

'Tell me about yourself,' continues the housekeeper. 'I believe you come from Lyon and both your parents have passed away?' She cuts a new length of thread and watches me closely while I mitre a corner of the flag.

'My father had a school in a small town outside the city,' I say, not wishing to disclose any more than is necessary.

'You have no family left?'

'Sadly, that is so.' I'm made uncomfortable by her questioning gaze.

'But you have both settled in well here?'

'I love it,' says Sophie.

'And you, Mademoiselle Moreau? Have you also made a new beginning at Château Mirabelle?'

I concentrate on rethreading my needle. 'We're fortunate to rent such a charming house.'

We're silent for a while until Madame Viard leans over to inspect my stitches. 'Very neat work,' she says. 'My son speaks highly of your natural grace and talents, and I see that he is right.'

Sophie glances at me with her needle poised in mid-air.

'How kind of him,' I murmur, wondering where this conversation is leading.

'I hear from Jean-Luc that the mayor will soon be calling for more volunteers for the army,' says Madame Viard. 'A mother can be very proud of a son who is serving his country, but nonetheless I should not care to see my Jean-Luc go to war. His role here as estate manager is too important for him to be spared, don't you agree?'

'Of course,' I murmur.

Madame Viard holds up the section of the flag that she's just completed. 'Perhaps you both hope to make your home permanently here at Château Mirabelle?'

'I can imagine nothing we should like better,' says Sophie.

I shrug. 'As to that, who knows what the future will bring?'

'Who knows indeed?' Madame Viard smiles at me as she nips off a thread with her sharp little teeth.

Chapter 24

14 July 1793

One evening the following week the carriage draws up outside our house and Jean-Luc and Etienne make a deal of fuss over Sophie, settling her comfortably inside.

'I feel as excited as a girl going to her first ball,' she says.

Colbert has been given strict instructions to avoid all potholes and the carriage makes stately progress on its way to Morville. The road is unusually busy and we're overtaken by a number of horses, carts and *charrettes*. Pedestrians crowd the roadside, all heading for town.

We rattle over the stone bridge as dusk descends and the sky fades from lavender to indigo. Colbert drives us to the bustling courtyard of the Lion d'Or.

It's only a step to the market square and an orchestra welcomes us, playing slightly off key but with a great deal of enthusiasm. Children run about squealing with excitement and the citizens are dressed in their best clothes, many of them wearing red caps or tri-colour sashes.

Tables and chairs have been set out around the square and we sit as far away from the band as we can so that we don't have to shout at each other. The remaining sultriness of the day can still be felt in the warmth of the cobbles beneath our feet and the air is smoky with the aroma of cooking sausages.

The Hôtel de Ville is bedecked with red, white and blue bunting, and the flag that Sophie and I helped Madame Viard to make flutters proudly from the flagpole.

'It looks very fine, doesn't it?' says Sophie to Jean-Luc.

'Excellent! The mayor was delighted to receive it.'

'The sausages smell delicious.' Sophie looks at the cloud of smoke rising from the brazier set up outside the church.

'Shall you eat one if I fetch it for you?' asks Etienne.

'Yes, please!' she says.

Etienne disappears to join the multitude gathered around the glowing brazier and Jean-Luc orders jugs of wine from one of the serving maids.

'The church is no longer boarded up,' I say.

Jean-Luc nods. 'There's a new priest now; one who supports the Revolution.'

I glance at Citoyenne Mathieu's house across the square. The door to Père Chenot's garden is firmly closed.

We sit at our table listening to the laughter and the voices simmering with excitement all around us, and watching the children running about without a care. Flickering lanterns are strung between the plane trees and bedeck the roof of the *lavoir*, where the young have congregated to flirt with each other, unimpeded by their parents' censure. As the sun sets a boy carrying a glowing taper moves from one table to another lighting the candles.

Etienne brings sausages and coarse bread wrapped in newspaper. His hair and clothes smell of hot smoky fat and I help him to tear the paper into four makeshift plates.

'This is unbelievably delicious,' says Sophie, her lips glistening with grease as she devours a sausage.

Jean-Luc's sausage disintegrates as he bites into it and a chunk bounces off his chest, smearing the front of his silken waistcoat before falling to the ground. He swears under his breath. 'Wretched peasant food! Look at my waistcoat . . . it's ruined!'

I dip my handkerchief into a glass of water and wipe away the worst of the staining. 'It really needs soap to take out the grease but that looks better.'

Jean-Luc captures my hand in his and kisses it.

I realise that Sophie is watching us with an indulgent smile while Etienne's face is pinched with disapproval. Pulling my hand away, I'm relieved when the orchestra strikes up a noisy military march full of crashing cymbals and banging drums.

After a while the orchestra begins to play dance music and we watch young couples leave the *lavoir* and begin to dance in the square, swiftly followed by their parents and even grandparents.

'Shall we?' Jean-Luc rises to his feet and holds out his hand to me.

We take our places amongst the other dancers and it is soon apparent that this is nothing like an elegant, formal dance in a London drawing room but an opportunity to forget the troubles of the world and lose ourselves in the moment. Two fiddlers stand at the front of the orchestra and enter into a competitive frenzy of speed, their bows scraping up and down almost too fast to be seen. Whirling around, I see Babette, her cheeks flushed and her eyes bright, dancing with Victor, and Madame Gerard is holding hands with her children as they spin in a circle, shrieking with glee.

Several dances later, laughing and breathless, we withdraw and Jean-Luc kisses me swiftly on the lips as we return to our table.

I can't help noticing Etienne's eyes upon me as I fan my overheated cheeks and drink my wine.

'Oh, I should so like to dance!' says Sophie wistfully.

'Perhaps if we wait for a more restrained tune we might take a turn together around the dance floor?' says Jean-Luc.

'Then I shall make a note on my dance card,' jokes Sophie, clapping her hands. 'And since it's dark no one need notice my condition.'

A portly man in a white wig approaches our table, his hand held out to Jean-Luc and a wide smile on his face. His yellowing teeth are slightly crossed at the front. 'Was that you I saw dancing with a pretty lady, Viard?'

'Indeed it was,' says Jean-Luc. 'May I present the lady in question, Mademoiselle Moreau? Madeleine, this is Monsieur Prudhomme, Mayor of Morville.'

He bows to my curtsey. 'And I believe you are one of the ladies we have to thank for the new flag for the Mairie?'

'Together with my friend Madame Levesque here.'

'It was an honour to work on the flag,' says Jean-Luc.

Mayor Prudhomme nods at Sophie. 'Naturally.' He turns to Etienne. 'And I hear you are attempting to save the grape harvest at Château Mirabelle by employing the village women, d'Aubery?'

'Indeed.' Etienne's voice is carefully neutral but I know him well enough to realise that he doesn't like Prudhomme any more than I do.

'Well, we shall see.' The mayor puffs up his chest, full of self-importance.

Prudhomme puts his arm around Jean-Luc. 'Will you be at the Jacobin Club tomorrow evening?'

'Most definitely.'

'Good, good.' The mayor makes a small bow to us all and saunters away to greet the people at the next table.

'For one with such influence, he is a most unassuming man, don't you think?' asks Jean-Luc.

Etienne's lips thin to a line. 'As the son of a pork butcher, he has worked assiduously to rise in society.'

Not wishing to fan the flames of potential discord I turn my attention to the moths fluttering around our candle flame. I'm relieved when the orchestra begins to play a lilting melody.

Jean-Luc stands up and bows to Sophie. 'A *boulangère*. I believe this dance is mine. Shall we?'

Giggling a little, Sophie stands and makes her curtsey to him.

Etienne holds out a hand to me. 'Madeleine?'

I hesitate, but where is the harm in dancing with him in a public place? I rest my hand on his arm.

He holds me lightly, the heat of his fingers searing through the thin muslin of my gown as he leads me towards the dancers. The lingering taint of sausage fat on his clothing cannot disguise the clean, soapy scent of his warm skin beneath.

The violinists play a sweet, melancholy air as the women dance around the circle, taking each man in turn by the hand and twirling him around, gradually returning to their partners. I'm circling with a man I recognise as the greengrocer. Two more steps and Jean-Luc is smiling at me and then I pass on to another man I don't know. Then Etienne's hand is in mine and we twirl slowly in the warm darkness, as lightly as thistledown on a summer's breeze. His breath is a soft sigh on my cheek as we move together and then apart. I close my eyes, wishing time would cease to exist and that I might remain for ever in this bubble of happiness.

The dance tune fades to a close. Etienne continues to hold my hand for a second or two after the music finishes but then he leads me back to our table.

'What a wonderful evening!' says Sophie.

'Isn't it?' I say, still feeling the lingering warmth of Etienne's fingers.

'And it's not over yet,' he says. 'They're preparing to light the fireworks.'

'Not too tired, Sophie?' I whisper.

She shakes her head, kneading her back. 'Though I rather wish I hadn't eaten all of that sausage.'

A sudden lightning bolt makes us gasp and look up. A vast shower of white stars is falling slowly from the velvet black of the sky above. Another series of explosive bangs follows, so loud that Sophie and I clap our hands to our ears, while some of the children scream in fright. Burning streaks of red, green and gold shoot across the sky, illuminating the night.

'Isn't it beautiful!' says Sophie, gazing heavenwards as a crackling starburst of violet drifts towards the earth, leaving a trail of sparks.

Great fizzing fountains of gold and silver erupt twenty feet into the air and whistling wheels of brilliant light whirl around, spitting sparks in all directions.

I clap my hands and laugh aloud. Then I feel the pull of Etienne's gaze and turn slowly to look back at him, the laughter fading from my face. The naked longing in his eyes makes me catch my breath. I cease to hear the crowd exclaiming as each new wonder bursts in a spectacular display of colour and light and see only Etienne. I stare back at him, speechless and unable to move for the yearning that tingles in my veins.

Jean-Luc touches my hand and says something that I can't hear over the crackling of firecrackers. There's a final rapid-fire of explosions and then only silence, while smoky drifts of gunpowder enfold us.

The crowd cheers and claps and whistles and the orchestra starts up again and children, fuelled by excitement, chase each other across the square while their parents call after them.

Sophie is leaning back in her chair, her eyes closed.

'Did you enjoy that?' Jean-Luc asks me.

'Very much, though perhaps it's time to take Sophie home.' I touch her wrist gently. 'Are you all right, Sophie?'

She opens her eyes and nods. 'It was wonderful but I'm suddenly very tired.'

Etienne rises to his feet. 'Let me escort you back to the carriage.'

There is a press of conveyances leaving the courtyard and plenty of good-natured jostling as we wait our turn to exit through the archway. Progress is slow until we pass the bottleneck of the river bridge but at last we are on the open road.

Sophie winces as we jog over every rut.

'This evening has been too much for you,' I say.

'I wouldn't have missed it for anything.' she says, and smiles wryly. 'I'm almost certain that my baby is coming.'

A cold wash of fear runs down my back. 'Oh, Sophie!'

Jean-Luc sits bolt upright and stares at her in horrified fascination. 'Good God, is that my fault for dancing with you?'

She laughs. 'Not at all.'

'We'll take you home as quickly as possible,' says Etienne calmly.

I hold Sophie's hand and she squeezes mine tightly. It seems an eternity until the carriage draws up outside the house.

'Thank you for your kind attentions,' Sophie says to Etienne and Jean-Luc as she descends from the carriage. 'I would be grateful if you would send a message to Widow Berger. I don't want Madeleine to walk to the village in the dark.'

'Absolutely not!' says Etienne. 'I'll fetch her myself.'

'Is there anything I can do?' asks Jean-Luc.

Sophie shakes her head. 'Nothing. Now it's all women's work. But thank you for a lovely evening.'

'Well then,' Jean-Luc rubs his hands together nervously, 'the next time we meet I hope to see you cradling your baby in your arms.'

'Indeed.'

The men leave and I smile brightly at Sophie, suddenly alarmed because I have no idea what to do. I've never been called upon to assist at a birth before.

'It'll be all right, Madeleine,' says Sophie gently. 'It took two days for Henry to present himself to the world so there's plenty of time for the midwife to arrive.'

'Tell me what to do.'

'Set a pan of water to boil and help me to put clean sheets on the bed.'

'You sit here quietly and I'll do that.'

She nods and looks at me with a beatific smile. 'Soon my baby will be here. I shall tell Charles I have adopted him, an orphan of the Revolution. Nothing and no one will ever make me give him up.'

An hour later Sophie is resting in bed. All the pans, jugs and tureens are full of hot water. Towels are folded beside the bed, along with a pile of clean rags. Her pains are coming regularly every ten minutes or so but she's riding the discomfort as well as can be expected.

Another hour later the pains are every two minutes apart and Widow Berger still hasn't arrived. Sophie is groaning and writhing on the bed. 'It's happening so quickly this time, Madeleine!'

I give her sips of water and stroke her hair, soothing and calming her as best I can without letting her see how very anxious I am.

Sophie groans and retches into a basin. 'I knew I should never have eaten that sausage,' she says as I wipe her face.

'Where is Widow Berger?' I pull the curtain aside for the tenth time and peer out into the dark, really frightened now.

'Madeleine!'

I turn back to Sophie to find that her eyes are closed. She reaches blindly for my hand and grips it so hard I think my fingers will break. Her knees are drawn up to her chest and she grunts, her whole body tensed. At last she lets out her breath in a long sigh. 'It's coming soon,' she says, falling back against the pillows.

'It can't be! Widow Berger isn't here yet.' There's an icy knot of terror in my stomach. I snatch open the casement and look outside yet again. An owl hoots in the oak tree but there is no sign of the midwife.

Sophie is labouring with heavy panting breaths.

'What shall I do?' I ask. My voice is high with fear. What if Sophie or the baby should die because I do the wrong thing?

Sophie groans but then her pain appears to ease again. 'So thirsty,' she whispers.

I help her to sip water and she nods gratefully. 'You need to take a look,' she says. 'It won't be long now.' She pulls up her nightgown and I peer between her thighs but there's nothing to see in the guttering candlelight.

Sophie grips my wrist. 'Another pain.' She grunts as her body convulses. After a few moments she lets out her breath in a sigh.

'Look again,' she says.

Feeling utterly helpless, I lift her nightgown with trembling fingers and catch my breath. 'I can see the top of the baby's head!' Not knowing what else to do, I wipe the sweat off her brow. I start to pray.

'Maddy, fetch a towel!' Sophie draws her knees up and takes a deep breath. Her face is screwed up as if in extreme pain and she lets out a yell. 'I can't push the baby out!'

'Yes, you can!' I say, though it looks an impossible task. 'Now push! Harder, harder! That's it!'

Sophie shuts her eyes and her face turns scarlet. Her whole body is shaking with the effort. She lets out a bloodcurdling scream and slowly the baby's head appears, the hair darkly matted with blood.

I stare at it in horror, wondering if she is going to bleed to death.

Sophie rolls her head wildly on the pillow. 'It hurts!'

'It won't be long now,' I say, stroking her hand and hoping I'm right. All the while I'm bargaining with God, praying that he won't desert us in our hour of need.

'It's coming again,' groans Sophie. She tenses all her muscles, bears down and then gives an almighty yell.

The baby slithers out and, with a gasp of surprise, I catch it in the towel.

Sophie sighs and collapses back against the pillows.

Into the ensuing silence comes the high-pitched wail of a newborn.

Sophie pushes herself up again, her face slick with sweat. 'Is it all right?'

The infant cries in lusty protest and, fearing she'll catch cold, I wrap her in the towel so that only her angry little face is showing. 'Sophie, you have a beautiful daughter.' Tears running down my face, I hand the wailing infant to her mother.

A sob rises in my throat and I have to sit down to quell the trembling in my knees. A moment ago we were two in the room and now we are three. I have seen something so momentous that I can't quite grasp it yet but I know that nothing will ever be the same again. I wipe the tears of emotion from my cheeks but they continue to fall.

Sophie, her face luminous with love, kisses her daughter's forehead and rocks her against her breast. A small fist frees itself from the wrappings and Sophie catches hold of it, kissing each of the perfect, tiny fingers. 'My precious little darling,' she croons. 'Quiet now and all will be well. Shush, sweetheart, I'll never let you go.'

'She's so beautiful,' I say. 'And she has your dimples.'

'So she has!' Sophie laughs and kisses her baby's button nose. 'I shall name her Marianne, since it's Bastille Day.' Slowly, Sophie counts the toes on each little foot. Finally, she begins to unwrap the towel, using it to wipe the infant's face and head. Suddenly she becomes utterly motionless and then looks up at me, her eyes round and tragic.

Fear grips me. Is the child not perfect in some way? 'What is it, Sophie?'

Now that the baby's head has been rubbed dry it's clear that she has a head of bright, copper-coloured down. Anyone who has met Jack Fielding will know instantly who fathered Sophie's child.

Chapter 25

The following afternoon little Marianne won't settle. Sophie is exhausted and I suggest she tries to sleep while I take the wailing baby downstairs. I'm walking round and round in the drawing room, rocking her in my arms, when I see Etienne at the open window.

'I've come to meet the new arrival,' he says.

I usher him into the drawing room and he bends over to look at the screaming infant's scarlet face.

'It makes me feel so helpless,' I say. 'Even the kittens run away, terrified by the noise she makes.'

'Poor little cabbage! May I hold her?' He takes the baby from me, holds her awkwardly against his chest and walks up and down, singing '*Au clair de la lune*' to her.

My heart melts to see him holding Marianne so tenderly.

After several minutes the baby's cries lessen and then cease. Very carefully, Etienne sits down on the sofa. 'I daren't move in case she wakes,' he whispers.

We sit side by side, watching the baby sleep, while Etienne strokes her copper hair.

'How is Sophie today?' he asks.

'Tired but relieved that the birth is over.'

'You must have been worried last night,' he says. 'Once I discovered Widow Berger had gone to the celebrations in Morville last night, I didn't waste time coming back to tell you that I was going to have to return there to find her. In retrospect, I should have sent a woman from the village to sit with you.'

'No harm was done,' I say. 'And Widow Berger pronounced both mother and child well.'

Etienne nods but his expression is distracted. After a moment he says, 'Forgive me, I have no wish to pry, only to help, but I must ask you ...'

'Yes?'

'Will Sophie's husband accept the child when she returns home?'

I hesitate. Clearly Etienne has worked out the difficulty for himself. 'I strongly doubt it,' I say. 'Sophie tells me she and her husband had not shared the marital bed for some time.'

'I confess I'd wondered previously about the child's paternity because of Sophie's absolute insistence on leaving England, even though she had to leave her son behind. And I knew she'd been devastated by the end of her affair with that scoundrel Jack Fielding. And now that Marianne is here and her hair is the exact colour of Fielding's ...'

'In the circumstances Sophie believed she had no other option but to leave the country.' I sigh. 'Etienne, please don't think too badly of her. Charles Levesque is a monstrously bad and violent husband and he taunted her about his mistresses. All she craved was a little attention, some love ...'

'I do not condemn her. God knows, this is an imperfect life and sometimes we have to shift for ourselves as best we can in difficult circumstances.' His voice is bleak. 'People often judge without knowing all the facts.'

I hold my breath, wondering if he will tell me about Isabelle at last. But he says no more, only strokes Marianne's cheek as she slumbers.

'The question is,' he says quietly, 'what is Sophie going to do about it?'

'I don't know. I'd imagined we'd find a family to adopt the baby but I don't know where to begin. We visited the orphanage but, having seen it, we cannot abandon Marianne there. Sophie had planned to tell her husband she'd adopted the baby in France, but there's her red hair to consider ... Charles may not have heard the rumours about his wife's red-headed lover but someone will soon tell him if she takes Marianne home. He'd have no hesitation in casting Sophie out then and she'd never see Henry again.'

'It's a terrible situation for her.' Etienne is silent while he thinks. 'Perhaps my old friend Dr Dubois might be able to help. He may know of a lady who longs for a child but has been disappointed.'

'Sophie is in no mind to ask you such a thing at present; she loved Marianne from the moment she saw her.' I touch the baby's tiny hand and, still sleeping, she clasps my finger. 'But I'd be grateful if you'd make enquiries because she'll have to make a difficult decision before long.'

Later that morning Jean-Luc brings flowers for Sophie but I'm too tired to make the effort to talk to him and he soon gives his excuses and leaves.

Sophie insists on feeding Marianne herself, even though Widow Berger offers to find a wet nurse.

'Charles made me send Henry to a nurse in the country almost straight after he was born but I will keep my daughter close,' she says, smiling down at the infant greedily sucking at her breast.

My heart is breaking when I see the love in Sophie's eyes because I know how impossible it is for this child ever to be a part of the Levesque family.

Babette, although young, is experienced with babies and remains calm and unruffled in the face of a fretful infant. I shall be able to continue working in the vineyard and the vegetable gardens for a few hours a day while Sophie is lying in, confident that Babette is on hand.

Marianne is asleep and I'm sitting at Sophie's bedside while we sip our coffee together one morning when Babette arrives. She's panting and out of breath. 'It's Père Chenot,' she says.

Instantly I feel a tremor of unease. 'What is it?'

'His sister has betrayed him.'

'Citoyenne Mathieu?' I remember the mean-spirited woman who was so unkind to her brother and who had been barely civil to me.

'Père Chenot was giving Mass to two old women in his garden shed . . .'

'His shed! But why?'

'He was under house arrest so couldn't visit them in their own homes and, of course, he's forbidden to enter the church or to take services.'

'But couldn't his parishioners take Mass in the church now that the Convention has sent a new priest?' asks Sophie.

'Not everyone likes the new priest.'

'So what has happened to Père Chenot?'

'He's in the gaol in the Mairie. He's to be tried today. Madame Porcher says they'll find him guilty.'

'Tried?' I say. 'But he's just a harmless old man! What threat can he possibly be to the revolutionaries?'

'Madame Porcher says he's committed a crime against the Revolution.'

'But the punishment for that is death!' Sophie frowns. 'Perhaps Jean-Luc would speak to Mayor Prudhomme?'

A short while later I ring the doorbell and a maid tells me that Jean-Luc has already ridden into Morville. I stand on the step, undecided as to what to do, when I remember it's Thursday. 'Is Madame Thibault here?' I ask.

'She's in the kitchen, Mademoiselle, if you would like to see her?'

I follow the maid down the kitchen passage and find Madame Thibault dressed in her market day hat.

'Ah, Mademoiselle Moreau!' she says. 'You will accompany me to Morville today?'

Ten minutes later we are in the *charrette* on the way to the market.

'Have you heard that Père Chenot is to be tried today?' I say.

Madame Thibault glances at me. 'I heard.'

'It's shocking.'

'Shhh! Don't let anyone hear you say that!'

'But I thought you liked Père Chenot?'

'That's as maybe but I don't want anyone thinking I support what he did or I'll be under suspicion, too. And you'd be wise to keep quiet on the subject.'

'Is it really as bad as that?'

White-faced, she nods and refuses to discuss it any further.

Morville is even busier than is usual on a market day. I call into the Lion d'Or but Jean-Luc is nowhere to be found, though I recognise his chestnut gelding in the stables. I walk amongst the market stalls, keeping my eyes open for him while I make my purchases.

Standing in the bread queue I notice Madame Thibault in earnest conversation with a soldier near to the *lavoir*. He has a recent, disfiguring scar down one cheek.

The cook glances up as if she feels my gaze on her and hurries away.

Once I have a loaf tucked under my arm, I purchase the available grocery items on my list and look again for Jean-Luc. Before long I come to the conclusion that he cannot be in the square or, since he's so tall, I'd see his head and shoulders above the crowd.

A large group of people are gathering on the opposite side and the sound of hammering can be heard above the bustle of the crowd. I draw closer and stand on tiptoe but I still can't see what is going on. The Hôtel de Ville is nearby and several people are gathered together at the top of its steps and looking over the crowd. I hurry to join them, hoping for a better view.

'What's happening?' I ask one of the men. He's wearing a red cap and a revolutionary cockade is pinned to his coat.

'They're building a scaffold to hang the priest and the old women.' He spits on the ground.

'But there's to be a trial . . . ' I say, shocked.

The man shrugs. 'That was early this morning. Guilty, of course.' He smiles, displaying blackened teeth. 'Caught red-handed they was, when a loyal citizen called the authorities. They never even put up a fight, so the Mayor's decided to be merciful and hang them straight away.'

'Merciful?' My voice is incredulous.

'Gets it over with, doesn't it?'

I'm saved from answering because the doors to the Hôtel de Ville open behind us. A dozen soldiers appear and I'm forced to flatten myself against the wall as they march past. The frail figure of Père Chenot follows, hobbled by chains and roped to two elderly women. The women weep, their grey hair loose upon their bony shoulders and their skirts dirty and torn.

Tears well up in my eyes but I dare not call out to Père Chenot. I'm upset to see that a purple bruise stains his jaw. Perhaps he senses my gaze because he glances up and sees me. As I reach out a hand to him, he shakes his head.

Another dozen soldiers march behind, prodding the prisoners with their rifles.

A group of well-dressed men follow, led by Mayor Prudhomme. Jean-Luc is close behind the mayor. He catches sight of me and steps back to allow the rest of the committee to continue down the steps.

'Madeleine, what are you doing here?' he hisses, grasping me by my wrist.

'I came to ask if you could help Père Chenot?'

'Help him? He's on his way to the hangman.'

'He's an old man!'

Jean-Luc's lips fold in a tight line. 'That doesn't absolve him from his crimes. He's had warnings and he deliberately set out to flout the law.'

'But …'

Jean-Luc shakes my wrist. 'Madeleine, say no more. You put yourself in grave danger. Do you want to find yourself on the gallows beside him?'

'I haven't done anything!'

'Please, I beg you, keep your voice down!' He glances fearfully over his shoulder. 'People are already looking. If you're suspected of sympathising with the priest, I won't be able to save you, even though I'm on the mayor's committee.'

The shock I feel on hearing this gives way to apprehension when I notice that several of the men on the Mairie steps are watching me through narrowed eyes. Suddenly I'm aware that Jean-Luc is not making vain threats.

Jean-Luc glances at the mayor and his men as they follow the soldiers. 'Come with me, Madeleine, and I warn you that you'd better look as if you are wholly in favour of these proceedings or it will be the worse for both of us.' He pulls sharply on my wrist and I am pulled along behind him until we catch up with the mayor.

'There you are, Viard!' says Mayor Prudhomme. 'I wondered where you'd disappeared to.'

Jean-Luc pushes me forward, still keeping a tight hold on me. 'By chance I saw Mademoiselle Moreau amongst the crowd and took the liberty of asking her to join us.'

Mayor Prudhomme looks me up and down. 'So you've come to see the traitors hang?'

I swallow the bile that rises in my throat. 'I was shopping in the market,' I say, evading the question.

'But like all good citizens,' says Jean-Luc smoothly, 'Mademoiselle Moreau will be gratified to see justice done.'

The mayor nods in approval. 'There's no place for squeamishness when there are traitors in our midst. Shall we take our seats with the rest of the committee?' He turns to lead the way.

Suddenly dry-mouthed, I shrink back, full of horror at the prospect of being forced to watch Père Chenot hang. 'I can't, Jean-Luc,' I whisper. 'Let me go and I'll keep out of the way.'

'Too late for that now.' His voice is harsh and the grip on my wrist grows stronger as I hurry along beside him over the square. Once or twice I trip on the cobbles and he has to drag me to my feet again. Then we reach a raised platform with a row of chairs facing the gallows.

I'm overwhelmed by disbelief. Morville is a commonplace little market town full of ordinary people. How is it possible that the sunny market square has been turned into a cruel place of execution for a kindly priest and two devout old women?

The soldiers have formed a cordon before us and the chattering crowd is kept back from the scaffold, where three gallows have been erected. I shiver as I see that nooses are suspended from the cross-beams, silhouetted darkly against the blue of the sky.

I'm aghast to discover that I have a perfect viewpoint for the proceedings in the front row of chairs. My gorge rises and I swallow hard. My knees begin to tremble with dread as I sink down on to the chair that Jean-Luc indicates.

He's still holding my wrist but his grasp loosens. 'Don't you dare disgrace me by fainting,' he whispers. 'You don't have to watch. Look above the gallows if you must but *do not* turn your head away.'

It seems impossible that violence could come to a place as peaceful as this. But then, the king, the highest man in the land, hadn't escaped the revolutionaries' wrath and had paid the ultimate price. A vision of his execution rises before me. I hear again the gleeful shrieks of the spectators and then the 'swish' that haunts my dreams as the blade falls. I picture the young executioner dancing across the scaffold with the king's head in his hands, spraying the crowd with royal blood.

'Jean-Luc, please . . .'

He strokes my hand, kind again. 'Madeleine, be calm!' he whispers. 'Remember, I bring you here only to keep you safe after your own impetuous behaviour.'

I cannot answer him and my stomach lurches again as Père Chenot and the two women, their hands tied behind their backs, stumble up the steps to the scaffold. A soldier pricks them with his bayonet to chivvy them into their places.

'Forgive them, Lord, for they know not what they do!' calls out Père Chenot.

A ripple of laughter runs through the crowd and someone jeers.

A soldier, little more than a youth, casually rams the butt of his rifle into the priest's stomach and I cram my knuckles into my mouth to stifle a cry of distress. The young soldier catches Père Chenot as his knees crumple and the hangman pulls a sack over his head.

One by one, the hangman slips the nooses around the prisoners' necks.

The throng ceases their catcalls and whistles, the noise dying down into a hum of anticipation.

Mayor Prudhomme, seated in the centre of our row of chairs, stands up.

All at once I'm icy cold, despite the heat of the sun. Spots of blackness dance before my eyes and my mouth is dry.

Mayor Prudhomme holds a white handkerchief above his head.

The crowd becomes eerily silent.

I glance at Jean-Luc's profile but he shows no emotion.

The mayor swiftly lowers his hand.

At the signal, the hangman pulls a lever.

The trapdoors fall open and the three prisoners drop.

The crowd screams in delight, roaring and whistling in approval.

I follow Jean-Luc's advice and look up high above the three figures jerking like puppets on the ends of their ropes. I stare, dry-eyed, at the wispy clouds floating in the lovely cerulean blue of the sky, wishing I had never set foot on French soil.

I hardly remember us taking our leave of Mayor Prudhomme. Jean-Luc holds my arm tightly as he leads me back to where Madame Thibault is waiting for me in the *charrette*.

Silently, I climb up to sit beside her.

She turns away and keeps her gaze firmly fixed on Colbert's back.

He flicks the reins and we roll forwards.

Jean-Luc rides alongside us on his chestnut gelding as we clatter over the stone bridge and leave the town behind.

Madame Thibault glances at me out of the corner of her eye now and again but neither of us mentions the hangings.

Some time later, she says, 'Mademoiselle Moreau?'

I blink to rid myself of the picture of the poor priest jerking in his death throes. 'Yes, Madame Thibault?'

'I've had a stroke of good fortune,' she says. 'I've been offered another sack of flour at a very good price. It will be delivered next week.'

'I thought flour was rationed?' I hardly care, so shocked am I by what I have witnessed.

Madame Thibault purses her lips. 'It is, in the normal way. However, Madame Viard hinted that she'd heard a soldier had some sacks of flour available and he might be found near the *lavoir*, so I went to seek him out. The flour has been confiscated from some anti-revolutionaries. In a way, you could say it's being redistributed to the people.'

I open my mouth to speak and then think better of it. But I can't help thinking that, whether Madame Thibault knows it or not, she must be buying her sack of flour on the black market.

Chapter 26

The day after the hanging, the evening sun is still hot and the air torpid as I leave the vineyard.

Jean-Luc is leaning against the *chai*, waiting to walk me home.

'Madeleine, I apologise if you thought me harsh yesterday,' he says as we set off, 'but I don't think you realised how dangerous your comments were. I was trying to protect you.'

I rub the bruises on my wrist from where he'd gripped me but my anger dissipates at the sight of his anxious expression.

'I wonder,' I say, 'since you grew up beside Etienne at Château Mirabelle and enjoyed the benefit of sharing his education, why you have so much sympathy for the new regime?'

Jean-Luc frowns. 'Regardless of my current position, I'm never allowed to forget that my mother is no more than a superior servant. There is a rot still festering in our society,' he says, his voice full of passion, 'and it must be cut out! Those rich, weak aristocrats, feasting on lark's tongues while they grind the faces of the poor underfoot, must be taught a lesson.'

There is a fanatical glint in his eye and I look away, suddenly uncomfortable. Père Chenot was not a rich aristocrat but I'm still too upset to argue the point. The first time I met Etienne he accused me having too little knowledge of the Revolution to make a proper judgement of a complex situation and I understand now that he was right. The complacent conversations I used to enjoy with friends and acquaintances in London drawing rooms about the events unfolding in France have in no way prepared me for the truth of the situation. It's confusing. Jean-Luc supports the revolutionary ideals despite his advantageous upbringing and extravagant tastes, whilst Etienne, although he has noble blood, toils beside his labourers in the fields.

'Nothing is black and white, is it?' I say. 'Only many shades of grey.'

Jean-Luc leans forward to clasp my hands. 'France is building a new and better society. There are bound to be difficulties initially but once these are swept away we'll all reap the benefits.' He lifts my hands to his lips.

I hope he's right.

'The sun has kissed your cheeks,' he says. 'You must take care not to spoil your complexion. I shall buy you a sunbonnet with a wider brim or you'll end up looking as leathery as the village women. I'll send to Paris for a pretty one in finely woven straw, decorated with silk ribbons.'

'Then I shall have to take care not to be taken for a rich aristocrat or I may come to an untimely end.'

Jean-Luc laughs. The breeze ruffles his brown hair and the sun paints it with shiny bronze highlights. He looks a picture of vigorous good health. 'Let me take you home.'

As the château comes into sight, Jean-Luc catches hold of my arm, drawing me to a halt. 'Look!' he says.

The sun paints the stonework with gold, and the conical roofs of the four towers make the château resemble a fairytale castle.

'Isn't it beautiful?'

'It's a privilege to live here.'

Jean-Luc nods. 'This place and the estate mean more to me than I can say.'

A little while later we reach the house and I remove my battered old sunbonnet and shake my hair free.

Jean-Luc grips me by my shoulders. 'You're so lovely, Madeleine.' He gathers me into his arms and kisses me. His lips are warm and urgent and I confess that desire stirs in me as I feel his broad chest pressed against me.

At last he lets me go. His eyes are gleaming as he runs his fore-finger slowly down my cheek and stops to touch my mouth. 'So soft,' he says, and kisses me again.

Resolutely, I banish the thought of Etienne from my mind and submit with some willingness to Jean-Luc's embraces.

Then the thin wail of a baby's cry comes from upstairs and I step back. 'I must go,' I say.

'Must you?'

I nod. But Sophie is right, I realise; I should forget my feelings for Etienne and think only about this man who is able to offer me a secure future.

'Tomorrow evening I dine with the mayor,' says Jean-Luc. 'I would be honoured if you'd accompany me.'

I don't like the mayor but I know that he matters to Jean-Luc. 'Thank you,' I say. 'I should be delighted.'

The following morning I peep into Sophie's room. Marianne clings to her mother's thumb, making contented little noises as she nurses.

Sophie smiles up at me. 'I swear she's grown since yesterday.'

'She's beautiful.'

Sophie turns her adoring gaze back to her baby's face and I qui-etly withdraw. It's too painful to contemplate what will happen to them in the future.

In the evening Babette carries a jug of hot water upstairs for me.

'I've laid out your dress and clean stockings on the bed. One of them had a small tear so I've put a stitch in it.'

Her earnest little face makes me smile. 'Thank you, Babette. You make an excellent lady's maid.'

She flushes and smiles. 'You must look your best for the mayor. He's a very important man.'

I strip off my work clothes and wash, paying particular attention to my fingernails, which are grimed with dust. I slip on my clean dress and take special care with arranging my hair. My father's moonstone ring, threaded on a ribbon, nestles between my breasts and I lift it up to stare into the milky depths. Do I wish to see into the future now? I'm not sure. Only if it is happy, I decide.

Downstairs, Sophie is watching for the carriage through the hall window with Marianne on her shoulder. In only a moment she cries out, 'Here he is!' and I hear the wheels on the gravel.

'Have a lovely evening,' says Sophie, kissing my cheek. 'And in the morning you must tell me everything that happens.'

I open the door and wonder with a momentary pang if Etienne knows that Jean-Luc is using his carriage to take me out for dinner.

'You look ravishing, Madeleine,' Jean-Luc greets me, taking my hands to draw me closer so that he can look at me properly. 'I shall be the envy of every man tonight.'

It's hard not to be flattered. 'And you have an elegant new coat,' I say, noticing how well it fits his broad shoulders.

A moment later we are bowling along the carriage drive. As we turn out of the gates a horseman carrying sacks in his panniers is waiting to enter. I glimpse his scarred face and recognise him as the soldier from the market place. He must be delivering Madame Thibault's black-market flour.

The Lion d'Or has reserved a private room for the mayor's dinner party. Mayor Prudhomme comes to greet us, clasping Jean-Luc's hands in his and full of loud exclamations of welcome. He kisses my hand and I try not to flinch away from his moist lips. 'It's a pleasure to meet you again, Mademoiselle Moreau.'

Madame Prudhomme proffers me two limp fingers and a suspicion of a social smile. Her cheeks are rouged and her fair hair has an unnatural tinge of yellow.

'Mademoiselle Moreau has taken it upon herself to teach the village children to read and write,' says Jean-Luc.

The mayor nods approvingly. 'We all must do what we can in the current struggles for equality. And education is the key.'

'I agree,' I say.

Mayor Prudhomme continues speaking without acknowledging my comment. 'Robespierre himself advocates education for children, even the girls.' He spreads his hands wide and smiles. 'Let no one say that he is not generous.'

'I hold the view,' I say, 'that girls who grow up with an education will pass that knowledge on to their children ...' My words fade away as the mayor turns his back on me. The door has opened to admit the innkeeper, bearing two bottles of wine.

'Nothing less than your best vintage, I hope?' says Prudhomme.

'Most certainly,' replies the innkeeper, uncorking the first bottle. He pours a little into a glass and offers it deferentially to the mayor, who takes a sip and makes a great show of rolling it around his mouth before swallowing it.

Still simmering with indignation at his rudeness, I hope he'll choke on it.

He shrugs. 'Passable,' he pronounces.

The saucy maid I met the last time Jean-Luc brought me to the Lion d'Or serves our dinner but her demeanour is meek this evening. Eyes downcast, she shoots an occasional anxious glance at the mayor.

The boiled leg of lamb and green beans is appetising and the dinner is only spoiled by Mayor Prudhomme's self-satisfied way of speaking, rarely allowing anyone else the opportunity to lead the conversation.

'Now that Maximilien Robespierre is elected to the Committee of Public Safety, we *will* have progress,' says Prudhomme. 'He will not allow himself to be swayed by emotion but will cut through all the uncertainties and act to end the uprisings and riots.'

'Robespierre won't stand any nonsense,' agrees Jean-Luc. 'He'll slice out the cankers in our society, cleanly and swiftly, with the guillotine. And then France will be a safe place for its citizens again.'

'Exactly!' The mayor's wig slips as he nods vigorous agreement and he reseats it with one podgy hand. 'When he's finished with the insurgents, Robespierre has promised that there will be nothing left of the Vendée but scorched earth.'

'Is that not a little harsh?' I ask.

Madame Prudhomme stops chewing and turns to look at me.

'Mademoiselle,' he says with a flash of his yellowing teeth, 'I fear you understand little of politics.'

I open my mouth to protest but catch sight of Jean-Luc's slight shake of the head and stare at my plate while my temper cools.

'Robespierre will send in battle-hardened troops.' Mayor Prudhomme snorts with laughter. 'They'll soon shatter the Vendéeans so-called Royal and Catholic Army, who fight with nothing more than pitchforks and wooden clubs.'

Jean-Luc nods his head in agreement. 'Robespierre is a catalyst for change.'

Mayor Prudhomme continues to drone on and I stop listening since he doesn't allow comments from a mere female to interrupt his flow.

Under the table Jean-Luc presses his foot against mine. He glances at me with a swift curving of his full lips and then turns his attention back to Prudhomme again.

My attention wanders until I hear Château Beaubourg mentioned.

'The Rocheforts are too full of ideas of their own superiority,' states Mayor Prudhomme. 'I've received reports that they ignore Robespierre's decree on the hoarding of food.' He smiles. 'But they will receive what they deserve when their storerooms are inspected.'

Jean-Luc puts down his fork. 'The workers are hungry and what little there is should be shared. The punishment for hoarding is death, I believe.'

'Just so,' says Prudhomme.

'Etienne d'Aubery is friends with Edouard Rochefort,' Jean-Luc says. 'Why, he came to take dinner at Château Mirabelle not two months ago.'

I stare at Jean-Luc. Surely it isn't wise of him to draw attention to that?

'Did he, indeed?' says Mayor Prudhomme. 'These nobles, despite giving up their titles, will always stick together, it seems.'

'I expressed then the sentiment that Edouard Rochefort is a pompous fool who has never shaken off his sense of privilege.'

The serving maid brings us apple tart, walnuts and cheese, and Mayor Prudhomme calls for more wine.

'Are you enjoying yourself?' whispers Jean-Luc.

I force a smile and resign myself to an interminable evening.

Some time later Madame Prudhomme excuses herself and when she returns I, too, take the opportunity to escape. On my return from the privy, I loiter outside the door to the private dining room, unwilling to return to the party.

'It will be hard to stop people from hoarding food,' I hear Jean-Luc say. 'A prudent housewife has always kept a little extra in the cupboard for hard times. Why, I cannot even guarantee that the cook at Château Mirabelle hasn't hidden a spare sack of flour or a few jars of olive oil in the cellars.'

'That will no longer be tolerated,' says the mayor. 'We cannot allow the army to go hungry, and the people need to know that the Republic will provide for them.'

I dare not delay any longer and enter the room.

'There you are!' says Jean-Luc, rising to his feet. 'It's growing dark so I shall call for the carriage. Madame Levesque will not wish me to keep you out too late.'

'No, indeed,' I say with relief, though Sophie is too besotted by little Marianne to notice if I'm late home. In any case, I suspect she would encourage any dalliance between myself and Jean-Luc.

Then we are outside in the balmy night air, climbing into the carriage.

Dusk is descending and I watch the countryside roll past while I mull over the evening's conversations. I don't like Jean-Luc's toadying support of Mayor Prudhomme and wonder how he reconciles his revolutionary theories with his privileged position as Etienne's estate manager.

'You're very quiet,' he observes.

'This evening gave me a great deal of food for thought,' I say.

Jean-Luc takes my hand. 'Soon we'll all have a golden future to look forward to,' he says. 'And I dare to hope that I can persuade you to remain at Château Mirabelle to share that future.'

A pulse beats in my throat and I am unable to look away. Is this merely an expression of friendship or am I correct in reading into it something more?

Jean-Luc smiles and I'm relieved when a moment later the carriage turns into the drive, devoid of its high gates now. Soon we draw up outside the house. The porch lantern has been lit for me and a candle burns in the window of Sophie's room.

Jean-Luc accompanies me as far as the porch.

'Goodnight, Madeleine,' he says softly. He makes no attempt to kiss me since Colbert is nearby, watching us as he holds the horses' heads. 'You look beautiful tonight,' he whispers, 'and I was proud to take you to meet Mayor Prudhomme.'

'It was kind of you to invite me,' I say.

'Until tomorrow, then.'

I open the front door and Minou and Mouche come to wind themselves around my ankles, mewing for attention. I wait while Jean-Luc returns to the carriage. Once it has rolled away into the dark, I go upstairs.

Sophie's door is ajar. She's sitting on the bed with Marianne lying on her knees. 'Did you have a good evening?' she asks, eager for information.

'Mayor Prudhomme is too full of his own opinions for my taste.'

Marianne gives a sudden cry and I pick her up so that her little head nods against my shoulder. I pat her back and bury my nose in the milky-sweet softness of her neck.

'And Jean-Luc?' asks Sophie. 'He had a smile in his eyes when he came for you this evening.'

'He indicated that he has hopes I'll stay at Château Mirabelle.'

'Maddy!' Sophie claps her hands together.

'I do find him very personable ...'

'But?'

I shrug. 'I'm not sure. His close acquaintance with Prudhomme and his committee makes me uncomfortable.' I kiss Marianne's downy head. She bats at my cheek with a tiny fist and all at once I'm overwhelmed by a flood of love for her.

'Maddy, your life will pass by while you wait for a man you can never have,' Sophie says warningly.

I cradle Marianne against my breast, tears starting to my eyes.

'Maddy? You're crying!'

'I'm so confused.'

'Come here.'

Hugging the baby tightly, I sit on the bed beside Sophie and she wraps her arms around us. 'Maddy, never forget, no matter what happens,' she says, 'you will *always* have Marianne and me.'

Chapter 27

I sleep badly, my head full of disturbing dreams of soldiers marching into Château Mirabelle and searching for hidden food stores. Awaking with a start at cockcrow, I lie in bed remembering the events of the previous evening. Suppose the mayor takes it into his head to make an inspection today and finds Madame Thibault's sack of flour?

I dress quickly and let myself out of the house. If I hurry, I might catch Etienne before he takes his morning ride.

The sun is a golden orb floating in a hazy sea of pearlescent sky and my spirits lift at the beauty of it. Underneath my feet the grass is wet with dew and the hem of my skirt is soaked before I have gone more than a few yards. I love this time of day when the world is unsullied and full of hope.

As I approach the stables I hear the squeak of the winch and the clatter of a bucket as Jacques draws water from the well. He catches sight of me and waves.

'Good morning, Jacques!'

Etienne must have heard my voice because he opens the door of Diable's box to greet me.

'You're bright and early today,' he says. 'Have you come to join me on my morning tour? We can have Minette saddled in a matter of moments for you.'

'I need to talk to you,' I reply.

'We could talk and ride at the same time.'

I glance across the park at the ethereal beauty of the mist rising from the ground and long to feel the wind in my hair. My resolve to avoid Etienne's company fades. 'I'll speak to Colbert about Minette while you finish saddling Diable.'

Colbert is in the tack room and I tell him what I need. He frowns at me but goes to saddle the chestnut mare. A few minutes later I follow him into the yard.

Etienne glances up as he tightens Diable's girth and then straightens his back and takes another look. He gives a shout of laughter as I walk towards him. 'I didn't recognise you,' he says. 'I thought you were one of the village boys.'

'I haven't time to return to the house to put on your sister's riding habit,' I say. 'And Colbert's spare *pantalon* fit me moderately well. It's early enough in the day that no one will see. I'm afraid he disapproves, though.'

'It will remain our little secret.' Etienne turns to the groom. 'Won't it, Colbert?'

Colbert grins and retreats to the tack room.

We mount our horses and leave the stable yard. It's a strange feeling sitting astride Minette but it's far more comfortable than using the sidesaddle, especially when we gallop across the park.

Slowing to a walk, we enter the sheep meadow and see a fox slink across the grass ahead of us and slip silently into the hedgerow. We guide the horses down towards the wide expanse of the river on the opposite side of the field. The water, a deep olive green, flows sluggishly and dried mud cakes the banks.

'The river is so low there won't be sufficient force to drive the watermills,' says Etienne. 'The hot summer has given us a badly needed good harvest of wheat this year, but it will be wasted if the grain stays in the granaries instead of being milled.'

'It's still hard to find bread to buy. And that's what I wanted to speak to you about. You know that Robespierre's latest directive is that hoarding food is punishable by death?'

Etienne raises his eyebrows. 'How does that concern me?'

'It concerns you if your cook is buying flour on the black market,' I say, 'and if the mayor implements a search of Château Mirabelle.'

Etienne draws on the reins and pulls Diable to a sudden halt.

'I went to the market with Madame Thibault and while we were there I saw her talking to a soldier,' I explain. 'Later, she told me that she'd arranged to buy a sack of flour from him, flour confiscated from insurgents. I didn't think too much of it until I heard Mayor Prudhomme talking last night.'

'You were with Prudhomme?' A frown creases Etienne's forehead.

'Jean-Luc and I were invited to dine with him in Morville.'

'I see.' All expression is wiped from his face.

'Etienne, I'm worried. Prudhomme is going to send soldiers to search Château Beaubourg for hoarded supplies. There was something about the way he said it . . . I believe he is seeking any excuse he can find to make an example of Edouard Rochefort.'

'It is true Edouard has never gone out of his way to endear himself to the majority,' says Etienne with a faint smile.

'I think Prudhomme intends to inspect Château Mirabelle, too. And if he finds Madame Thibault's sack of flour . . .'

'Let's return there at once.' Etienne's expression is grim. 'I'm going to speak to Madame Thibault and then warn Edouard Rochefort.'

The following day, one of the kitchen maids runs up the hill to the top of the vineyard shouting, 'Come and get it!' while she bangs a metal ladle on a cooking pot.

The women and older children put down their buckets and pruning knives and we amble down towards the *chai* in a chattering group.

The rich scent of sheep fat pervades the heated air, becoming stronger as we approach the glowing fire pit. Smoke billows on the breeze and another kitchen maid flaps her apron at it. Madame Thibault is cutting thick slices from the roasting meat, her brow beaded with sweat.

The younger children race about between our legs, squealing with pleasure.

'It's too hot to run, Solange,' says Madame Gerard, catching up one of the little girls clamouring for her attention.

Etienne is standing outside the wide doorway greeting everyone as they enter the cool dimness of the *chai*.

I linger behind after Madame Gerard and Madame Porcher have gone inside. 'Did you manage to warn Edouard Rochefort yesterday afternoon, Etienne?' I ask.

He nods. 'I did, but he didn't take a blind bit of notice. His exact words were that he wouldn't be threatened by "the trumped up son of a butcher with airs above his rank". He said he'd have Prudhomme whipped at a cart's tail if he so much as set foot inside Château Beaubourg.

'You've done all you can,' I tell him. I lift my head to sniff the air. 'The roasting meat smells delicious.'

'I thought slaughtering one of my sheep was a worthwhile sacrifice to make, in the circumstances.'

Inside the *chai*, long tables have been laid with white cloths and decorated with bunches of wild flowers and bowls of salad. Golden-crusted loaves of bread formed in the shape of bunches of grapes are piled up in great pyramids and earthenware jugs of wine and water are placed at intervals along the tables.

Widow Berger holds court at one end of the *chai* and exchanges pleasantries with the mothers as they collect their children. Sophie is helping her today, with Marianne wrapped in a shawl tied across her chest.

'She's sleeping, in spite of all the noise,' I say, kissing her forehead.

'I've just fed her,' says Sophie, smiling indulgently at the sleeping baby. 'And now it's time for us to eat.'

Madame Gerard, with baby Albert in her arms, comes to greet Sophie. 'Babette never stops talking about Marianne,' she says. 'And I have to agree, she is very pretty. Not like this great lump!' She ruffles Albert's fair hair and he crows in delight.

'What a handsome little fellow!' says Sophie, tickling him under his chin.

Etienne follows the last of the workers into the *chai* and raps on the table for everyone to pay attention.

Gradually the babble of voices ceases and he steps forward.

There is a 'Huzzah' from Emile, quickly muffled by his mother's hand.

Etienne smiles. 'The men here know what it is to work hard in the vineyard, but this year, since so many of the usual workforce have joined the army, it would not have been possible to keep the vines productive without the help of the women and the older children of the village.'

One of the men waves a fist in the air and shouts, 'Long live women!'

Etienne laughs. 'Indeed. Where would we men be without them? It has been a long, hot summer and you have all risen magnificently to the challenge. This celebration is to thank you for what you have achieved so far. I shall delay you no longer. Please, enjoy your dinner.'

A buzz of conversation and laughter breaks out as everyone finds a place. Etienne comes to sit beside me and Sophie is on my other side. Madame Gerard and Claudette Porcher sit opposite us.

Madame Thibault and the kitchen maids move amongst the

tables passing round platters of thickly carved meat, running with pink juices and studded with garlic and rosemary.

'Such a feast!' says Madame Gerard. 'And it's not even the end of the harvest.'

'It's all right for him,' says Madame Porcher, nodding at Etienne, 'born into luxury and probably ate his bread and milk off a silver spoon when he was a babe. I expect he has such fine meals all the time while we struggle to feed our children.'

Etienne pretends not to hear. 'May I pour you some wine, Madame Porcher?'

Grudgingly, Claudette Porcher pushes her wine glass towards him and turns away rudely once it is filled.

'Etienne, have you seen Jean-Luc?' I whisper.

He shakes his head. 'He had a meeting at the Jacobin Club last night and went out early this morning, before I could tell him about the celebration dinner today. In any case, I prefer him not to know about Madame Thibault's sack of flour.'

'Far better he isn't troubled by the knowledge,' I agree. 'He thinks a great deal of Mayor Prudhomme and I shouldn't wish him to find his loyalties divided.'

The roast lamb is delicious and after the juices have been mopped up with crusty bread there are second helpings for all who wish it. Wine flows freely. The plates are collected and great wheels of glistening apple tarts are passed down the table, followed by ewe's milk cheese served on a bed of vine leaves.

One of the old men, made merry by the wine, stands up and begins to sing. A moment later another joins him and before long the rest of us are joining in with a rousing chorus. Sophie and Madame Gerard sway in time to the melody with their babies in their arms.

'I think we can agree that the party is a success,' I say.

Etienne's smile warms my face, just as if the sun had shone upon me. 'It was worth butchering one of my sheep to see them all having a good time,' he says. 'And Madame Thibault has excelled herself.'

'She was so upset yesterday morning when she realised the implications of buying that sack of flour, I wasn't sure she'd be in a fit state to cook,' I say. 'But then she rallied and was up half the night baking all this bread from it. I doubt many of the people here today have ever eaten so well in their lives.'

'They deserve every mouthful,' says Etienne.

A shadow falls over us then and I glance up to see Jean-Luc. I notice that he carries with him the acrid scent of bonfires and there is a smudge of dirt on his usually pristine coat.

'What's been going on here?' He turns to look at those of the company who are still singing, the children playing on the floor and the piles of dirty plates.

'I called for a celebration dinner to show my appreciation of the workers' efforts in the vineyard,' says Etienne.

'But the grapes won't be harvested for another month or more!' Jean-Luc sits down on the bench beside me.

'Then we'll have another celebration.'

'No matter.' Jean-Luc shakes his head. 'I come on more important business. Mayor Prudhomme asked me to accompany him and his men to Château Beaubourg early this morning.'

Etienne looks at Jean-Luc, his face guileless. 'Why was that?'

'He'd received a report that food was being hoarded there and wanted a reliable witness.'

To avoid meeting Jean-Luc's eyes, I gather up some of the remaining bread, a couple of slices of lamb and some salad, and put the plate before him. Absentmindedly, he spears a chunk of lamb and eats it.

'And did you find such a hoard?' asks Etienne.

'We did,' says Jean-Luc, tearing apart the thick chunk of crusty bread and biting into it.

'And the Rochefort family?' I ask, suddenly afraid for them.

'Gone. Somehow they must have got wind of the mayor's intention to search the château. One of the servants said he heard a deal of shouting in the stables and then horses galloping away from the back while we were searching the kitchens. And Madame Rochefort's maid said her mistress had fled in her nightclothes and taken her jewel case with her.'

'Did Mayor Prudhomme send a man after them?' Etienne's face is tight with tension.

Jean-Luc shrugs and reaches for more bread. 'Of course, but they were nowhere to be found. And they'll not be back.'

'Surely they'll have to return eventually?' I ask.

'I doubt it. Once the food hoards were located, the mayor directed the servants to share the items equally amongst themselves, but then matters spun out of control.'

'In what way?'

'Edouard Rochefort was not liked. The villagers and his servants were angry when they realised that, while they starved, Rochefort and his family feasted on white bread, coffee, fine brandy and sweet-meats, so they took matters into their own hands and put Château Beaubourg to the torch.'

I gasp.

'I expect it's still burning. It's an old property and it's been a hot, dry summer. Edouard Rochefort is unlikely to show his face round here again.' Jean-Luc mops up the last of the gravy with a morsel of bread and pops it in his mouth. 'Etienne, I came to find you because the mayor's men are searching the kitchens here now, looking for stockpiled food supplies.'

'There aren't any,' he says. 'You of all people, Jean-Luc, know that we eat moderately here.'

'Then you have nothing to worry about, have you?' Casually, Jean-Luc drapes an arm around my shoulders. 'It's best to let the mayor carry out his search without interference.'

Etienne stands up abruptly and drops his napkin on the table. 'Despite that, I don't care for Prudhomme and his men rummaging through my property without my express permission.'

269

'My mother is with him and saw no reason to refuse him entry.'

Etienne says not another word but turns on his heel and marches from the *chai*.

Jean-Luc looks amused. 'Oh, dear, the master's feathers are ruffled.'

I stare at his gloating expression then push his hand off my shoulder. 'Shall we go and see what's happening?'

Few words are exchanged between us as we make our way back. My dress is clinging damply to me, partly due to the heat of the afternoon and partly from apprehension.

There is a confusion of horses in the courtyard and the stench of dung and hot horseflesh fills the air. A couple of soldiers in blue coats watch curiously as Jean-Luc leads me up the steps. The front door stands wide open. As we enter the coolness of the marble-floored hall, I hear booted footsteps overhead and raised voices coming from the kitchens.

'Are they searching all of the château, Jean-Luc?' I ask. 'Not just the store rooms?'

'It would appear so.' We walk along the corridor, past the servants' staircase and into the kitchen.

Madame Viard, her hands folded neatly against her trim waist, is standing beside Etienne and Mayor Prudhomme. Every cupboard door is open and all the contents have been swept to the ground.

Etienne glances at us, his face white and his jaw set.

'What news, Mayor Prudhomme?' asks Jean-Luc in a jovial tone of voice that jars in the silence.

'Nothing.' The mayor's self-satisfied smile makes me itch to slap his face. 'But we haven't finished yet.'

The sound of splintering wood and then the crash of breaking crockery comes from the corridor to the storerooms.

Etienne mutters an oath and takes a step forward.

I snatch hold of his shirtsleeve and feel the tension in his arm. 'Best to stay here,' I say, as calmly as I can.

Madame Viard glances at him, her dark eyes unfathomable.

Etienne subsides and I let go of his arm.

A soldier clumps his way into the kitchen, bearing a plate with a hambone upon it in one hand and half a loaf in the other. 'There are only a few dried beans and this, Mayor Prudhomme,' he says.

The mayor sighs. 'Put them back.'

'So you are satisfied that there is nothing untoward here?' says Etienne abruptly.

Regret passes over the mayor's face. 'It appears that our information was incorrect.' He narrows his eyes. 'But you will understand, Monsieur d'Aubery, that any dwelling place, be it a château or a peasant's hovel, is subject to being searched at any time if we are led to believe stockpiling of provisions is taking place. The consequence of such a misdemeanour is death by hanging. Do you understand?'

'Perfectly,' says Etienne crisply. 'My housekeeper will show you out.'

'No need,' says the mayor, 'since I know the way.'

'Nevertheless,' says Etienne, 'Madame Viard, accompany Mayor Prudhomme off the premises, if you please.'

The tramp of boots on the staircase prevents any further conversation and Jean-Luc and the mayor leave the kitchen with Madame Viard close on their heels.

Etienne sinks on to the edge of the kitchen table and lets out his pent-up breath. 'I don't know how I managed to contain myself,' he says. 'All I wanted to do was to batter the smirk off Prudhomme's fat face.'

'I'm glad you didn't,' I say. 'He's dying to find an excuse to cause trouble for you.'

'Even though we knew Madame Thibault had used up the sack of flour for the bread today, I prayed that Prudhomme's men wouldn't find anything else. I was suddenly fearful that false evidence might have been planted here to discredit me.'

'I don't trust Prudhomme either,' I say.

271

'Confiscated châteaux are being purchased for a pittance all over the country by men such as Prudhomme and his cronies, who have risen to power quickly since the Revolution. I wondered if he was looking for an excuse to step into my shoes.' Etienne rubs his temples. 'Thankfully, he didn't ask where the food for our celebration meal came from. I'd have had a hard time explaining that.'

'And, what's more,' I say, 'Jean-Luc helped to eat the last of the evidence.'

Etienne gives a shout of laughter. 'So he did. But then, Jean-Luc always has had the château's best interests at heart.' He catches hold of my hand and pulls me towards the door. 'Come on, back to the party! I'll give the workers the rest of the afternoon off and you and I will celebrate with a glass of wine.'

Chapter 28

August 1793

As the summer reaches its zenith the weather continues to be unusually hot. The languorous heat and the mindless work lull me into a torpor as I walk slowly up and down tending the vines all afternoon. The sun beats down but the wide brim of the finely woven straw bonnet Jean-Luc gave to me protects my face from sunburn. In every other way the bonnet is entirely unsuitable since it has feathers and pink roses around the brim and wide silk ribbons to secure it under my chin.

The vine leaves stir on the opposite side of the row and then I hear voices.

'... giving us a good dinner once in a while doesn't make things equal.'

The women are out of sight but I recognise Madame Porcher's complaining tone.

'It's all right for him, isn't it?' she continues. 'Living in that great house with servants to wait on him, eating off fine porcelain with his crest on every plate, he's no idea what it's like to worry where the next crust of bread's coming from.'

I stand on tiptoe to peer over the vines and catch sight of Madame Dufour's coarse straw hat and Madame Porcher's battered green bonnet.

Then there is silence apart from the rustling of the leaves until Bertille Dufour speaks. 'I wonder what *did* happen to the master's wife?'

I duck down behind the vines again and keep still, listening.

'He must've murdered her,' says Claudette Porcher. 'No one's seen her since he said she'd gone missing. Men don't know their own strength when they lose their temper.'

'That Moreau girl doesn't seem to care if he's a murderer. She's always making sheep's eyes at him.'

'I can't understand why she's working in the fields with the rest of us. Perhaps she can't bear to be apart from him. And I'll tell you what, if she's d'Aubery's whore, I don't want her teaching my children and poisoning their minds.'

'I thought she was doing it with Jean-Luc Viard?'

'Very likely, I'd say. He's always hanging around her like a fly on a dunghill. I'm told he sent to Paris for that fancy hat she's taken to wearing. As always, it's one rule for the rich and another for the rest of us.'

Scarlet-cheeked, I remember Mama telling me that eavesdroppers never hear any good of themselves.

'My husband told me the Revolution would bring us equality,' says Bertille Dufour. 'Don't see any sign of that, do you?'

'And one big dinner isn't enough to see us through the winter.' Claudette laughs. 'Tell you what though, Bertille, perhaps we could help another of Etienne d'Aubery's sheep on its way? I reckon we could manage to butcher it together, don't you?'

'If any more of our men are taken to be soldiers and we're left alone to provide for our children, we may not have any choice.'

Mortified, I creep away but make a mental note to warn Etienne to keep an eye on his sheep.

At the end of every working day I look forward to returning to the house and spending time with Marianne before working in the vegetable garden. At six weeks old she's growing fast. Her little body and cheeks are filling out and once or twice I think I catch a suspicion of a smile on her face. Her blue eyes try hard to focus on mine as I sing '*Au clair de la lune*' to her.

It's impossible to deny that my love for her grows with every passing day and I dread the time when we must find her a new family. Sometimes I catch Sophie rocking her baby against her breast while tears make rivers down her cheeks and I know she's thinking the same thing.

'Perhaps we should stay in France,' she says one day. 'I like it here. I don't care if I never see Charles again, if only I could fetch Henry.' There is yearning for her son in her voice.

'I could settle in France,' I say, 'except that I don't like the atmosphere of unease and that won't change until the political situation improves.'

'Surely nothing bad will happen to us here, tucked away in the countryside?'

'It already has,' I say unhappily. 'Look what happened to Père Chenot, and it frightened me that Etienne and Madame Thibault could have been executed for hiding that sack of flour.'

'You don't think the mayor really would have carried out his threat?'

'He's fanatical about carrying out Robespierre's directives.'

'Maybe that would be the case in Paris but in the country ... '

I shrug. 'I'd hoped that the dinner at the vineyard would form a closer bond between Etienne and the villagers than it has.'

Sophie looks at me enquiringly. 'Did it not?'

'Madame Porcher and her cronies are huddling together and whispering about the luxurious life they imagine Etienne leads. They ignore the fact that he works longer hours than anyone.' I refrain from mentioning what they think of me.

'There will always be those who are happiest when they are grumbling about something or other,' says Sophie comfortingly.

The following morning I wake up with a banging headache and return to bed. Dozing in the half-light of the shuttered room, I'm awoken by a frantic hammering on the front door. A moment later I hear a rising babble of female voices followed by Babette's loud cry of distress.

Downstairs in the kitchen I find a tear-stained Madame Gerard with Albert on her hip, talking to Babette and Sophie.

'What has happened?' I ask.

'It's Victor,' weeps Madame Gerard.

Sophie puts an arm around her. Albert begins to cry, burying his face in his mother's neck.

'He's been taken for a soldier,' says Babette, her voice trembling. 'The press gang came to the workshop and took Victor and his master away.'

'The mayor had instructions from Paris to send more men to be soldiers,' weeps Madame Gerard. 'Victor's only just sixteen!'

Sophie makes strong coffee and stirs in the last of our sugar, for the shock. When they are a little calmer, we send them home.

'I'm going to see Jean-Luc,' I say.

A short while later one of the housemaids admits me to the estate office.

Jean-Luc is lounging back in his chair with his feet on the desk. His shirtsleeves are rolled up to expose his muscular arms as he studies the ledger laid across his knees. A smile lights his hazel eyes when he sees me. 'Well,' he drawls, dropping his pen on to the desk and closing the book with a snap, 'this is an unexpected pleasure.' He waves his hand for me to sit down and removes his feet from the desk. 'Is something wrong?'

'Victor Gerard has been pressganged. His mother said that Mayor Prudhomme received instructions from Paris.'

'The *levée en masse*.'

'But what is that?'

'Each *department* has received instructions from the Convention to supply a proportional number of conscripts. All unmarried, able-bodied men between eighteen and twenty-five must join the army.'

'Jean-Luc, Victor's barely sixteen!'

He shrugs. 'Then he will perform his patriotic duty a little sooner than some.'

'You have influence with Mayor Prudhomme. Can't you ask him to release Victor?'

'It won't do any good.'

'Please!'

He sighs and rubs his nose. 'Very well. I'll try, Madeleine, for you, but I can't promise anything. The truth is, we need soldiers so badly to quell the uprisings, both within France and to defend our borders, that sixteen year olds will be sent to war within a few weeks anyway. Etienne and I are both without wives to support and, at twenty-six, I suspect it will be our turn next.'

Cold sweat breaks out on my forehead at the thought. 'But they can't take you; you're both needed here to keep the estate functioning!'

'I've already had that conversation with Mayor Prudhomme but we'll have to see what transpires.' Sighing, Jean-Luc pushes himself to his feet.

Since there is nothing more I can do at present, I return to the house.

Sophie and I take our supper in the garden to enjoy the last drowsy warmth of the day. It's quiet except for the cicadas, the muted chink of our spoons against the soup bowls and our murmured conversation.

Minou and Mouche are curled up in the flowerbed in a patch of sunshine.

As we are finishing our vegetable soup I hear the latch on the garden gate and then see Etienne striding towards us.

'I came to see if you are feeling any better, Madeleine?' he says. 'Jean-Luc mentioned that you were unwell.'

'Nothing more than a headache,' I say.

'Sit down with us,' says Sophie.

Etienne sits beside me and stretches out his long legs with a sigh.

'You sound weary,' I say.

'It's been quite a day.' He delves inside his shirt and pulls out a letter. 'I brought this for you, Madeleine.'

Frowning, I take it from him. 'I don't know anyone here who would write to me.' I turn the letter over and see that it is addressed simply to *Mademoiselle Moreau*, *Château Mirabelle* in spidery black ink. 'Who brought it?'

'I have no idea, except that it was a man of middle years. He rode into the stables this afternoon and gave Jacques a few sous to make sure that I received it and then rode away again. Intriguing, isn't it?' Etienne smiles, the weathered skin crinkling at the corners of his eyes.

I unfold the letter.

Dear Mademoiselle Moreau

I dare not call you Madeleine or Granddaughter since our last, and only, meeting was so unhappy. I send my last remaining faithful manservant to you with this letter to beg for your help since your Uncle Auguste is too proud to ask.

I have no pride any more, having spent my life being beaten down by your grandfather and then by Auguste. In truth, if you do not help us, I shall turn my face to the wall and hope that the Good Lord will soon release me from my pain.

The peasants have finally rebelled against your uncle's harsh

278

regime. Auguste and I are imprisoned in the dungeons at
Château de Lys and I fear for our lives. I remember your
father's compassionate nature and hope that, if you have
inherited even a small part of it, you may be able to persuade
Comte d'Aubery to come to our aid.

Whatever happens, I send you my sincere wishes that your
life will be happier and more fulfilled than my own.

Aurélie Moreau

'Madeleine? What is it?' Sophie's brown eyes are full of concern.

Wordlessly, I hand her the letter. After she has read it, I pass it to
Etienne.

He asks me, 'What do you wish to do?'

'Auguste can rot in his dungeons for all I care,' I say, 'but it makes
me uncomfortable to refuse an old lady's plea for help.'

Sophie's face is full of indignation. 'She allowed your grandfather
to treat your papa abominably.'

'But what if she dies there? I'd be tormented by guilt for the rest
of my days if I made no effort to help her. I couldn't save Père
Chenot but perhaps there's some way to rescue Grandmother
Moreau? Surely, as my grandmother, I owe her that?'

'She's cruel and selfish and you owe her nothing at all.'

'But is she cruel?' I ask, unhappily. 'When Auguste expelled us
from Château de Lys I wondered ...'

'What?' demands Sophie.

'I saw something in her eyes, sorrow or regret, perhaps. I wondered if she was too frightened of Auguste to welcome me.'

'Surely you can't mean to help them, not after the way they
treated you?'

'It's not my decision, is it?' I look at Etienne.

He sighs. 'You would like me to extract your uncle and your
grandmother from the dungeon and escort them to safety?'

'I know it's a great deal to ask.'

'Such an undertaking would be fraught with danger. After my friends died I vowed never to act as escort again, not while France is at war with Britain.'

'I don't want to expose you to such a risk.' I shudder at the thought. 'But if we can at least rescue them from the dungeons then they'll have to make their own arrangements.'

Etienne drums his fingers on the table and sighs again. 'I shall leave early tomorrow morning.'

'*We* shall leave early tomorrow morning,' I say, firmly.

'Certainly not.' His expression is uncompromising.

'Madeleine, you cannot go unchaperoned,' says Sophie, 'and I cannot accompany you since Marianne is too young to travel.'

'Then Babette shall come with us.'

Sophie opens her mouth to argue but we hear the garden gate open again.

The rays of the setting sun slant low across the path and I squint into the light to see Jean-Luc walking towards us.

'Good evening! It's as I suspected, Madeleine,' he says, sitting down beside us.

'You've spoken with Mayor Prudhomme?' I ask.

He nods. 'It's too late to fetch Victor back.'

'Oh, no!'

'He's already on his way to Paris.'

'Victor is *where*?' asks Etienne.

'He was pressganged into the army this morning,' I say. 'Madame Gerard and Babette were most distressed.'

'But Victor isn't old enough to go soldiering.'

'Mayor Prudhomme has his quota to fill,' says Jean-Luc. 'The Committee of Public Safety has invested in him unlimited powers and authority to act as he sees fit in his district, in line with the Committee's directives.'

'Poor Victor!' says Sophie.

'So you and I may be next?' says Etienne.

Jean-Luc shrugs. 'Let's hope it won't come to that.'

Etienne stares at the sunset. 'Well,' he says at last, 'there's no benefit in worrying about what may never happen and there are other matters on my mind at present.'

'Yes?' says Jean-Luc.

'I go to Paris again to arrange the sale of our wine. I would have left it until after the harvest but Madeleine has been called away to visit her sick grandmother. I shall accompany her there tomorrow morning.'

'Your grandmother?' asks Jean-Luc, studying my face. 'You haven't mentioned her before.'

I shake my head. 'We aren't close but she has no one else.' I pick up the letter. 'She has asked for help.' If I'm going to tell lies, I find it's always better to keep close to the truth.

'Where does she live?'

'A small village between Pithiviers and Fontainebleau.'

'A day's travel then. How long will you be away?'

'That depends on how Madame Moreau fares,' says Etienne. 'I shall continue on to Paris and on my return escort Madeleine back here.'

'Will you take your maid, Madeleine?' asks Jean-Luc, frowning.

'But of course.'

'I would have offered to accompany you myself but I have an important meeting with the committee tomorrow.'

'We will have an early start,' says Etienne. 'I suggest you retire early tonight, Madeleine.'

'I will,' I say, 'but first I must tell Babette that I need her to come with me.'

'I'll do that,' he says. 'I'll tell her that you require her services by seven o'clock tomorrow morning.' He stands up. 'We should go, Jean-Luc.'

Chapter 29

At seven o'clock the following morning, Babette and I arrive at the stable yard. Etienne is adjusting Diable's girth while Colbert hauls buckets of water for the horses' last drink before we depart.

The carriage sets off at a steady pace with Etienne and Diable leading the way. The weather is dry so we need not fear becoming trapped in mire, which is a blessing, but the constant motion as the carriage jolts over the road, the mud baked hard by the sun, is unpleasant.

Babette, pale-faced and her eyes red from weeping, sits beside me staring out of the window. She makes no complaint about the rough journey but every now and again she wipes tears from her cheeks.

When the sun is high we stop in a small town to allow the horses to drink from a trough in the market square. It's hot and noisy and crowded with soldiers and horses.

Babette scans every uniformed man who walks past, her face full of hope, as Etienne leads us into the inn on the square. We find a table in the crowded taproom. There are a few groups of farmers and their wives but most of the customers are soldiers. Some are playing cards or dice and most are drinking and making ribald comments to the barmaid.

Babette whispers to me and then slips away to the privy.

'I'm hungry,' says Etienne. He calls to the barmaid and asks for a platter of bread and cold meats.

'But no, M'sieur,' says the barmaid. 'There is nothing I can offer you. The troops are billeted in the town.' She rolls her eyes. 'How those men can eat! Our kitchen stores were empty after twenty-four hours and all supplies within ten miles have gone. Even our children go hungry,' she says indignantly.

Etienne shakes his head in sympathy. 'We have travelled a long way already today. Might you be able to find us a pot of coffee?'

The girl simpers at his winning smile and taps her nose. 'I'll see what I can do, M'sieur.'

'I've brought some bread and cheese in my basket,' I say.

'How sensible! Then we'll travel a little further and make another stop,' says Etienne. 'In any case, the horses will become tired in the heat.' He smiles wryly. 'Besides, if you bring out a picnic here, I expect the soldiers will descend like a biblical plague of locusts and devour it in seconds.'

Five minutes later we are sipping scalding coffee and energy begins to course through my veins again.

I glance towards the door, wondering if Babette is unwell as she's not yet returned, when I see her talking earnestly to a young soldier.

'It's Babette, not I, who needs a chaperone,' I say to Etienne, pushing back my chair.

He rests his hand on my wrist. 'Stay here,' he says.

My gaze follows his retreating back while I savour the warm touch of his fingers. As he approaches Babette, the young soldier puts his arm around her and plants a kiss firmly on her mouth. She pushes him away.

Etienne speaks curtly to the soldier. I can't hear what is said but the boy, for he is little more than that, steps back sharply. Etienne takes Babette's arm in a firm grip and leads her back to our table.

'I wasn't doing anything wrong,' she says, her cheeks scarlet with mortification. 'I only asked if he'd seen Victor.'

'Unfortunately, young men see it as an open invitation if a pretty girl approaches them,' says Etienne gently, 'especially if she's alone.'

'Don't worry, Babette,' I say, 'there's no harm done.'

We return to the carriage and continue our journey.

In the evening we come to another town and I heave a sigh of relief as I recognise it as the place we stayed when we last visited Château de Lys. A faded inn sign that depicts a cockerel hangs above an archway. We drive underneath it and into the cobbled courtyard.

An ostler hurries to take the horses and Babette and I climb stiffly down from the carriage. The aroma of some kind of meaty stew drifts from the kitchen window and mingles with the reek of fresh horse dung. Suddenly, I'm ravenously hungry.

The innkeeper appears from the kitchens, wiping his hands on a grimy apron as he directs us to the dining room. We take a table by the window and a young woman lights the candles and brings us bread, a carafe of rough country wine and bowls of mutton stew. There's a contented silence until after we have mopped up the last of the gravy with coarse brown bread.

Babette, worn out by the long journey, begins to nod and I send her up to bed, secretly pleased to be alone with Etienne.

'I'm anxious about tomorrow,' I admit as we linger over the last glasses.

Etienne stares into the dregs of his wine and I study his long fingers as he twirls the glass. I grip the stem of my own glass to prevent myself from reaching out to touch him.

'I'll find a way inside,' he says. 'Perhaps I can bribe a servant into unlocking the dungeon. You will stay here.'

'I'm coming with you!'

Etienne catches hold of my wrist and his eyes glitter in the flickering candlelight. 'This isn't a game, Madeleine. It's dangerous.'

His hand is warm on my skin and I can feel the slight roughness of his work-hardened palms. 'I'm coming with you,' I insist. 'And don't glare at me like that, Etienne.'

'You are an impossible female!'

'Perhaps no one will notice us if we look like servants?' I shiver as Etienne rubs his thumb in tiny circles against the inside of my wrist. 'I could borrow Babette's cap,' I say, as if his touch isn't making me melt with desire, 'and my dress is plain enough to pass under an apron borrowed from the kitchen.'

Etienne sighs.

'Then that's settled,' I tell him.

'If you must come, you will do as you are told and we will leave here before first light.' He stands up and gathers my hands to his chest. 'Now go and get some rest!'

'Goodnight, then.' I meet his eyes, so dark that I could lose myself in their obsidian depths. I don't want to leave and he makes no move to let go of me.

At last, he touches the back of one finger against my cheek in a feather-light caress. 'Until the morning, then. Goodnight, Madeleine.'

I drop my gaze. 'Goodnight, Etienne,' I whisper, and turn reluctantly away.

It's still dark the following morning when we leave the inn, although faint streaks of pale blue are beginning to lighten the sky in the east. A cock crows nearby but no lights show in the tumbledown houses as we walk through the sleeping village of Villeneuve-St-Meurice and up the steep hill towards the château.

The stone eagles atop the gateposts still guard the drive. The magnificent wrought-iron gates are gone, however, torn from their hinges by revolutionaries, no doubt, to melt down for arms.

We creep past the gatehouse, where not a soul stirs, and begin the long trek up the carriage drive. The sun is only just peeping above the horizon and the grass is beaded with dew. Deer graze on the parkland in the grey early-morning light, lifting their heads to stare at us as we walk silently past. Ahead of us, the forbidding grey bulk of Château de Lys sits squarely on top of its hill.

A shudder runs down my back at its inhospitable appearance and my steps falter. How can we possibly hope to enter such a fortress and release Auguste and Grandmother Moreau?

'Madeleine?' Etienne's voice is low. 'You can change your mind, if you wish.'

'I will not,' I say. Damn the man! Does he always sense what I'm thinking?

Five minutes later we reach the drawbridge. The massive stone walls and turrets that loom so far above us are reflected darkly in the moat. A dejected-looking swan drifts by, its head bowed. The water level in the moat is low and the barred windows to the dungeons are safely above the waterline. At least the Moreaux are unlikely to drown but I wrinkle my nose at the stench of the brackish water.

Etienne nods at the great oak doors. 'Look,' he says, softly, 'they're open.'

We walk silently over the wooden drawbridge and I expect at any moment that someone will shout a challenge. Crossing the gravel forecourt as quietly as we can, we climb one of the curved stone staircases to the balustraded terrace and head for the entrance.

The studded doors are flung wide. Entering the vestibule we find a set of inner doors.

Etienne grasps hold of one handle, turns it and lifts his eyebrows in surprise as the door swings open. 'Someone is very careless,' he murmurs.

As we tiptoe over the inlaid marble floor of the hall, he catches hold of my sleeve. 'I can't remember the way to the dungeons, he whispers, 'but if we can find the kitchens perhaps we can find a way down.'

'We know it's not that way,' I nod to the corridor leading off the hall to our right, 'because we went that way last time.'

Moving stealthily along the left-hand corridor, our feet sink into the thick pile of the carpets. Paintings depicting hunting scenes punctuate the walls, interspersed with boars' heads and sets of antlers. We peer into a vast, empty ballroom with a polished oak floor and glittering chandeliers suspended from the painted and gilded ceiling. Next we find a library and, in another life, another place, I would long to spend time curled up in one of its comfortable velvet chairs, leafing through the leatherbound volumes. But cobwebs festoon the ceilings and the furniture is grey with dust. I infer that my Uncle Auguste isn't a great reader.

Etienne opens another pair of doors and we step inside.

I catch my breath at the splendour of the enormous dining room. The walls of the chamber are covered with red silk damask. The black marble chimneypiece is exuberantly carved and the gilded mirror that sits above it reflects the swagged and braided silk at the windows. Glittering chandeliers a yard in diameter hang from the high ceiling over a table surrounded by enough chairs to seat a hundred people.

A repugnant smell of putrefaction pervades the air. The table is dressed for a party but the chairs are not neatly tucked under the table and the imposing flower arrangements positioned along the length of the table consist of roses with browning petals and dead foliage. The water in the crystal vases is green and slimy.

Etienne makes a sound of disgust and I turn to see him peering at a silver platter.

'What is it?' I ask.

'Maggots.'

Sickened, I touch my hand to my mouth. It's only when I step nearer to the table that I see pyramids of apricots and grapes tinged with powdery green mould and a half-eaten jelly that has collapsed into a yellow puddle and overflowed the dish. There are traces of decomposing food on the delicate porcelain plates. Crystal glasses have been overset and red wine stains bleed into the starched linen cloth. Flies crawl over the surface of the remains of a weeping cheese.

'What happened here?' I whisper.

Etienne shrugs. 'It looks as if the guests simply walked away and the servants never cleared the table.' Then his eyes widen as he looks over my shoulder. He puts his fingers to his lips.

My heart in my mouth, I spin around and see that two men are sitting on the floor in the far corner of the room. I dare not move in case they notice me but then I see that there are several bottles beside them on the parquet floor.

'Drunk?' I mouth to Etienne.

He nods and we steal from the room, closing the door softly behind us.

At the far end of the corridor, the luxurious carpet gives way to bare floorboards as we find ourselves in the servants' passage. A few paces further on is the kitchen.

An immense pine table dominates the room, crowded with piles of unwashed dishes, chicken carcasses and mouldering crusts. A myriad of copper cooking utensils are arranged on the shelves of the dresser, ranging from one large enough to boil half a pig to one small enough for a single egg.

All at once I stop dead and clutch at Etienne's sleeve. Curled up on the floor before the great hearth lies a turnspit dog. He opens one eye and emits a throaty growl.

'Good dog!' I say warily, as he sprints towards us, hackles raised and teeth bared.

Etienne snatches up an abandoned ham bone from the table and holds it out to the dog, who sniffs at it warily. 'Open that door,' Etienne whispers.

I unlatch the door to a store cupboard and Etienne throws the bone inside. The dog follows and Etienne closes the door smartly. I'm not quite sure but I think he smirks.

Then I gasp as a voice behind me says, 'Who are you?'

A girl is staring at us from the doorway. She's very thin and her hair hangs down in greasy locks around her sallow face.

'Where's the cook?' asks Etienne. 'I've a delivery for her.'

The girl shrugs. 'Asleep upstairs, I shouldn't wonder. We don't have to get up early to wait on the master no more.' She goes to the hearth and picks up the poker. 'You're very early.'

'It's a busy day for us,' says Etienne briskly.

'It's strange,' the girl says. 'Since the changes I don't have to rise before first light to kindle the fires but I still wake early. I'm not used to such a soft bed.' She stirs the embers into sulky flames, takes a handful of kindling from the hearth and feeds it into the fire.

'What has changed then?' I ask.

'Everything,' she says simply. 'It started when the master held a grand dinner. All of us servants worked for days to prepare the state dining room and cook the food.' Her eyes gleam. 'I'm only a scullery maid but I saw roasted venison, whole suckling pigs, dishes of partridges, great hams, soups, custards, jellies and tarts, all carried up to the dining room. There was a coach and horses made from sugar to amuse the guests. Beautiful it was.' Her voice fades away.

'And then what?'

'Carriage after carriage rolled up the drive and the gentlemen and ladies came in, all dressed in sparkling diamonds and silk.' Her narrow face clouds over. 'Two of the men from the village had called on the master the day before to plead with him to give the children some bread, but he refused. The men were whipped.'

'What happened then?' Etienne's face is dark with anger and I'm filled with shame to be related to Auguste Moreau.

'That night one of the children died of hunger, his poor little belly all swollen. His father went mad with grief and the rest of the men came here in the middle of the night and battered down the door. The master's guests had gone by then and they dragged him from his bed and threw him and his mother into the dungeon.'

289

'Serves him right!' I say.

The girl smiles. 'So now everyone from the village has moved into the château. I have a room to myself with a silken quilt on the bed. Imagine!'

'Imagine,' I echo.

In the distance, I hear the sound of voices coming along the passage. I glance fearfully at Etienne.

'We'd better be going,' he says.

The girl frowns. 'What did you say you're delivering?'

The sounds grow louder.

'We'll come back later,' I say.

We dash out of the door and scurry along the servants' passage. Etienne grasps my hand and pulls me through a warren of rooms until we can no longer hear the voices.

I lean against a wall to catch my breath while the sound of my heartbeat rings in my ears.

'No time to stop,' whispers Etienne, and we are off again, peering into larders, storerooms, dairies and coal stores. At last I find a studded door with a metal grille set into it. When I open it there's a narrow stone staircase leading down into darkness.

Chapter 30

'This is it,' says Etienne, a muscle tightening in his jaw. 'I'll never forget this place. It gave me nightmares for years when I was a boy.'

'Then I hope Auguste suffers the same in the future.' Anger simmers in my breast as I follow Etienne down the spiral staircase. The stone steps, worn hollow by the passage of generations of feet, are treacherous and the walls seep moisture. The narrow space makes me shudder. Etienne turns and takes my hand as he reaches the bottom.

It's cold and smells of mould and excrement but a little light filters in from a barred window above. We stand motionless while our eyes grow accustomed to the shadows. All sound is deadened and I shiver as I imagine the thick walls pressing in on me. I cling tightly to Etienne's hand.

Into the silence comes the clank of metal chains and the rustle of straw. I whirl around and see that there is a barred cell behind us.

'Auguste?' says Etienne.

'Who is it?' replies a voice, high with fear.

'D'Aubery.'

'Thank God! I thought you'd come to torture me. Unlock the door and let me out of here!'

'Where is your mother?' I ask.

'Let me out!'

'I said, where is Grandmother Moreau?'

A whimper comes from the far corner of the cell. 'I'm here,' a voice whispers.

'Are you all right?' I ask.

'Now that you have come ...'

'The keys are behind you!' Auguste's voice is on the verge of hysteria. 'Those bastards put them where I could see them purely to torment me.'

'And who can blame them?' retorts Etienne. He runs his hands over the wall until I hear the rattle of a bunch of keys.

A moment later the gate is open and Etienne is unlocking the leg irons that shackle Grandmother Moreau to the wall while I try not to look at the overflowing bucket beside her. The air in here is thick and I feel the stirrings of panic.

'Release me at once, you dolt!' orders Auguste with barely repressed fury.

Etienne stands over him, jangling the keys in his hand. 'Perhaps I'll leave you here. What do you think, Madeleine? We could open the sluice gates until the moat rises.'

I look at Auguste's corpulent figure with loathing. 'An excellent idea, in my opinion.'

Auguste moans. 'Don't jest!'

'I'm not,' says Etienne.

'Please, I beg you to free us both,' says Grandmother Moreau.

I help her to rise from the ground and she stands trembling beside me.

Etienne kneels down and unlocks Auguste's shackles, pulling him roughly to his feet. 'You can thank your mother for this,' he says. 'I'd far rather leave you here.'

I gasp as a sudden shout comes from above, followed by another, and then there's the tramp of footsteps clattering down the staircase and a wavering light appears.

Auguste cries out, 'They're coming for me!'

Etienne shakes him so hard his teeth rattle. 'Take control of yourself, man! Is there another way out?'

'No!' Auguste pulls himself free from Etienne's grip.

I glance despairingly at the barred window. Full of dread, I flatten myself against the wall.

Whimpering, Auguste retreats into the cell and crouches on the floor with his hands over his ears.

A crowd of men and women surges down the stairs. They surround us, waving sticks and flaming torches. One man pinions Etienne's arms roughly behind his back and another prods me in the stomach.

Grandmother Moreau staggers and sinks to the ground.

A torch is thrust into my face and a man yanks my head back by the hair, his face contorted with anger. 'What are you doing here?' His breath reeks of garlic.

There's a babble of questions as we're shoved back against the cold stone of the wall. I'm shaking, terrified that they'll lock us up in this terrible dungeon.

Etienne struggles, frees an arm, punches his captor on the nose and receives a blow to the head for his pains.

'Look, they've unlocked Moreau's chains!'

Seven or eight men form a circle around Auguste and he screams in high-pitched terror as he's hauled to his feet and pushed from hand to hand like a child's plaything.

'String 'im up from the nearest tree, I say!'

'Hanging's too good for him. Shove a red-hot poker up his arse!'

Suddenly, over the tumult and the taunting, there comes an ear-splitting whistle.

The mob is stopped in its tracks.

The whistle is repeated and all eyes turn to Etienne. He removes his fingers from between his lips. 'Stop!' he commands.

The grip on my hair relaxes and I pull myself free and crouch down to help Grandmother Moreau to her feet. She clings to my hand, trembling uncontrollably.

'Let the ladies go!' says Etienne. 'They have done nothing to harm you.'

Anger sweeps over me in a red tide. 'You should all be ashamed of yourselves,' I shout, fixing my gaze on one face after another. 'Look at this old lady, frightened half to death! Would you do this to your own mothers and grandmothers?'

The men mutter amongst themselves and then one calls out, 'She's the Devil's mother!'

A ripple of laughter echoes around the dungeon.

'And who are you to come here and try to free the duc?' shouts another man over the rising cacophony. 'Lock them all up!'

'No!' I struggle but I'm lifted up, carried into the cell and dumped on the floor. A moment later, Etienne lands beside me.

A cacophony of jeers and whistles nearly deafens me as I push myself to my feet in rising panic. Terror at being confined in a small space squeezes the air from my lungs and I gasp for breath.

Then one voice rises above the others. 'I know these people!'

The muttering dies away and a young man pushes to the front of the throng and holds his torch aloft.

'You came to see the duc and he had you thrown out.'

At once I recognise the footman who escorted us from the premises.

He laughs and I see that he's little more than a fresh-faced youth. 'I remember how you stood up to that useless piece of shit.' He nods at Auguste, cowering in the corner. 'You're Philippe Moreau's daughter.' He turns to the others. 'She has the Moreau ring.'

An old woman waving a large stick peers at me. 'Philippe's daughter? Is it possible?'

'Philippe Moreau was my father.' I stand up tall and try to still the

294

trembling in my knees. 'And I'm proud of that. I'm anything but proud, however, to be associated with his brother Auguste.'

The woman pushes her way through the tightly packed throng until she's standing in front of me. 'You're Philippe's girl?'

I nod.

'Bring me light!' she says. She snatches a torch from one of the men and studies my face closely. After a long silence I see tears glinting in her rheumy eyes. 'Yes, you have Philippe's likeness.'

I reach inside my collar, fish out the moonstone ring and hold it up to show her.

'That's mine!' shrieks Auguste.

'No, it isn't,' I say. 'You stole my father's inheritance and this ring is all that he took from this terrible place.'

The elderly woman reaches out to touch my hand. 'I was your father's wet nurse. I loved him and watched him grow up, frightened he would be tainted by the rest of his family.' She shakes her head. 'But he never was.'

I frown, trying to remember. 'Are you Thérèse? Papa rarely talked about his past but he did mention his beloved childhood nurse sometimes.'

Thérèse lifts my hand to her cheek. 'I helped him escape when the old duc locked him in the dungeon. They left him here to rot when he demanded justice for my brother after the old duc beat him to death. If I hadn't freed Philippe, he could have died here. I knew he'd never give up demanding justice for André.'

'I couldn't help him, Thérèse!' says Grandmother Moreau, her voice agonised. 'Do you think I wanted Philippe to be imprisoned in this place? But I dared not flout my husband's wishes. I tried that once,' she whispers, 'and lost the child I carried.'

A man in a brown coat sticks out his unshaven chin and narrows his eyes at me. 'What d'you want here? This place is ours now.'

'I don't want the château.' I shudder. 'And neither did my father.'

'Mademoiselle Moreau and I have not come here to cause any of you trouble,' says Etienne. 'You are welcome to the château as far as . . .'

'Shut up, d'Aubery!' yells Auguste. 'It's not yours to give away. And you, Gaston, I'll have you horsewhipped for your insolence!'

One of the men slams Auguste back against the wall.

Etienne continues as if he hasn't been interrupted. 'Mademoiselle Moreau wants nothing but to remove her grandmother and uncle from your presence.' He glances at me. 'And I solemnly undertake to escort them both out of France.'

I catch my breath.

'You can't make me go!' Auguste struggles furiously in his captors' arms.

'Oh, I think we can,' says Etienne, looking meaningfully at the others. 'Don't you?' He catches the footman's eye. 'As you say, Auguste is a useless piece of shit and I can save you all the trouble of having his blood on your conscience.'

The men and women begin to argue fiercely amongst themselves, and I hear Thérèse's pleading tones above the growl of the men's deeper voices. I glance fearfully at Etienne.

His mouth is set but he darts a smile at me. 'Courage!' he whispers.

'Quiet!' Gaston glares at the crowd. 'We shall discuss this upstairs.'

'A trial!' shouts a voice.

I cry out in terror as Gaston slams shut the iron gate of the cell and our captors march away up the stairs.

I grasp the iron bars and shake the gate but it's immovable.

And then there is only the sound of receding footsteps and my grandmother's weeping.

The air is fetid and my heart is fluttering as I picture the great mass of the château pressing down upon us from above. Panic constricts my chest. I dare not scream or I may never stop. I sit on the filthy straw with my arms wrapped tightly around my knees to still the shaking.

Etienne sits close beside me. 'I should never have let you come,' he says.

'I'm frightened,' I whisper. 'I hate small spaces.'

'I don't like them much myself,' he says, putting his arm around my shoulders.

He appears perfectly composed but I can feel the slight tremor in his fingers and remember that this is a recurrence of his worst childhood nightmare. I lean against him and for his sake force myself to breathe slowly and try to empty my mind of anxious thoughts.

I don't know how much time passes but eventually the glimmer of light begins to fade from the barred window.

'It seems they're not going to release us tonight,' says Etienne, a muscle flexing in his jaw.

I shudder as I fight down the panic I feel.

Grandmother Moreau and I take it in turns to suffer the indignity of squatting over the bucket and then we lie down on the hard floor to sleep.

The absence of light becomes total and soon Auguste's snores reverberate around the cell.

Wide-eyed with fear I stare into the suffocating blackness, my pulse hammering in my chest and my breathing ragged. Etienne's hand reaches out to me and I grip it, holding on to him as the one safe thing in this terrible place.

The straw rustles as he turns over and I don't resist when he gathers me to him. We lie on our sides facing each other, with our foreheads and knees touching and our breath mingling. Gently, he strokes my hair, smoothing it off my forehead and lulling my fevered thoughts. Little by little, the tension drains from my muscles and I let it go with a long sigh.

He caresses my cheek, tracing the line of my jaw with a touch as light as thistledown. I banish all thoughts, forgetting my terror and the hard floor beneath us. There is only this moment and the soft touch of Etienne's finger on my lips. Powerless to resist, my mouth opens a little.

He makes a small sound and then he is smothering my throat, my eyelids and my mouth with hot kisses. Perhaps it is the total darkness that makes me so shameless but I press the length of my body against his and return his kisses with abandon. Cupping my face in his hands, he kisses me until rising desire makes me tremble with longing.

At last he draws away a little, his breath fast and uneven. He touches his lips against my forehead and enfolds me in his arms so tightly that I couldn't escape, even if I wanted to. Gradually, his hold slackens and he sighs deeply. Turning on to his back, he settles my head on the hollow of his shoulder and rests his hand against the curve of my hip.

I listen to the regular thud of his heartbeat and think that if the mob murders me in the morning, at least I shall have had one night in his arms.

As I drift off to sleep I hear him whisper, 'Goodnight, my love.'

My eyes flutter open. A glimmer of grey light filters through the barred window and there's a pain in my hip from lying on the hard ground.

Etienne lies beside me, looking curiously young in repose. His jet black eyebrows are finely drawn and thick lashes fringe the curve of his closed eyelids. Heavy stubble shadows his jaw.

He opens his eyes and a sleepy smile curves his mouth as he picks a piece of straw out of my hair.

Auguste groans and passes wind and I'm brought back to the full realisation of our plight.

I sit up and stare around the cell, my heart thudding with dread. 'What's going to happen to us?' I whisper.

Etienne puts his arm around my shoulders but doesn't answer.

We sit like that for a long time, deep in our fearful thoughts.

Into the quiet comes a murmur of voices.

Etienne's hand grips my waist as he listens.

Grandmother Moreau whimpers and tucks herself further into the corner while Auguste snores.

The sound of voices swells and now we can hear footsteps.

Etienne pulls me to my feet and we stand side by side facing the stairs. I'm rigid with fear.

Heavy boots clump down them and then the small chamber is full of people again.

Gaston pushes his way through the crowd and stands with his hands on his hips in front of us. 'Thérèse has pleaded for you,' he says, 'and we don't want blood on our hands. Though, God knows, Auguste Moreau and his family have made us suffer.' He points to a young man with ragged hair. 'Joseph's child died for want of a little compassion from that bastard.'

'Then let me take Auguste away,' says Etienne. 'You'll never be troubled by him again.'

There is silence while Gaston glances at the others. One by one, they nod their heads and I let out my breath very slowly.

'If we see any of you again,' says Gaston sternly, 'you'll be hung up by your ankles from the clock tower. We'll disembowel you and make you eat your own hearts. Is that understood?'

Etienne nods.

One of the men kicks Auguste until he squeals assent.

Gaston unlocks the iron gate and two men drag Auguste to his feet and frogmarch him up the stairs. Etienne is surrounded next and then Grandmother Moreau and I are bundled after them. I trip and panic for a moment as the press of bodies threatens to engulf me, but all at once we are in the corridor and I gasp for breath before we are off again, jostled from all sides.

Grandmother Moreau is weeping as she stumbles along and I reach for her hand.

More and more villagers and servants arrive until the corridor is jam-packed. Men on either side of me lift me by my elbows so that my feet barely touch the ground and Grandmother Moreau's hand slips from my grasp. She looks over her shoulder at me with terror in her violet eyes as she's carried away by the mob.

A woman's voice starts to sing the unofficial anthem of the revolutionaries as we're swept along.

'*Ah! ça ira, ça ira, ça ira.*'

The song echoes in my head with every step we take. 'Ah! It'll be fine, it'll be fine, it'll be fine.' My vision is spotted and I'm dizzy.

The horde, trebled in numbers now, bursts through a door and surges into the light outside.

'*Ah! ça ira, ça ira, ça ira.*'

I gulp in deep breaths of fresh air. The mass isn't so closely pressed now and I regain a little equilibrium, but the singing grows in volume as more people join in.

'Where are we going?' I shout. The men to either side ignore me as they sing along with the refrain.

'*Ah! ça ira, ça ira, ça ira.*'

We reach the stables and gather in the yard. An ancient, swaybacked Percheron horse is taken out of his box and hitched up to a rotting wooden cart. Hands lift me up as if I'm on the crest of a wave and thrust me into the cart.

'*Ah! ça ira, ça ira, ça ira.*' The singing reaches a crescendo.

A moment later Etienne is sprawling at my feet and then a weeping Grandmother Moreau is lifted up high and thrown in after us. She lands in a crumpled heap and Etienne and I pull her on to the bench seat beside me.

'*Ah! ça ira, ça ira, ça ira,*' roars the crowd.

I put my hands over my ears but still the singing reverberates in my head. The cart jolts as people push against it. I see the girl we met in the kitchen, with her eyes shut and her head thrown back as she sings, completely swept along by the moment.

Two men clamber on to the cart and tie our wrists with rope,

300

lashing them to the wooden seat so tightly that we cannot escape.

A terrified scream erupts over the clamour.

Etienne leans against me and nods. I follow his line of sight and see Auguste flailing his arms as a sack is pulled roughly over his face. Then his hands are tied behind his back and a noose looped over his head.

'What are they doing?' I shout.

The man called Gaston ties the other end of the noose to the rear of the rickety cart. Then he holds up his hands and shouts for silence.

Gradually, the singing dies away, leaving my ears ringing.

'A fitting mode of transport for these aristocrats, don't you think?' he says.

'A tumbril would be better!' calls out one of the women.

A ripple of laughter runs through the crowd.

'Joseph?' Gaston beckons to the father of the dead child, who pushes his way towards him. 'In memory of your son,' he says, handing him a horsewhip.

Joseph takes the whip and looks at the hooded figure with burning hatred. 'For my son,' he echoes, and then raises the whip, bunching the muscles in his arms.

Grandmother Moreau lets out a desperate cry. 'Don't!'

The whip lashes across Auguste's back and he utters a yell of shock and outrage. Joseph's hand falls three more times and Auguste sags to his knees, his screams of agony subsiding into sobs. Blood trickles from his lacerated shirt.

'One for each year of my son's life,' says Josef. 'I'm a more merciful man than you.'

Gaston drags the moaning Auguste to his feet and pulls off the hood. 'Now it's up to you to save your own life,' he says, face twisted in an ugly smile.

Another man whacks the big grey horse on the rump. It snorts and tosses its head as the cart jerks forwards.

'Etienne!' I cry. 'Look at Auguste!'

Gaston shouts encouragement to the horse, grabs its bridle and runs alongside as it begins to trot.

The cart bumps violently over the cobbles and we're knocked together. Auguste stumbles along behind, his mouth wide open in a silent scream. The noose around his neck stretches in a straight line to the rear of the cart.

Etienne struggles to free his wrists but the knots are too tightly tied.

The people whistle and jeer, throwing clods of horse dung at Auguste.

Unused to physical exercise, he's panting for breath and nearly trips over but rights himself just in time.

I look at Etienne in horror. 'If he falls he'll be dragged by his neck. He'll hang!'

The crowd whoop and yell, smacking the horse's flanks until it rolls its eyes in terror and begins to trot even faster.

We rumble along the carriage drive with the crowd running beside us, all shrieking abuse. Joseph jogs along behind, flicking the whip across Auguste's back from time to time.

He screams every time he is lashed and heaps curses upon his tormentors until his breath runs out. Scarlet-faced, he concentrates on staying upright.

Gaston leads the horse just fast enough to prolong Auguste's agony.

Grandmother Moreau moans and calls out to her son but he is oblivious to her cries.

At last we reach the gateposts and Gaston pulls the cart to a shuddering halt.

Unable to stay upright any longer, Auguste collapses to the ground, sobbing.

Several men gather him up and throw him in the cart behind us. One of the men spits on him and I stare fascinated as the gobbet slides gently down his face, mixing with his own tears and snot.

Then Gaston jumps on to the cart and leans towards me, brandishing a knife.

Frozen, I cannot even scream.

But he reaches for my left wrist and saws through the rope binding it to the seat. I whimper as the knife nicks my skin. My right wrist remains tied.

Gaston pushes his face towards me. 'If you ever show yourselves here again we'll flay the flesh from your bones and feed it to the fish in the moat. May you all burn in Hell! Now get out of our sight!'

The cart rocks as Gaston jumps off. He throws the reins into my lap and slaps the horse on its rump again. The crowd jeers and cat-calls but I see Thérèse lift her hand in farewell to me.

The cart rolls forward and I snatch up the reins as we quickly gather speed down the steep hill and career along the winding lane towards the village.

Auguste writhes in agony as he's thrown about on the floor of the cart and Grandmother Moreau shrieks as she is rocked from side to side.

I trap the reins between my knees and stretch out with my left hand to press the brake lever on my right but it's just out of reach. I push Grandmother Moreau unceremoniously out of the way and lean over as far as I can, stretching out my fingers, but I still can't reach it. The reins slip through my knees.

'Hold tight, Madeleine!' warns Etienne, as I snatch them up again. He lifts his knee as high as he can and crashes his booted foot again and again on to the slatted wood of our seat.

I manage to keep the cart in the centre of the lane as it barrels along but as we round a sharp bend we teeter for one agonising moment on two wheels.

Etienne throws his weight to the left and the cart regains its balance and crashes to the ground with a bone-shaking thud. The horse rears up, whinnying in terror, and gallops off, dragging the cart behind at break-neck speed.

Brambles slash at our faces as we hurtle down the hill along a narrow lane and Grandmother Moreau screams in terror.

Etienne finally smashes through the slats of the seat, which collapses under us so that we tumble to the floor. Pulling his wrists free of the splintered wood, he launches himself over me and Grandmother Moreau and drags on the brake lever with both hands. There is the scream of metal upon metal and sparks fly up from the wheels.

I pull hard on the reins and a moment later the cart comes to a shuddering halt.

Chapter 31

We remain at the nearby inn for several days while the wounds on Auguste's back begin to heal. He is not at all grateful to me as I bathe and dress the stripes on his fat, white body, and as each day passes I learn to loathe him a little more.

'I shall return to Château de Lys, burn down the village and have the servants flogged,' he pronounces.

'And who do you think will assist you?' asks Etienne, goaded beyond endurance at last. 'Not I, nor anyone else of my acquaintance. Think yourself lucky that your niece has interceded for you. I would just as soon have left you in the dungeon so that the servants could ram a red hot poker up your arse.' He strides from the room and slams the bedchamber door so hard that bits of plaster fall down like snow.

After supper that evening I sit by the open window in the dining room of the inn, reading in the newspaper disturbing stories of rioting and political unrest in Paris. I keep half an eye on the street outside, glancing up every time I hear the clatter of horses' hooves.

Etienne has not been seen since he stormed out of Auguste's bed-chamber.

Grandmother Moreau sits at an adjacent table, playing piquet with Babette. They have formed an unlikely comradeship, which relieves my conscience as I don't feel obliged to entertain her myself. I have tried to talk to her about Papa but she simply shakes her head and says that it was all too long ago. I'm deeply saddened and disappointed that there is no warmth of affection between us.

I stare listlessly out of the window. A large black horse is crossing the square and I sit up straight as I realise that the rider is Etienne.

A short while later he enters the dining room, bows to Grandmother Moreau, and after a brief exchange of pleasantries comes to stand, ramrod straight, before me. 'I apologise,' he says. 'My behaviour earlier today was inexcusable.'

'Not at all,' I say. 'If you hadn't spoken to Auguste in that way I should have been obliged to do so myself.'

'I went out with Diable,' says Etienne in a low voice as he glances at Grandmother Moreau, 'to ride off my temper.'

'I should have liked to have done the same,' I say, 'instead of sitting here in a stuffy inn, fuming and reading about atrocities.' I sigh. 'I never imagined that the Revolution would bring such horror with it.'

'In Paris, they call the guillotine the National Razor,' he says. 'Any person associated in the smallest way with an anti-revolutionary act is being denounced. People betray family and friends to save themselves, and more heads are falling day by day.'

'Nothing feels safe any more.' Depression settles over my shoulders like a mantle. 'Shall we go out? I'm so tired of being cooped up indoors.'

The air is balmy as we amble around the town square and we nod to several other couples also enjoying a walk. Old men sit in groups outside the inn, drinking wine and arguing about politics, while a couple of dogs scrap over a bone under the tables. Everything appears so tranquil here it's hard to believe that this is a country in the grip of war.

Crossing the square we take the road behind the church until we come to a bridge. We lean on the sun-warmed stone and watch the river flowing below. The evening light slants low across our vision and the sky is streaked with orange.

'The nights are beginning to draw in,' I say. 'It's almost autumn.'

'There's a certain *tristesse* as the summer fades,' says Etienne, echoing my own feelings.

A little of the day's tension disappears as I watch a duck paddling slowly downstream.

'Is Auguste well enough to travel yet?' asks Etienne.

'If you can stand to listen to him moaning.'

A smile flickers across Etienne's face. 'I'm anxious to fulfil my promise and escort him and his mother to England as soon as I can. The grapes will be ready in two weeks and I must return in time.'

I bow my head. 'I'm so sorry, Etienne, that my family are causing you to face such a hazardous journey.' The worry of it knots my stomach. 'I don't know how you found it in your heart to help Auguste.'

'Don't you?' Etienne's dark eyes are gazing steadily at me. 'I should have thought it was obvious.'

Slowly, warmth rises in my cheeks. It's impossible for me to look away.

He reaches out and covers my hand with his and I study his long fingers and his clean, oval nails, remembering how he held me in his arms all night in the dungeon and soothed my fears.

'Madeleine, you must know that you have captured my affections,' he says in a low voice. 'The journey to England will be fraught with danger and who knows what will happen? My heart is too full of you to go away and say nothing.'

'Etienne . . .' I whisper.

He holds up his hand. 'I know. You love Jean-Luc.' He shrugs.

'How could you not? He has always been able to make women fall in love with him.'

My heart is fluttering and bumping against my ribcage. 'I wish you had told me about your wife,' I blurt out.

'Isabelle?' Etienne frowns. 'But you knew about her. The scandal had reached as far as Lady Georgiana's salon in London.'

'But I believed she was dead. You never mentioned her to me. Ever!' Suddenly I'm white hot with anger. 'You knew I was falling in love with you and you never told me that Isabelle is probably still alive! Jean-Luc informed me, as a friend, because he thought it right I should hear the truth.'

Etienne releases my hand. 'I thought you already knew.' His voice is bleak. 'Besides, when I realised you had fallen in love with him, there seemed little point in disclosing my feelings for you.'

Briefly, I remember the unsettling scene in the stable yard when Etienne returned from his travels to find me in Jean-Luc's arms.

'No, I hadn't fallen in love with him,' I say. 'Though I did try to, it was hopeless when I already loved you.'

Etienne draws in his breath sharply and reaches for me, sudden joy transforming his face.

I move back, out of his reach. 'Will you tell me about Isabelle now?'

His hands fall to his sides. 'She was beautiful . . .'

'Madame Viard showed me her portrait.'

'Did she now?' He sighs. 'I moved it upstairs because her eyes appeared to follow me. I wasn't sure if she was mocking me or trying to tell me I'd failed her.'

'What was she like, Etienne?'

He looks out over the river, remembering. 'My mother chose her for me and I wasn't unhappy with her choice at first. But Isabelle wanted to live in Paris, which caused great difficulties between us. I grew tired of the endless quarrelling but, even so, I hoped that in time we might have grown fond of each other. She was accomplished and elegant but her foremost duty was to provide me with an heir, a son to inherit Château Mirabelle.'

Inside, part of me is singing. Accomplished and elegant Etienne's wife might have been, but he doesn't sound like a man in love. I look out over the river where a cloud of midges hovers. I watch them as they dance above the water while I summon the courage to ask the question that has to be asked. For good or bad, I have to know. I take a deep breath. '*Did* you murder her, Etienne?'

He looks at me, all expression wiped from his face.

I stare straight back into his eyes. 'Did you?'

He's silent for an aeon and it's at this moment that I understand I will still love him no matter what he tells me.

'Do you think I did?' he asks, pain etched into his face.

I don't answer him straightaway. I remember how he and Papa laughed together as they shared a bottle of wine, how he gave Sophie and me a home at a time of crisis, how he cared for the people on his estate and how deeply he wanted a son. It's as if the veil of doubt has finally been lifted and now I can see the truth.

A heavy weight falls from my shoulders. 'No,' I say. 'Of course not.'

He lets out his breath in a long sigh. 'But people talk and half the villagers still believe I killed her.'

'What do you think happened?'

'That's the most terrible thing. I have no idea. Isabelle had become ... ' Etienne shakes his head. 'Evasive. We always had different interests. Painting and music occupied her and she wasn't interested in the workings of the estate. But she became unusually light-hearted and sometimes I heard her singing to herself. I wondered if she'd found a lover. Then one day she told me that she was expecting a child.'

Jealousy slices into me. 'The news you'd been hoping for,' I say.

Etienne bows his head over his clasped hands. 'She was happy for once and I was ecstatic. But then, a day later, she simply disappeared.

I looked everywhere. All the villagers and servants turned out to help and we searched every nook and cranny of the château and the estate.' He runs his hands through his hair, leaving it sticking up. 'I even dragged the lake.'

'It must have been a dreadful time for you.'

'Not as bad as what was to follow. It was then that the rumours began that she'd had a lover and that I'd killed her in a fit of jealousy. For a while it was as if everyone was whispering about me. A room would fall silent if I entered. It was torment. I couldn't sleep or eat.' Etienne's complexion is ashen. 'And the child Isabelle carried. Was it mine or not? How could I be sure any more?'

'And you never discovered where she went?'

He shakes his head. 'I made enquiries at all the nearby towns and offered reward money in all the inns and posting houses for news of her. Not a trace of her. Nothing.'

I see the anguish in his eyes.

He reaches blindly for my hand. 'But if losing Isabelle was terrible,' he says in a low tone, 'it was nothing compared to the agony of falling in love with you and knowing that we can have no future together.' He turns my hand over and traces the blue veins of my wrist with one fingertip until I shiver. 'I may never be free to marry you.'

The terrible words hang in the air between us and it's all I can do not to weep.

The sun has almost dipped below the horizon now and a cool breeze has sprung up. Unbearably sad, I shiver and rub my arms. 'We'd better return to the inn,' I say.

The lamps are lit when we arrive and Grandmother Moreau and Babette are tidying away the cards before going to bed.

'Madame, we will leave tomorrow morning,' Etienne says to Grandmother Moreau. 'Please inform your son of my decision.'

She inclines her head in assent. 'I bid you goodnight, Mr d'Aubery, and you too, Mademoiselle Moreau.'

Babette follows her upstairs.

Etienne draws me away. 'Madeleine, for all that your grandmother is so proud, she is an old lady and too frail to ride. I must convey her to the coast in my carriage. Besides, it's wiser to keep Auguste out of sight as much as possible. I'm not comfortable having to abandon you in this way and it leaves the question of whether you prefer to stay at the inn until I come back for you or if you and Babette will feel safe returning to Château Mirabelle on the diligence?'

'We'll return on the public coach. It stops here at the inn so please don't look so worried, Etienne.'

'Then sleep well.' He turns my hand over, kisses the palm then folds my fingers over the kiss. 'Until the morning.'

I awake, heavy-eyed, to find that it is raining. Outside in the square the church clock chimes and I hurriedly wash and dress.

Downstairs Auguste and his mother are seated in the dining room with Etienne and Babette, their breakfast nearly finished. I notice that Auguste wears one of Etienne's coats, the buttons straining across his flabby stomach.

'I'm still not sure that I wish to go to London,' says my uncle, ignoring my presence. 'I went there once as a young man and found it a most disagreeable place.'

'Less disagreeable than Paris,' says Etienne shortly, 'at least if you want to keep a head on your shoulders.'

'But you say you will take us to other nobles in the same plight as ourselves?' asks Grandmother Moreau.

Etienne nods. 'The other *émigrés* will advise you on how to find lodgings and employment …'

'Employment!' Auguste nearly chokes on his bread.

Etienne raises his eyebrows. 'How else are you going to afford your lodgings? Or do you have funds in London?'

'Since we have no more than the clothes we stand up in and

311

currently rely upon your charity, we will do what we have to do,' says Grandmother Moreau, putting a restraining hand on her son's arm. 'Won't we, Auguste?'

I'm pleasantly surprised that she is standing up to him, in however small a way.

Half an hour later Etienne waits to accompany Babette and myself to the diligence while I say goodbye to Auguste and my grandmother.

'Madeleine, I do thank you for coming to our rescue,' says Grandmother Moreau. 'We had no reason to expect your help, even though our plight was so desperate.'

Her eyes are anxious and I'm filled with sorrow for what might have been. Impulsively, I lean forward and kiss her papery old cheek.

Her eyes fill with tears and she whispers, 'You are so very like Philippe.'

I turn to Auguste and force myself to say, 'I wish you well in your new life.'

He ignores my outstretched hand. 'Once the troubles are over I shall reclaim my birthright,' he says, scowling, 'and then those peasants will rue the day they insulted me!'

To hell with him!

'Shall we go?' says Etienne. He picks up my holdall and offers me his arm.

A little while later we shelter from the rain under the gallery in the courtyard waiting for the diligence. The sky is as leaden as my mood and drizzle patters down on the cobbles.

'Babette,' says Etienne, 'will you run to the baker's and see what you can find for yourself and your mistress on the journey?' He hands her a fistful of coins. 'And you are to keep the remainder in recognition of your discretion over what you have seen and heard on this journey.'

Babette looks at the gold coins resting in the palm of her hand and her mouth drops open. She bobs a curtsey. 'Thank you, M'sieur but I wouldn't have said anything anyway.'

'Off you go then, before the diligence arrives.'

'That was kind of you,' I say, after she has gone.

'Madeleine, will you be my ears and eyes in the vineyard?'

'Of course I will.'

'All being well, I'll stay at the house in Paris for a day or two on my return.' He smiles faintly. 'I shall have to justify my disappearance from home by the sale of a decent quantity of this year's vintage. And I'll take the opportunity to speak to Dr Dubois about finding a good home for Marianne.'

'I can hardly bear to think of giving her up,' I say, 'but I believe it is for the best. I shall pray that your crossing is uneventful and that Auguste isn't too offensive.'

'If he is, he may find himself swimming across the Channel,' Etienne says, his eyes gleaming with amusement.

Suddenly fear gets the better of me. 'Etienne, what if there are warships ...'

He touches a finger to my lips. 'Hush, Madeleine! It's no use worrying about something that may not happen.'

'I couldn't bear it if ...' My voice trails away as I swallow back tears.

'If I should not return, go to Armand Dubois.' Etienne grips my shoulders. 'I trust him implicitly and he knows of your situation. He lives in Rue Dauphine near the Pont Neuf on the south side of the river. Promise me?'

I nod, unable to speak.

The mud-spattered diligence, drawn by six horses, lumbers into view through the archway and my heart turns over at the imminence of our departure. The ostlers hurry to change the horses as the passengers alight. Porters begin to heave trunks on to the roof and chain them in place.

Anxiously, I look out for Babette through the teeming courtyard and am relieved to see her hurrying towards us with a small loaf tucked under her arm.

I mount the steps into the coach and claim a seat by the window. Babette settles beside me.

Etienne stows the baggage in the net suspended overhead, while four other passengers jostle for a seat. I begin to feel sick with dread at the thought of our parting and the dangers he may experience afterwards.

Etienne descends from the coach and I open the window and lean out.

He reaches up for my hands and kisses my fingers. 'Goodbye, Madeleine. Safe journey.'

I cling to him, fearful again for his safety and that this might be the last time I see him.

'Be careful, Etienne, for my sake,' I whisper.

I keep my gaze fixed on him until we exit through the archway into the square. Then he is gone from my sight.

Chapter 32

The sun has appeared again by the time we arrive. I'm stiff and weary from hours of travel as we climb down from the cart I hired in Orléans to convey us on the last stage of our journey. Babette droops with exhaustion beside me as I pay the carter.

'Go straight home, Babette,' I say, conscious that she has spent little time with her mother since Victor was conscripted. 'We can manage perfectly well if you wish to stay with your mother for a few days.'

Her face is lit by a wan smile. 'Thank you, Mademoiselle.' She bobs a curtsey and hurries away as I let myself into the house.

Sophie is in the garden and hugs me with a squeal of delight. 'I missed you,' she says.

'And how is Marianne?'

'Asleep.' My friend leads me to the wicker cradle under the apple tree.

Marianne lies on her side, her plump cheeks flushed with sleep and one little fist pressed to her chin. I stroke the peach-soft skin of her forehead very gently so as not to wake her. 'She's so beautiful,' I whisper.

'Isn't she? But come and tell me all the news! How was your journey? Is Etienne with you? Did you find your grandmother?'

It pleases me to see the old Sophie again, with her dimples flashing and her brown eyes full of laughter. 'Let me start from the beginning...'

'You and Etienne were both so brave,' she says, half an hour later.

I nod while anxiety gnaws at me. 'I pray they cross the sea without being blown up by a warship or being denounced as spies.'

Sophie glances over my shoulder. 'Here's Jean-Luc,' she says. 'I'll go inside while you talk to him.'

I rise to meet him and find myself swept up against his broad chest. He kisses both my cheeks and lowers me to the ground again. 'Jacques told me you'd returned on a common cart. Why didn't you come and find me?'

'I've only been back a little while.'

'And is your grandmother well again?'

'As well as an old lady can be.'

'But where is the carriage?'

'In Paris with Etienne,' I say. I'd had plenty of time to prepare my story whilst travelling. 'He intended to collect me from my grandmother's home on his way back but, once I realised that the severity of her illness had been greatly exaggerated, I wanted to return to Château Mirabelle straight away. So Babette and I came by the diligence.'

Jean-Luc flashes his strong teeth in a wide smile. 'So you couldn't wait to see me again?'

I lower my eyes modestly. Better he should think that than learn the truth. 'What's happening at the vineyard?'

'The grapes will soon be ripe. I've arranged a party for the workers in a couple of days' time.' He shrugs. 'It's important to keep them sweet, don't you think? But will Etienne return for the harvest?' Jean-Luc shakes his head. 'Is he really in Paris? I don't understand why he would go now, when he should be monitoring

316

the grapes every day. It's far too soon to find buyers for the new wine and we've already sold most of the previous vintages to cover some of the debts.'

'Debts?' I look at him sharply.

'There are the new taxes and we're paying more generous wages than before. He really should be here. There are whispers . . .'

'What whispers?'

He sighs. 'The villagers are in a sullen mood and there's a growing lack of respect for Etienne. He needs to be very careful. For all that he professes to believe in equality, he's of noble blood, and I believe his frequent absences are a cover to help members of the nobility flee the country.'

'What makes you think that?' I ask, suddenly wary.

'He made no great secret of it a few years ago but I sincerely hope he isn't continuing such ill-judged pursuits. If Mayor Prudhomme should suspect that Etienne is a traitor to the Revolution or, worse still, a spy . . .'

'Of course he isn't a spy!' My heart begins to beat faster.

'How can you know?'

'He . . . he cares too much for the estate to take any risks. And he's sure to return soon.'

Jean-Luc sighs. 'Etienne doesn't confide in me like he used to. It's time he accepted that the changes brought about by the Revolution have seen the end of the *ancien régime* for ever. Madeleine, you would tell me if you thought he was playing a traitor's game, wouldn't you?'

'He isn't!' I say.

Jean-Luc's eyes bore into me but I don't allow myself to flinch. 'I must go,' he says. 'Maman has dinner waiting for me.'

'I'll walk to the gate with you.'

As we part he kisses my cheeks again. 'I simply want to protect you, Madeleine,' he says. 'Don't forget that.' He walks off along the path.

I close my eyes for a moment, while my heart bangs against my ribs, then return inside.

Sophie is waiting for me in the hall. 'Was Jean-Luc pleased to see you?'

I nod.

'Maddy?' Sophie grips my wrist. 'I've been thinking. I love it here. I don't want to return to England. Charles ...'

'But what about Henry?' I ask.

She swallows. 'I'm going to ask Etienne to help me. If he can take your uncle and grandmother to England, he can take me.'

'It's dangerous,' I say flatly. 'His friends died when they made the crossing. We don't even know if Etienne will return. Besides, you're still nursing Marianne and she's too tiny to risk exposing her to such a voyage.'

'But next spring, you could look after her for me.' Sophie sticks out her chin. 'I'm going to fetch Henry and bring him here.'

'Are you mad? Charles will come after you.'

She shakes her head. 'Not if he doesn't know that I'm the one who took Henry. Maddy, I'm happy for the first time in years. Or I would be if only I could have both my children at my side. We can stay here if you marry Jean-Luc ...'

'I can't.'

She looks at me with imploring eyes. 'But, don't you see, that would solve all our difficulties? I took coffee with Madame Viard again while you were away and she indicated she'd approve if you and Jean-Luc made a match.'

I'm astonished. 'She hardly knows me.'

Sophie shrugs. 'You like Jean-Luc, don't you? And he'd look after you.'

'That's not enough for me,' I say, picturing Etienne's face.

'Please, Maddy! We haven't anywhere else to go. Perhaps, in time ...'

'No!'

She stares at me. 'Maddy, I'm so frightened. I *have* to find a way to keep Marianne and I *cannot* abandon Henry. The fear of losing either of my children is tearing me apart.'

'Sophie, don't make me responsible for your happiness at the expense of my own.' Suddenly I'm close to tears. 'How can I stay here, so close to Etienne, knowing he can never be mine?'

The following morning I rise late. Once I'm dressed I find Sophie sitting on a blanket in the garden with her sketchpad on her knee. Madeleine lies beside her and Minou is stretched out in the sun nearby.

'I'm sorry we quarrelled last night,' I say, sitting down beside her.

'I'm sorry, too. I shouldn't have asked it of you. Friends again?'

I cannot resist her infectious smile. 'Of course.'

She hugs me and I kiss her cheek.

'Have you been drawing?' I ask.

'Marianne was watching the butterflies,' she says, showing me her sketches of the baby.

I pick up Marianne who nods her little head as she focuses on my face. 'She's really trying to look at me,' I say, delighted.

'You love her, too, don't you?' says Sophie.

'How could I not?'

Sophie's face clouds over. 'It frightens me how much I love her. Promise me you'll always be her guide and friend as she grows up?'

'Of course, I will.' I kiss Marianne's red-gold curls and she yawns widely. Laughing, I replace her on the blanket. 'I'm going to see what's been happening at the vineyard.' I step back and see that the kitten is inquisitively licking Marianne's cheek. 'Oh! Look at Minou!'

Sophie squeals and shoos the cat away. She glances up at me, her cheeks dimpled as she laughs.

I wave farewell and set off.

The sun is hot on my back as I pass the *chai* and climb the hill between the vines. The grapes appear ripe now and are covered in a dusty bloom. Some of the leaves are already tinged with gold, reminding me that soon autumn will be here and it will be time to open the schoolroom again.

I walk between the rows of new vines planted to the west side of the vineyard and see that they are growing strongly. The ground under the plants is still moist from the recent rain.

Marcel Viard is working at the other end of the row but I have no intention of engaging in conversation with him. As I retreat he straightens up, shades his eyes against the sun and stares at me. His unsmiling stare makes me uneasy but I lift a hand to wave. He doesn't respond but simply turns away.

I continue my tour but see only a few women working. Smiling a greeting, I approach Claudette Porcher and Bertille Dufour.

'So, you're back, I see,' says Claudette. She straightens up. 'We heard you went off on a jaunt with the master.'

My smile fades and warmth rises in my cheeks at the blatant hostility in her tone. 'I went to visit my sick grandmother.'

'The master never came back with you. Had a quarrel with him, did you?' asks Bertille, a knowing smile on her lips.

'Monsieur d'Aubery went on business to Paris while Babette and I stayed with my grandmother.' Damn the woman, why does she make me sound so defensive?

Claudette raises her eyebrows. 'Ah, well, I believe you, though thousands wouldn't.' She turns her back on me.

Bertille looks me up and down. 'We know your sort,' she says. 'For your own good, I hope you don't have the nerve to show your face at the vineyard feast this afternoon. You may act like a lady but we know what you are and don't want you teaching our children no more.' She spits on the ground near my feet.

I gasp at the insult but it's obvious that it's pointless protesting my innocence. I walk away, my heart pounding with anger, the women's mocking laughter echoing in my ears.

I'm still seething as I stride down the hill again and don't see Jean-Luc, elegant in a cornflower blue coat, lounging in the doorway of the *chai*, until he calls out to me. 'What's the matter, Madeleine?

'I appear to be the source of some malicious gossip amongst the village women.'

'Ah!' Jean-Luc runs a finger over his chin. 'I'd hoped you wouldn't hear that.'

Suddenly I feel close to tears. 'They said they don't want me to teach their children. Bringing literacy to the villagers is the most useful thing I can do to help them.'

'Madeleine, perhaps it *is* best to delay resuming lessons for a while, at least until the rumours fade away. There's a deal of turmoil amongst the villagers now and I suggest you avoid the vineyard, too. Perhaps you can find something else to occupy your time?'

'I've no intention of taking up some fanciful pursuit like shell-work, if that's what you mean.' There's a distinctly acid tone to my voice.

Jean-Luc holds up his hands. 'I'm simply concerned for your safety. Weren't you writing a treatise on education for girls? Madeleine, take my advice and keep within doors for the next few days, will you?'

I glance at him sharply. 'Why?' There's something in his tone that makes me apprehensive.

He frowns. 'I can't quite put a finger on it but there's something hostile in the air, as if the villagers scent blood. And you and Sophie are new to the area. Perhaps if Etienne were here he'd be able to settle things but his continuing absence feeds the flame of speculation.'

'I've already felt that hostility today.'

'So heed my warning!'

I nod. 'I've left some of my books in the schoolroom,' I say. 'I need them if I'm to work on my treatise.'

'Then I'll come with you to fetch them.'

I'm grateful for his presence close to my side as we walk towards the château as it suddenly seems as if every servant we pass stops to stare at me. We enter by the servants' door and Jean-Luc accompanies me up the back staircase.

On the landing, Madame Viard is closing the door to her apartment. She smiles as we approach.

'Don't be late for dinner, *chéri*,' she says to Jean-Luc. 'You shall have your favourite veal *ragoût*.'

Jean-Luc puts his arm around her and hugs her to his side. 'I won't be late, Maman.'

She turns to me. 'Mademoiselle Moreau, perhaps you would care to join us for dinner tomorrow?' Madame Viard's expectant smile is warm.

Surprised, I hesitate. Perhaps Sophie is right and Jean-Luc's mother is match-making. I'm about to give a polite refusal but then decide it might be sensible to find out more about the cause of the unrest. 'Thank you,' I say, 'I should like that very much.'

Madame Viard nods and makes her way downstairs and we go through the servants' door. We walk down the deserted corridor and at last reach the schoolroom. Jean-Luc ushers me inside.

The air is stale and he unbolts the shutters and throws open a window.

I take the books I need from the large oak cupboard. The slates are neatly stacked inside, ready for the children to resume their lessons. Standing still for a moment, I fancy I hear echoes of their voices in the silence.

'I'm saddened that the mothers won't allow me to help their children any more,' I say, suddenly close to tears.

'I promise you, better times are coming.' Jean-Luc takes the books from my arms and puts them on the table. Then he leans towards me and presses his lips against mine.

I freeze. I don't want this but I have no wish to antagonise him.

He laughs. 'Still so modest, Madeleine?' He cups my face in his

322

hands. 'You have such extraordinarily beautiful violet eyes. They ensnared me from the very first and hold me still in thrall. I cannot blame Etienne for falling in love with you since you would tempt any man,' he whispers, and kisses my lips again.

I pull back but he's captured my wrists.

'Madeleine, I was going to wait for an appropriately romantic moment but I shall wait no longer.'

'Jean-Luc . . .'

'Shhh!' He touches a finger to my lips. 'I never thought to put my neck in the matrimonial noose until I met you, Madeleine. You have made my desire to remain free evaporate into thin air. I must have you.'

I'm filled with dismay by his declaration. How could I ever have considered marrying a man who appears to think I wish to entrap him and who proposes in such an unromantic way? I must put an end to this at once. 'Please, Jean-Luc . . .'

'Madeleine, I have such plans for us, far greater than you can imagine!' He pulls me into his arms and kisses me, his tongue flicking into my mouth.

I shrink away but I'm trapped against the heavy cupboard.

He frowns and pinches my chin between his finger and thumb, forcing me to look at him. Then he smiles. 'So, you want me to coax you?'

'Please, release me,' I say, my voice quavering.

He bends his head and kisses me again.

I try to turn my head away but his hand is in my hair and he holds me fast, his tongue in my mouth again. Repulsion overwhelms me and I struggle to free myself but I'm no match for Jean-Luc's strength. Panicking, I clamp my teeth together over his tongue and bite down. I taste blood.

'You little vixen!' There's blood on his teeth.

I shudder at the sight of it. 'Please, Jean-Luc, you're frightening me!'

'Madeleine, be calm!' His grip on my arms grows tighter. 'My intentions are honourable.'

'Then release me!'

He lets me go. 'Tell me that you'll marry me?'

'No, I cannot!'

The smile fades. 'I'm not asking you to be my mistress, I'm proposing marriage. Both Mayor Prudhomme and my mother have given their blessing. I have *chosen* you.'

I shake my head.

'You refuse me?'

His expression is incredulous and it is in that moment, as I look into his eyes, that I realise he is unhinged. Shock and disbelief ripple over me in an icy wave.

'You cannot!' He jams his forearm across my throat, shoving me back against the cupboard again. 'The daughter of a no-account schoolteacher refuses me, *me*, the estate manager of Château Mirabelle and a member of the Mayor's Convention? Don't you understand that I am a person of consequence?'

'Let me go!' It's hard for me to breathe and my eyes are watering from the effort.

His breath hisses between his lips. 'I see it now. It's Etienne, isn't it?' His face is so close to mine that I feel the fine spray of his saliva on my cheeks. 'Despite all I've told you, you still love him, don't you?'

His arm is across my windpipe and the breath rasps in my throat.

'I am taller and stronger than he. I have an education. I have danced attention and favour upon you. Tell me, what does Etienne have that I do not?'

I look wildly towards the door, hoping beyond hope that someone will save me.

'Is it the château?' he demands, and bares his teeth in a rictus grin. 'Of course it is! What girl would not have her head turned by such a place? Well, let me tell you, Madeleine, it won't be his for long.' He removes his arm from my neck and air fills my wheezing lungs again.

'What do you mean?' I croak.

'Hah!' Jean-Luc is triumphant. 'Soon the château will be mine. It *is* mine by right. And when it's in my possession, then you will *beg* me to marry you.'

I fold my mouth in an obstinate line.

Fury flares in his eyes and he kisses me again, his teeth grinding painfully against my lips. His hands roam over my breasts and waist while I try to fight him off, but my cries only serve to anger him further.

'No one will hear you if you scream.' He bends to nip my throat and I pull his hair. He swats my hands away and tears at the neckline of my dress, ripping the muslin and exposing my breasts, barely covered by my chemise.

Suddenly he pulls back, uttering a muffled curse. 'What the hell is this?'

I catch my breath as I see he holds the moonstone ring in his hand.

Holding it up to the light, he examines the crest. 'Where did you get this?'

I refuse to meet his eyes.

Jean-Luc raises his hand and strikes me.

Pain reverberates through my skull. Stunned, I shake my head to clear the buzzing in my ears and a trickle of blood runs from my nose and drips on to my chemise.

'This is the Limours signet ring.' Jean-Luc raises his fist. 'I'll ask you again, where did you get this?'

I flinch away from him. 'It was my father's,' I whisper.

Jean-Luc's face blanches and he drops the ring as if it were a burning coal. '*Your father?* Your father is the lost heir, the one who stole the ring and ran away?'

Reluctantly, I nod, closing my hand over it.

'The story was that he went to England.'

I lower my eyes so that he cannot see the fear in them.

'Madeleine? By God, I see it all now. You're one of those arrogant aristocrats.' Jean-Luc shakes his head as if to clear his thoughts. 'And I remember that I heard you defending the British to the children, right here in this schoolroom! You didn't grow up in Lyon, did you? I wondered if there was something about the way you speak that didn't ring true ... You and Etienne are both spying for the British, aren't you?' He shakes me so hard my teeth rattle.

I hold my head up high. 'I'm not a spy and my father was the most honourable of men.'

The shock of the second blow, when it comes, sends me spinning into merciful darkness.

Chapter 33

My head is throbbing insistently, my throat hurts. I'm lying on the floor.

A shadow falls across me. 'So, you're awake,' says Jean-Luc. He pulls forward a chair and straddles it, arms folded on the backrest. He sighs heavily. 'Why did you have to make it all so difficult, Madeleine?'

My mouth is dry and my heart is thudding as I pull myself into a sitting position and lean against the wall. I'm filled with disbelief at this turn of events. 'I'm not a spy, Jean-Luc.'

He stands up abruptly and strides over to the window. 'I thought you'd jump at the chance of marriage to me. Even Maman approved of my choice of a wife.'

Something is worrying me. 'What did you mean when you said the château is yours by right?'

Jean-Luc chews his bottom lip. 'I hadn't thought ever to tell anyone the truth but it's been painful keeping it all to myself for so long.'

'Tell me!' I whisper, humouring him.

He begins to pace the floor. 'On my fifth birthday Maman took me to the library to see the old comte. He bent down and said, "And what have you to say for yourself, young Viard?"

'I looked around the library and asked, "Have you read all these books?" The comte laughed and said he hadn't but perhaps I would like to? I said that I would. A few months later I joined his sons for their lessons.'

I glance at the door, wondering if I can make a run for it.

'Some might say I was lucky to be given an education but they never had to bear the slights and insults that I did, a servant's child raised above his position. Our tutors thrashed me for small misdemeanours, whilst Laurent and Etienne were rarely punished.' He turns away. 'I didn't fit in anywhere,' he says, his voice bitter, 'being neither a gentleman nor a peasant. And Laurent, three years older than myself, made me miserable by continually taunting me with my lowly beginnings.'

I can almost find it in my heart to feel sorry for him. 'That must have been hard for you.'

'Don't interrupt!'

His voice is so harsh that I dare not speak again. I judge the distance to the door at the other end of the schoolroom but calculate I would never reach it before Jean-Luc caught me. Despair makes me shiver.

'By the time I was twelve years old the comte had elevated my mother from parlour maid to housekeeper and my father was overseer in the vineyard.'

Jean-Luc's gaze rests on me for a moment but I sense that he doesn't see me.

'It was one day when I was twelve and after my father had whipped me for some imagined misdemeanour that everything changed. I crept away to lick my wounds but later, as I returned to our apartment, I heard Maman scream.' Jean-Luc stops and stares at his feet.

'What happened?' I ask. I must keep him talking and persuade him to release me.

Jean-Luc starts as if I've awoken him from his reverie. 'I rushed into the sitting room to find my father raping Maman.'

I gasp. 'No child should witness such a terrible thing.'

'It *was* terrible,' he says. 'I grabbed the poker and hit him with it. Knocked him out cold. Maman was sobbing and as I bathed her bruises she told me the whole story. Thirteen years before, the comte, Etienne's father that is, had seduced her. When she realised she was pregnant she threatened to tell the comtesse unless he looked after her. His answer was to marry her off to Marcel Viard.'

My head aches and I struggle to think clearly. Then shock renders me speechless for a moment as I realise the implications of Jean-Luc's statement. 'So you are Etienne's half-brother?' I picture them both together but there is no obvious family likeness. 'Did no one suspect the truth?'

'Since the comte was not usually a philanderer,' says Jean-Luc, 'perhaps no one suspected.'

'It must have been a very unhappy situation for you and your mother.' A new escape plan has occurred to me. The tower door is a few paces away and the key is kept on the architrave above.

'Everything changed from that day,' says Jean-Luc. 'Once I knew that I was the comte's son I couldn't rest. Laurent and Etienne had everything to look forward to but all I could hope for was to be some kind of superior servant, like Maman.'

'That must have been galling for you.'

'It was.' He begins to pace up and down again. 'Then, when I was sixteen, Laurent and I decided to row to the island. I can picture him now, looking at me with that supercilious smile of his and saying, "Row faster, serf!"' Jean-Luc narrows his eyes at the memory. 'All the hidden hatred I felt for his patronising ways boiled up in me.'

I'm almost afraid to ask. 'What happened then?'

'It was over in minutes. I hit him with an oar, pushed him in the water and held him under while he drowned.'

I catch my breath at the casual way he tells me this and all at once I'm very afraid again.

'It was easy to explain a boating accident,' says Jean-Luc. 'Laurent had been drinking his father's wine and was fooling about. He banged his head on the side of the boat as he fell into the lake. I said I dived in to save him but it was too late.'

'I still don't understand.'

'So that made me the comte's eldest son,' says Jean-Luc. 'I worked hard at my studies and learned to be a gentleman. I was always charming and good-natured. I soon realised that the role of estate manager was an important one and would give me an element of control so I started to visit old Monsieur Auger in the estate office and make myself indispensable. When he retired I asked the comte to allow me to take over the position.' Jean-Luc smiles. 'And very lucrative it has been for me. Especially since Etienne had never been very clever at book-keeping.'

Outraged, I bite my lip.

'The next part of my plan didn't go so well.' He frowns. 'I decided, in view of my success, that I had become a son the comte should be proud of. So, since I was now his eldest child, I asked him to make me his heir.'

'And what did he say?'

Jean-Luc's expression is full of anguish as he remembers. 'He laughed at me.'

All at once I know what he's going to tell me and a cold shiver runs down my spine.

'I couldn't have him mocking me so . . .'

'There was a carriage accident?' I say.

'Clever girl!' Jean-Luc looks at me approvingly. 'The comte had recently bought himself a new curricle. A pretty thing, canary yellow with shiny black trim, the very latest design. It was simple for me to find out where he was to take it on its first excursion and to wait in the bushes until it passed by. A crow-scarer did the trick. The horses bolted and the curricle tipped over in the ford.'

I try not to picture the poor comtesse trapped under the coach in the water. 'What about Isabelle?'

'The marriage wasn't much of a success. I befriended her with a view to becoming her lover. It was imperative she didn't produce a legitimate heir and I planned her disgrace very carefully.'

'And *did* she fall into your arms?' I hold my breath.

'No,' he snaps. 'Condescending little bitch! She was attracted to me and we flirted a great deal so I had high hopes. One day I took her to the island for a picnic, hoping to seduce her with strawberries and champagne. She laughed when she realised my intentions and told me that she was already carrying Etienne's child.' Jean-Luc fixes me with a basilisk stare. 'Well, I couldn't allow the child to be born, could I?'

It's almost too much to comprehend but, despite the horror of his revelations, I have to ask. 'Did she die?'

'Oh, yes,' he says, in a light, conversational tone. 'Etienne had extended the west side of the vineyard that spring. Maman had the clever idea of burying her where the earth was already freshly turned.'

'Your *mother* helped you?'

'She always intended that I should take up my rightful place at Château Mirabelle.' He smiles. 'It amused me that Etienne took such pains to nurture the new plants and how well his care was rewarded. You may have noticed that the vines grow especially thick there?'

I close my eyes but the tears still seep out. Poor Isabelle! And poor Etienne, his life blighted by scandal and still tortured by the mystery of what had happened to his wife and unborn child.

'Maman soon spread the word about a mysterious horseman seen leaving the château on the day Isabelle disappeared,' says Jean-Luc. 'As long as she couldn't be found, Etienne wouldn't be able to marry again and produce a legitimate heir. And since he and Isabelle argued so often, others assumed he killed her in a fit of rage. It was really rather clever of us, wasn't it?'

331

'Devilishly clever.'

'And now the Revolution will complete my work for me. Once I expose Etienne as a spy, that will be the end of him and the château will be confiscated by the state.'

Terror bubbles in my chest. 'But then you couldn't inherit this property.' I'm willing him to walk to the other side of the schoolroom, to give me a chance of reaching the door to the tower.

'Once Etienne has been despatched, Mayor Prudhomme will listen favourably to my request to buy Château Mirabelle for a reasonable price. I've saved the funds from my careful manipulation of the accounts.'

'I thought you were in favour of the Revolution?'

Jean-Luc smiles. 'Only in so far as it furthers my own aims. And don't forget, half the blood that flows in my veins is noble.'

My fingers twitch with the urge to slap the complacent expression off his face. 'The villagers will never accept you in Etienne's place.'

'Oh, I think they will,' says Jean-Luc calmly. 'They're already angry and discontented. While Etienne has been away, I've discreetly let it be known that he has no intention of sharing the profits from the next vintage with the workers, as he promised.'

'You lying, misbegotten toad! You know that's not true! Look how hard he's worked . . .'

'Shut up!' Jean-Luc slaps my cheek and I gasp as my head jerks back. 'I thought I'd arranged Etienne's downfall when Prudhomme came to inspect the kitchens. Maman had given Madame Thibault a push in the right direction by letting her know where she could buy black-market flour, but it came to naught. It took me a while to realise how Etienne got out of that one. And you helped him, didn't you?' He grasps my shoulders and gives me a shake.

I will not look at him.

'So that brings me back to what to do with you,' he says. 'I think you'll rest very comfortably under the vines next to Isabelle, don't you? But there's still the little problem of Sophie and her brat. Once you've disappeared, I really can't allow her to tell people that you were with me this morning, can I?'

'Leave Sophie out of this!'

'Too late for that, I'm afraid. I could hand you both over to the mayor and tell him you're spies, but now I've told you how I brought the noble d'Aubery family to an end, I'm not prepared to risk you blabbing about it. No, I shall make it look as if you both ran away. And now it's time to set my plan in action.'

'What plan?' My teeth are chattering together with fear but I must find out what he has in mind.

'The peasants are increasingly resentful of Etienne. Maman and I did an excellent job of drip-feeding poisonous thoughts into their simple minds while you were both away. They're like a keg of gunpowder just waiting for a lighted taper.'

'What could you say that would make the villagers distrust him? He's always been such a good master.' I'm burning with outrage.

'It was a challenge,' says Jean-Luc, nodding in agreement, 'but Etienne used to travel regularly to London and now the villagers and servants are convinced he must be a spy. Combined with the knowledge that he intends to cheat them out of the profits from the wine, when he arrives here they'll either hang him or turn him over to the mayor.'

Jean-Luc walks to the window and I take the opportunity to draw my knees up, ready to push myself to my feet and run.

'It's nearly time for the party,' he says, taking out his pocket watch and glancing at it. 'It will take place in the dining room of the *château*, not the *chai*. The wine will flow freely, judiciously laced with brandy. Once the peasants are in their cups the petty grievances will rise to the surface and I shall be there to encourage them. It's so wrong that Etienne lives alone in a huge palace, eating off silver plates, with silk at the windows and gilded furniture, while the peasants struggle to survive in their mean little hovels, don't you think?'

'You seem to have it all worked out.' I cannot prevent the hatred I feel for him from showing in my eyes.

He scowls. 'I wanted you at my side as my chatelaine. I intended us to build a new dynasty together but you've proved yourself unworthy of me.' He turns to close and bolt the shutters.

Heart in my mouth, I grab the opportunity. I spring to my feet, tiptoe to the tower door and stretch up to fumble for the key on the architrave.

Behind me the shutter bolts grate home.

The key is in my hand! Fumbling, I shove it into the keyhole with trembling fingers.

The casements squeak as Jean-Luc pulls them shut . . . and then he bellows in rage.

The tower door swings open and I snatch the key from the lock.

Jean-Luc's footsteps pound across the room.

I slip through the doorway into the small, dark space, slam the door behind me and turn the key.

Blows rain down upon the other side.

Eyes tightly shut, I lean against it, gasping at each thump, terrified he'll break the door down. Then there is silence, except for the sound of Jean-Luc's heavy breathing.

'Madeleine!'

Knuckles pressed against my mouth, I say nothing.

'Very well,' he snaps. 'But it will be the worse for you when I return, so don't say I didn't warn you.'

A moment later I hear the sound of something heavy being dragged across the floor, which then thumps against the door. 'Don't forget, I'm coming back for you later!' His voice is muffled now and I remain frozen in fear, listening to his footsteps fading away. Then there is the sound of the schoolroom door slamming behind him.

I'm trapped as securely as if I were in a dungeon and panic grips me. I scream and beat on the door until my hands are bruised. At last

I sink to the ground with my arms folded over my face. My throat is raw and my cheeks sodden with tears.

The rackety tattoo of my heart slows a little and I lick my dry lips. If I can't exit through the door, I must go up the stairs into the turret room. Although I can't escape from my prison, at least there will be more space there. I will be able to breathe freely.

The winding stairs are so narrow that they brush my shoulders on both sides as I climb. Shuddering, I emerge into the small, circular chamber. Dust motes float in a shaft of light and I hurry to open one of the windows and lean out to draw in the fresh air.

The lake shimmers in the sunlight. On the opposite shore I see the house, with the gentle slope of the vineyard rising behind it. I yearn to be in the safety of the garden with Sophie and Marianne instead of trapped here in the tower like Rapunzel.

A movement in the distance catches my eye. Full of dread, I recognise the faraway figure of Jean-Luc in his cornflower blue coat as he walks up the path to the house. A moment later the front door opens and he goes inside. My stomach clenches in fear for Sophie and Marianne.

Helplessly, I continue to stare while tears roll down my cheeks. Now that I know how ruthless he is, I fear the worst.

Ten minutes later my breath catches in my throat when Jean-Luc emerges from the side gate. I watch him hurrying away along the lakeside path back towards the château until he is no longer in my view.

Time passes slowly as I agonise about Sophie and wrack my brains thinking of ways to outwit Jean-Luc when he comes back for me. Discarding every idea as impractical, it's impossible for me not to despair. I have no weapons and the turret room is bare.

At last exhaustion overtakes me. I sink to the floor and wrap my arms around my knees. My aching head begins to nod and I rest it upon my folded forearms. Before long, I sleep.

Chapter 34

When I awake, the light has already begun to fade. A fly is buzzing against one of the windows, as desperate to escape as I am. I open the casement and let it free. A breeze wafts in through the open casement, carrying with it a hint of smoke. Rooks are circling in the sky and settling into the chestnut trees as dusk approaches.

I remember Jean-Luc telling me that he and Etienne used to climb out of the turret window with their bows and arrows to shoot at the birds. I lean out over the rotting window frame and see there is a ledge eighteen inches wide some six feet under the window. It's a long way beneath it to fall to the ground. My heart begins to skip and flutter at the very thought of attempting to escape that way.

How did the youthful Jean-Luc and Etienne reach the ledge? I hang on to the worm-eaten mullion of the window, praying it won't splinter under my weight, and stretch right over the sill. Stone dragons embellish the walls of the tower, their wings spread and tails entwined. There are several bands of decorative stonework below the window, carved into a rope pattern. It is deep enough for a boy's, or a woman's, toes to find a foothold.

Either I can wait for Jean-Luc to arrive and hope there will be a chance for me to escape or I can climb out of the window. Either way I'll probably die. The villagers' party will soon be over and time is running out. Panic rises in me. I *have* to take the only choice that gives me a slim chance of survival.

I don't allow myself to think of what else might happen. I clamber on to the sill, my legs dangling over the edge. I roll on to my stomach, gripping the mullion so tightly that my knuckles turn white, while my feet flail around searching for the first foothold. I stub my toe and realise I've found it. I hook one arm around the mullion and loose the other hand, stretching below the sill until I can grab hold of a dragon's head.

Gradually, I lower myself over the sill, stretching down with my other foot until I find the next foothold. I snatch hold of the dragon's wing and, one foot after the other, work my way down until at last both feet are resting on the ledge. I face the stonework with my arms outstretched and fingers clawed. I begin to edge along, inch by inch. Flattened against the wall, my cheek is grazed by the abrasive stone. My eyes are closed. I dare not risk looking down.

Time ceases to have any meaning for me as I concentrate on my task. I hum '*Au clair de la lune*' as I step, crab-like, along the ledge, refusing to think of anything at all but Etienne's face when he crooned the melody to Marianne.

After an aeon my fingers touch a projecting piece of stone and I risk a fleeting glance sideways. A dragon! Above it is another tower, identical to the one I have left behind. I grasp the dragon's forked tail and shuffle closer. Using the beast's great, clawed foot as a step, I heave myself upwards until I can grab its wing. My feet find toeholds on the carved rope and I climb up until I'm facing a closed window. Humming loudly, I bang on the frame with my fist. It is as rotten as the one in the schoolroom turret but it doesn't budge.

The trick to staying sane is not to think of what might happen if I fall but to concentrate fiercely on just one second at a time. I continue to thump the window frame until the timber splinters and the casements swing inwards. I climb up the last foothold and launch myself over the windowsill. I land on the floor inside in an undignified, quaking heap. After a moment I pick myself up and take a deep breath.

This turret, although the same size as the one over the schoolroom, is an entirely different kettle of fish. The walls are lined with duck-egg blue silk and there is a soft rug on the parquet floor. An easel stands beside the window and paints are laid out on a side table. Can this be the turret above Isabelle's room?

I hurry down the spiral staircase and cautiously open the door. Isabelle's bedchamber is unchanged since my last visit. It's still and shadowed and there's a faint scent of roses. Her portrait still hangs on the silk-covered walls and I pause for a moment to look at it. She regards me with cool blue eyes but now, unless I'm being too fanciful, it seems to me that there is a hint of an encouraging smile lurking at the corners of her mouth. I smile back at her and then tiptoe across the thick carpet and let myself out into the silent corridor.

Stealthily, I continue until I come to the main staircase. I take the stairs two at a time but stop, panic-stricken, at the sound of laughter when I'm halfway down. Two women stagger across the hall, chattering excitedly, their arms piled high with silver dishes. A small boy trots behind, carrying a velvet cushion. I hold my breath but they don't see me.

After they have left by the front door I hurry down the rest of the stairs to the hall. The door to the dining room is ajar and a buzz of voices comes from within. Peering through the narrow gap I can see that the grand dining table is covered with the remains of Jean-Luc's promised feast. Several men are asleep with their heads on the table. Two small boys squabble as they have a tug-of-war with a large crystal vase, the flower arrangement trampled underfoot.

Shrill laughter comes from a knot of women intent on pulling down the silk curtains, and others are piling up the silver serving platters and wrapping them in their aprons to carry them away. Marcel Viard lies unconscious on the floor in a puddle of vomit, a bottle of brandy clasped in his fist.

Backing away, I cross the hall, slip out of the front door and run down the steps. Outside, it's dusk and the air is full of smoke. A great bonfire is blazing away in the centre of the knot garden, watched by a chattering crowd. The carriage drive is thronged with people running hither and thither. Paintings, furniture and ornaments are being passed out of the drawing-room windows and carried away by villagers. I seethe with anger as I realise that Jean-Luc's plan is succeeding. The estate workers have lost their allegiance to Etienne and are stripping the château in an orgy of avarice. There is nothing I can do except run away as fast as I can.

I come to a skidding halt on the gravel when I see that servants are pouring out of the full-length doors from the library, carrying armfuls of books and throwing them on the bonfire. Emile Porcher is amongst the watching crowd, whooping in delight as a shower of orange sparks shoots up into the darkening sky.

Rage at the desecration of Etienne's books makes me step forward again but then my blood turns to ice in my veins. Jean-Luc is standing with his back to me, rallying the crowd.

Waving his fist in the air, he shouts, 'We must never allow that traitorous oppressor Etienne d'Aubery to return to Château Mirabelle. No longer shall you endure him sitting like a king in his castle while your children starve!'

Bertille Dufour steps forward. 'He's a murderer, everyone knows that, and if the mayor doesn't hang him, we will!' she yells.

'And that Moreau whore of his by his side,' shrieks Claudette Porcher.

'He's a spy,' shouts Jean-Luc, 'and traitors to the Republic deserve to die!'

Terrified that they'll see me, I turn tail and sprint in the opposite direction.

I'm out of breath when I reach the house. I throw open each door in turn, shouting Sophie's name, but there is no sign of her. I peer into every cupboard and look under the beds but she is nowhere to be found.

I stand stock still at the top of the stairs, holding my breath and listening. The silence sings in my ears. I can't leave until I've found her. Perhaps she's hiding in the woods with Marianne, waiting for me to come and find her?

Hastily, I pack a bag, cramming in clean shifts, combs and shoes, all mixed up with a supply of baby napkins and nightgowns. As an afterthought I throw in Sophie's sketchbook before changing my torn and filthy dress.

As I close the kitchen door behind me, I catch a glimpse of something white under the apple tree. I squint into the gloaming. Hesitating a moment, I hurry to investigate. My heart lifts as I see that Sophie is sitting on the rug, her back against the trunk of the apple tree and her head bowed.

'Sophie! I've been so worried. Didn't you hear me calling you?' She doesn't respond and sudden apprehension makes my stomach lurch as I realise there's something about her posture that isn't right. Crouching down, I touch her shoulder.

Her head lolls and she slips sideways.

Despite the failing light I see that livid bruising marks her throat like some terrible necklace. Crying out, I cup her chin in my hands and lift her face.

Her swollen tongue protrudes through blue lips and she stares back at me with bloodshot, lifeless eyes.

Horror and disbelief overwhelm me. I let out a howl of anguish and gather her cold body into my arms, rocking her against my breast. Sophie has been my friend for nearly all my life and I cannot imagine a world without her.

I don't know how much time passes. Except for the silvery moonlight, it's dark when I wipe my eyes and lay her carefully on the ground. I close her eyelids, fold her hands over her breast and cover her with the blanket, tucking her up as carefully as if I were putting a child to bed.

And then I remember Marianne.

Frantically, I run around the garden, looking under bushes and even disturbing the chickens in the coop, but I cannot find her. I haven't heard her cry, not once. Defeated, I can only assume that Jean-Luc has strangled the baby too and concealed her tiny body. My hatred for him burns with a steady, white-hot flame.

I must lose no more time in warning Etienne that Jean-Luc has betrayed him. My best chance of finding him must be at his house in Paris. If I can reach Orléans I can take the diligence from there. Snatching up my hastily packed bag, I kiss Sophie's shrouded form for the last time and set off along the lakeside path towards Château Mirabelle.

The lake is inky black but the reflection of the moon touches it with liquid silver. I've almost reached the boathouse when a figure carrying a lantern comes into view on the moonlit path. Is it Jean-Luc come to look for me?

If I run, I can reach the boathouse in time to hide. I throw my bag into the long grass, sprint ahead, open the boathouse door and slip inside.

I stand stock still while my eyes adjust to the moonlight filtering through slipped roof tiles. A moment later the jetty judders beneath my feet.

Someone is coming.

Flattening myself against the wall, my hand brushes against rough timber. It's a ladder. Suddenly I remember Jean-Luc climbing this same ladder up to the cushion store. Quick as a flash, I unhook it and climb up to the little platform overhead. I pull the ladder up behind me, just as the boathouse door creaks open.

I lie flat, my face pressed into thick dust, praying I won't sneeze.

'Mademoiselle Moreau?'

It's a woman's voice.

I'm hardly breathing. My muscles are rigid and every nerve is straining.

'Don't think I didn't see you. I know you're there,' says the voice. 'Perhaps I should call you *Miss* Moreau?'

I stifle a gasp.

'I was on my way to the house to hide your friend's body when I saw you.' A throaty chuckle comes from below. 'Oh, yes, Jean-Luc told me all about you,' says Madame Viard. 'You stupid little bitch! If you'd married him you could have saved him from being sent to be a soldier and been mistress of Château Mirabelle yourself. But you're not good enough for my beautiful boy.'

I lift my head a little and see Madame Viard below, holding her lantern aloft.

'I shouldn't like to be in your shoes,' she says, 'when I tell him you've escaped from the turret.' She chuckles in a way that makes my blood run cold. 'He'll know the best way to hurt you. There's no longer any need for *me* to whisper in his ear to encourage him to destroy his enemies.'

It's pointless trying to hide any longer and I sit up. 'So it was you who corrupted him? You're the puppet-mistress behind the murders he committed?'

'I always intended my boy to be master of Château Mirabelle. After all, he has noble blood,' says Madame Viard, 'and as the comte's eldest son the château should be his.'

'It could never have been inherited by a bastard.'

'Don't you dare call him that! Jean-Luc's father loved me. And if it hadn't been for his whey-faced wife, he'd have married me. I should have done away with her years ago. Life would have been very different for us then.'

I shake my head. 'He'd never have married you.'

342

She rests her hands on her hips. 'Get down here, you little trollop,' she spits.

'My, what a fishwife!' I say. 'It's plain to see that, despite your genteel ways, the veneer is very thin.'

'You'll be sorry for that!' She kicks at the walls of the boathouse, levers off several pieces of timber and then disappears under the platform.

It's quiet for a while and then Madame Viard reappears. 'This'll teach you a lesson!'

And then I smell smoke. Light dances up the wooden walls and reflects on the water in the dock. Within seconds I hear flames crackling. Fear grips me as I realise she's used the lantern to set a fire underneath the platform.

Madame Viard looks up, cackling. 'I'll watch and laugh as you burn.'

Rage bubbles up in my chest and I lose all reason. This woman and her son have cut a swathe through the d'Aubery family, bringing them nothing but sorrow. They have murdered my best friend and her baby and deprived me of the man I love. I want revenge. I'll not let this woman stop me from warning Etienne of Jean-Luc's traitorous acts. I'll fight her with my bare fists if I have to.

I push the ladder so that it teeters on the edge of the platform.

Madame Viard looks up at me, still laughing.

I let out a shriek of fury and swing the ladder over the edge, so hard that she's knocked sideways.

She lets out a grunt, staggers and slips over the side of the boat dock to sink below the water without a sound.

I stare at the water, horrified. Have I killed her? I scramble down the ladder and run to the dock. Nothing.

Flames are leaping up to lick the platform now and the wooden floor is glowing orange all around the source of the fire. Acrid smoke makes me cough and my eyes stream.

I wrench a loose plank from the wall and run to the edge of the dock again. Madame Viard has floated to the surface now but she isn't moving. Sobbing, I lean out over the water and use the plank to pull her towards me. I'm able to grab hold of her clothing and lift her face out of the water. Blood streams from her head and her eyes are closed. I drag out first an arm, a leg and then another arm until I'm able to heave her on to the dock.

Behind me, the platform collapses with a crash, sending up a shower of sparks. The flames are roaring and I'm perspiring in the heat and choking on the smoke as I grasp Madame Viard's ankles and drag her towards the boathouse door.

Outside, I lean over her with my hands on my knees catching my breath. She coughs and I let out a sob of relief. I'm not a murderer, after all.

I leave her there, collect my bag from the long grass and disappear into the night.

Almost every window is aglow with candlelight as I hurry stealthily past the château. The sound of drunken laughter, music and carousing comes from within but I don't stop to peer in. My deepest fear is that Jean-Luc will have discovered I'm no longer imprisoned and be looking for me.

No light burns in the room above the stables. I cross the yard and creep inside. I stand still while my eyes grow accustomed to the shadows but there is sufficient moonlight to enable me to see that most of the stalls are empty. The matched greys and the carriage are with Colbert, but Minette, the piebald horse and the *charrette* are missing, requisitioned perhaps to carry away Etienne's possessions to the village.

A rustle of straw comes from the last stall. Jean-Luc's chestnut gelding and I look at each other in the moonlight while I decide if I dare to ride him. He's big, far bigger than Minette or any horse I've ridden in Rotten Row. Tentatively, I stroke his velvety nose. He flares his nostrils.

I find his saddle and put it on, tightening the girth underneath and warily stepping back when he shifts his weight from foot to foot. I remove his halter and attempt to slip on the bridle but he tosses his mane at me and snorts so I back away to find him a bucket of water. While he's drinking, I rummage through a variety of clothes hanging from a peg in the tack room. I find the pair of loose trousers I borrowed once before, a shirt, coat and a soft cap. Quickly, I dress in Colbert's clothes, twisting my hair into a plait and hiding it in the cap. I bundle up my dress and stuff it into my bag. I hope that, disguised as a youth, I'll attract less attention than a lone female.

It takes me a minute or two to persuade the gelding to allow me to put on his bridle but, at last, he's ready. I lead him to the mounting block and climb up. He prances from side to side and shakes his head but I cling on with my knees and hold the reins firmly. A moment later we are clopping across the stable yard.

The following morning the sun is rising by the time I reach Orléans. I'm exhausted, having lost my way in the dark several times. Once I began to fall asleep in the saddle I was forced to spend a couple of cold and frightening hours dozing in a copse. Every movement in the undergrowth, bark of a fox and hoot of an owl, made me sit bolt upright, wondering if Jean-Luc had found me. I'd never felt so alone. In the end I cried myself to sleep, reliving my last moments with Sophie while she was alive, picturing the sun shining on her glossy curls and her eyes full of laughter.

More by luck than judgement, I find the inn where the diligence set me down last time and discover that the coach for Paris will leave at ten o'clock. In the hope that it will put Jean-Luc off my trail, I decide against stabling his horse at the inn but ask one of the ostlers where I might find the nearest livery stable.

An hour later I pat the chestnut gelding on his flank and leave the livery with a pocketful of coins. I didn't get the best price for him since the owner clearly thought the horse must be stolen. I made no attempt to argue the point and took what was offered.

Returning to the inn, I spend some of my ill-gotten gains on a slice of rabbit pie and a glass of vinegary red wine. As soon as I've finished my breakfast, I lean my head back against the settle and fall into a doze.

A rumbling of wheels, a clatter of hooves and a great deal of shouting wakes me and I surmise that the diligence has arrived.

The courtyard is milling with passengers. By the time all the arriving travellers have alighted and found their baggage, the horses have been changed and I climb aboard.

Every seat in the diligence is taken and the passengers are tightly crammed together. I don't stow my bag in the luggage net overhead but rest it on my feet, conscious that although I've changed into male attire, my shoes are decidedly feminine. It's hot, and the stout woman pressed against my side reeks of stale sweat. She takes her embroidery out of her bag to while away the journey. A man in a frowsty wig lights up a cigar and in a few minutes the coach is filled with acrid smoke.

The diligence rolls forward and as we sway out of the courtyard and jolt off down the road, I begin to wish I hadn't eaten the rabbit pie.

Hours later, the man in the wig pulls down the window of the diligence and looks outside. 'Another twenty minutes, I estimate,' he says, sniffing the air.

I remember the smell of Paris from last time: sulphur and excrement, pigs' blood and decaying fruit, river mud and perspiration, all overlaid with smoke from a thousand fires.

The journey has seemed endless. I've feigned sleep for most of the time, afraid that if I speak the passengers will realise I'm not a youth. With my cap pulled down over my face I can conceal my tears. It's impossible not to keep reliving the terrible events of yesterday. Hatred of Jean-Luc burns in my heart.

The stout woman at my side gives me a sharp look and I realise that my knee is jiggling up and down with impatience. I cannot rest until I find Etienne and warn him of the danger that awaits him.

The road improves as we approach Paris and the bone-shaking jolting of the diligence lessens. Peering out of the window some time later, I see that we have left the suburbs and are on a wide street lined with town houses.

Over the usual city noises comes the sound of shouting, growing increasingly loud. A snatch of music from a penny whistle drifts by and the staccato beat of a drum comes from the distance. The diligence slows and then comes to a screeching halt. A crowd of chanting people surges past us, making the horses rear up in terror.

A youth in a red cap bangs his fist on the half-open window and yells, '*Vive la Révolution*!'

The stout woman starts, a hand clasped to her breast. 'There's no excuse for frightening me half to death, not even for the Revolution,' she says.

Another young man jumps up and down in front of the window and pulls grotesque faces at us before running off, hooting with laughter.

A thick-set passenger with a florid complexion leans out of the window, treading on my toes in the process. 'A tumbril is coming,' he says, 'on its way to visit Madame Guillotine, I expect.' He pushes his way back to his seat again. 'I hear going to the executions makes a good day out. You can buy a programme with a list of the condemned and see what crimes they committed against the Revolution.'

Another man nods his head. 'My neighbour and his wife took their children last week. There were pie and fruit-sellers going amongst the crowd with their baskets just like a summer fair.'

The jeering and catcalls of the rabble grow louder and then a cart with slatted sides trundles by, accompanied by soldiers. A dozen of

347

the condemned are crammed together in the cart and one of them, a dark-haired young woman, has fainted. The tumbril passes very close and, as I glimpse her bone-white face, I feel a wave of nausea as I picture Sophie's face in death.

'The Revolutionary Tribunal's been busy again,' says the stout woman.

'Enemies of the state, every one of them,' says the man in the wig.

The last of the shouting mob runs past and then the diligence jerks forward and we are on the move again.

Shortly afterwards we rattle over the Pont Neuf. The passengers begin to put away their books and newspapers and my neighbour folds up her embroidery. Very soon the diligence turns into the court-yard of an inn and stops.

There's the usual commotion as the passengers collect their luggage and I'm able to slip away without drawing attention to myself. I'm unsure of my direction and anxious about finding the Rue de Richelieu, where Etienne's town house is situated.

It's noticeable that there are far fewer smart carriages and sedan chairs about than on my previous visit and more pedestrians, most of them plainly dressed. A group of young men swagger by, wearing the ubiquitous loose trousers, tricolour cockades and red caps.

Jostled from side to side, since everyone seems to be in a hurry, I try to find my bearings. A beggar, dragging his legless body along behind him on a little wheeled cart, snatches at my knee and mutters an obscenity when I pull away.

Several of the streets look familiar but I'm still not sure of my way. Eventually, I find Rue St Honoré. The dusty street is lined with imposing town houses and I pass high-walled gardens on my left before I see the Palais Royal further ahead on my right. My spirits lift as I remember that the Palais is on the corner of Rue de Richelieu. I turn the corner and, freed from the restraint of skirts, sprint up the street, hardly able to contain my impatience.

I come to a halt when I reach Etienne's house, filled with dismay. The shutters are closed and not a wisp of smoke comes from the chimneys. Then I catch my breath as I notice the front door. A bucket of paint has been flung at it so violently that it has spattered the stonework and run down the steps in an ugly yellow waterfall. Here and there great gouges have been dug out of the door, splintering the wood in places, as if a madman has tried to smash his way in with an axe.

Hesitantly, I walk up the steps but the paint is quite dry. I pull on the iron ring and the bell jangles somewhere inside. I listen intently but there is no sign that the house is anything but empty. Disappointment and fear rise in me in a tide. In my desperate flight to warn Etienne, I hadn't considered what I would do if I couldn't find him.

Dread has me in its grip now as I realise the full implications of my plight. I'm alone in a strange city where the slightest suspicion that I am not what I seem could find me in a tumbril on its way to an appointment with Madame Guillotine. It will be dark in a few hours and I have nowhere to go.

Then I remember something Etienne said to me before he left to escort my uncle and grandmother to London. *'If I should not return, go to Armand Dubois.'*

I rummage in my bag and find a stub of pencil and Sophie's sketchbook. The book falls open at a drawing of little Marianne and it makes me catch my breath with a sudden sharp stab of loss. I leaf past it to tear out a clean page and write a note for Etienne telling him that I will return but also that I shall visit Dr Dubois.

I slip the note under the door and hurry away.

Chapter 35

It's not hard to find the Seine and follow it until I come to Pont Neuf. I cross the bridge and Rue Dauphine is directly in front of me. A young maid is hurrying towards me with a basket on her arm and I stand in her way so that she has to stop.

She looks up at me with frightened eyes and I remember that I'm dressed as a youth.

'I beg your pardon,' I say, 'but can you direct me to the house of Dr Dubois?'

'Dr Dubois?' She points down the street. 'The one with the black door.'

I thank her and she scurries off.

Dr Dubois's home is a solid three-storey townhouse. I ring the bell and, while I wait, study the polished brass plate engraved with the doctor's name.

A maid, neatly turned out in a clean apron and cap, opens the door.

'Is Dr Dubois at home?' I ask.

She shakes her head. 'But no, M'sieur.'

A blush rises to my cheeks and I speak in as gruff a tone as I can manage. 'When will he return? It's most urgent that I speak with him.'

The maid shrugs and sticks out her bottom lip. 'Who can say? Tomorrow, perhaps?'

All hopes of a safe refuge flee and there's a tremor in my voice as I ask, 'Do you know where he went?'

The maid looks at me curiously. 'Are you quite well, Monsieur?'

I grip the doorpost with trembling fingers. 'May I have a glass of water?'

'I don't think . . .'

'Please.' I don't have to feign dizziness. Terror digs sharp claws into me as my last hope fades.

'Wait here!' The door closes in my face and I sink on to the step, my head between my knees, while pinpricks of light dance behind my closed eyelids.

I don't have long to wait. An elderly housekeeper opens the door and helps me to my feet.

'You know Dr Dubois, you say?' she asks me. Her face is pinched with suspicion.

I nod. 'He treated my cousin Sophie Levesque earlier in the year when she had an infection of the lungs. We were staying with Monsieur d'Aubery at his house in Rue de Richelieu.'

'Monsieur d'Aubery?' The housekeeper's expression lightens. 'Ah, I know him. He has been here many times to visit Dr Dubois. And you are . . .'

'Mmm . . .' I stutter. I hadn't prepared a new name for myself to go with my disguise. Then I have it. 'Michel Moreau,' I say. The housekeeper's face fades in and out and I close my eyes.

'You'd better come in for a minute, Monsieur Moreau.'

A short while later I'm ensconced in a comfortable armchair with a fragrant tisane at my side.

'When you are feeling better I shall bring you notepaper and you

351

may leave a message for the doctor,' says the housekeeper. She withdraws from the room and closes the door behind her.

Shivering with delayed shock, I sip the tisane, my teeth chattering against the edge of the cup. I put it on the tray, bury my face in my hands and weep. I'm frightened and grief-stricken over Sophie and Marianne and terrified that Etienne is already on his way to Château Mirabelle. If he arrives there with no warning he'll face certain death. During the past year I've lost everyone I've ever loved and to lose Etienne now, knowing at last that he no longer belongs to another woman, would be unendurable.

When there are no tears left, I wipe my swollen eyes on my cuff and curl up in the armchair, trying to shut out the world.

It's dark when voices awaken me. I stretch out my cramped limbs and stand up, anxious that it's grown late and I must still find somewhere to stay. The voices outside the room grow louder and I peer into the hall and see Dr Dubois's broad back as he talks to his housekeeper.

'I cannot see anyone now, Madame Brochard.'

The housekeeper catches sight of me. 'Ah, there he is!' she says. 'Monsieur Moreau, I was just telling Dr Dubois that I hadn't the heart to awaken you when you were sleeping so deeply.'

I step forward. 'Dr Dubois, may I speak with you in private?'

He turns to face me. 'I have a patient waiting, Monsieur. Come back tomorrow, will you?'

'Please, Dr Dubois! I'll not take a moment but it's a matter of life and death.'

'That's very dramatic.' A frown creases his forehead. 'Have we met before?'

I hesitate, glancing at Madame Brochard.

He stares at me and then asks, 'Do you have a sister?'

I shake my head.

'I see. Madame Brochard, please will you prepare the guest room with all haste while I speak with Monsieur Moreau?'

'Very good, Dr Dubois.'

After the housekeeper has bustled away, Dr Dubois waves me into the waiting room again and closes the door behind us. 'Well?' he says. 'It is Mademoiselle Moreau, I presume?'

I nod.

Dr Dubois smiles, humour sparkling in his grey eyes. 'You had me fooled for a moment. May I ask why you're dressed in this fashion?'

'I thought it would be safer.'

'Safer?'

'After I escaped from Château Mirabelle I was obliged to travel to Paris alone. It's imperative that I find Etienne and warn him that his home has been taken over by the villagers. His estate manager has denounced him as a spy.'

The smile fades from Dr Dubois's face. 'Is this true?'

'Of course it's true! But I couldn't find Etienne at his townhouse. I was so sure he would be there by now and I'm frightened we might have missed each other on the road between Orléans and Paris. If he goes home ...' My chin begins to quiver as I fight back tears.

'But I know Jean-Luc Viard,' says Dr Dubois. 'He's Etienne's friend.'

'It's a long story but we're wasting precious time! When is Etienne expected to arrive in Paris? Or has he already left?'

Dr Dubois grasps my shoulders. 'Stay calm, Mademoiselle Moreau! Etienne is here.'

My jaw drops. 'Etienne is *here*? But your housekeeper never said ...'

'I brought him with me a few minutes ago.'

'Thank God!' I sigh in relief. 'Where is he? I must talk with him.'

'That may not be possible,' says Dr Dubois.

'But I've told you, I *must* see him!'

'Mademoiselle, Etienne is in no condition to talk to anyone. I

353

have removed a musketball from his shoulder but unfortunately the wound had already festered.'

I swallow. 'Is it serious?'

'He has a high fever.'

'I must go to him at once!' My voice is shrill with anxiety.

The doctor looks at me for a moment. 'Come with me, then.'

I follow him along the servants' passage where he opens a cupboard and takes his time withdrawing a long roll of canvas from amongst a motley collection of boxes, vases and old travelling capes.

I have to bite my tongue to stop myself from shouting at him to hurry up.

He picks up a lamp from a shelf by the back door and we go outside into the night. He lights our way along a gravel path running through a garden. Low hedges, wet with dew, brush against my knees and the scent of moist earth and damask roses overlays the city stench. Before us a low building is silhouetted against the moonlit sky.

A figure looms out of the shadows, making me jump.

Dr Dubois holds up his lamp and I recognise the other man as Etienne's groom.

'How is he, Colbert?' asks Dr Dubois.

'Still asleep.'

'Then we shall carry him upstairs.'

I follow Colbert and Dr Dubois into the stable. Etienne's carriage is stowed at one end and his horses are in the loose boxes, jaws working as they munch their hay.

Dr Dubois unrolls the canvas on to the clean straw underfoot. There are wooden poles slotted through loops either side of the narrower ends.

Colbert opens the carriage door.

Etienne is slumped inside.

Pushing past Colbert, I bend over Etienne. He has a ragged cut on his cheek and his left arm is tied up in a sling. He smells of brandy, and sweat, and the metallic tang of blood. I smother his burning forehead with kisses, stroking his face and whispering words of love, but he remains motionless.

'Etienne!'

He sighs at the sound of my voice but doesn't awaken and I'm frightened again.

'Please step down,' says Dr Dubois, 'and allow us to remove him from the carriage.'

Reluctantly, I hover impatiently while Colbert and Dr Dubois manhandle Etienne on to the stretcher. 'Be careful!' I say as his arm falls and his knuckles scrape along the steps. I lift his hand and place it across his chest.

'Shall I fetch a footman?' asks Colbert, eyeing the doctor as he catches his breath.

Dr Dubois shakes his head. 'The servants would recognise your master and I don't care to risk the news travelling abroad that I am harbouring a noble under my roof.'

I glance anxiously at Etienne, who lies unmoving on the stretcher. 'Shall I go on ahead and see if the coast is clear?'

'Take the lamp but don't worry about Madame Brochard,' he says. 'She's faithful to the end.'

The two men carry the stretcher behind me with its precious burden. At the back door I hold up a hand to stay their progress as a maid hurries past with her coal bucket and then beckon them to follow me.

We arrive at the top of the stairs and the doctor indicates the guest room with a nod of his head. Once inside, Etienne is laid upon the bed.

Dr Dubois lifts Etienne's wrist and takes his pulse. 'I'd hoped the fever would pass now the ball has been removed,' he says. 'Being jolted about in a carriage hasn't helped him but I thought it better to bring him here rather than to leave him in an inn.'

'Please, let me nurse him,' I say.

Colbert looks at me and frowns as he peers at my clothes. 'That's my coat!' Then his eyes open wide in surprise. 'Well, by all that's holy! Is it really you, Mademoiselle Moreau?'

I hold a finger to my lips.

'What's going on?'

'Terrible things have happened at Château Mirabelle and I came to warn Monsieur d'Aubery.'

Dr Dubois holds up his hand. 'Later. My first concern now is for my patient. Mademoiselle, you will please turn your back while Colbert and I undress him. Once he is comfortable you may sit beside him.'

I move out of the way while the men strip off Etienne's blood-stained clothing and place him, naked, in bed and cover him with a sheet. Fresh blood seeps through the bandage from his shoulder.

'I must change the dressing tomorrow,' says Dr Dubois, 'but for tonight I shall leave him undisturbed. Colbert, your work is done for the present and you may sleep in the loft over the stables.'

I rest my hand on Etienne's forehead again. 'He's so very hot, Doctor.'

Before long I have a small table set up beside me with a basin of water, lavender soap and clean cloths. I fold the sheet down to Etienne's waist and sponge his face and neck. He mutters and a flash of white shows through his slightly parted eyelids but still he does not wake.

'I gave him a substantial dose of laudanum to dull the pain while we travelled,' says Dr Dubois, 'so he may sleep for some time.'

'I shall remain with him until then,' I say.

Dr Dubois purses his lips and then shrugs. 'There are blankets and pillows in the armoire and I will send up some supper for you. After you've eaten you should rest while your patient sleeps. Call me if there is any change.'

'Thank you, Dr Dubois.'

He bows and closes the door behind him.

The housekeeper brings me a tray of soup, bread and a slice of apple tart, together with my bag of belongings. As soon as the door closes behind her I fall upon the tray, suddenly realising how long it has been since I last ate.

Ten minutes later I dab my mouth with the napkin. Perspiration beads Etienne's forehead and heat radiates from his body. I squeeze out the sponge and start to wipe him again. The cut on his cheek has begun to heal, but the surrounding skin is still inflamed. I rinse the cloth and slowly wipe it over his throat, tracing it down the cords of his neck to the delicate skin in the hollows above his collarbones. Blood stains his bandages. Etienne's chest is lightly covered in silky black hair and I cannot supress a shiver of desire as I see, lower down, that it forms a dark whorl around his navel and then disappears beneath the sheet.

Concentrating only on this task, refusing to imagine what might happen if he doesn't recover, I gently wash each well-muscled arm, first the skin of his forearms browned by the sun and then the paler skin above. The reek of stale sweat and blood is gradually replaced with the clean scent of lavender soap.

One by one I wipe his fingers, washing away crusts of dried blood. The skin on his hands is rough from working in the vineyards and his palms are heavily callused. I fold the sheet upwards and wash his feet and legs, drying carefully between his toes. At last, I dab him dry with a clean towel.

I pour a clean basin of water for myself and, hesitating only a moment to check that Etienne still sleeps, strip off my borrowed clothes and wash myself from head to toe. Reluctantly, I dress again in the same soiled shirt and trousers, feeling that it would draw too much attention if I appeared in a dress now.

I pull the armchair close to the bed and watch Etienne sleeping. It's strange to be able to study him in such detail, to learn every plane of his face, to see the faint blue veins in his eyelids without him watching me. I press my lips to his cheek. 'Goodnight, my love,' I whisper.

A muscle twitches in his jaw and his eyelids flicker but still he sleeps. I curl my hand around his.

The room is quiet. Only a few city sounds, a barking dog and a passing horseman can be heard through the window. A clock ticks sonorously on the mantelpiece and I breathe in and out to the same rhythm.

I sleep.

I hear my name and wake with a start. Light is creeping through the edges of the shutters. I yawn and then realise that Etienne's eyes are open.

'Madeleine,' he says, his voice like a caress. 'I dreamed of you last night but it seems it wasn't a dream after all.'

'Etienne, I was so worried! I couldn't wake you.' I touch my fingers to his neck. 'Thank God! The fever's broken.'

'Where are we?'

'Dr Dubois brought you here to his house.'

Etienne frowns in concentration. 'I remember now. I crossed the Channel in a fishing boat and landed in a small cove under cover of darkness. The captain was expecting to load a fresh cargo of brandy and sail off again to England with the morning tide, but the militia was waiting for us.'

I grip his hand in fear of what might have been.

'Several men went down,' he says, 'and there was such confusion ... I was shot in the shoulder but escaped.' He closes his eyes for a moment, his breathing agitated.

I stroke his forehead. 'Shhh, now!'

'Somehow I found my way back to the inn where Colbert was waiting for me. He carried me upstairs and put me to bed. My shoulder hurt like the very devil and he tried to remove the ball but it only made things worse. We daren't call for a doctor. Colbert rode Diable, hell for leather, back to Paris to fetch Dr Dubois.'

'You're quite safe now,' I say.

He smiles faintly. 'I have nine lives, like a cat. But how did you come to be here? Is Sophie with you?'

I shake my head and tears well up in my eyes. I must not think of Sophie or little Marianne yet. 'I came to warn you.' I'm unsure how to break the news of Jean-Luc's betrayal. 'All is not well at Château Mirabelle.'

'Is Jean-Luc with you?'

Mutely, I shake my head.

'You came all the way to Paris, alone?' He tries to sit up and I restrain him. 'What has happened?'

'So much that I hardly know where to begin.' I'm reluctant to recount the truth in case the shock is too much for him, in his weakened state.

Etienne takes my hand. 'Madeleine, you must tell me. Otherwise I shall only imagine something worse than it is.'

'It's very bad, Etienne. The worst news you can imagine.'

He shakes his head. 'As long as you are safely by my side nothing else matters.'

I kiss our entwined fingers, feeling a tiny shaft of pleasure amongst the sorrow. 'It's Jean-Luc,' I say.

He squeezes my hand tightly, his eyes shadowed with sudden fear. 'Not dead?'

'If only it were so,' I say, my voice full of bitterness.

'Madeleine, what are you saying? Jean-Luc is my closest friend.'

'He's no friend to you! He has done you incalculable harm.'

He stares at me. 'You must have misunderstood . . .'

'Misunderstood?' The anger swells in my chest until I cannot contain it. 'Etienne, Jean-Luc has been a secret poison in your life for years. He murdered Sophie and Marianne, and your wife and family!'

He grips my hand. 'He killed Isabelle?'

'And he tried to kill me and has turned the villagers against you.

Even now they have taken over Château Mirabelle and are burning the books in your library and stealing all your treasures. Jean-Luc has denounced you as a spy and if you return there you will be executed.'

Etienne stares at me, his mouth slack with shock. 'I can't . . .'

'I know it sounds as if I'm raving,' I say. 'It's hard to believe the depths of his treachery, but I promise you that I'm telling the truth.'

'Could you be mistaken?'

'I wish I were.'

'But *why*?'

'Because Jean-Luc is your half-brother and wants what is yours.'

'My half-brother?' His expression is incredulous.

'Let me tell you the whole story.'

Half an hour later Etienne leans back against the pillows, white-faced, while his fingers pluck at the sheet folded over his chest. The sight of his distress hurts me and I sit on the bed beside him and wrap my arms around him.

'I can hardly comprehend it,' he whispers. 'If it had been anyone but you telling me this story I should not have believed them.'

The door opens and Dr Dubois enters. 'I see my patient is awake. I'm sorry to disturb such a touching scene but we'd better have a look at that shoulder, Etienne.'

Pink with embarrassment, I slide off the bed.

Dr Dubois keeps up a flow of conversation while he deftly unwinds the bandages.

'The wound is still angry, Etienne,' he says, 'but there is less infection.' He smiles at me. 'You have a good nurse in Mademoiselle, or should I say Monsieur, Moreau? She may keep you company if you wish?'

'I'm not letting her out of my sight,' says Etienne, reaching out for my hand. 'Not after what has happened.'

'You never told me the turn of events that brought you here, Mademoiselle Moreau,' says Dr Dubois.

I render a brief version of the facts and at the end of it he shakes his head. 'After recent happenings here in Paris, the beheadings and the terrible atmosphere of suspicion, with neighbour denouncing neighbour, you can trust no one, Etienne.'

'I'm beginning to understand that,' he says. 'When the Moreaux and I arrived at my house in Rue de Richelieu to break our journey to the coast, a mob of revolutionaries threw stones at us. Once we were inside they tried to force their way through the door. Your grandmother nearly died of fright, Madeleine. When we left, I instructed my housekeeper to close the house and go to stay with her daughter until I send for her again.'

'You escaped lightly,' says Dr Dubois. 'The new Law of Suspects has made terror the order of the day. Anyone whose neighbour has a grudge against him has reason to be frightened since little proof is required when charged with a crime against the Revolution. Punishment is fast and merciless. The tumbrils are rattling their way to the guillotine daily.'

Etienne rubs his eyes in despair.

Dr Dubois sighs. 'I have other patients to attend to now. I will see you at dinner.'

Chapter 36

Later that afternoon Etienne insists on getting up. 'I shan't sleep tonight if I don't get some fresh air. Anger against Jean-Luc is seething inside me and I must take my mind off it. Where are my clothes?'

'They were so torn and soaked with blood that we had to burn them.'

'Then fetch my bag, please.'

It's useless to argue with him when his mouth is folded in that line of grim determination.

In his travelling bag I find a shirt stiff with seawater and sweat and help him to ease it over his bandages.

Discreetly, I turn my back while he struggles into loose workmen's trousers and ties the waist with cord. Then I pass him a shabby homespun coat with a limp red, white and blue cockade pinned to one shoulder.

'There's a revolutionary sash in the pocket,' he says. 'I'd better put it on, if only for the benefit of the servants.'

Unsteadily, he stands up and runs his fingers through his tousled hair. 'I need a shave,' he says. 'I must look like the worst kind of peasant.'

'Tomorrow,' I say, tucking my pigtail inside the man's cap I wear. 'Now take my arm.'

We make slow progress and Etienne is pale and shaking by the time we reach the garden. A blackbird sings in a tree, the liquid notes full of joy. We sit side by side on a bench in the knot garden. I stretch out my legs and some of the tension of the past days drains away. For now I decide to put aside sadness and revel in the company of the man I love.

I watch Etienne carefully as he draws in deep breaths, eyes closed and face turned up to the autumn sunshine. He's pale under his tan and the fierce stubble on his chin is blue-black. His hair falls in dishevelled curls over his forehead but he's still the handsomest man I've ever seen.

A smile spreads across his face. 'I can feel you watching me.'

'You're exhausted. I should have made you stay in bed.'

He shakes his head. 'Blood loss has made me weak but I'll be well again soon. Meanwhile, I must plan what we are going to do.'

'We can't go back to Château Mirabelle,' I say.

Etienne sighs deeply. 'Everything I thought was true has turned out to be a sham.' He turns to me. 'Except for you, Madeleine.'

I cannot help but laugh. 'You say that when I'm sitting beside you disguised as a youth?'

'You make a very fetching youth, if I may say so.' He curls his fingers around my hand.

The sound of an altercation drifts out of the kitchen window, disturbing the peace.

'Perhaps Cook has burned the dinner,' says Etienne, closing his eyes again.

A man shouts and then a girl screams. A door slams violently and I sit up in alarm. 'Shall I go and see what's happening?'

Then the doors from the drawing room open and footsteps crunch over the gravel path.

'Etienne!' I whisper, my heart somersaulting in my chest.

Dressed in his fine coat of cornflower blue silk, matching knee breeches and white stockings, Jean-Luc is strutting towards us.

'Well, well,' he drawls as he comes to a halt. 'Look at the love-birds!' He shakes his head in mock consternation. 'People will spread terrible rumours about you, Etienne, if you're seen holding hands with a young man. I understand now why my enquiries for a lady travelling alone came to naught.'

Etienne struggles to his feet. 'How dare you show your face here?'

'Has Madeleine been telling tales out of school? She's cleverer than I gave her credit for, but still stupid enough to leave a note at your townhouse letting me know where to find you.'

The familiar scent of Jean-Luc's musky hair pomade almost makes me gag.

'I thought we were friends, Jean-Luc?' Etienne's voice is low and I can hear the hurt in it.

Jean-Luc's face twists into a bitter smile. 'We were, up to a point. But did you not think how galling it was for me to be ever at your side but never your equal?' His voice grows hard. 'I'm older than you and our father should have passed on the estate to me. Still, everything is different now,' he says. 'It took me years to formulate and carry out my plans but I had to act swiftly when Isabelle told me she was breeding.'

'You bastard!' Etienne is white and shaking with rage.

'That, of course, was my problem,' says Jean-Luc. 'Despite that I've turned the situation to my best advantage. And the Revolution has evened up the odds for me. Château Mirabelle is mine now.'

'Not for much longer!'

Jean-Luc's smug smile makes my fingers itch to slap his face.

'You have cause to be grateful to me. Now that you know Isabelle is dead, you're free to pursue your affair with Madeleine,' he says. 'And you're welcome to her since she's proved herself unworthy of me. What a shame that you'll have so little time together.'

'You're not fit to utter her name!' Etienne's hands ball into fists but beads of perspiration break out on his forehead.

'Idle threats, my dear Etienne. She will be made to suffer.' Jean-Luc fixes me with a hard stare. 'No one who harms my dear mother shall escape retribution. I've presented a letter from Mayor Prudhomme to the Committee of Public Security here in Paris. It states that he has information you're a spy for the British.'

'You cannot prove that,' says Etienne.

Jean-Luc pulls a gold watch on a chain from his pocket and glances at it.

Etienne draws in his breath with a hiss. 'That's my father's watch! I searched everywhere for that. Where did you find it?'

'I took it from his body after he met with his unfortunate accident,' says Jean-Luc calmly. 'I was determined to have something to remember him by. It gave me a curious sense of satisfaction to know that, just like Isabelle, it was so close to you but you couldn't see it.' He smiles broadly.

'My father meant me to have it!'

'Our allotted time is up,' says Jean-Luc, glancing at the watch again. 'There are men here with a warrant for your arrest, waiting only for my signal.' He lifts up his arm and the French doors burst open and three soldiers run towards us. A man in a dark coat and a badly powdered wig follows at a more leisurely pace behind.

'They allowed me five minutes alone with you to say goodbye,' says Jean-Luc, 'since we are such old friends.'

Etienne shakes off my restraining hand and swings his fist at Jean-Luc.

Jean-Luc utters a muffled curse, his nose blossoms scarlet and blood drips on to his fine coat.

Two of the soldiers grasp Etienne, who groans in pain as his arms are wrenched roughly backwards.

'Be careful!' I shout.

One of the soldiers imprisons my wrists. 'Shut up and listen while we read the charges.'

'Let go of me!' I twist in his grip. 'I've done nothing!'

'Don't struggle or it'll be the worse for you!' He grins, his teeth blackened stumps. 'Never could abide a pretty boy and who would blame me if I have to hurt you? After all, I'm only doing my job.'

The man in the wig clears his throat and holds up a piece of paper. Clasping his lapel with the other hand, he strikes a pose in front of Etienne. 'I am Citoyen Hugo Furet, empowered by the Committee of Public Security to inform you of the charges to be brought against you.'

'I am innocent of any crime against the Revolution,' declares Etienne.

One of the soldiers yanks his arm higher behind his back. 'Don't speak until you're spoken to!'

I cry out as Etienne's knees buckle and his eyelids flutter with the pain.

'Shall we continue?' Citoyen Furet clears his throat again. 'It has come to the attention of the Committee of Public Security that you, Citoyen Etienne François Guillame d'Aubery, former noble of Château Mirabelle, near Orléans, have unlawfully travelled to Britain, France's mortal enemy, for the purpose of aiding the escape of traitors to the Revolution. Furthermore, you are accused of hoarding food supplies at Château Mirabelle, in direct contravention of the revolutionary principle of equality.'

Etienne sways in his captors' hold. 'I tell you again that I am no traitor.'

I had believed the worst was over but now I'm shaking with terror and disbelief.

Citoyen Furet looks sternly at Etienne. 'You will be taken to a place of confinement until your trial tomorrow.'

Etienne shakes his head, as if to clear it. 'I'm not a traitor,' he mumbles. His face is as white as whey and I expect him to pass out at any moment.

Fright nearly chokes me. Etienne is too ill to defend himself and my mind races as I try to think of a way out. Then, as Jean-Luc pulls a lace-edged handkerchief out of his pocket to dab his bloody nose, I have it.

'Citoyen Furet!' I call.

Hugo Furet raises his eyebrows. 'You address me?'

'Yes, M'sieur, I do. You're making a mistake.'

'I do not make mistakes.' He turns away.

'You have been misinformed, M'sieur. You have accused the wrong man.'

Furet turns back. 'Explain yourself.'

I struggle to free my wrists from the soldiers' grasp.

'Release him,' says Furet, 'for the moment.'

I draw myself up to my full height and take a deep breath. I must not falter now. Looking Furet in the eye, I speak in tones as deep as I can manage. 'My name is Moreau. I work in the vineyard at Château Mirabelle. And this man,' I point to Etienne, 'is Jean-Luc Viard.'

'What cock and bull story is this?' asks Jean-Luc, laughing.

I ignore him. 'Citoyen Viard is the housekeeper's son and a labourer in the vineyard and on the estate. But this man, 'I point to Jean-Luc, 'is the traitor and spy Comte Etienne d'Aubery, who feasts off suckling pig from golden plates while his estate workers' children die of starvation.'

Citoyen Furet narrows his eyes. 'Why would I believe this story?'

'Sir, I am only a poor peasant but you must believe the evidence of your own eyes.' I turn my hands palm up. 'See the rough skin and broken nails from honest labour.' I snatch up one of Etienne's hands and thrust it towards Furet. 'Look at the scars and calluses! Is this the hand of a nobleman?' I demand.

Furet's face remains expressionless for a moment then he addresses one of the soldiers. 'Bring the other one to me.'

One of the soldiers takes Jean-Luc's arm and frog-marches him to Furet.

Jean-Luc, scowling, struggles in his grip. 'What nonsense is this?'

The soldier grasps him roughly by the wrist and holds out Jean-Luc's hand for Furet to examine.

My mouth is dry and my pulse thunders in my ears. 'Citoyen Furet, now you have seen the hands of these two men, Jean-Luc Viard and Comte Etienne d'Aubery, you know which one has the hands of a working man and which the soft-skinned hands of a noble.'

Jean-Luc laughs. 'This is ridiculous! I am Jean-Luc Viard.'

'Liar!' I spit on Jean-Luc's polished shoes. 'You attempt to save your own cowardly skin by placing the blame for your crimes on a poor peasant who has sweated for long hours in the fields every day to make you rich. Now the worm has turned! Monsieur Furet, I appeal to you. Is *this* man, scented with perfume, wearing a silk coat and carrying a lace handkerchief, a common labourer?' I turn to Etienne. 'And *this* man, in his ragged and filthy clothes and shoes with flapping soles, how can you possibly believe him to be Comte Etienne d'Aubery?'

'We're wasting time,' says Jean-Luc. 'Take d'Aubery to meet the Revolutionary Tribunal and see what they have to say.'

'Don't speak again until I give you leave!' barks Furet.

Jean-Luc flinches and the soldier holding his wrist jerks his arm up behind his back.

Slowly, Furet looks me up and down. 'For one so young you think yourself quite a lawyer, don't you?'

'I believe in justice and the revolutionary ideals of equality and liberty for all, Citoyen,' I say quietly.

'And you,' Furet turns to Etienne. 'What do you have to say for yourself?'

He gives Jean-Luc a long stare of naked hatred. 'I say this man is a tyrant and a coward, whose greed drives him to prey on those weaker than himself. He has violent fits of madness; everyone knows it runs in the family. And for further proof of his identity, I suggest you look at the pocket watch he always carries. It belonged to his father, Comte Guillaume d'Aubery. No labouring man could honestly own such an expensive timepiece.'

'Check his pockets,' Furet says to the soldier.

'Take your filthy hands off me!' bellows Jean-Luc as the soldier snatches the cornflower blue coat open and withdraws the watch.

The sun glints on the chased gold case as Furet flicks it open. 'It is engraved with the entwined initials FGd'A.'

'François Guillaume d'Aubery,' says Etienne.

'Now do you see the truth, Citoyen Furet?' I hold my breath until black spots dance before my eyes.

Citoyen Furet sighs.

'Listen to me, you stupid little bureaucrat!' says Jean-Luc. 'Can't you see they're lying!'

Citoyen Furet casts a look of dislike at Jean-Luc and addresses me again. 'I believe you have prevented me from being the instrument of a miscarriage of justice, Citoyen.' He nods to the soldier who holds Etienne. 'Release him. And take up the other.'

I feel no triumph as Etienne stumbles away from his guard, only overpowering relief.

'No!' screams Jean-Luc. 'This is all your fault!' He launches himself at me, twisting and bucking as the soldiers attempt to restrain him. 'I'll make you pay for this!' He lashes out with his feet and elbows as he tries to reach me. 'It's her fault! She's destroyed all my plans.'

I catch my breath in fear and glance at Citoyen Furet.

'Silence!' he thunders.

'Etienne's the noble!' shouts Jean-Luc. 'Take him before the Tribunal. He must be condemned!'

It takes two soldiers to bind Jean-Luc's wrists behind his back while he yells and struggles. Spittle froths his mouth and his face is red and contorted with fury. Wild-eyed, he turns to Furet. 'I'm telling you, that's Comte Etienne d'Aubery and his whore Madeleine over there!'

369

'He's having another of his fits of lunacy, Citoyen Furet,' says Etienne. 'I warn you, he may become extremely violent. As you can see, he's a big man and very strong when the madness takes him.'

Jean-Luc lashes out with his foot. 'Shut your mouth, Etienne! You and that little bitch won't get away with this. By God, just you wait until I get my hands on you ...'

'Enough!' shouts Furet, striking him across the face with the flat of one hand.

Jean-Luc gasps and then snatches Furet's wig askew before yelling a torrent of abuse at him, fighting against the guards all the time.

Citoyen Furet glances at me, frowning. 'Who is Madeleine?'

Etienne shrugs. 'He often sees people who aren't there. Who knows what goes on in the mind of a madman?'

Furet straightens his wig. 'As you say, Citoyen, the man is a lunatic. Guards, take him away!'

Fighting and screaming, Jean-Luc is dragged up the path towards the house. Digging his heels into the gravel, he looks back at us over his shoulder as the soldiers push him through the doorway. 'A curse on you all! May you burn in hell!'

Etienne, Furet and I look at each other as the racket fades away and finally the garden is quiet again.

'I can almost find it in my heart to feel sorry for him,' I say.

'It is disconcerting to see how an apparently sane man can be overcome by madness in a matter of moments,' says Furet, shaking his head. 'I shall tell the Tribunal what I have witnessed and, if he is not found guilty of the crimes of which he is accused, I shall recommend that he be incarcerated for the rest of his life.'

'There are many who have suffered at his hands who would be relieved to hear that,' says Etienne.

'Indeed,' says Furet. 'I shall take my leave of you.'

Once he has disappeared indoors, Etienne collapses on the bench, his face as grey as ashes.

370

My knees give way and I flop down beside him. Shock and relief make my teeth chatter.

Etienne wraps his arms around me. He rests his chin on the top of my head and utters soothing, nonsense words. We hold each other in silence for a long time while I try to banish the image of my last sight of Jean-Luc, spitting fury and with venom in his eyes.

At last Etienne tips up my chin so that he can look into my face. 'My brave and clever Madeleine,' he says.

And then he kisses me.

The trembling and shaking of my limbs ceases as the warmth and sweetness of his kiss works its magic. I press myself against him, drawing strength from his closeness and feeling the blossoming of joy inside me.

Then there is a scream and the sound of shattering china.

We break apart to see Madame Brochard with her hand to her mouth and shock in her eyes. A silver tray lies on the gravel with an overturned coffee pot and shards of broken china all around.

I jump up to go and help her but she holds up her hand in horror. 'Sodomites!'

'Madame Brochard . . .'

'Get away from me!' She picks up her skirts and runs back indoors.

Etienne looks at me and a corner of his mouth twitches. 'Poor woman, what a shock for her to find two men canoodling in her garden.'

'Etienne, it's not funny!' But then a giggle bubbles up in my chest.

'No, of course not,' he says, chuckling.

We collapse into each other's arms, whooping with laughter.

A few minutes later I wipe tears of merriment from my eyes. 'I think it's time I went to put on a dress and curl my hair again, don't you?'

Chapter 37

October arrives, bringing heavy rain that sweeps over Paris, turning the street dust to mud and causing the citizens to hurry by with sacking held over their heads. Etienne and I sit beside a small fire in the drawing room of Dr Dubois's house but it does little to dispel the damp chill in the air.

Etienne sits close to the hearth, apparently reading a book, while I stare out of the window, waiting, and making bets with myself as to which drop of rain running down the glass will reach the bottom first.

Madame Brochard has forgiven us for the shock we gave her when she came upon us in the garden and, although it has taken two weeks for Etienne's wound to heal, at last he has regained his strength. Despite that, we are both suffering from a malaise as heavy as the leaden sky outside.

Etienne stares morosely into the flames, lost in thought.

For my own part, anxiety and disappointment make me dejected. Regardless of Jean-Luc's confession that he murdered Isabelle, Etienne hasn't proposed to me, even though he's now free to do so. I try to comfort myself by thinking that he's still recovering from the shock of Jean-Luc's betrayal.

I go to the window and stare miserably outside at the rain until I see a figure in a brown greatcoat hurrying along the street.

'Etienne, he's coming!'

He drops his book in his haste to reach the window.

A few minutes later there are footsteps in the hall and then the drawing-room door opens. Dr Dubois shakes rain from his hair as he comes towards us.

Etienne's fingers close around my hand in a grip so tight it makes me wince. 'Well?' he asks.

Dr Dubois nods, his face grave. 'It is done.'

I hear Etienne's breath slip away in a long sigh. His eyes glitter with sudden tears.

'Was it very terrible?' I ask.

'Jean-Luc ranted and raved to the end,' says Dr Dubois. 'His bitterness and fury before the Tribunal only served to convince them that he'd lost his reason. They had to chain him to carry him to the guillotine. But it was swiftly done and all his troubles are at an end now.'

'It appears he always coveted my name,' says Etienne, 'and finally he achieved his ambition, if not in the way he wished. Now the man known as Etienne d'Aubery is no more,' he says in a low voice. 'So where does that leave me? Who am I now?'

My heart bleeds for him, hearing such grief in his voice.

Dr Dubois opens the cupboard and takes out a bottle of brandy and three glasses.

The spirit stings my throat but then warmth courses through my veins.

'It's strange,' says Etienne, cradling his glass in his palm, 'but it's hard to feel anything but sorrow for him now. I know Jean-Luc murdered most of the people I loved, I know he incited an uprising, stole my estate and betrayed me, but all I can think of is the boy with the infectious smile who grew up by my side. I remember us shooting ravens from the tower and swimming in the lake and

373

sharing midnight feasts in the stables. Where did that boy, my best friend, go?'

I can hardly bear to hear the anguish in his voice and take him in my arms. His shoulders heave and he clings to me.

A moment later Etienne regains control of himself and I judge it best to leave the two men with their brandy.

Etienne and Dr Dubois are already at breakfast when I come downstairs the following morning.

Etienne smiles at me but there are deep shadows under his eyes.

'It doesn't look as if you slept any better than I did,' I say, pouring myself a cup of coffee.

'I'm going back to Château Mirabelle,' he says.

Coffee slops from my cup on to the starched tablecloth. 'Etienne, you can't!'

He blots the stain with his napkin. 'I have to.'

'But . . .'

'I think he must,' says Dr Dubois. 'He will never rest until he sees for himself what the situation is there.'

'You don't understand! I *was* there and I saw how Jean-Luc turned the servants and villagers against Etienne. They'll kill him if he returns.'

We argue for nearly half an hour but he is determined to have his way and I grow angry with Dr Dubois, who supports him. It's no use wasting my breath any more and I retire to the morning room while Etienne packs for his journey.

I sit hunched in an armchair by the fire, listening to his booted feet moving about in the guestroom above. Then he comes to say goodbye.

'Please understand that I must do this.'

'Then take me with you!'

He shakes his head. 'Too dangerous.'

There's no alternative for me but to accept the inevitable. 'Then Godspeed and come back safely.'

The following week drags by painfully slowly. A deep depression has settled over me and despite Dr Dubois's sleeping draughts I am tormented by dreams of Sophie and Marianne crying out to me for help. But the worst part of my misery is fear for Etienne.

As we move into the second week of Etienne's absence there's still no word from him and a sliver of ice grows in my heart. Has the horde inhabiting Château Mirabelle captured and killed him? I've lost everyone I've ever loved and am lonely and fearful for the future.

One day I catch sight of my reflection in the hall mirror. I have grown thin and pale and there are shadows under my eyes. I look very different from the self-confident young woman I had been a year ago and I don't like what I see. But then I had Mama and Papa to love me, my teaching to give me a purpose in life, and no concerns as to what the future might bring.

A week later there is still no word from Etienne. Most days I sit by the window waiting for him and watching the endless tumbrils rattle past, taking the convicted to the guillotine, while I grow more and more frightened.

At dinner one day I say to Dr Dubois, 'I've decided I must make plans for the future.'

'There's time enough for that when Etienne returns.'

'But what if he doesn't return? After all this time I can only fear the worst. I'm homesick. I have no family to care about me. I'm uncertain and afraid here in Paris so I shall travel back to London as soon as I can find a way to do so.'

Dr Dubois shakes his head. 'It's far too treacherous.'

'If Etienne managed it then I'll find a way.'

'But can you return to the life you left behind?'

Dubois has voiced my innermost fear. 'I shall return to teaching. And then there's Sophie's son. I loved little Marianne but I haven't forgotten Henry. To have lost his mother is a very dreadful thing for a child. I want him to grow up knowing that she loved him, and that I will always be his friend as well as his godmother.'

Dr Dubois sighs. 'I beg you not to make any imprudent decisions.'

'I can't stay here living on your charity for ever.'

'Etienne would never forgive me if I let any harm come to you.' Dr Dubois rests his hand on my shoulder for a moment. 'Wait a while. If he hasn't returned in another week, I'll go and look for him.'

One morning when Dr Dubois is out visiting a patient, I'm afraid when a chanting mob marches down the road, rattling the shutters, hammering on the door and leaving a trail of destruction in its wake. Later, Dr Dubois returns with the news that Queen Marie Antoinette has been beheaded on trumped-up charges of incest with her son.

Sickened by this society corrupted by its hunger for power, I determine to find a way to return to London. But how can I contemplate leaving France until I know what has happened to Etienne? In my heart I believe he's dead, killed by the very villagers he strove so hard to provide for, their minds poisoned by Jean-Luc.

Later that afternoon I'm in the morning room when I feel a draught on the back of my neck. I turn, expecting to see Madame Brochard with my coffee tray, but instead, leaning in the doorway, is Etienne.

I stare at him, wondering for a moment if I have summoned him up out of my hopeful imagination.

'Madeleine?'

And then I'm in his arms and he's smothering my face and throat with kisses and murmuring words of love in my ears.

'You were away so long we had almost given up hope of you.' My

376

knees are trembling so much that, if he weren't holding me tightly, I would be unable to stand.

'Did you not receive my letter?'

I shake my head.

'It must have gone astray.'

'I was sure you were dead.' Tears roll down my cheeks and he kisses them away.

'I wouldn't have worried you for the world.'

'I was so frightened that you'd been caught and executed.'

He sits on the sofa and draws me on to his knee. 'As you see, I'm safe but I've lost the estate and the château. Most of my wealth has gone with them.' His face is as expressionless as a mask.

Anger at the injustice of it cuts me like a knife. The hurt and loss that Etienne must be experiencing are unimaginable to me. Generations of the d'Aubery family have lived at Château Mirabelle and now all that tradition counts for nothing. 'I'm sorry,' I say. The words are totally inadequate for the magnitude of his loss.

'The place has been emptied of anything of value. The villagers ran wild,' continues Etienne, 'and drank all the wine stored in the *chai*. Mayor Prudhomme has taken the opportunity to confiscate my home, allegedly for the benefit of the Republic, and is now in residence there with his wife. I daresay he pays a small rent to the state for the privilege.'

'That's no more than legalised theft. I never trusted that man!'

'I've come to the conclusion that he used Jean-Luc.'

'In what way?'

'I believe Prudhomme encouraged him and his mother to stir up the villagers' resentment and always had the intention of taking over the château once they'd done their worst. Prudhomme's making the villagers suffer now by paying reduced wages and threatening to turn them out of their homes.'

'So can't you persuade them to throw him out and then you can take the château back?'

'Not now that it's been confiscated by the state. The Committee would have my head if I tried. Besides, it's still on record that I'm a traitor to the Revolution. As it is, Prudhomme thinks I've been guillotined. No one, except Madame Viard, seems to care that Jean-Luc has vanished without trace.'

'What about the vineyard?'

Etienne turns up the palms of his hands and shrugs. 'The recent heavy rain destroyed most of the crop. It will be a very small harvest this year.'

'After all our hard work! But how did you find out what was happening?'

Etienne smiles briefly. 'Madame Gerard. She kept her family away while the rioting went on and gave me shelter when I reached the village. There is one piece of good news, though. Victor has been returned to her.'

'The army have let him go?'

'Invalided out. He was shot in the leg. He limps so he's no use for marching, but he'll still make a fine carpenter.'

I cannot contain myself. 'Etienne, why were you away for so long? I've been mad with worry.'

'I couldn't walk away from my estate until I knew there was no hope of recovering it. But there was an even more important issue at stake. I had to find out about Isabelle.'

'But Jean-Luc told us he murdered her.'

'He told so many lies I had to be absolutely sure about this. It took time as I had to work under cover of darkness but I found her body. And I have proof of her identity.' He reaches into his pocket and then uncurls his fingers. A gold and sapphire pendant rests on his palm.

I stare at it. 'I remember this from her portrait.'

'Her grandmother left it to her and Isabelle always wore it.' His face is unutterably sad. 'I'm haunted by guilt. She and I did not have a perfect marriage but she was my wife and I should have been able to protect her.'

'How could you have known that the man you trusted was capable of murdering again and again?'

'Nevertheless, it was important to me that she should have a proper burial. She never was happy at Château Mirabelle.' Etienne puts the pendant back in his pocket. 'Isabelle has now been interred in her own family's vault. It delayed my return to you but I had to do this for her.'

'So, at last, you have an end to your torment?"

He nods. 'Madeleine, there's something else too. I found Sophie, lying beside Isabelle.'

Tears start to my eyes. 'Jean-Luc said he'd make it look as if we'd run away.'

'I've had her buried in a pretty country churchyard. In due course we'll arrange a headstone for her and I'll take you there to pay your respects.'

'Thank you, Etienne.' My heart aches as I picture her smiling face but I hope she is at peace. 'What will you do now?'

'A year ago I could not have survived the anguish of losing my home and the estate. They meant everything to me. One after another members of my family died and it became more and more important to me to maintain their traditions while the foundations of my world were swept away. But now,' he looks at me, his dark eyes intent upon my face, 'I feel a curious sense of lightness that all that responsibility has gone and I am free to make a new beginning.'

'What will that be?' I ask.

'That depends on you.'

I become very still and a pulse begins to beat wildly in my throat.

He tucks one of my curls behind my ear, tenderness in his eyes. 'Madeleine, it's very clear to me now what is essential to my happiness. It isn't Château Mirabelle or my estate. It isn't riches or a title or fine clothes, and it doesn't matter to me if I live in England or in France.'

The knot of misery I've carried in my breast over the last weeks begins to unravel and I feel the sweet dawning of hope.

Reaching for my hand, he turns it over and kisses the soft skin of my inner wrist, sending a shiver running up my arm. 'My dearest girl, I love you with all my heart and soul and I shall never know true happiness unless you are by my side. Madeleine, sweet Madeleine, please say you will be my wife?'

A sob of pure joy escapes me. 'Oh, yes, Etienne,' I say.

He exhales on a sigh and gathers me in his arms. His lips are as warm and sweet as honey. He winds his hands though my hair and time ceases to have any meaning as I drown in his kisses. I slide my hands around his neck and press myself against him, melting against the hardness of his muscular chest, feeling the heat of him through his shirt. All the anxiety and uncertainty of the past weeks drains away and I feel myself born anew in the wonder of our love.

'Madeleine? I have no fortune or estate any more . . .'

'But I have,' I say. 'Or I will have once I'm twenty-five. And we shall live perfectly comfortably on it.'

Etienne's eyes open wide. 'You have surprised me yet again. I'm not entirely penniless, however, as I still have several smaller properties. Then, if you have no objections, I wish us to be married very soon.'

'The sooner the better,' I say, nearly bursting with happiness.

'Good.' He kisses the tip of my nose. 'Because I have arranged for us to be married at the Mairie tomorrow.'

'Tomorrow!'

'I want to make you mine without delay,' he whispers, his breath tickling my ear. 'But there's another reason. Stay here for a moment.' He releases me and goes into the hall.

I hear a murmured conversation.

Curious, I follow him and then stop dead. My heart begins to beat very fast.

Etienne is talking to Madame Gerard who holds a baby in her arms. A baby with copper curls as bright as a new penny.

'Babette found her,' says Madame Gerard, smiling at me. 'She returned to your house to see if you needed her and saw Monsieur Viard throttle Madame Levesque. She ran inside and snatched Marianne from her crib before he could find her. I've been nursing her ever since and she's thriving.'

Etienne carefully takes Marianne from Madame Gerard and cradles her against his shoulder.

My knees buckle and I cling to the newel post.

'Steady!' says Etienne. He wraps me tightly in the circle of his arms with Marianne between us. He strokes the baby's cheek with infinite gentleness. 'So now you can see why I'm in such a hurry. This little orphan of the Revolution needs a family as soon as possible, don't you think?'

Historical Note

I began to research *The Chateau on the Lake* with the vague thought that it would be interesting to write a novel set at the time of the French Revolution. I didn't know much about it but everyone knows that the starving poor rebelled against the greedy aristocrats and beheaded Louis XVI, don't they? Except that, once I started my research, I quickly discovered that it was nothing like as straight-forward as that.

What caused the Revolution? France had been involved in several of the wars that took place in Europe and America in the forty years leading up to the Revolution and the financial implications of this were considerable. The cost of maintaining the army severely depleted a treasury already drained by royal extravagance and the country was almost bankrupt.

The bourgeoisie and the poor, known collectively as the Third Estate were resentful and angry because the wealthy clergy, (the First Estate), and the nobility, (the Second Estate), owned land, had fortunes and paid no taxes. This was manifestly unfair. The bour-geoisie began to rally support in the *salons* of Paris and London to bring about change.

By 1789 it became apparent that the First Estate and the Second Estate had no interest in using their privileged position to assist the

Third Estate. The frustrations of the bourgeoisie reached boiling point. The final straw came when severe weather caused the harvest to fail and the poor went hungry.

The discontent grew and an angry mob stormed the Bastille and took control of the armoury. Later that year the women of Paris marched to Versailles to complain about the food crisis. In 1790 the nobility was abolished. Two years later the royal family was arrested and in January 1793 Louis XVI was guillotined. Soon France was not only at war with Austria, Prussia and Britain but had to contend with bitter civil war and rioting within the country.

In simplistic terms, there were two main rival factions, the Girondins and the Jacobins. The Girondins were a group of radicals who campaigned for the end of the monarchy and represented the idea of a democratic revolution. The Jacobin's power was most often felt through their influence with the Parisian underclass, the *sans-culottes*, so-called because they wore loose working mens' trousers rather than the knee breeches of the gentry and aristocracy.

The Girondins became dismayed by and resisted the spiralling momentum of the Revolution. The *sans-culottes* were by now out of control and changed their rallying cry from 'Liberty!' to 'Equality!' while the idealist Jacobins led by Robespierre, were prepared to take aggressive action to further the aims of the Revolution. Robespierre seized control of the Committee of Public Safety and set about targeting anyone whose views differed from his own. The Reign of Terror had begun.

It is often perceived that most of the victims trundling their way to the guillotine in a tumbril were powdered and patched aristocrats but this wasn't the case. The great majority were of working class background who had taken up arms against the Revolution, most notable in the Vendée. Those nobles who had chosen to emigrate and then returned to France were also executed as they were assumed to be spies. Priests who had refused to take an oath of loyalty to the constitution were also seen as enemies of the Revolution and guillotined. Many ordinary people were denounced for very little reason and an atmosphere of suspicion and fear prevailed. Even those who orchestrated the Revolution were not immune and Robespierre himself was guillotined in 1794.

Finally the populace had had enough. It was impossible to continue to live in such a heightened state of fear. The civil wars and revolts were supressed and the necessity for a government ruled by terror was lessened. The Committee was disbanded and the Jacobin club closed down.

It's impossible to perfectly distil the facts of the Revolution in so few words and the description above is, of necessity, vastly simplified. For those of you who are interested in finding out more, I have added a list of some of the books I kept constantly to hand while writing *The Chateau on the Lake*. Not all of these contain information about the French Revolution but were the sources I used to gain a wider picture of the world in which Madeleine Moreau lived.

Acknowledgements

I'm grateful to everyone who helped me to bring this story to life; all the team at Piatkus but especially my wonderfully encouraging editor Lucy Malagoni, Caroline Kirkpatrick and Lynn Curtis. My thanks also to my lovely agent, Heather Holden-Brown, and to my hugely supportive writers' group, WordWatchers, who supplied cake and bracing comments in equal measure. My love, as always, to my husband Simon for accepting that I've spent most of the last year in another century. Again.

Suggested Further Reading

History of the French Revolution from 1789 to 1814 by Francois Mignet
The Journal of a Georgian Gentleman by Mike Rendell
Ladies of the Grand Tour by Brian Dolan
A Tale of Two Cities by Charles Dickens
Behind Closed Doors – At Home in Georgian England by Amanda Vickery
The English – A Social History 1066–1945 by Christopher Hibbert
The Glass Blowers by Daphne du Maurier
Fatal Purity – Robespierre and the French Revolution by Ruth Scurr
War and Society in Revolutionary Europe 1770–1870 by Geoffrey Best
A Place of Greater Safety by Hilary Mantel

Do you love historical fiction?

Want the chance to hear news about your favourite
authors (and the chance to win free books)?

Mary Balogh
Charlotte Betts
Jessica Blair
Frances Brody
Gaelen Foley
Elizabeth Hoyt
Eloisa James
Lisa Kleypas
Stephanie Laurens
Claire Lorrimer
Sarah MacLean
Amanda Quick
Julia Quinn

Then visit the Piatkus website and blog
www.piatkus.co.uk | www.piatkusbooks.net

And follow us on Facebook and Twitter
www.facebook.com/piatkusfiction | www.twitter.com/piatkusbooks

piatkus